*Letters of* HENRIK IBSEN

# HENRIK IBSEN

# LETTERS OF
# HENRIK IBSEN

*Translated by*

JOHN NILSEN LAURVIK
*and* MARY MORISON

NEW YORK
DUFFIELD AND COMPANY
1908

THE PREMIER PRESS
NEW YORK

# INTRODUCTION

On the 31st of May 1880, Henrik Ibsen wrote to his publisher, Frederik Hegel, that he had begun a little book in which he intended to give some account of the outward and inward conditions under which each one of his works had come into being (Letter 147). It was to be called *From Skien to Rome*, and was to give descriptions of his life at Skien and Grimstad, Bergen and Christiania, Dresden, Munich, and Rome.

As Hegel offered various objections to this project, Ibsen declared himself quite willing to relinquish it for the time being (Letter 149). But he did not give up the idea altogether. In the spring of 1881, in Rome, he said to his friend Professor L. Dietrichson, as the latter has recorded in his Memoirs (*Svundne Tider*, i. 363, 364): "People believe that I have changed my views in the course of time. This is a great mistake. My development has, as a matter of fact, been absolutely consistent. I myself can distinctly follow and indicate the thread of its whole course—the unity of my ideas and their gradual development; and I am writing some memoranda which will prove to the world how exactly the same I am now as when I first found myself."

Towards the close of this same year he wrote to another Norwegian friend, Professor O. Skavlan, that he had for some time past been busying himself at intervals with writing a record of his experiences, in the form of a work conceived in the half-sportive, half-serious style of the Preface to *Catilina*. He suggested publishing passages from this in Skavlan's periodical (Letter 155). Up to the present time, however, no such memoranda have been given to the public, with the exception of some reminiscences of childhood to be found in Henrik Jaeger's book on Ibsen (pp. 6–16).

The idea of the living, inward connection of all his work was again insisted on by Ibsen in March 1898, in the address to his readers in the first volume of the complete edition of his works. And in the same month, in his speech at the festival in Christiania on the occasion of his seventieth birthday, he announced that he was once more thinking of writing a book which should " connect his life with his works, and make of them one self-explanatory whole." But this time, too, the project was postponed. What he himself designated " dramatic follies " (*dramatiske galskaber*) pressed their claims too importunately. And when, in 1899, the author had completed his " epilogue," it proved to be his last work—illness was at hand, to prevent the now aged man from writing more. All the documents from his own pen which throw trustworthy light upon his outward and inward life are, unfortunately, mere fragments—such as the prefaces to *Catilina*, to the *Feast at Solhaug*, and to *Love's Comedy*, his speeches, and some of his newspaper articles. To these may be added the diaries which he kept when travelling, and which he frequently mentions in his Letters, more particularly in a letter to Hegel dated December 14, 1869 (Letter 62).

The collection of Letters now presented to the public will, in many respects, take the place of the contemplated autobiography. Ibsen's Letters, extending over a period of more than fifty years, provide us with a direct presentment of the man during the changing conditions of his life and of his friendships, and contain much, of both biographical and literary interest, that has never before been made public. They were written without any thought whatever of publication, and there is, therefore, nothing of the literary character about them—now they are ponderous, clumsy, official communications, now spontaneous, or even violent expressions of the feeling of the moment. But this very lack of literary finish endows them with the charm of real life, and makes them of inappreciable value as sources from which to derive knowledge of Ibsen. We have in these Letters that unreserved expression of his personal feelings which has hitherto been, to a great extent, withheld from the public; we see him in his human weakness and greatness; we learn that his proverbial reserve is not in reality an essential element of his character; and a wonderful light is thrown upon the development of his theories of life and art, and upon the germination and growth and aim of his works. Into some of his most private feelings and most intimate relations with others it is not permissible to allow the public any insight; common consideration for the author who could never bear to strip himself completely in public (see Letter 17) forbids it. For the present, at least, our knowledge must remain incomplete.

And there is another respect in which this collection of Letters is unavoidably imperfect. It has been impossible to include a single letter *to* Ibsen—as none are to be found. In a case of the same kind, namely, at the time of the publication of the letters of Julius Lange, Ibsen himself wrote (Letter 233) that "it is not conducive to the understanding of a dialogue that we should hear only the one interlocutor's speeches, and be obliged to guess at those of the other." The fact that Ibsen must appear in the character of a monologist makes our understanding of his frames of mind incomplete. The Introduction and the Notes appended to the Letters are intended to remedy this defect, as far as it is remediable. No attempt is made to point out all the new data provided by the Letters and to deduce conclusions from them; this must be done in some more elaborate biographical or critical work. All that we aim at is to assist our readers to a better understanding of the Letters, by providing, as it were, the background against which they ought to be seen. The fact that each one of them is an isolated utterance renders some indication of the general connection between them necessary. What we give is no complete biography, but only an account of some of the relations into which Ibsen has entered in the course of his life —relations with society in

general, with great and with small circles, with individuals
and with ideas.  But even such an account will throw light,
here and there, on the process of his development as a man
and an artist.

*       *       *       *       *       *

Henrik Ibsen left Skien and his father's house at an early
age.  After his confirmation, at the age of 14, he was obliged to
support himself, as his family's once ample means were entirely
exhausted.  He was taken into the employment of the
apothecary at Grimstad, with whom he remained for six years
(1844–1850), first as apprentice and then as assistant.  To Skien
he returned only to spend short holidays; and his connection
with his family became slighter and slighter as years passed.
As a grown man, he never wrote to his parents.  We know of
two reasons for this.  In the first place, many years passed
before he was in a position to be able to help his family, and
when he did reach that position (Letter 134), he was already
"half a stranger" to them.  In the second—and here we doubtless have the chief reason—he felt that in the course of his
development he had acquired a new basis for his spiritual life,
in a totally different sphere from that in which ideas moved at
home; and to him, with his imperious craving for "completeness,"
a half-understanding was intolerable (Letter 44).  In his
father's house, strict biblical piety reigned, whereas he himself
had cast off the yoke of every outward authority, and valued
freedom of thought above all else.  Ibsen regarded talent not
in the light of a property, but of a duty (Letter 45); and when
he separated himself from his parents and other relations, he
did it for the sake of his life-work.  The step was an outcome
of that "full-blooded" egoism about which he once (Letter 84)
wrote to George Brandes, which "forced him for a time to regard
what concerned himself as the only thing of any consequence,
and everything else as non-existent."  Here we observe in
Ibsen himself a good deal of "Brand."

It was, to take the matter from the other side, quite natural that the uncompromisingly radical principles which displayed themselves ever more clearly in the young author's works, should alienate his family from him. But there was never any actual breach. And there was one of his family with whom Ibsen always kept up some connection, namely, his sister Hedvig, who married Captain Stousland of Skien, of the merchant service. It was this sister whom he took as model for the beautiful child-character, Hedvig, in *The Wild Duck*, and it was of her Björnstjerne Björnson said, that after making acquaintance with her, he understood how much of Ibsen's inclination to mysticism was hereditary. A woman of delicate, warm feelings and much strength of character, she gradually attained a standpoint of gentle, considerate tolerance; she was able to understand her elder brother's spiritual development, different from her own as it was; and she was always a loving sister. To her in his early youth he confided his plans for the future. In his twentieth year, on one of his last visits to Skien, he told her that his desire was to reach "the highest, most perfect, attainable degree of greatness and understanding," and then to die. And it has been his sister's joy to see him working his way to an ever higher, clearer view of life, to see the goodheartedness of his childhood asserting itself ever more and more in the grown man's judgments of his fellow-men.

By his marriage with Susanna Thoresen, Ibsen entered into new family relations. The Letters now published tell little about his married life; except for the love-letter to her in verse (Letter 5), almost the only important mention of his wife that is to be found is a clever sketch of her character in Letter 74, which throws a flash of light on her significance to his life and work. We learn more of the author in his capacity of father; we see him making careful provision for his son Sigurd's education, planning his reading and his studies (Letters 119, 138, 168), and taking energetic steps to open up an official and political career for him (Letter 175). For his son's sake he often sacrifices his

own wishes; he repeatedly makes the choice of a place of
residence entirely dependent on the advantages offered for
Sigurd's education.

As to the other members of the Thoresen family, we find
Ibsen in business relations with one, his brother-in-law, J. H.
Thoresen, and carrying on a literary correspondence with
another, his mother-in-law, Magdalene Thoresen. But the only
one of them with whom he was at all intimate, and who had any
personal influence on himself and his work, was his sister-in-law,
Marie, who died comparatively young. She lived in his house
in Dresden for several years (Letter 98).

\*          \*          \*          \*          \*          \*

Some of the most important years of his youth were spent
by Henrik Ibsen at Grimstad, a little town of about 800
inhabitants—more a village than a town in outward appearance.
Its interests and traditions were chiefly connected with the sea.
Its best society was formed by a few old families, whose heads
were shipowners, merchants, or sea-captains; these families
held themselves aloof from the "common people," and assumed
a coldly suspicious attitude towards all new-comers to the town.
Ibsen, young, penniless, and reserved, had not the entry of this
superior circle, and led a rather solitary life for the first years.
Besides, as he himself tells in the Preface to *Catilina*, he
speedily stood on a war-footing with the leading citizens of the
little town; the apothecary's little "'prentice" had a dangerous
trick of making comic verses about them; and his caricatures,
too, were a source of annoyance to many worthy men. In the
course of a year or two, when he was about nineteen, he began
to make friends among the young men of his own age; but
although several of his intimates belonged to the best families of
the town, Ibsen himself never became a member of the select
circle—he was too poor and of too unfavourable notoriety. His
sharp tongue and pen were always getting him into trouble,
and he and his friends played too many "mad and riotous

pranks" (Letter 74) to come up to the town's standard for well-behaved young men. Traditions of this Grimstad life were published in 1900 in the Christiania paper, *Eidsvold* (Nos. 233, 235, 238).

Among Ibsen's Grimstad friends, special mention must be made of two—neither of them natives of the town—who stood faithfully by him in his first attempts to make his way as an author. One was Christopher Lorentz Due, the son of the principal custom-house officer in the neighbouring small town of Lillesand, and himself employed from a very early age in the custom-house of Grimstad. The other was the law-student, Ole Schulerud, whose father was appointed principal custom-house officer of Grimstad in 1846, and who himself came to the town in 1847, after passing his second examination. To these two, Henrik Ibsen confided his poet's dreams. Due was musical. He set to music a poem which Ibsen wrote in 1848 ("Vaarens minde"—Memories of Spring; printed only in German, in the *Sämtliche Werke*, I. 195, 196); and it was he who made the fair-copy of *Catilina*. With this copy in his possession, Schulerud went to Christiania in the autumn of 1849, to offer the play to the Theatre and to try to get it published. He was, as is well known, unsuccessful both with the Theatre and the publishers; but he lent Ibsen the necessary money, and the drama appeared in April 1850, published at the author's own risk. Ibsen has told all this himself in the above-mentioned Preface to the Second Edition of *Catilina* (1875), in which he makes several quotations from Schulerud's letters regarding the position of matters. Due in 1904 contributed some reminiscences of Ibsen's Grimstad years to the Christiania *Aftenpost* (Nos. 560, 574, 588).

\*     \*     \*     \*     \*     \*

At the time when *Catilina* appeared, Ibsen had already left his situation at Grimstad and come to Christiania to study for the University matriculation examination. He passed part of it in the summer of 1850, but failed in two subjects. One of these was Greek—so that he wrote the truth when he wrote of himself (Letter 100) that he was no great Greek scholar. As he never went up for these two subjects again, his name was never inscribed on the University roll. His pecuniary position was anything but satisfactory; it was fortunate for him that he and his unselfish friend Schulerud lived together, as the latter had a small monthly allowance. For a short time after Ibsen's arrival in Christiania a third young man shared the rooms. This was Theodor Abildgaard, who had just begun to take part in the first Norwegian working-men's movement, organised by Marcus Thrane. The social and national struggles of the years succeeding 1848 had, before he left Grimstad, exercised a "powerful and maturing" influence on young Ibsen's mind; and this working-men's movement strongly approved itself to him, because it boldly attacked the very foundation of existing society. He and Abildgaard became friends; he was introduced by Abildgaard to Thrane and other leaders of the working-men, took part in the meetings and demonstrations, and even wrote once or twice in the *Arbejder-Foreningernes Blad*, the organ of the working-men's unions. When Thrane and Abildgaard were arrested in July 1851, Ibsen was afraid that he also might be imprisoned; but his letters to Abildgaard and other implicatory documents were burned by the business-manager of the newspaper before the police could get hold of them (Letter 210).

After this, Ibsen helped the temporary editor, Bernhard Hansen, a journeyman mason, to put his thoughts into suitable language—more particularly when it seemed best to express them in verse; but later in the same year Hansen, too, was arrested, and, as Ibsen immediately afterwards left Christiania, his connection with the "Thranites" came to an end. But he retained his sympathy for the working-men's movement, even though he never again took any active part in it, and would never espouse either one side or the other in the theoretical and practical disputes connected with it. The workmen themselves, however, have always regarded his works as their influential allies in the struggle for a new ordering of society; and in

Ibsen's letters of the Eighties and Nineties (Letters 200 and 215), and in one or two of his speeches, particularly the speech to the workmen of Trondhjem in 1885, and the speech delivered at Stockholm in 1887 on the subject of "the third kingdom," there is plenty of evidence of his characteristic attitude towards the cause of the working-man.

* * * * * *

One of the first acquaintances Ibsen made when he came to Christiania in March 1850, and took his place on the benches of old Heltberg's "studenterfabrik" (a famous "cramming" establishment), was Aasmund Vinje, a man of peasant birth, who had been a schoolmaster, and already possessed experience in journalism and many other things. Though ten years older than Ibsen, Vinje was studying at Heltberg's at the same time with him for the matriculation examination; he had an insatiable thirst for knowledge; and he was preparing himself with obstinate industry to take an active part in the Norwegian intellectual conflicts. He too was, like Ibsen, in a stage of spiritual ferment; in spite of his thirty-two years he was not yet the grown man. In conversation with him, Ibsen heard forcible and characteristic expression given to an intellectual tendency towards which he had some inclination himself—the bitter scepticism which poured contempt and ridicule on the endeavours of the age, and irreverently trampled all its ideals underfoot. Vinje had arrived at the consciousness that all truth is only relative—that truth is always in a condition of growth and development. His recognition of this produced his "tvisyn" (double-vision)—which could see right and wrong in the same thing; and this in its turn produced the originality of his ironic style—a style that scratches and pats, laughs and cries, at the same time—that, as he himself remarks, "dances on the edge of a knife midway between heaven and hell," without allowing itself to be caught either by the one or the other. It was an unhealthy scepticism this, which preyed upon the soul;

and in the merry dance of words, personal responsibility was apt to be forgotten. Herein lay a great danger both for Ibsen and Vinje. They had had to fight their way to the strength of scepticism ; now they had to fight their scepticism. A kinship of soul in this matter was what drew them together, and they were soon friends. But it does not seem as if their friendship had ever been very intimate. In this collection of Ibsen's Letters, Vinje's name is only mentioned once (Letter 4); and the two authors in their maturer years grew ever farther apart— Vinje, the nationalist language-reformer, had little in common with Ibsen, the "Scandinavian"[1] and "Teuton." But in both, the indomitable will of the fighter triumphed over doubt in its unhealthy form. They retained their scepticism as far as any subjection to authority was concerned; but they freed themselves from its weakening power and became devoted combatants in the war for ideas. Self-satire was not uncommon with Ibsen at a later period, but he never became so addicted to it as Vinje, in whose style it was the life-giving element. It is not impossible that in writing *Peer Gynt* Ibsen at times had Vinje in his mind, as the man who always kept a retreat to a new position open for himself—and even in Peer Gynt's manner of expressing himself there is something that recalls Vinje.

\*　　\*　　\*　　\*　　\*　　\*

Another acquaintance made by Ibsen in Christiania in 1850, and one with whom he was ultimately much more closely and intimately connected than with Vinje, was Paul Botten-Hansen. Botten-Hansen, who, like Vinje, was of peasant extraction, was at this time a student, and also already engaged in literary work. He was a better educated man than Vinje, a passionate book-lover, and an independent and original thinker. He represented to a great extent the same school of thought as Vinje—was a satiric, half *blasé* sceptic. But his scepticism

---

[1] Adherent of the party which aims at the unification of the interests of the three Scandinavian kingdoms.

was not so aggressive, and his satire was milder and more humorous. Vinje, who was a competent judge, said that few, indeed, were the writers who owned such an admirable two-edged style as Botten-Hansen. And in the matter of style, especially the style in which *Love's Comedy* and *Peer Gynt* are written, Ibsen learned more from Botten-Hansen than from any one else. The poetic efforts which the latter printed in 1851 in *Andhrimner* (the periodical published by the three friends), his national fairy-poem, " The Fairy Wedding " (Letter 66), and the satirical peasant-story, *Norwegian Mysteries*, undoubtedly had a good and lasting influence both on Ibsen's ideas and his style. The style on which Botten-Hansen had modelled his, was Ludvig Holberg's; this made its appearance again, fresh and daunt-less as ever, in Hansen's journalistic writings. And Hansen taught Ibsen, too, to love Holberg. In Letter 54, Ibsen tells us that he never wearied of reading Holberg, an assertion which is borne out by many references to that author's works in other Letters (see Letters 59, 74, 79, and others). A real spiritual kinship existed between the Norwegian genius whose eman-cipatory labours in the eighteenth century entitle him to be called the father of Danish - Norwegian literature, and the poet in embryo whose emancipatory struggles and labours were to aid in creating a new era in Norwegian literature and Norwegian spiritual life, and were to extend their influence far beyond Norway.

Significantly enough, both Botten-Hansen and Ibsen were known in the circle of their friends by nick-names taken from Holberg. A comrade happened to give expression to his feelings regarding Botten-Hansen's luck in picking up all kinds of rare books, in the following quotation from *Jakob von Tyboe*: " Fie on the Dutchman. He has his spies everywhere!" After this, Botten-Hansen always went by the name of "the Dutchman." He, again, always called Henrik Ibsen "Gert Westphaler"; for though Ibsen often sat perfectly silent among a company of friends, if he once began to talk, he was not easily stopped— he would treat his friends both to "Arius and the seven

Electors" and the "Journey from Haderslev to Kiel"[1] (Letters 79 and 80).

In the Fifties and Sixties Botten-Hansen was the central figure of a circle which became known by the name of "learned Holland," or "the Dutchmen," or "the Westphalians." Its members were chiefly learned and literary men, most of them still young, but nearly all of them destined to play, in some department or other, an important part in the life of their day. Ibsen did not actually assist in founding this "Dutch" society, for in November 1851 he left for Bergen to be play-wright and stage-manager of the newly established "Norwegian Theatre," and when he returned to Christiania in 1857, it had almost attained its full dimensions. At its reunions he met again his old friend Vinje, who, however, was gradually finding other supporters and other points of departure for his pioneer literary work, and who, in private intercourse as well as in other matters, was a person of very irregular habits. Another person who made an occasional appearance when he happened to be in Christiania, was Björnstjerne Björnson; and at a time J. S. Welhaven would come, to have some point in the history of literature cleared up for him by Botten-Hansen, the book-learned. A large proportion of the members were historians. Even the most eminent representative of that profession, Professor P. A. Munch (at whose grave in Rome Ibsen was, in the days to come, to speak heartfelt, moving words of remembrance and farewell), sometimes came, to inspect Botten-Hansen's literary treasures. More regular attendants were M. Birkeland and H. J. Huitfeldt, both future Keepers of the Royal Archives, and Oluf Rygh and Ludvig Daae, future professors. The last-mentioned, the Latinist of the society (Letter 116) and one of its liveliest members, a great Holberg lover, and an eager collector of old curiosities, has provided "the Dutchmen" with an enduring literary monument in his sympathetic article on Botten-Hansen in the periodical, *Vidar* (1888). From this

[1] Stock subjects of conversation with "Gert Westphaler, the loquacious barber," the hero of Holberg's comedy of the same name.

article, which is full of interesting detail, we have drawn largely. Amongst the historians we must not omit to mention Björnson's and Vinje's friend, J. E. Sars, who, however, in the Sixties himself became the central figure of another and very different circle—a circle in which national questions were of all-prevailing interest. To Botten-Hansen's reunions came other men, whose labours were chiefly directed to the furtherance of the national renascence—such as the fairy-tale collector P. Chr. Asbjörnsen and the gifted philologist Ivar Aasen; and more regular attendants were two eager, active "Scandinavians"—O. A. Bachke, who rose to be Chief Judge of the Supreme Court and Minister of Justice, and took an active part in the promotion of reciprocity in legal matters between the three Scandinavian kingdoms; and Jakob Lökke, schoolmaster and philologist, one of the principal supporters of the movement in favour of changes producing more uniformity in the three languages.

In this circle, as we see, very varied interests were represented; it was wide enough to contain men of the most contradictory literary and political opinions. Whilst Ibsen was still in Christiania (1857–1864), these antagonisms had not developed all their force; there had not yet begun that open, general warfare between the old and the new opinions, which in the Seventies and Eighties produced a complete change in almost every domain of intellectual life in Norway. But there were already signs of the coming struggle; the essentially Radical and Nationalistic elements were by degrees eliminated from the circle, so that it in time came to represent mainly Conservative and "Scandinavian" opinion. Some of its members, such as O. A. Bachke and Ludvig Daae, actually became the foremost opponents of the democratic, free-thinking, Nationalistic movement, the leaders of which were Johan Sverdrup, Sars, and Björnson. During this struggle, Henrik Ibsen's position was rather a solitary one; siding with neither party, he was claimed now by the one, now by the other, under circumstances which will be described hereafter.

The friendships which Ibsen made among the "Dutchmen"

proved valuable to him in many ways.   Through them he came
into contact with the most widely differing intellectual tendencies
of the day; and it is to this that his being in touch with all
modern movements is chiefly due, though he himself, in a letter to
George Brandes (No. 81), ascribes it to his fortunate "instinct."
But from a purely practical point of view, too, his "Dutch"
friends proved of use to him.   Lökke helped him to collect
his poems (Letters 63 and 73); Birkeland assisted him in both
pecuniary and literary matters (Letters 28, 35, 85, 95); Daae
helped him with Greek and Latin for *Emperor and Galilean*
(Letters 100 and 103); Bachke facilitated his son's entrance
into Government employment.   His best helper was, however,
Botten-Hansen himself; for Botten-Hansen was for many years
a literary power in Norway.   From the beginning of 1851 to
the end of 1866, almost without interruption, he conducted
the weekly *Illustreret Nyhedsblad*; and by the literary criticism
which he wrote regularly for this paper, he introduced a new
feature into Norwegian journalism.   His judgment in literary
matters was sound, and his criticisms soon came to be held in
much estimation.   His two friends, Ibsen and Vinje, required
and received a special amount of literary support from him.
He found room for their productions (especially Ibsen's) in the
*Nyhedsblad* (Letters 6 and 74); and in its columns their books
were reviewed capably and at length (Letter 6), and the first
biographical sketches of the two authors appeared (1863).   In
the days of Ibsen's poverty, Botten-Hansen helped him to find
publishers, and even himself undertook the publication of two
works (*Lady Inger of Östraat*, 1857; and *The Vikings at
Helgeland*, 1858.   See Letter 7).   And in 1866, when a movement was set on foot to procure a Government pension for
Ibsen, Botten-Hansen did everything in his power to assist
(Letter 33).   For these services Ibsen never publicly thanked
his friend, but the letters to him now published give unmistakable testimony to the depth of his gratitude.

\*        \*        \*        \*        \*        \*

The life which Ibsen led during his seven years' residence in Christiania was a life burdened with many cares. The worst were the pecuniary difficulties. He left debts in Bergen, and in Christiania he contracted more (Letter 13). His salary as "artistic director" of the "Norwegian Theatre" in Christiania was the reverse of ample for a man with a wife and child; and the failure of the theatre in 1862 meant to him not only the loss of his situation, but of money as well. In 1863, when he was "æstetisk konsulent" of the old "Christiania Theatre," his salary was not only smaller, but was not paid in full when the receipts of the theatre were insufficient. It was, in the strict sense of the word, a struggle for existence which Ibsen carried on during these years; and amongst those from whom he was obliged to seek help were money-lenders of the usurer type.

He had not as yet won much recognition as an author, and was a comparatively unnoticed literary man at the time when Björnstjerne Björnson, his junior, was already receiving the homage of his countrymen as their national author. But there was one conspicuous member of Christiania society who already openly interested himself in Ibsen. This was the eminent barrister, Bernhard Dunker, one of the men who influenced both the social and intellectual tone of the day. His interests were as widespread as his influence—he was the most intimate friend of Welhaven the poet; he knew Björnson well; he was a "Scandinavian"; and yet he repeatedly gave active support to the policy of national independence. Both to Ibsen and Björnson he was a capable, discerning adviser in literary matters; and his distinguished patronage was of great importance to them socially.

Ibsen had another good friend in an eminent man belonging to a different party—namely, Johan Sverdrup, the new leader of the Liberals, a politician of European fame. Sverdrup's interest in everything national led him to occupy himself with the affairs of the "Norwegian Theatre" in Christiania, and this, in turn, probably led to his becoming personally acquainted

with Ibsen. It is certain that Ibsen wrote several letters to
him, and, when Sverdrup's papers become accessible, these
letters will doubtless be brought to light. All that we have
at present is a mere note, written in 1883, which shows that
their political differences had not effaced from Ibsen's memory
a grateful remembrance of the friendly help given him by
Sverdrup in his time of need.

For so miserably poor was Ibsen, that he was obliged to accept
direct pecuniary assistance from richer friends (*Saml. værker*,
x. 507). When, in the spring of 1864, a Government travelling-
grant of £90 enabled him to go to Rome, private individuals
had to come to his assistance before he could leave Christiania,
and also help to support him in Italy. Sverdrup was of the
number (Letter 20); but Dunker did more than anyone else—
and this Ibsen never forgot (Letters 17 and 23). Reserved and
retiring, he would, however, very probably never have received
such assistance if he had not had an ardent, indefatigable
friend to plead his cause—Björnstjerne Björnson.

In all Norwegian history there is no record of a more
remarkable personal relationship than that between Ibsen and
Björnson. In its changing character, it mirrors a whole epoch
in the intellectual life of the country; and since the first really
clear light is thrown upon it by Ibsen's Letters, as now
published, some preparatory information must here be given.

Very soon after Ibsen first came to Christiania, in the
spring of 1850, he and Björnson met—the latter having arrived
at almost the same time, also to study at Heltberg's "studenterfabrik." No particular intimacy, however, existed between the
two young men when Ibsen left Christiania for Bergen in
1851. But it was during this period of separation that their
future close connection was prepared for; in the following
years, during the struggles of the national awakening, no
two men worked together in more brotherly fashion than did
Ibsen and Björnson.

"They lifted together"—to quote an article written in
*Verdensgang* (1884, No. 112) on the occasion of their joyful

meeting after a separation of many years—"they lifted together when the old Saga had to be lifted into our literature again. They brooded over the same thought and both developed it in their poetry—the 'kingship thought'—who was to be king in Norway? It was the thought embodied in Björnson's first play. 'Let that man be king who has something to be king of,' is what we read in *Between the Battles*. Victorious King Sverre was the hero of Björnson's youth. And it was in describing kingship that Ibsen emancipated all his mighty powers. The leader, the king of men, was he who was not tied down merely to reviving the old, but who could steer boldly out into the new, the unknown, the future, Saga, because he was the fortunate mortal who had been seized by the thoughts of the age as by a passion.

When *The Feast at Solhaug* appeared (1856), Björnson hastened to direct public attention to this new and genuinely Norwegian contribution to the dramatic literature of the country; and when *The Vikings at Helgeland* was refused by the Christiania Theatre (1858), he ardently supported Ibsen's demand that the play should be performed. But it was some time before the two men had much personal intercourse. Ibsen returned to Christiania in the summer of 1857, but shortly afterwards Björnson left for Bergen to succeed him in the management of the "Norwegian Theatre" there; and it was not till the autumn of 1859 that Björnson settled in Christiania again. From this autumn dates the intimate friendship between the two authors—a friendship which was apparent both in public and private life. In the beginning of 1860, Björnson stood godfather to Ibsen's only son. In November 1859, Ibsen and Björnson together founded the "Norwegian Society"; the initiative was taken by Ibsen, and Björnson was President of the Society during the short period of its existence. In May 1860, Björnson went abroad, remaining away for three years. He sent home the play, *King Sverre* (1861) and the great lyric-dramatic trilogy, *Sigurd Slembe* (1862). The latter work was reviewed by Ibsen in the *Illustreret Nyhedsblad*; and this

2

is the only evidence we have of the connection between the two
authors during these three years.

They met again in Bergen at the Festival of Song in the
summer of 1863, and both spent the following winter in
Christiania. Their intercourse during this year brought them
closer to each other than they had ever been before. They felt
that they were inspired by the same ideas and the same hopes;
and they suffered the same bitter disappointments. With
anguish they watched the Danish "brother" nation's desperate
struggle against the superior power of Germany, and saw a
province with a population of Scandinavian race and speech
taken from Denmark and incorporated in a foreign kingdom,
whilst the Norwegian and Swedish kinsmen, in spite of solemn
promises, refrained from yielding any assistance. This was a
disappointment both as regarded Scandinavia in general and
their own country in particular; and the experience left its
marks on the minds of both—Ibsen being perhaps the more
deeply affected of the two, because he had seldom had such
bright hopes.

During all these years doubt and despondence had been
gnawing at Ibsen's soul. He had been consumed by the fear
that he might never attain to the "completeness and clearness"
which had been the dream of his youth. Was he never to feel
himself free and whole? Were all kinds of outward bonds and
considerations to hamper his development, so that he should not
be able to break through what he himself called (Letter 44)
"the crust of folly and frowardness"? Was he to be merely a
"clever author," and not a champion of great ideas? With this
question he fought a solitary, silent fight. And his critical
scepticism regarding the ideas which prevailed in the world
around him made the fight all the harder.

Then Björnson came to his assistance.

Abundant testimony has been borne to the wonderful
influence exercised by Björnson's powerful personality, even in
his youth, on all those with whom he came into contact. This
power was the result of the unfailing *faith* which radiated from

his whole being. *He* was no doubter; he had the natural, simple confidence of a child in himself, in his fellow-men, in all good powers; and it was almost impossible to help sharing his confidence—there was something contagious in it. From Björnson's faith, Henrik Ibsen derived strength for the battle with himself. He learned from it to have faith himself, and to risk everything for his faith. It was not a bright, glad faith like Björnson's; but it meant a courage that never failed, a life-resolve that lasted a lifetime. It became confidence in his own power "to realise himself" (Letter 110), and a "complete and firm belief in the self-propagating and self-developing power of high ideals" (*Saml. værker*, x. 517); and the practical outcome of it was a dauntless endeavour to arouse his people and set them on the way to a freer, richer future. To his own struggle to attain this standpoint Ibsen gave poetic expression in the dramatic contrast between Duke Skule and King Hakon; both "Pretenders" he found in his own soul—Hakon was the new element in it, which he owed to Björnson. When Björnson's life-work comes to be estimated, it will not be reckoned one of his least deserts that, at a difficult and dangerous crisis, he helped Henrik Ibsen to "find himself."

In outward matters, too, Björnson spared no trouble to assist Ibsen; he procured money for him from public and private sources (Letters 18, 20, etc.), helped him to go abroad in March 1864, and in the autumn of 1865 introduced him to the principal publisher of the Scandinavian countries, Frederik Hegel, the head of the "Gyldendalske Boghandel" in Copenhagen. These two things—the getting away from the narrow social conditions prevailing in Norway, and the acquiring of a high-minded man of business as his publisher—Ibsen felt to be a kind of release from bondage. It had always been difficult for him to get his books published, and in the middle of the Sixties the Norwegian publishing trade was at the lowest possible ebb. Old Johan Dahl was resting on the laurels won in past days, and Christian Tönsberg, in the course of his too daring ventures, had suffered shipwreck. All the younger publishers were as yet afraid of embarking on any large undertaking. It was a national loss to Norway that her authors were obliged to go abroad with their books; but the authors themselves were undoubtedly fortunate in being able to find such good headquarters for their work. Hegel had begun in 1858 to enlarge his publishing premises, in the expectation of doing business with all the Scandinavian countries. From 1861 onwards he published Björnson's books; and in 1865, on Björnson's recommendation, he agreed to publish for Ibsen too. It can never be denied that by so doing he gave a stimulus to the development of the whole intellectual life of Scandinavia.

Ibsen always felt that it was a piece of great good fortune to have Hegel for his publisher; and he regarded their connection not only from a purely personal, but also from a Scandinavian point of view. On the 16th of March 1866, the day after *Brand* was given to the public, he wrote to Hegel from Rome: "I hope in the years that are to come, to enjoy the honour and satisfaction of being connected, as an author, with you, as a publisher. It is my intention to connect myself as much as possible with Denmark. Norwegians and Swedes have a capital crime to atone for to your nation; and I feel that it is my life-task to employ the powers which God has given me in arousing my countrymen from their lethargy and obliging them to see in what direction the great questions of life point." And in 1870, when the "Gyldendalske Boghandel" celebrated the hundredth anniversary of its foundation, Ibsen expressed himself to the same effect, both in his letter of congratulation to Hegel (Letter 72), and in the poem he wrote on the occasion (*Saml. værker*, IV. 371, 372). In a letter dated Munich, December 10, 1875, he reminds Hegel of the days, ten years earlier, when he was anxiously awaiting the arrival of *Brand*. "Thanks for all you have done for me since then," he continues. "No one has contributed so much as you to the difference for me between *then* and *now*. You may be certain that I never forget this." Hegel was undoubtedly much more to his authors than their publisher and paymaster; he was their quiet, faithful friend, ever ready with advice and practical help in time of need. He generously undertook all the trouble connected with the proper investment of the money which Ibsen in time made by his writings.

The long residence abroad and the satisfactory business connection with the "Gyldendalske Boghandel" placed Ibsen in the independent circumstances which were necessary for his development; and he felt exceedingly grateful to Björnson, to whose assistance this favourable position was largely due (Letters 17 and 18). Nevertheless, before many years had passed, the two friends had quarrelled, and for a long time all connection between them was broken off.

The causes of this breach were partly personal, partly connected with the public affairs of the day. Ibsen's Letters (Letter 44) tell of the misunderstanding which followed on the publication of *Peer Gynt* in 1867, and indicate what powers were at work separating the two authors. In Norway party divisions were beginning at this time to be more sharply marked; a Right and a Left, in both political and intellectual matters, were forming. Björnson without hesitation espoused the cause of the Left, and rushed enthusiastically into the fight for national independence and popular government. Ibsen was "far away," and his political interests were not the same; his hopes lay in the direction of a Scandinavian union; and he had no sympathy with the peasant party, which was now striving for power in Norway. It was therefore natural that his "friends of the *Morgenblad*" (Letter 45), his old "fellow-Dutchmen," should attempt to win him for their side and make use of him to further the interests of the Right. They declared *Peer Gynt* to be a satire on all nationalistic endeavours, and received *The League of Youth* as a piece of party-writing— Right against Left.

To Ibsen it was exceedingly disagreeable, nay painful (*Saml. værker*, x. 520), to be thus regarded as the poet of a party; it seemed to drag all his work down to a lower level and to place

him in a false position. For although, as regarded the
political questions of the day, he might with perfect justice be
considered to belong to the Right (Letters 95 and 98), yet his
fundamental principles, his radical demand for liberty, were not
at all in conformity with the arguments and aims of that party.
Contradictions such as these are natural to the human soul;
Ibsen himself has given expression to the truth that one cannot
think out a thought to the end without coming upon self-
contradictions (*Henrik Ibsen, zum* 20 *März gewidmet von der
Freien Bühne*, pp. 14, 15). In reality he was a "solitary *franctireur* at the outposts" (Letter 161); and he was inclined to
regard everything of the nature of a party as antagonistic to
his philosophy of life. He considered it to be a necessity of
life for a poet "coldly to turn his back on all parties and take
up a position for himself" (Letter 57); it was in his nature to
be "the enemy of the people." This is the explanation of his
displeasure at seeing Björnson ally himself with the Norwegian
peasant-Left. He could not detect in their opinions "an atom
more of real liberalism than in those of the ultramontane
peasant population of the Tyrol" (Letter 178). He feared that
the pursuit of politics would lead Björnson to lay aside his
work as an author (Letter 68), and thereby to neglect the duties
imposed on him by his gifts.

It very soon appeared to him, too, as if his old friend were
proving unfaithful to the "Scandinavian" ideal. This was
when Björnson, in the autumn of 1872, called on Denmark to
"alter her signals" in the direction of Germany, and give up
all thought of revenge and the reconquest of Danish Schleswig.
In anger that the dream of years should thus be relinquished,
Ibsen wrote his wrathful poem, "Nordens signaler" (*Saml.
værker*, x. 567–569)—a poem aimed directly at Björnson, that
"weather-cock" who had now become "the priest of Pan-
Germanism." It is not what Adolf Strodtmann called it (*Das
geistige Leben in Dänemark*, p. ix.), "a disdainful defiance of
Germany," but a bitter outcry against the men who had proved
traitors to the "Scandinavian" ideal (Letter 104).

Björnson, on his side, was enraged by the "assassination" (*snigmord*), which in his opinion was attempted in *The League of Youth* (Letter 62, and note to same). It was a great cause of offence to him that Ibsen accepted orders and decorations (Letter 45); and, as he himself at this time still accepted the doctrines of Christianity, it was a grief to him to see Ibsen inclining ever more and more to "atheism" (Letter 107).

Here were causes enough for a breach between the two authors — and there was an open one from 1868 onwards. Ibsen more than once had a reconciliation in view. In 1870 he thought of dedicating the new edition of *The Pretenders* to Björnson (Letter 65), but was prevented from doing so by information received from his "friends of the *Morgenblad.*" In 1877 he actually made an attempt towards a renewal of friendship, after Björnson had expressed himself sympathetically on the subject of George Brandes's writings. Björnson's favourable estimate of a man who in many, nay most, matters was his opponent, atoned in Ibsen's eyes for a great deal; and from Munich, on the 28th of October 1877, he sent, through Hegel, a little note (unfortunately lost) to Björnson, along with a copy of *The Pillars of Society.* It does not seem, however, that this step led to any result. Though Björnson, when travelling in Germany in the last months of 1872, passed through Munich, where Ibsen was then living, he did not go to see him.

Yet during these years the two authors were approaching each other, in a very real sense, in their works. In 1875 Björnson began to occupy himself with the problems of modern life as dramatic subjects. He wrote *The Editor* and *A Bankruptcy.* Towards the close of the Seventies, after a hard inward struggle, he finally relinquished his old Christian faith. Henceforth, to him, as to Ibsen, freedom of thought and the personal quest of truth were the highest good. In his speech to the Christiania students on the 31st of October 1877 he had already formulated his famous motto: "At være i sandhed"— (Be in truth!)  In 1877, in *The Pillars of Society*, Ibsen turned his attention, as a dramatist, to the same kind of subject. The germs of social drama which were contained in *Love's Comedy* and *The League of Youth* began to mature; and he pursued his assault upon existing society with implacable consistency in *A Doll's House* and *Ghosts*. Whilst the attacking columns were appearing on the field, each new arrival with heavier guns, the party of the Right was becoming more and more suspicious of "its" poet; and when, in 1881, *Ghosts* appeared, Ibsen was with blast of trumpet and beat of drum cast out of its ranks. It turned all the moral indignation at its command to bear upon his godless, immoral works, with their society-dissolving tendency. And for a number of years he had to bear his disgrace as best he could.

This turn of affairs in itself helped to bring Björnson and Ibsen together again. They had now learned to understand and value each other as they had never done before; and the winter of 1880–81 saw their friendship firmly re-cemented. Björnson was at this time travelling in America. Towards the close of 1880, in an article in an American periodical, he wrote as follows of Henrik Ibsen: "I think that I have a pretty thorough acquaintance with the dramatic literature of the world, and I have not the slightest hesitation in saying that Henrik Ibsen possesses more dramatic power than any other play-writer of our day. The fact that I am not always partial to the style of his work makes me all the more certain that I am right in my judgment of him" (Björnson: *Den norske Forfatningskamp*, pp. 14, 15). Ibsen, on his side, felt himself, in spite of all that at all times repelled him in Björnson, once more irresistibly attracted by the man's mighty personality. In the spring of 1881, having heard that Björnson, while in America, had had a narrow escape with his life from some great danger, he wrote him a letter (unfortunately now lost), in which he declared that his feeling when he heard the news was, that if his friend had died, he himself could never have written any-thing more (communicated verbally by Fru Mathilde Schjött, *née* Dunker). When, soon after this, *Ghosts* was published and every one turned against the recklessly belligerent poet, Björnson stood forth boldly and defended him—which drew from Ibsen the highest possible commendation: "He has in truth a kingly soul" (Letter 161). They both now began to understand that they had in reality, each in his own way, been fighting for the same cause; and Ibsen gave expression to this thought when he telegraphed from Gossensass in the Tyrol on the 10th of August 1882—the day of Björnson's "author's jubilee": "My thanks for the work done side by side with me in the service of freedom these twenty-five years!" By degrees Ibsen, too, became interested in the Norwegian political struggles in which Björnson was taking part with heart and soul. When the Norwegian Left really followed up its words with actions, the frame of mind of the man who had written contemptuously of "the screaming politicians at home," was one of anxious expectation; during the winter of 1883–84 his attention was so much occupied with the political complications at home that (as he wrote to Hegel on the 21st of April 1884) he was unable to make any real progress with the dramatic work he had in hand.

An adherent of the Left, in the party sense of the word, Ibsen of course never became; but the general development of events led to his writings forming a component part of the work of emancipation which was going on in Norway—political emancipation included; and there was, therefore, to men of every shade of liberal opinion in the country, something symbolic in the meeting between Ibsen and Björnson which took place in September 1884 at Schwaz in the Tyrol. It set, as it were, a public seal upon the alliance of the powers of freedom, in pursuit of a common aim. The two old friends themselves were deeply affected by this meeting after a separation of more than twenty years. Their renewed friendship has stood the test of all the changes that years have brought. In 1892 the marriage of Ibsen's only son with one of Björnson's daughters added close family ties to those of friendship. When Björnson came to congratulate Ibsen on his seventy-fifth birthday, Ibsen said, with tears in his eyes: "After all, it is you I have loved best."

\*　　\*　　\*　　\*　　\*　　\*

Ibsen left Norway in 1864. The first important outcome of his residence abroad was the dramatic poem *Brand*, which appeared in March 1866. The earliest outward sign of the influence of this book was the granting to its author of the state-pension which he had so long been endeavouring to obtain. It was conferred on him by the Norwegian Government—unanimously voted by "the pocket-edition souls" from whom he expected no comprehension—as a public recognition of his literary labours. Although, in the matter of this pension and other grants, Ibsen was among the authors to whom the state-authorities showed most favour, his attitude towards the state has always been one of decided opposition. Such an attitude is the natural result of his conception of the relation between the state and the individual, a conception to which he has frequently given distinct and forcible expression in his works—for example, in the famous funeral speech in *Peer Gynt*—and upon which he dwells in many of his Letters. The life of the nation, its independent intellectual and moral development, was of more consequence in his eyes than the constitution of the state; in fact he could not see any reasonable necessity for the existence of the state (Letter 79), or of the present "political and social ideas" (*Saml. værker*, x. 516). To him the single steps towards liberty for the citizen, made by revolutions within the state, were meaningless. The revolution in which he was ready to take part, must be one which would utterly destroy the state and secure for all time to come unlimited liberty for the individual.

Holding such opinions, it was naturally his aim to withdraw himself as much as possible from the hampering influence of the state; and this explains to us why he kept away from Norway during so many important years of his life—how he felt it to be almost a necessity for him to live at a distance from the home-country and its social conditions. "Go abroad, carissimo!" he cried to Björnson (Letter 45). "Both because distance gives a wider range of vision, and because much more value is set upon the man who is out of sight." And he gave the same advice to all those of his countrymen and country-women in the development of whose minds and characters he took a special interest—such as Magdalene Thoresen (Letters 42 and 47), Laura Kieler (Letter 71), and Christian Elster (Letter 144). He himself found his most peaceful home in Rome, where no politics, no commercial spirit, no militarism had set their stamp on the population (Letter 22). As long as Rome had not yet become the capital of a Kingdom of Italy— as long as it was not yet "taken away from us human beings and given to the politicians" (Letter 77), he could hardly understand how it was possible to live anywhere else (Letter 47). It is characteristic of this aversion of his from the state-principle, that he could never persuade himself to settle for any time in Prussia, which, especially after the successful war of 1870, was to him the type of a state, the strength of which was bought by "the merging of the individual in the political and geographical concept" (Letter 79).

Abroad, released from the yoke of the state, he could more freely feel as a Norwegian and write as a Norwegian. For, as he said in his speech to the Christiania students in 1874: "A poet belongs by nature to the race of the long-sighted. Never have I seen home, and the living life of home, so distinctly, so circumstantially, and so closely, as from a distance and in absence" (*Saml. værker*, x. 511). It was just about this time, in the middle of the Seventies, that Ibsen's literary activity entered, with *The Pillars of Society*, upon a new phase, during which, with a firm foothold in Norwegian social and intellectual life, he describes Norwegian people and Norwegian conditions. He kept home affairs as present with him as possible by reading the Scandinavian newspapers regularly and carefully, corresponding with friends and ac-quaintances in Norway (correspondence in which he very

certainly received more than he gave), and embracing the many
opportunities which offered of meeting and associating with
travelling Norwegians. During the twenty-seven years of his
voluntary exile, his longing for his native land led him to visit
it twice. On the occasion of his visit to Christiania in 1874,
he observed with joyful satisfaction—so he wrote to Hegel—
that " every one received him with remarkable friendliness," " that
all displeasure with him had vanished." He did not, however, at
this time feel any temptation to settle down at home again.
" As I sailed up the fjord," he wrote to Björnson afterwards
(Letter 182), " I felt a weight settling down on my breast, a feeling of actual physical oppression. The feeling lasted during my
whole stay. I was no longer myself beneath the gaze of these
cold, uncomprehending Norwegian eyes at the windows and in
the streets." At the time he wrote this (1884), the author of
*Ghosts* and *An Enemy of the People* was already openly at war
with the political and social powers at home; and his second
visit to Norway (in 1885) ended in a jarring dissonance (Letter
188). He had, however, employed part of his time in making
careful studies of men and manners, which he employed in the
construction of the rousing conflict - drama (" kampdrama ")
*Rosmersholm* (Letter 191).

Ibsen's antagonistic attitude to his native country, his
adoption of the rôle of " state-satirist " (Letters 45 and 98), was
in reality only the other side of his patriotism. Although in
his dramas of modern life he is primarily the poet who sees
and creates human characters and human destinies, and has
an unquestionable claim to be judged as poet, there is unmistakably a tendency in his poetry—he felt it to be his life-
task in Norway " to arouse the nation and lead it to think great
thoughts " (Letter 26). This enemy of the state was at one
time led so far by the tendency in question as to draw up, in
a letter (Letter 178), a whole little political programme, based
on the idea that all the " unprivileged " should unite in insisting
on their claim to liberty being acknowledged. But in general
he felt very " doubtful to what extent it would be possible to

rouse the good Norwegian people, and reform them by instalments"; what seemed to him of most importance was
"thoroughly to weed and cleanse the spiritual ground in every
direction" (Letter 141), in other words, "the revolution of the
mind of man" (Letter 77). The artist in him speaks in the
declaration that there is little hope for a nation which "considers it of more importance to build meeting-houses than
theatres, and is more ready to support the Zulu Mission than
the art-museum" (Letter 141). What supports him, in spite
of everything, in the struggle for a higher national standard
of civilisation, is his hope in the young generation (Letter 189),
which he, like his master-builder Solness, will not be afraid of,
when it comes and knocks at his door. For he was certain, as
he told a young Norwegian friend in 1885 (*Dagbladet*, 1885,
No. 203), that "what may appear like madness in the young,
is what will in the end prove victorious"; and he promised to
march along with the youth of Norway as "left file leader."
He has lived to see that the practical reforms which he proposed
in 1884—the introduction of manhood suffrage, the emancipation of woman, the abolition of the Church's control of the
national schools—have to a great extent been actually carried
out in Norway.

In a moment of anger Ibsen might resolve "to sever all ties
with Norway and never set foot on her soil again" (Letter
85); but when complete self-expatriation became a practical
question, he shrank from it as a too "serious step," which it
would be "unspeakably hard" for him to take. "I must come
home again, after all," he wrote to Björnson as early as 1875
(Letters 20 and 33 in combination); and we know that "from
the land of sunshine and flowers, every night in the silent
hours, a homeless rider hied him forth, towards the huts of the
snowy north" (*Saml. værker*, IV. p. xvii.). In 1891 Ibsen
came back to Norway and settled in Christiania. He was at
home once more among his own people. The secret longing,
which was always drawing him homewards, had taken the form
of a longing for that sea which he had learned to love in the

days of his youth at Grimstad. "Of all that is wanting to me down here," he wrote both from Munich and from Rome, "the want of the sea is what I have most difficulty in becoming reconciled to" (Letters 149 and 187). But life at home did not permanently satisfy his longing. "The man who has made himself a home in many lands, never in his heart of hearts feels at home for good anywhere—not even in his native country" —such was the mournful conclusion to which he himself came after seven years' residence in Christiania (*Saml. værker*, x. 520). It was no longer possible for him to acclimatise himself. He did not find the free, open sea at home. He found " all the 'sounds' closed, and all the channels of comprehension blocked" (Letter 230). And once more the old poet longed to be off—out into the wide world. This time it was Denmark that attracted him—the country where, in 1887, he had re-discovered the sea and rejoiced in it. But now he was tied to Christiania; and in Christiania he has been obliged to remain.

\*     \*     \*     \*     \*     \*

We have poetic testimony from Ibsen's own pen which proves how early he felt himself more than merely a Norwegian —felt himself a Scandinavian. It was in the days of his youth that the movement which goes by the name of "Scandinavism" began, and developed vigorously, both as an intellectual and a political movement. As a youth of twenty-one, Ibsen wrote a passionate appeal to the "brothers of the North" to unite in defending South Jutland (Schleswig).[1] And in 1863 he again conjured his countrymen to stand by their Danish brother "in the hour of danger, on the day of battle" (*Saml. værker*, IV. 300–303.) The "Scandinavian" ideal never lost its place in his heart, and it more than once inspired his poetry. Unification was the leading thought in *The Pretenders*; and in *Peer Gynt*

[1] Fragments of this poem were printed in the *Tilskuer* in 1903, pp. 300–303. It is to be found in its entirety in German (*Sämtl. Werke*, I. 198–204).

Ibsen opposed himself to all Norwegian separatism and self-sufficiency. The "Scandinavian" idea appears clearly both in the long poem written in 1872, on the occasion of the celebration of the thousandth anniversary of Norway's existence as a kingdom (*Saml. værker*, IV. 424–432), and in the remarkable little cosmic picture, "Stars and Nebulæ" (*Saml. værker*, IV. 434–435.) Even in his old age he has not been able, as his speech made in Stockholm in 1898 proves, to relinquish his "old idea of a united Scandinavia as a spiritual unit." Ibsen's letters furnish a long series of testimonies to the depth and ardour of his feeling in this matter of unification; he never tired of bringing it forward.

Of the Scandinavian countries, Sweden was the one which had least influence on Ibsen's own development. Although he visited Sweden several times, and even made a special study of its institutions (Letter 87), he never penetrated at all deeply into the spirit of Swedish intellectual and social life; and there was always to him something foreign about it (Letters 47 and 94). Carl Snoilsky, the lyric poet, was the only Swedish friend with whom he ever became really intimate. They made each other's acquaintance in Rome in 1864, and were able more than once to renew the ties of friendship. In 1885 they met at Molde (Letter 191); and their last meeting was in 1898, at Stockholm, when Snoilsky made a speech in honour of his brother-poet. It was Snoilsky who, by drawing the attention of his relative Count Prozor to Ibsen's works, really brought about their introduction to the French reading public. Prozor was the first translator of Ibsen into French.

A much stronger, in some respects a decisive, influence was exercised on Ibsen's life by Denmark, and Danish intellectual conditions. Inspirations from Denmark reached him very early—before he had ever set foot in the country. The first periodical with which he was connected in Christiania, *Andhrimner* (which Ibsen, Botten-Hansen, and Vinje started in 1851), was a direct imitation of a famous Danish polemical periodical, M. Goldschmidt's *Corsaren*. And in *Andhrimner*

Vinje wrote a long article on Goldschmidt—an article in praise
and defence of the spiritual leader of the new generation, the
man who had taught the young men of his day an attitude of
manly doubt towards all authorities and all infallible truths,
taught them to judge unbiassedly, without regard to party
considerations or to the verdict of majorities.  At a later period
Ibsen made the personal acquaintance of this teacher of his
youth; in the beginning of 1867 he received a "very admirable
and cordial letter" from him (Letter 40), and in 1872
Goldschmidt went to Dresden for the sole purpose of visiting
the young Norwegian by whom his ideas had been developed
with such genius.

Soon after the *Andhrimner* time, in the spring of 1852,
Ibsen paid his first visit to Denmark, for the purpose of
studying theatrical art as practised at Copenhagen (Letters
3 and 9).  It is probable that even then he experienced the
feeling which he once described in a speech (*Saml. værker*,
x. 521)—"the feeling of having escaped from the dark into
the light—from the thick mist through a tunnel into the
sunshine." He was giving expression to his own private
experience when he called Copenhagen the "real centre of
Scandinavia" (Letter 22).  But—as was only right—this feeling
could not and did not prevent him from openly opposing any
unjust pretensions in intellectual matters on the part of Denmark in general or Copenhagen in particular.  He demanded
of the Danes that they should respect the first and essential
principle of Scandinavism—the complete equality of the three
Scandinavian nations, and the independence of each, subject
to the conditions of the union (*Saml. værker*, x. 437, 438).
He aimed at emancipating the Norwegian stage **from** all such
Danish influence as tended to obliterate its national characteristics (Letter 3); and he could and did write most satirically of
Copenhagen pretentiousness, and conceit, and ignorance of
Scandinavian affairs — and of the narrow-mindedness which
took no interest in anything "beyond the bridges and ram-
parts" (Letter 113)   These were the things which prevented

Copenhagen from taking its place as the chief city of the North.

None of the works written by Ibsen in the Fifties and the first half of the Sixties had made any lasting impression in Denmark, but with *Brand* he at once took a prominent position in Danish literature. And this position was rendered more secure by his connection with the Gyldendalske publishing firm in Copenhagen. But the æsthetic standard then established in Denmark at first prevented any appreciation of the most characteristic and essential qualities in Ibsen's poetry. The leading critic of the day, Clemens Petersen, refused to acknowledge *Peer Gynt* as poetry, and relegated this great work to the same class of literature as *Corsaren*, a polemical newspaper. This utter want of understanding drew from Ibsen the memorable words: "My book *is* poetry; and if it is not, then it will be. The conception of poetry shall be made to conform to the book" (Letter 44). Denmark did not succeed in imposing her "conventions of beauty" on this original poet (Letter 59). It was, on the contrary, Ibsen who entirely refashioned the Danish conception of the nature of poetry.

In Denmark Ibsen was soon to find an able ally, who awakened an understanding of his quality as a poet not only in that country but throughout Europe. This was young George Brandes. Ibsen's attention was directed to this future intellectual pioneer at a very early period in his career. He heard in Rome from Brandes's friend, Ludvig David, of the new critic who was preparing to raise the banner of the future (Letter 27). And he felt strongly appealed to by the gallant manner in which Brandes, then only twenty-four, had thrown down the gauntlet to both orthodoxy and the philosophy of Rasmus Nielsen, which aimed at a compromise between religion and science, at "a recognition of the undoubted value of science, along with a retention of the ideal requirements of faith" (R. Nielsen, *Det aandelige Liv i Nutiden* [*The Spiritual Life of the Present Day*], p. 253). It was clear to

3

him that "this man would play a prominent part in the
intellectual life of Scandinavia" (Letter 43). Brandes, too, was
undoubtedly hampered at first by the traditions of Danish
æstheticism. He regarded *Peer Gynt* from the same standpoint
as Clemens Petersen; he wrote in the strongest terms of condemnation of Ibsen's habit of "moralising," and he declared
the poem to be "neither beautiful nor true" (Brandes, *Samlede
Skrifter*, iii. 271). To this Ibsen replied that he was utterly
indifferent to æsthetical conventions; that to him, conventional ugliness, if it were full of character, might actually be
beautiful—"by virtue of its inherent truth" (Letter 60). And
to this view Brandes allowed himself to be easily converted,
because his own personal inclinations lay in the same direction;
life soon extended the range of his vision and of his sym-
pathies, and he "got rid of all the prejudices which were due
to education and tradition" (Brandes, *Samlede Skrifter*, iii. 239).
And so, when Ibsen called on him to be a leader in the great
spiritual revolution (Letter 77), Brandes answered with a fiery
poem of homage, in which he declares himself ready to take
part in the fight, as the born follower and squire of Ibsen,
his "matchless leader" (Brandes, *Samlede Skrifter*, xii. 366–367).

The new conception of art, which made truthful human
character-drawing the first and highest requirement, was formulated by Brandes, in his famous lectures on "Main Currents
in Nineteenth Century Literature," more distinctly than by
any other writer. The First Series of these lectures appeared
in book form in 1872; and how strongly Ibsen now, in his
turn, was influenced by Brandes, we learn from many passages
in his Letters. "No more dangerous book could fall into the
hands of a pregnant poet," he wrote at once to Brandes in
1872 (Letter 91). And what constantly occupied his thoughts,
disturbing even his night's rest, was not the historical subject
of the book—"the Emigrant Literature"—it was the manner
in which Brandes, from the starting-point of literature, "re-
volted" against existing conditions (Letter 109), and, eager
for the fray and inspired by a heaven-storming desire for

liberty, assaulted the prejudices of society,—his manner, for example, of treating suicide, or unlawful love. This is what Ibsen means when he says that the book "places a yawning gulf between yesterday and to-day" (Letter 91). It may almost be asserted that Brandes's work, which created a new school of literature in Denmark, was also "epoch-making" in Ibsen's literary career. It gave him new strength at the time when he was beginning to devote his whole productive energy to the drama of modern society. And on the path of development on which Ibsen now entered, Brandes followed him, step by step, as his faithful defender and interpreter, at home and abroad. After the first years of impassioned warfare, the aggressive tone in Ibsen's works gradually died away, giving place to the mood of the true poet, who does not judge men, but tries to understand them. This was what he himself in 1871 had declared to be his task—to see and describe life in its tragic and comic developments (Letter 81). With *The Wild Duck* he entered upon "new paths" in his dramatic production (Letter 181), and, in following them, succeeded in fulfilling the task which he had set himself. After having unburdened himself, in *Rosmersholm*, of something which it was "a vital necessity" to him to proclaim publicly, even though he knew that there were many to whom it would give offence (speech at Molde, September 4, 1885), he no longer took the same eager interest in the polemics of the day (speech at Gothenburg, September 12, 1887); and a new, more purely psychological stage in his writings began. Now, again, he found Brandes at his side—for the new element, the "element of the future," which Ibsen considered that Brandes had introduced into the writing of history (Letter 172), was exactly this same capacity of *seeing* —it was the artistic, intuitive revivifying of past times and people. This was the quality in Brandes's works which in Ibsen's estimation constituted them "poems" (Letters 172 and 233).

Whilst the poet and the critic were thus gradually approaching each other in the course of their development (Letter 179), their brotherhood in arms was becoming more and more of a real, personal friendship (Letter 107). And, obstinate and combative men though they both were, each in his own way, the friendship has been an unbroken one. Brandes was often annoyed by Ibsen's neglectfulness in the matter of correspondence; but the feeling of spiritual kinship always drew him again to the side of his literary friend and "chief"; and Ibsen on his side never allowed any feeling of annoyance to produce a change in the old relationship; for he always felt that from Brandes he received that understanding which to him was of more value than any praise. "I do not require," he wrote to him, "the kind of agreement upon which the preservation of a friendship usually depends" (Letter 64). It was a higher kind of unanimity which formed the tie between these two men.

\*　　\*　　\*　　\*　　\*　　\*

On the subject of one mental evolutionary process, Ibsen wrote to Brandes: "I began by feeling myself to be a Norwegian; then I developed into a Scandinavian; and I have ended in *Teutonism*. And it was his firm belief (expressed in a speech to be found in the *Sämtliche Werke*, I. 527) that it was necessary for an author to become a denizen "of the great Teutonic house," in order to ensure victory for his ideas in his own native land. "It is abroad," he cried to Brandes (Letter 96), "that we Scandinavians are to win our decisive battle; a victory in Germany, and you will be master of the situation at home!"

Ibsen's own connection with Germany began very early. On his tour in the interests of theatrical art in 1852, he spent two months in Dresden, to make himself acquainted with the German theatre; and his recollections of this stay were "among the pleasantest and brightest" he possessed (Letter 25). And yet neither at that time nor for long afterwards did he permit any spiritual influence from Germany to reach him. For, unnatural as he himself recognised the position to be, even in those early days he regarded the Germans as the "hereditary enemies" of

Scandinavia (Letter 25)—principally because he believed that the
dependence of the Danes upon Germany in intellectual matters
had hindered the independent development of Scandinavian
intellectual life. His study of the subject had shown him
that for the last fifty years the reactionary currents in theology,
in philosophy, and in literature, had almost all come to the North
from Germany, whereas very few progressive movements had
had their origin there. And the next time he set foot on
German soil, on his way to Rome in 1864, the events of the
war had violently inflamed his Scandinavian patriotic feelings;
we see from his letters to Björnson and Fru Thoresen (18 and
22) that he was almost maddened with indignation. His
sympathy with the unfortunate Danish "brother nation," and
feeling of anger and shame at the behaviour of Norway and
Sweden, found expression in Rome in heated private and public
speech, and even in the almost childish form of caricature-
drawing (L. Dietrichson, *Svundne Tider*, i. 334, 335, 342). In
his well-known speech at P. A. Munch's grave, on the 11th of
June 1865, addressing the Danes, he cried : " Root out, with word
and with spiritual deed, that party in your country which does
everything with its eyes turned to the south, as if its home-land
lay there ! " (*Saml. værker*, x. 505).

In the spring of 1868 Ibsen set out, it must be confessed
most unwillingly, on his homeward journey from Italy. He
broke it at Munich and at Dresden—settling down in the last-
mentioned town to spend the winter of 1868–69. As he became
accustomed to them, Germany and the German spirit and conditions proved to have considerable attractions for him ; and the
winter visit was lengthened into a residence of years. No
doubt one consideration which strengthened his determination
to make a long stay in Germany was the facility there
offered for the education of his only son ; and he was probably
also influenced by the strained relations existing at this time
between him and those friends at home from whom he would
naturally have sought support on his return.

Ibsen was in Dresden during the Franco-Prussian War and

the subsequent political developments in Germany—Germany's
"great period" (Letter 198). The stirring events made such an
impression on him that he could not collect his thoughts
sufficiently to be able to write (Letters 75 and 80); and during
this period of enforced idleness he formed an entirely new
estimate of Germany. It was borne in upon him what a
wonderful thing the "discipline" is, to which, in his opinion, the
honour of the Germans' victory and their consolidation into an
empire were due. That ideal of unification which he had so
ardently longed to see realised by the three Scandinavian peoples,
he now saw in realisation in Germany. And the impression of
the tremendous power for progress which lies in strict national
discipline was never effaced from his mind. In his speech to
women (May 26, 1898) he besought mothers to regard it as
their highest task to serve their country by awakening in their
children "a conscious feeling of culture and discipline" (*Saml.
værker*, x. 526). In this manner did Ibsen receive his first
great spiritual gift from Germany. The old "Scandinavian"
became a "Teuton"—but without relinquishing his Scandinavism; the difference being that he now regarded it as only a
preparation for a higher spiritual race-unification.

During his residence in Dresden, Ibsen was, as is well-known,
accused (in 1871) of having mentioned Germany in a very hostile
manner in his *Poems*, which had just been published. In his
"defence" (*Sämtliche Werke*, I. 506–509) he maintained with
perfect justice that it was unfair to attack a man holding the
views which he did now, for what he had written at a time when
his standpoint was a perfectly different one; and he averred,
moreover, that he had never entered the lists *against* Germany,
but only *for* Scandinavia.

"Under German intellectual influences" (Letter 198) Ibsen
at last succeeded in writing the long-planned drama, *Emperor
and Galilean*; and whilst he was completing it, he saw
with his own eyes the violent struggle between state and
church, between the kingdom of this and the kingdom of
the other world, reproduced in the German "Kulturkampf."

His drama "became more suited to the times" than he himself had expected it to be (Letter 109); the characters of the poet's imagination fitted in with the reality of the new spiritual movement, and gained thereby in force and influence.

Except for a shorter and a longer stay in Italy (1878–79 and 1880–1885) Ibsen lived in Germany from 1868 to 1891, first in Dresden and then, for a longer time, in Munich. This in itself is sufficient evidence that he had learned to feel at home in Germany. But we have it in his own words. On the 13th of November 1885 he wrote from Munich to George Brandes: "I feel quite at home here, much more so than in my own home, so-called." In Germany the foundation of his universal fame was laid; of his victorious career in Germany itself we find some account in his Letters. Curiously enough, it was a Norwegian who first thought of translating Ibsen's works into German—John Grieg, a man of artistic and literary interests, a brother of Edward Grieg, the composer. In 1866 Grieg translated *The Pretenders* into German iambics. (This idea of Grieg's has a curious counterpart in Edmund Gosse's assertion that *Emperor and Galilean* ought to have been written in verse [Letter 110]). But his translation was never published. Three years later a literary amateur, P. F. Siebold, of Cassel, made a well-intentioned, but not quite so well executed, attempt to introduce Ibsen to German readers by means of a translation of *Brand* (Letters 54 and 56). Various circumstances combined to prevent this translation appearing before 1872, in which year Adolf Strodtmann, a man with more literary taste and a more poetic mind, translated and published *The Pretenders* and *The League of Youth* (Letter 90).

Ibsen's plays began to appear on the German stage in 1875 and 1876—thanks to the pioneer work of the "Meiningen" actors and to the exertions of his friends in Munich, notably Fräulein Emma Klingenfeld. *The Pretenders* and *The Vikings at Helgeland* were the two then acted. But these attracted little notice; they did not appeal by anything remarkably new to the German artistic sense. It was with *The Pillars of Society*,

*A Doll's House*, and *Ghosts*, that Ibsen became a power in German intellectual life. In 1878 *The Pillars of Society* was put on the stage, not only in Berlin, but in many of the other large towns of Germany; and this work made a decisive impression upon the generation which was afterwards to forward Ibsen's cause in Germany. "Our young eyes were opened by it," wrote Paul Schlenther many years afterwards (Ibsen's *Sämtliche Werke*, VI. pp. xvii.-xviii.), "to all the theatrical artificiality of the day. We trembled with joy. We revisited the theatre time after time; and we could sit all day reading the play in Wilhelm Lange's bad translation. Neither the unpoetic, stiff German nor the manners of the actors in the suburban theatre could do away with the power of the drama. Until then Ibsen had been to us an empty name. This play taught us to love him—to love him for life. I may affirm for many of my contemporaries, as well as for myself, that it was the influence of this modern realistic work, at a decisive period in our development, which determined the tendency of our taste for the rest of our lives. Here, in our era of marvellously realistic politics, we had come upon correspondingly realistic poetry. Now it was a joy to live, for there was living together with us a poet who had the strength and the courage to face the questions of the day." Similar testimony to the impression produced by *The Pillars of Society* is borne by Otto Brahm (*Neue Freie Presse*, May 10, 1904): "We received from it the first idea of a possible new poetic world; we felt ourselves for the first time in the presence of fictitious characters of our own age in whom we could believe; and from this comprehensive criticism of the society of the day we saw ideals of liberty and truth emerging victoriously, as 'pillars of society.' From that hour we were adherents of this new school of realistic art; we had found our æsthetic creed."

But the deeper Henrik Ibsen probed into existing conditions, the more violent, in Germany also, did the outcry against his plays become. Much was written against *A Doll's House*, much

more against *Ghosts*.  The translation of *Ghosts* was a really
daring literary deed.  The play had been in existence for three
years before any one ventured to translate it—then Frau Marie
von Borch was courageous enough to make it accessible to the
German reading public.

Two Danes, George Brandes and Julius Hoffory, have unobtru-
sively acted, as it were, the part of agents and interpreters of
Scandinavian thought in Germany ; they have, in particular, done
much, both as critics and by their personal influence, to forward
Ibsen's cause.  Brandes, who during a residence of more than five
years in Berlin (1877–1883) won for his own work and aims the
favour and support of the young literary generation, produced,
by his essays on Ibsen, a real understanding of the Norwegian
poet's writings and greatness.  Hoffory introduced some system
into the work of translation—particularly of the newer dramas ;
and his own powerful, original character enabled him to convert
many of Ibsen's opponents.  Ibsen's great polemical drama,
*Ghosts*, had divided Germany into parties for and against him ;
and when the play came to be performed, the dispute became
most violent.  The first theatrical manager who ventured to
stage *Ghosts*, was August Grosse, director of the Augsburg
Theatre, who did it at the instigation of the Ibsen circle in
Munich.  Then the Duke of Meiningen ordered its performance
at his theatre.  But the triumph of the play, and the spread
of the new conception of life and art which had produced it, were
not assured until it had been performed in Berlin on the 9th of
January 1887 (Letter 196).  On this occasion it was Hoffory
who inspired the leaders of the undertaking with courage ; and
he also took an active part in the necessary preparations.

In 1887 no fewer than three critical works on the writings
of Ibsen were published in Germany.  But the first great
German literary portrait of the Norwegian author had been
given to the public four years previously by Ludwig Passarge,
who was peculiarly qualified for his self-imposed task by his
thorough knowledge of the country and people of Norway.
Passarge was also courageous enough to make such a character-

istically Norwegian work as *Peer Gynt* accessible to his countrymen by means of a translation (Letter 146).

Thus Ibsen won, slowly but surely, an established position
in the German literary world and on the German stage.
Translators sprang up like mushrooms. Ibsen had only too
good reason for writing to Rudolf Schmidt on the 31st of August
1892: "I have, unfortunately, far more German translators than
I desire." He soon began to publish "authorised German
editions" of his new works simultaneously with the first
Norwegian editions (Letter 141), in order to protect himself
from being taken advantage of by unauthorised and uncon-
scientious translators and publishers (Letter 151). It was not
until the Nineties that an end was put to the lawless condition
of matters. In Berlin Ibsen found a publisher who assisted
him in asserting his rights; and it was in Berlin that the
complete German edition of his works was planned and
published (Letter 231). One aim of this edition was to show
German readers the inward coherence of Ibsen's work, by giving
them his plays in chronological order; another was to substitute
for the stiff book-language of many of the older translations
a reproduction of the characteristic, animated language of the
Ibsen originals. Especially in his poetic dramas and his poems,
much injustice had been done him; and here, not mere translators, but poets, were required, to give the poet his due.

But Ibsen has not merely presented the German reading
public with books and the German stage with a repertory;
he has done what is of infinitely greater importance—he has
re-fertilised the literature of the country and released productive energies which, but for his mighty creative word, might
never have become conscious of themselves, or rather of their
tasks. On the soil which he has prepared by his theories and
his practice, a whole new literary school has arisen, of which
the powerful and beautiful works of Gerhart Hauptmann entitle
him to be considered the chief. There is no question of imitation
—in Hauptmann's case the word would be peculiarly inapplic-
able—only of a free and independent further-development of

ideas received. The selection of *Ghosts* for the opening performance of the "Freie Bühne" of Berlin, on the 22nd of September
1889, gave public expression to the feeling that Ibsen has been
the literary leader of young Germany.

    *       *       *       *       *       *

Neither in England nor in France has Ibsen had the same
powerful, life-awakening influence, though in these two countries
also, gifted critics have endeavoured to interpret his works,
accomplished translators have tried to spread them among
their countrymen, and theatrical managers and actors have
done their best to make room for them in the stage repertories.
The discoverer of Ibsen for England was Edmund Gosse, a
man of letters in whom learning and critical severity are com-.
bined with poetic feeling. He first named the name of Ibsen
to the English public (Letter 90), and offered that public, in
excellent translations, the first specimens of his poetry. Following in Gosse's steps came William Archer, who undertook the
systematic translation of Ibsen's dramas into English, and
who succeeded, assisted by the Norwegian-English journalist,
H. L. Brækstad, in introducing them on the English stage. In
the same year in which Archer's main propaganda was beginning in England (1888), a Russian diplomatist in France, Count
Moritz Prozor, a highly-cultivated man with literary tastes,
began a series of French translations, which finally included
almost all Ibsen's dramas of modern life.

The courageous pioneer, Antoine, in his "Théâtre libre,"
made the first attempt to place Ibsen's characters on the French
stage. Lugné Poë, the manager of another independent theatre,
"L'Oeuvre," was the next to undertake the task; he, in course
of time, made Ibsen plays the specialty of his theatre. There
has been a more vigorous development of "Ibsenism" in France
than in any other country; something almost of the nature of
a sect is formed by those who discuss the poet and the meaning
of his works. And among French dramatists Ibsen has found
many imitators, who have made their characters discuss social

problems on the stage with more or less intelligence and more
or less effective dialogue; but all of these have, nevertheless, in
essentials adhered to the limitations of the older French drama.
No French dramatist has as yet perceived and appropriated the
essential feature of "Ibsenism"—the representation of human
character.

Still slighter is the influence which Ibsen has exercised on
the development of the drama in England.  But there is one
dramatic author at least, namely, George Bernard Shaw, whose
clever and original works show that he has received impulses from
Ibsen, and that he has rightly comprehended the Norwegian
master.  In London also, on the 13th of March 1891, an "Independent Theatre" opened its doors to the public with a performance of *Ghosts*.  This theatre, however, had but a short
existence, and, contrary to what had happened in Berlin, none
of the regular theatres endeavoured to carry out its ideas.  The
men who in England have striven, with courage, insight, and
fidelity, to bear Ibsen's banner onwards, are generally regarded
as "men of the lost causes."

In Italy, some of Ibsen's plays were known earlier than in
France, but it was not until the Nineties that he really made
his mark there.  Now, except in their Scandinavian home and
in Germany, there is no country where his dramas of modern
society, especially *A Doll's House* and *Ghosts*, are so often and
so widely played as in Italy, where the most eminent scenic
artists have found some of their principal rôles in Ibsen's characters.  No new Italian school of literature has followed in
Ibsen's footprints; but the great social questions which his
plays have raised have become the subject of eager and widespread discussion.  On the students of the universities, in
particular, his books have exercised a powerful influence.  He
has acted as a stimulating force in the process of national social
regeneration.

*       *       *       *       *       *

The letters from Ibsen herewith presented to the public—

letters to Scandinavians, to Germans, to Englishmen, to semi-Frenchmen—show us how his fame and his influence have spread from country to country. They do not give a complete description of the process, but convey it to us in characteristic fragments. The degree in which Ibsen has impressed himself on the national consciousness as an artistic and intellectual power has varied very much in the different countries. But a poet of world-wide fame he has undoubtedly become at last—the Norwegian author whose struggle was at first such a hard one. The prophetic, determined words which he wrote in 1866, before even *Brand* was published—"I will and shall have a victory some day" (Letter 24)—these words he himself has converted into historic fact.

# LETTERS

## 1.

*To* OLE SCHULERUD.[1]

GRIMSTAD, 15*th October* 1849.

MY DEAR FRIEND,—Your last letter has given me pleasure in more ways than one; in the first place, it leads me to expect a speedy accomplishment of our undertaking; in the second, it proves, by your characterisation of my letter to you as the product of a momentary, hasty impulse, that you are my true friend. Your lenient judgment makes me hope that you have put yourself in my place, and realised the point of view from which I have looked at the matter. I hope you have realised the disappointment I have had every mail-day, and have understood that it put me into an exceedingly unpleasant humour. I was unable to divine the reason of your silence, and the uncertainty could not but give rise to a thousand doubts, all the more painful because I could not in my heart acknowledge one of them as well founded.

Your letter has explained everything that seemed doubtful in your conduct; and I should ill deserve your friendship if I did not, with the utmost readiness, take back everything in my own that could be construed as an offensive doubt of the honesty of

[1] Ibsen's friend, Ole Schulerud (1827–1859), at this time a law-student, had gone to Christiania in the beginning of September 1849, taking with him a copy of the manuscript of the drama, *Catilina*, as author of which Ibsen assumed the pseudonym of " Brynjolf Bjarme." Schulerud offered the play to the Christiania Theatre, and tried to find a publisher for it; but the theatre refused it, and no publisher cared to bring it out. Ibsen's impatience had found vent in an angry letter (unfortunately destroyed), for which the above is an apology.

your intentions. I therefore again beg you to overlook the whole thing as something that can have no effect upon our future friendly relations, and I hope to receive in your next letter an assurance that you do.

I have not time to write more to-day. Due [1] asks me to thank you for the guitar; he is expecting it with impatience. I also thank you very much for the trouser material. I had not given it further thought, and believed that the matter had escaped your memory too; but it is very acceptable, for I must needs save as much as possible nowadays. The first act of *Olaf Tr(ygvesön)* [2] is virtually finished; I think it will be really good, and trust that this play will prepare less unpleasantness for us than *C(atilina)* did. Farewell!—Your affectionate friend,

HENRIK IBSEN.

*P.S.*—Do me the kindness of consigning my last letter to the flames; it vexes me to know that it is in your possession!


## 2.

*To* OLE SCHULERUD.

GRIMSTAD, *5th January* 1850.

MY DEAR FRIEND,—Your last letter conveyed to me *Catilina's* death sentence. It is a blow to me, but there is no use in losing courage. You are quite right in saying that this apparent defeat is not really to be looked upon as one. *C.* was only intended to be a forerunner of those other things of the same kind which we had planned; and it may still fulfil its purpose. I am of precisely the same opinion as you, namely, that it will be best to sell the play; and I think its rejection by the

---

[1] Christopher Lorentz Due, Ibsen's other intimate friend, had been the copier of the manuscript.

[2] During the winter of 1849-50, Ibsen was engaged in writing a drama, with King Olaf Trygvesön as its hero. It was never finished.

Management will rather do good than harm, since, from the terms of the letter, it was apparently not for lack of merit that it was refused. The sale of the play you will, of course, manage as you think best. I will only observe that to me it seems better to sell the right of publication than to publish ourselves. In the latter case we should have to advance a considerable sum of money to cover the cost of printing, and should have to be content to receive the profits by gradual instalments; in the former we have nothing to do but accept payment; however, we must allow ourselves to be governed by circumstances.

Now a few words about my literary labours. Of *Olaf T(rygvesön)*, as I have no doubt already said, the first act is practically finished; the little one-act play, *Normannerne*,[1] is rewritten, or rather will be so immediately, for I am now busy with it. In its new form it will clothe a more developed idea than that for which it was originally destined. I have made use of some Telemarken legends and stories for a few short poems adapted in their metre to well-known popular melodies— thus making an adventure in the national line.[2] I have also half finished a longer and, perhaps, somewhat extravagant poem entitled " Ball-room Memories," which owes its existence to my imaginary infatuation of last summer.[3] But what has been really my most important work since your departure is a national historical novel, which I have called *The Prisoner of Akershus*, and which treats of the sad fate of Christian Lofthus.

No doubt the story of this man's life is familiar to you; in case it is not, here is a short sketch of it. C. L. lived on his

---

[1] *Normannerne* was the name given to the first draft of *Kaempehöjen* (*The Hero's Mound*). In the revised form mentioned in this letter, the little play was acted in the Christiania Theatre in the autumn of 1850. It was never printed, but a written copy of it is preserved at the National Theatre, Christiania.

[2] The only existing poem of Ibsen's in which a Telemarken legend is employed, is an unpublished one of 1850, "The Miller's Boy."

[3] This poem is preserved in manuscript in the Christiania University Library. It is translated in full in the German edition of Ibsen's *Sämtliche Werke*.

4

property of Lofthus, near Lillesand, in the latter part of the last century.  The Danish Government officials were more tyrannical there than anywhere else; and Lofthus, at that time still a young man and very generally respected, decided to espouse the cause of his oppressed neighbours.  He prepared a list of grievances against the officials and set out for Copenhagen, where he appeared in person before the King, and pleaded the cause of the people so forcibly that a commission was appointed and the most hated of the officials were discharged.  This was more than his enemies could bear ; he was accused of negotiating with the Swedish King, of aiming to assist him to the Kingdom of Norway on consideration of receiving part of it as an independent kingdom for himself.  As a result, warrants were issued for the arrest of Lofthus; but no sooner did the fact become known than a host of armed peasant farmers prepared to defend him.  He fortified his house and sustained an actual siege, until he was treacherously lured to a neighbouring house, captured, and conveyed, in a ship that lay in readiness, to Christiania. Here he remained imprisoned in Akershus Fortress, without trial, for ten years—until 1797.  His friends worked for him in secret, and finally secured his pardon; but too late; just before it arrived, death had released him.  These are the historical facts of the case, as I have discovered from an old document which has fortunately come into my possession.  Don't you think that something may be made of this ?[1]

I consider it necessary to supply *Catilina* with a short introduction, and therefore request you to copy and insert the following

### PREFACE.

"The following play was originally intended for the stage. The Directors of the Theatre, however, have not considered it

---

[1] Of *The Prisoner of Akershus*, Ibsen wrote only one whole chapter and part of a second.  The manuscript, of 21 pages, is no longer accessible ; but an account of the composition was given by J. B. Halvorsen in 1898, in Nos. 52 and 53 of the Norwegian periodical, *Ringeren*.

suitable. Although the author has grounds for believing that the chief reason for the rejection of the play was not its want of merit, it is not without a very natural anxiety that he presents his work to the public, from whom he hopes, however, for that lenient criticism to which the first publication of a beginner may reasonably lay claim." [1]

*N.B.*—Be sure you do not let any misprints escape you. I should like to have the manuscript returned to me; and please also send me two copies of the play when it is printed. Farewell!—Yours ever,

HENRIK IBSEN.

### 3.

*To* THE MANAGEMENT OF THE NORWEGIAN THEATRE AT BERGEN.[2]

COPENHAGEN, 16*th May* 1852.

SIRS,—In my last letter I could only briefly indicate what, in accordance with my instructions, I have accomplished here; to-day I shall permit myself to be more explicit.

I have engaged as a dancing teacher for H. Nielsen, and also for Brun and his wife,[3] the solo-dancer Hoppe, of the Theatre

---

[1] This preface was not used.

[2] Ibsen had, in November 1851, been appointed dramatist to "The Norwegian Theatre," established in 1850 at Bergen by Ole Bull. In April 1852 the management sent him to visit various foreign theatres, making him a grant of 200 specie-dollars (about £90) for his travelling expenses. At Copenhagen he met with a most friendly reception from the director of the Theatre Royal, Councillor Heiberg, the well-known Danish author.

[3] The actors Johannes and Louise Brun had also received a grant to enable them to spend six weeks at Copenhagen, improving themselves in their art under Ibsen's direction. Johannes Brun (1832–1890) became the most famous of Norwegian comic actors. Fru Brun excelled in romantic rôles. Nielsen acted at Bergen and Trondhjem.

Royal, who is regarded as the leading member of the ballet, and who, besides, as I had taken care to ascertain, has had great experience in teaching. The dance in which they are to receive special instruction is the minuet; and along with it they are to be taught whatever else may contribute to an elegant deportment on the stage, Herr Hoppe bearing always in mind the method of instruction employed in the dramatic school here. He has arranged that the course of instruction is to last three weeks, with a lesson of one hour every day. The charge for this, for the three persons, is to be twenty-four rix-dollars, or about twelve specie-dollars in Norwegian money [1]—a sum which certainly cannot be regarded as unreasonable.

With regard to the proposed engagement of a dancing-master for the rest of the Bergen actors, I beg leave to state that the position of matters is as follows: Bournonville, the ballet-master, left for Christiania almost immediately after my arrival, and I had only an unsatisfactory conversation with him in the theatre the evening before his departure; at the end of this month most of the members of the ballet follow him to Christiania. The solo-dancer, Gade, who remains here, might be willing to go to Bergen this summer, but in that event he would require you, sirs, to guarantee that he will not run the risk of financial loss. Remembering your discussions on this subject, I have no reason to suppose that you will give such a guarantee. As far as I understood it, your plan was that the dancing-master in question should cover his travelling expenses by giving private lessons, the theatre only paying for the time he devoted to the instruction of the company. But it will be impossible to engage any dancer on these conditions, unless he can be assured that you have made arrangements for a certain and sufficient sum being derived from the private teaching The ballet begins its work again in August, and then every member must be back here; if, therefore, you, sirs, believe that the arrangement here suggested could be made in time for it to

[1] £2, 12s. The calculation of the specie-dollar throughout is approximate.

be of any use this year, I beg that you will let me know as soon as possible. If you decide to the contrary, Herr Hoppe has expressed his willingness to go' to Bergen next year with some members of the ballet, provided that an agreement is arrived at in good time. He demands, as one of its terms, that, during the time the theatre is not in use, he may have it for a certain number of subscription-performances, which would have to be announced beforehand; of course, the company would meanwhile receive a complete course of instruction in dancing.

This latter arrangement certainly has its advantages, but it entails losing a whole year; and it is undoubtedly desirable that the public should, in this matter also, be able as soon as possible to see the good results of the measures taken by you this year for the improvement of the theatre. If, therefore, you think that you can offer a sufficient guarantee to the dancer who is inclined to go to Bergen this year (which might be done by securing him a certain number of private pupils in advance), I beg, once more, that you will let me know.

H. Nielsen and Brun and his wife are showing great interest in the dancing lessons, and, better still, realise perfectly the necessity for them.

Speaking of H. Nielsen, I do not know what to do in regard to procuring him free admittance to the theatre. Contrary to my expectation, he was not here when we arrived; and neither the previous letters from the Management to Councillor Heiberg nor the communications which we brought with us made any mention of him. Moreover, his trip was an entirely private undertaking, which might, for anything we knew, have been given up after our departure from Bergen, so that I dared not undertake anything in his behalf before his arrival, which I looked for every day. He did not appear, however, for more than a fortnight; and, when he came, he again disappointed my expectation by bringing no written credentials with him, so that I have been unable to do anything in the way of obtaining a pass for him. He has, of course, been at the theatre every evening since he came; the cost of admittance to the pit is

trifling, and I leave it to you to decide if it is necessary to
secure for him the privilege which has been granted us. I
would only observe that, as the season ends in the last week of
the present month, he could, supposing he received the pass,
make use of it only for a few days.

Herr Overskou [1] is helping me to an acquaintance with the
interior arrangements of the theatre, the stage-management,
machinery, etc.

Works on costumes are not to be obtained here, but Herr
Overskou will give me a list of such as are procurable elsewhere, with information as to where they are to be had, so
that I may purchase them in the course of my travels. It is
impossible to tell exactly what they will cost, but I imagine
that from ten to twelve specie-dollars would enable me to
procure what the Bergen theatre requires. I have bought only
one new play, namely, *Ten Years Ago*, by Carl Bernhard.
A small sum should be allowed for this item also, as I
shall in all probability come across things in Germany worth
securing. With the assistance of Sichlaus, the actor, I hope to
procure a good deal of second-hand music. I am, however, in
uncertainty in this matter, for, being practically ignorant of
what your theatre already has, I might lead you into unnecessary outlay. If you can let me have a list of the music
which I must not buy, I shall be much obliged.

I have a strong and well-grounded apprehension that my
allowance for travelling expenses will not be sufficient for my
needs. During my stay in Hamburg I had a foretaste of what
it means to travel in Germany; and Brun would have found
himself in an embarrassing predicament if he had not been
enabled by the kindness of our fellow-traveller, Dr. Hofmann,
to continue his journey to Copenhagen. I therefore venture to
petition you, sirs, to advance 48 specie-dollars of my salary,
which (along with the 12 specie-dollars that I applied for
before my departure, and which I hope you have granted) can
be deducted from my salary at the rate of 5 specie-dollars

[1] Stage-manager of the Theatre Royal.

per month. Should you consent to this, I trust in your having the kindness to send my money here, along with the sum due to Herr Hoppe and whatever may be voted for the purchase of books, music, etc.[1]

With regard to the repertory, we have been very fortunate. We have seen *Hamlet* and several other Shakespeare plays, some of Holberg's, *Bataille de Dame* (Scribe and Legouvé), *A Sunday in Amager* (Johanne Luise Heiberg), *The Relatives*, (Buntzen), and others.

As a matter of course we acquaint ourselves with everything that is of artistic interest. The Danes are exceedingly courteous and obliging to us, and, far from feeling any displeasure at our attempt to free ourselves from their influence upon our theatre, are surprised that we have not made the effort sooner. I have become acquainted with H. C. Andersen, who advises me very strongly to go on to Vienna from Dresden, to see the Burg Theatre. Perhaps he may be there himself at the same time, and be able to show me about; if not, I hope that Professor Dahl will come to my assistance.[2]

Trusting that you, sirs, will answer this communication at the earliest possible moment, I beg to subscribe myself—Yours most respectfully,

HENRIK IBSEN.

*P.S.*—Councillor Heiberg desires to be kindly remembered to you all, and also to Judge Hansson.

---

[1] The advance of salary was not granted.

[2] The Norwegian painter, Professor J. C. Dahl, procured for Ibsen the introductions necessary to enable him to study the arrangements of the Dresden Court Theatre. At that time Emil Devrient and Bogumil Dawison were playing there. In August (1852) Ibsen returned to Bergen, without having visited Vienna.

4.

To PAUL BOTTEN-HANSEN.

BERGEN, *5th August* 1853.

MY DEAR FRIEND,—I write these lines in the greatest haste; you ought to have heard from me long ago, but——. If only I could master that demon of procrastination that goes about like a roaring lion and devours all my good intentions, I should become the most punctual man in the world. How are things with you? Are you pregnant with anything? May not "The Fairy Wedding" soon expect a little brother or sister? I myself am fairly prolific, as you will learn during the course of the winter. You must be sure to send me a copy of "The Fairy Wedding," which I cannot procure here, and also the numbers of *Andhrimner* in which "Helge Hundingsbane" appeared. Now don't forget![1]

Remember me to that nationalist, Vinje.

You will soon hear more from me. If you can do anything for the bearer of this (I mean especially in your capacity of critic), then spare no pains; he very much desires to make your acquaintance.[2]—Yours most cordially,

HENRIK IBSEN.

What news of Abildgaard[3]?

[1] Since the autumn of 1851 Botten-Hansen had been publishing a Christiania weekly paper, the *Illustreret Nyhedsblad*. During the first nine months of 1851 he, Ibsen, and Vinje had co-operated in the production of a weekly paper, the above-mentioned *Andhrimner*, one of Ibsen's contributions being the poem, "Helge Hundingsbane," and one of Botten-Hansen's, the dramatic poem, "The Fairy Wedding." For Botten-Hansen and Vinje and their influence on Ibsen, see Introduction, pp. 9, 10, 11.

[2] The bearer of this letter was the actor, Ole Bucher.

[3] For Abildgaard, see Introduction, p. 8. After a long previous period of confinement, Abildgaard was, in 1855, sentenced to five years' imprisonment with hard labour.

5.

*To* SUSANNA THORESEN.

[BERGEN], *January* 1856.

TO THE ONLY ONE.

THE ball-room glitters resplendent,
  Already the dance moves fast;
Ladies in rainbow clusters,
  Airily decked, go past.
High overhead the music
  Scatters its witchcraft fine;
Each dancer's in festal humour,
  Each lamp hath a festal shine.


Hark to the ball-room courtships,
  Whisperings soft and low—
All that the moment prompts of all
  Dreamt or heard long ago.
And the ladies smile demurely
  As memory's album receives
Speeches, fiery and tender,
  Nor speaker nor hearer believes.


Throughout the crowded ball-room
  There's naught but gladness and mirth;
Not one of them all that hath felt it—
  The weary burden of earth;
Not one of them all that hath felt it—
  Not one that could ever guess
How, under the veil of rejoicing,
  Lurks the horror of emptiness.

Ah yes! there is one, one only,
  Among so many but one.
Her eyes have a secret sadness;
  I read in them sorrow begun—
I read in them dreaming fancies
  That rise and sink without cease—
A heart that longs and throbs upwards,
  And finds in this world no peace.

Dared I but rede thee, thou riddle
  Of youth and deep dreamings wrought;
Dared I but choose thee boldly
  To be the bride of my thought;
Dared I but plunge my spirit
  Deep in thy spirit's tide,
Dared I but gaze on the visions
  In thy innocent soul that hide;

Ah, then what fair songs upspringing
  Should soar from my breast on high;
Ah, then how free I'd go sailing
  Like a bird toward the coasts of the sky!
Ah, then should my scattered visions
  To one single harmony throng;
For all of life's fairest visions
  Would mirror themselves in my song.

Dared I but rede thee, thou riddle
  Of youth and deep dreamings wrought;
Dared I but choose thee boldly
  To be the bride of my thought.

  *     *     *     *     *
    *     *     *     *     *
  *     *     *     *     *
    *     *     *     *     *

                              HENRIK IBSEN.

6.

*To* PAUL BOTTEN-HANSEN.

BERGEN, 17*th April* 1857.

MY DEAR OLD FRIEND,—First of all, accept a friendly greeting! Along with it I send you a few observations on the ancient Norwegian heroic ballads, with the request that they may appear in your paper. If you think you can make use of my article, please publish it in as large portions as possible; above all, divide it at the most suitable places, and also see to it that the spelling and punctuation are correct. For you will notice that I have had a clean copy made of my manuscript, and this I have only been able to glance through hurriedly.[1]

I have often thought of writing to you, but have always put off doing it; I thought once, too, of sending you some sketches of my travels; but nothing came of that either. For this summer, however, I have long wanderings in prospect, and I may be able to send you something useful. I know of nothing interesting in my own affairs here to tell you, except that last year I became engaged to a daughter of Dean Thoresen, of this town. Her step-mother is the author of *A Witness,* and several other plays which you have noticed in the *Nyhedsblad* at the time of their appearance.

My very best thanks for your notice of *The Feast at Solhaug.*[2] I sent my new play, *Olaf Liljekrans,* to the Chr(istiania) Theatre several months ago; but Borgaard is

[1] The article on the ancient ballads appeared in Botten-Hansen's newspaper, the *Illustreret Nyhedsblad,* in 1856. It is to be found in vol. x. of the Norwegian complete edition of Ibsen's works.

[2] *The Feast at Solhaug* was written in the summer of 1855, and played at the Bergen Theatre in January, and the Christiania Theatre in March, 1856. It was then immediately published by Tönsberg; and Botten-Hansen wrote a long and favourable notice of it in the *Nyhedsblad.*

not the man to hurt himself by hurrying. He has refused to add my best play, *Lady Inger of Östraat*, to the repertory until various changes, to which I will not consent, have been made.[1] I sent it to Chr. Tönsberg[2] about the beginning of January, asking him to publish it; but he does not see his way to doing so at present; and as it is highly important for me that this, my best work, should be brought out, I put the matter in your hands, and beg of you to do what you can for me. The play is at Tönsberg's; read it through and get me a publisher! I care nothing about the conditions—I will willingly forego any remuneration if only you succeed in getting it printed. I am sure, if you will use your good offices for me, that you will succeed. It has occurred to me that the play might possibly be published for the benefit of the building-fund of the Students' Union; I should in this case like to introduce it with a little prologue dedicated to Young Scandinavia. Dear friend, let me count on your help! I give you full liberty to do as you please with *Lady Inger*. Urge a publisher until he gives in![3] It would be kind in you to send me a few lines as soon as possible. Give me news of yourself and our mutual acquaintances in Christiania.—Yours always,

HENRIK IBSEN.

[1] C. P. Borgaard, a Dane, was "artistic director" of the Christiania Theatre from 1851 to 1863. He never produced *Olaf Liljekrans* (which was played in the Bergen Theatre in 1857); and when he also refused to produce *The Vikings at Helgeland*, Ibsen had a heated controversy with him.

[2] Tönsberg was a well-known publisher in Christiania from 1845 to 1861, and from 1875 to 1891.

[3] *Lady Inger of Östraat*, written in 1854, and played at Bergen in 1855, was not printed till 1857, when it appeared in five successive numbers of the *Illustreret Nyhedsblad*, and subsequently as a separate publication.

7.

*To* PAUL BOTTEN-HANSEN.

BERGEN, *28th April* 1857.

DEAR FRIEND,—Only a few lines to-day, for it is almost post-time. Call my article, if you see fit: "On the Ancient Ballad, and its influence on the Art of Poetry." I cannot, at the moment, think of any title that more clearly indicates the contents. "A few words on," etc., would not be bad, for I have material for an article ten times as long on the subject; but since the expression smacks of Ole Vig, we'll have none of it![1]

Your proposal to bring out *Lady Inger* in the *Nyhedsblad*, and to publish it independently as well, seems to me an excellent one. The play, however, is too long to appear in two numbers of the paper; I think you should give one act at a time. I rely upon the publication in book form being done attractively and in good taste. I give you authority to dispose of the play as if it were your own property. I enclose a note for Mr. Tönsberg, which you will present when applying for the manuscript, which I sent him some time ago.

I should like to have *Olaf Liljekrans* published in the same manner, as soon as it has been performed at the Christiania Theatre; but so far I have not heard a word from Borgaard about it. I am much tempted to attack him on the subject of his refusal to produce *Lady Inger* in its present form. He writes himself that he considers the play "poetic, full of good character studies and strong dramatic situations"; but nevertheless—. Well, you will understand his reasons when you read the play.

[1] Ole Vig (1824–1857) was a noted member of the sect of Grundtvigians, and a clever and zealous advocate of the enlightenment of the people and of the use of the old Norse idiom. The titles of some of his essays begin with the expressions: "A Little About," "A Few Words On." He and Ibsen were friends.

As to terms, etc., I leave myself entirely in your hands, and shall be satisfied with your arrangement, whatever it may be. One thing more. Several times in *Lady Inger* I have called the deceased husband of the lady, "High Steward Henrik Gyldenlöve," although his name, as I have since discovered, was "Niels Henriksen Gyldenlöve." But as there are two other Niels in the drama already, will you, please, simply call him "High Steward Gyldenlöve," without any Christian name. I should be particularly glad if, as soon as you have read it, you would let me have, in a few words, your opinion of the play.

If you meet O. Schulerud, remember me to him. And Abildgaard—what is the real state of matters with him? Do you never think of taking a little trip in this direction? I can assure you it is one worth taking—glorious scenery; everything quite out of the common. Farewell for the present. I feel sure of your looking after my interests in the best possible way.—Yours ever,

H. I.


I have already a new dramatic work under way, the tone and subject-matter of which will be quite different from those of my earlier productions.[1]

H. I.


### 8.


*To* CARL JOHAN ANKER.[2]


CHRISTIANIA, *30th January* 1858.

DEAR FRIEND,—What must you think of my having delayed so long sending a few words in answer to your three friendly

---

[1] The new drama alluded to is *The Vikings at Helgeland*, which was finished in the autumn of 1857.

[2] Carl Johan Anker (1835–1903), at his death a lieutenant-colonel in the Norwegian army, was from 1856 to 1860 a lieutenant in the Norwegian Guards at Stockholm. He had a strong literary turn, and

letters—for I really have received them all, and as yet not answered one of them? What do you think of me? I myself am certain that I am less guilty than I seem. At all events, my long silence is not the result of indifference, but rather of an egotistical feeling to which one often succumbs because of the want of real inclination to combat it.

Dear Anker, perhaps you do not understand me; but the fact is that I have been so near you every day in my thoughts that anything more seemed superfluous.

Believe me, I often live over again the days of our short acquaintance. The trip to Hardanger is a bright remembrance for me, one of those delightful episodes in a man's life from which he draws spiritual nourishment for long, long afterwards.

I have often wondered what opinion you really formed of me at that time; if you did not find me hedged about with a sort of repelling coldness that made any close approach difficult. And yet it was infinitely easier to me to attach myself to you than to any one else, because there was a youthfulness of soul in you, a joy in life, and a chivalrous way of looking at things, that did me good. Preserve all this! Believe me, it is not agreeable to see the world from the October standpoint; and yet there was, strange to say, a time when I wished for nothing better. I had a burning desire for, I almost prayed for, a great sorrow which might round out my existence and give life meaning. It was foolish, and I have fought my way out of that phase—and yet, the remembrance of it is never effaced.

A thousand thanks for all your trouble with my play.[1] I shall soon send you a new one, *The Vikings at Helgeland*, which is to be produced here shortly, and perhaps in Copenhagen as well.

wrote several historical works. He and Ibsen took a walking-excursion together in 1856; and the chivalrousness which Ibsen observed in him on this occasion, continued to the end to be one of the most distinguishing features of his character.

[1] Probably *The Feast at Solhaug*, which was played at the Theatre Royal of Stockholm in 1857.

I have published in the fourth number of the *Nyhedsblad* a poem entitled " To the Memory of Carl Johan," which has won approval here. It is dedicated to the Carl-Johan League, a society with the aim of which you are of course familiar.[1]

It is not unlikely that I shall go to Stockholm this summer. Shall I meet you there, or are you, too, perhaps planning to travel?

I beg you to convey to Herr Hyltén-Cavallius[2] the assurance of my sincere regard and of my gratitude for the favourable notice which he has taken of my early productions; it would give me great pleasure if he could make use of my new work. I have not as yet communicated with Fougstad[3] on the subject of the Swedish play, but shall do so now.

Dear Anker, do not exercise your right of retaliation, but send me a letter as soon as you can. I am disturbed by a bad conscience because of my long silence; a few friendly words would reassure me.—Yours most sincerely,

HENR. IBSEN.

### 9.

*To* THE NORWEGIAN GOVERNMENT.

CHRISTIANIA, *6th August* 1860.

To THE KING!

Henrik Johan Ibsen most humbly petitions that he be granted a sum of 400 specie-dollars (£90) out of the fund voted for artists' and scientists' travel abroad, in order that he may spend six months in visiting

[1] Carl Johan Bernadotte, one of Napoleon's generals, adopted by the childless Charles XIII., succeeded that king on the throne of Sweden and Norway. The aim of the League was to preserve his memory. The poem in question was never reprinted.

[2] Director of the Theatre Royal of Stockholm.

[3] Member of the board of management of the Christiania Theatre. Ibsen's commission was to procure the performance at Christiania of the play in question.

London, Paris, the larger German cities, Copenhagen, and Stockholm, with the special purpose of studying dramatic art and literature.

During ten years of literary activity, and also whilst preparing for the same, most of my time has been devoted to dramatic art and literature, the principles, systems, and history of which have formed my chief study. I venture to believe that the reviews of my dramatic works which have been published during this period by both Norwegian and foreign critics, contain sufficient evidence that my studies have not been unfruitful; and I trust that the favour with which the public has received my plays (some of which have been produced in Sweden and Denmark as well as in Norway), may be taken as evidence of ability in my chosen calling.

Toward the end of the year 1851 I was appointed stage-manager of the theatre at Bergen, then newly established. In the beginning of 1852 a grant voted to me by this theatre enabled me to devote five months to visiting Copenhagen, Hamburg, Berlin, and Dresden, chiefly with the object of acquainting myself with the technique of dramatic art, the principles of its practice in the different places and in its various forms, together with everything pertaining to the management of theatres.

I held my appointment at the Bergen Theatre until the summer of 1857, when I accepted that of "artistic director" of the Norwegian Theatre here, a position which I still hold.

Of late years the opinion has become more and more prevalent that the development of art and poetry, in their various forms, cannot but concern the state; which has therefore, with ever-increasing readiness, assisted our painters, sculptors, and musicians; two of our poets, moreover, have benefited by a not inconsiderable travelling-grant. The reason for the drama having hitherto received no state aid, is not to be sought in any repudiation on the part of the state of the claims of this art; on the contrary, the state has, by giving its support to

5

poetry, plastic art, painting, and music, distinctly implied its recognition of the drama, which is, by its very nature, a unification of all these other forms of art. Moreover, the experience of all other countries has sufficiently established the fact that dramatic art, in every age in which it has been cultivated, has, in a higher degree than any other, shown itself an important factor in the education of the people—a very obvious explanation of which fact is to be found in the drama's more intimate and direct relation to reality; in other words, in its greater intelligibility and in its easier and more general accessibility to the whole people.

The reason for state aid having been withheld from the theatre in this country must, therefore, judging from the utterances of the authorities on the subject, lie in their disapproval of the form which applications for help have taken,—disapproval, namely, of requests for direct contributions to the working expenses of individual theatres, or to building funds, and the like. The opinion has been expressed that any theatre ought to be self-supporting, provided it does not lack capable artistic management and a national dramatic literature.

Endorsing this view of the matter, I, as dramatic author and manager of one of the theatres of the capital, present this, my most humble petition.

I must not omit to point out that, if the state has, as above indicated, tacitly acknowledged the right of dramatic art to existence, it ought also to be interested in knowing that the institutions of scenic art are managed with the greatest possible ability and insight, especially at a time like the present. The national drama is in process of development in this country, and the direction which it takes now and in the near future must vitally influence the forms which it will assume at a more established stage.

I venture to consider that I, having ten years behind me of activity as a dramatic author, and nine of practical work in theatrical management, experience gained on an earlier journey taken with the same object, and having many acquaintances formed partly on this journey and partly in the course of business, must be regarded as possessed of the main qualifications for undertaking another journey to good advantage; and I therefore hereby petition for a grant of 400 specie-dollars to enable me to spend six months in visiting London, Paris, Copenhagen, Stockholm, and the large German cities, for the purpose of increasing my knowledge and understanding of dramatic literature and art.—Your most humble servant,

HENR. IBSEN.[1]

10.

*To* THE COUNCIL OF THE UNIVERSITY OF CHRISTIANIA.

CHRISTIANIA, 14*th March* 1862.

HONOURED SIRS, — Permit me herewith respectfully to petition for a grant of 120 specie-dollars (£27) from the fund set apart for scientific research in Norway, to enable me to travel for two months this summer in western Hardanger and the districts surrounding the Sognefjord, thence proceeding northward to Molde and returning through the Romsdal—the object of the journey being the collection of the songs and legends (both ancient and more modern) which are still current among the people. It is impossible to give, in advance, a more detailed itinerary, since the information and experience obtained at each place visited must decide in what direction the researches are to be further prosecuted. My intention is, however, provided my request be granted, to explore chiefly those remoter coast-districts which, in so far as regards the object I have in view, have received less attention than any others.—Your obedient servant, HENR. IBSEN.[2]

[1] This application led to no result. Travelling-grants were voted in 1860 for Björnstjerne Björnson and A. O. Vinje.

[2] In answer to this application a grant of 110 specie-dollars was made to Ibsen on the 24th of May 1862. The following letter tells how he employed it.

## 11.

*To* THE COUNCIL OF THE UNIVERSITY OF CHRISTIANIA.

CHRISTIANIA, *6th March* 1863.

HONOURED SIRS,—I herewith intimate respectfully that the grant made me last year was applied to the purpose mentioned in my application for the same. The reason why the report which it was incumbent on me to make has not been made sooner, is that immediately upon my return I contracted with one of the publishers of this city for the publication of a collection of Norwegian popular legends, to be brought out during the course of the winter—a work which would have been the clearest evidence of the results of my journey. Circumstances, however, have hindered the publication of the book. I therefore take the liberty, pending this publication, to inform you that in the course of my tour I succeeded in collecting, for the most part in Nordfjord and Söndmör, from seventy to eighty different and hitherto unpublished legends, of which several specimens have been printed in the *Illustreret Nyhedsblad.* I also found a few songs and fairy-tales, for the most part only variants of those already known through Landstad's, or Moe's and Asbjörnsen's collections. My collection of legends, now in preparation, will be submitted to you, Honoured Sirs, as soon as it is published.—Your obedient servant,

HENR. IBSEN.[1]

[1] The book of legends for which Ibsen had contracted with the publisher, Christian Tönsberg, never appeared. Tönsberg was winding up his business at this time, and, as a matter of fact, failed. A few of the legends collected were printed in the *Illustreret Nyhedsblad.*

12.

*To* THE COUNCIL OF THE UNIVERSITY OF CHRISTIANIA.

CHRISTIANIA, 6*th March* 1863.

HONOURED SIRS,—I, the undersigned, hereby respectfully petition for a grant of 120 specie-dollars (£27) from the fund voted for scientific research in Norway, to enable me to travel for two months in the summer of the current year in the fjord and outer coast districts of Trondhjem, and also, if possible, in Nordland, with the object of further prosecuting the collection of popular legends and songs begun last year with the aid of the grant vouchsafed me then.

My first tour was, under the circumstances, by no means unsuccessful. In the course of it I took down, in Nordfjord and Söndmör alone, seventy to eighty different legends, all hitherto unpublished. This, along with other incidents of the tour, leads me to hope that researches in the districts above indicated may be undertaken with profit.

Permit me, in this connection, respectfully to call your attention to the fact that last summer, immediately after my return from the country, I contracted with one of the publishers of this city for the publication of as complete a collection as possible of Norwegian popular legends. It is specially intended to be a popular collection, of which it must be allowed that we stand in need, since A. Faye's, the only one in this country, hardly satisfies present requirements, and is, in any case, much inferior to the collections which neighbouring countries have long possessed. My book, on which I have been constantly occupied during the winter, is now pretty well advanced; yet, as I have gone on with it, I have seen more and more clearly that the material in hand is far from sufficient for the production of anything like a complete work; hence its publication must depend upon whether or not you, Sirs, by granting this petition, enable me to supply the deficiencies in my material.

My idea would be to go from Opdal through Sundal, and

thence out along the Fjord, and northwards through Nordmör; but it is impossible to give any detailed itinerary in advance. The direction of a tour, with the object which mine would have, must necessarily be influenced by information acquired on the journey itself.

As to the amount of the grant, permit me respectfully to observe that I am asking what seems to me the lowest sum possible, taking into consideration the fact that the route which the object of my journey would oblige me to follow entails a good deal of boat hiring, which adds considerably to the necessary outlay.—Your obedient servant,

HENR. IBSEN.[1]

13.

*To* THE NORWEGIAN GOVERNMENT.

CHRISTIANIA, 10*th March* 1863.

TO THE KING!

Henrik Ibsen most humbly petitions that a proposal with the royal signature be laid before the Storthing now assembled, to the effect that the petitioner be granted a yearly salary of 400 specie-dollars (£90) from the exchequer, to enable him to continue his literary activity.

As justification for this my most humble application, permit me to submit a short sketch of my life and literary labours.

I was born at Skien on the 20th of March 1828, and, my parents being without means, I had to support myself from the age of fourteen. I obtained a situation first as apprentice and later as assistant in the apothecary's shop at Grimstad, where

---

[1] In answer to this application a sum of 100 specie-dollars (£22, 10s.) was granted. Ibsen spent it in the course of the summer, but does not appear to have rendered any account of it.

I remained until the end of 1849, employing all the time left me from my duties to prepare myself for the matriculation examination of the University of Christiania, which I passed in the summer of 1850. By that time, besides a few minor poems published in the *Christiania Post*, I had written and published *Catilina*, a three-act drama in verse, which was very favourably noticed by the reviewers, especially in Lange's *Tidsskrift for Videnskab og Literatur* (Literary and Scientific Journal). My next work of any length was *The Hero's Mound*, a dramatic poem in one act, which was produced in the Christiania Theatre in September of the year in which it was written (1850), and which was also favourably received by the professional critics. Toward the close of the year 1851 I was engaged by the Norwegian Theatre, established in Bergen the year before, first as playwright, and then as manager also. During the summer of 1852 I went, at the Theatre's expense, to Copenhagen and several of the large German cities, for the purpose of studying art and literature. From this journey I brought back with me a new three-act play entitled *St. John's Night*, produced later, but still unpublished. In 1854 I wrote *Lady Inger of Östraat*, a historical drama in three acts, which has been played often in various theatres, and has been published in Christiania. *The Feast at Solhaug*, a drama in three acts, written in 1855, has also been produced with much success in all the theatres of this country, at Copenhagen, and in the Theatre Royal of Stockholm, where it was chosen as the festival play for the celebrations on the 4th of November 1857. *The Vikings at Helgeland*, a play in four acts, appeared in 1858, and received much and remarkably favourable notice from the reviewers in Denmark and Sweden, as well as in this country; this play, too, has been acted in all our theatres. This year I have published a three-act play in rhymed verse, entitled *Love's Comedy*. Moreover, I have, in the course of these years of literary activity, written a number of minor poems, of which a complete edition is now in preparation.

I resigned my appointment at the Bergen Theatre in 1857, and at once accepted that of "artistic director" of the Norwegian Theatre here in Christiania, which I held until last summer, when the theatre was given up and its affairs came into the bankruptcy court. Since the 1st of January of the present year I have held a temporary appointment as adviser in artistic matters to the Christiania Theatre. In 1858 I married a daughter of the late Dean Thoresen of Bergen, and I have one child by this marriage.[1] My salary at the Bergen Theatre was only 300 specie-dollars (£67, 10s.) per annum, and I had to leave the town in debt. My appointment at the Norwegian Theatre in Christiania brought me in, on an average, 600 specie-dollars (£135) per annum, but the failure of that theatre meant a loss to me of over 150 specie-dollars, as well as the loss of steady employment. At the Christiania Theatre my nominal salary is 25 specie-dollars (£5, 12s. 6d.) monthly: but the payment of the full amount is contingent upon the theatre's making larger profits than it has done this year. It is an impossibility to live entirely, or even chiefly, on literary work in this country. My best paid work, *The Vikings at Helgeland*, which occupied my whole time for nearly a year, brought me in all 227 specie-dollars (£31). Owing to this condition of matters I have contracted debts amounting to nearly 500 specie-dollars (£112), and, being unable so far to see any prospect of improving my position in this country, I have been obliged to make preparations for emigrating to Denmark this spring.

To leave my native land and give up what I have hitherto regarded, and still regard, as my real life-work, is, however, an unspeakably painful step for me to take; and to avoid it, if possible, I now try the last means in my power, by most humbly petitioning that a proposal signed by the King be laid before the Storthing now assembled, to the effect that a yearly allowance of 400 specie-dollars (£90) be granted me out of the exchequer to enable me to continue labours in the

[1] Sigurd Ibsen, Henrik Ibsen's only child, was born in Christiania on the 23rd of December 1859.

service of literature which I have reason to believe the public does not wish to see interrupted.—Your humble servant,

HENRIK IBSEN.[1]

## 14.

#### *To* THE NORWEGIAN GOVERNMENT.

CHRISTIANIA, 27th *May* 1863.

TO THE KING !—In a previous humble petition to your Majesty (praying that, according to the procedure followed in the case of another Norwegian author, a proposal with the Royal signature should be laid before the Storthing now assembled, to grant me a yearly allowance from the exchequer) I have given a sketch of my literary activity during the last thirteen years or thereabouts, and also of my private circumstances. To this sketch I take the liberty of referring, in once more making humble application to Your Majesty. The great and numerous difficulties with which an author has to contend in this country are increased still further by the almost complete lack of opportunity for acquiring that foundation of general culture which is generally everywhere esteemed indispensable, if a man is to be successful and to do his best in the career to which I believe myself called.

Making bold to observe that similar travelling allowances have been granted to all the Norwegian writers who have made authorship the business of their lives, except myself, I hereby most humbly petition that I may be granted, from the fund for scientists' and artists' travel abroad, a sum of 600 specie-dollars (£135) to enable me to spend a year, for the most

---

[1] On the 28th of March the Government decided "to take no steps " in the matter of Ibsen's petition. The Ecclesiastical Department had, however, intimated to him on the 18th that it was probable he might receive a travelling grant.

A pension of 400 rix-dollars was conferred on Björnson in April of this year, 1863.

part in Rome and Paris, studying art and the history of art and literature.—Your obedient servant,

HENRIK IBSEN.[1]

15.

*To* RANDOLPH NILSEN.[2]

CHRISTIANIA, 24*th June* 1863.

MY DEAR FRIEND,—At this very hour a week ago we were bidding each other farewell. The festive mood, thank God, remains with me, and I hope it will long continue to do so. My hearty thanks to you and your dear wife for your inexpressibly great kindness and friendliness to me. The festival itself, and the many lovable, unforgettable people I met at it, acted upon me like an inspiring church-service, and I hope and believe that the feeling produced will not be a mere passing one. They were all so good to me in Bergen. It is not so here, where there are many who seek every opportunity to pain and wound me. The powerfully uplifting impression, the feeling of being ennobled in every thought, was shared, I believe, by all the guests at our festival of song; indeed only a very hard and wicked soul could resist such an influence. Herein, perhaps, lies the greatest power for good in such a meeting.

I received your telegram as I was leaving Stavanger; for this friendly attention, too, accept my thanks. I will not

[1] In answer to this application the Norwegian Government, on the 12th of September 1863, made Ibsen a grant of 400 specie-dollars (£90); and in the spring of 1864 he went, *viâ* Copenhagen and Berlin, to Rome, where he resided till the spring of 1868.

[2] In June 1863 the fifth great "Festival of Song" was held at Bergen. Both Björnson and Ibsen took part in it, and wrote poems on the occasion. During his stay in Bergen, Ibsen was entertained by Randolph Nilsen, the shipowner, in whose house he met many of the well-known citizens of the town, including those here named.

tell you anything now about our homeward journey; I hope soon to describe it in one of our newspapers. Farewell for the present. Let me hear soon from you. Remember me to all whom I met—to Chr. Grans, the W. Mohrs, your brothers, Blytt —every one, in short. If Jakob v. d L(ippe) comes here, we two will hold a memorial celebration. Nor do I give up the hope of seeing you and your dear wife again. In the meantime I send you both the most sincere and cordial greetings.—Do not forget Yours gratefully,

HENRIK IBSEN.

## 16.

### To BERNHARD DUNKER.[1]

COPENHAGEN, 17th April 1864.

DEAR SIR,—Permit me to offer my heartfelt thanks for the remittance sent me. On Wednesday I leave here for Lübeck, and go thence to Trieste. I have derived much pleasure and profit from my stay here. As soon as I arrive in Rome I shall begin a new five-act drama, which I expect to finish in the course of the summer.[2] I hope the affairs of the Theatre will be in good order by that time; and it would please me very much if it were possible for the season to open with the production of my new work.—Yours most gratefully,

HENRIK IBSEN.

---

[1] Bernhard Dunker, a very eminent barrister, and after 1859 State Counsel, at the Supreme Court in Christiania, was for a number of years chairman of the board of management of the Christiania Theatre. The state of Ibsen's finances at the time of his leaving Christiania obliged him to accept assistance from private individuals (notably Bernhard Dunker) as well as from the state. Björnson procured several private donations for him.

[2] This projected drama was never written.

17.

*To* BJÖRNSTJERNE BJÖRNSON.

ROME, 16*th September* 1864.

DEAR BJÖRNSON,—Dietrichson has shown me your letter.
It seemed very extraordinary to me that you should not, at the
time you wrote it (toward the end of August), have known of
my reply to the offer made by the management of the Theatre;
but that you should for a single. moment have felt uncertain
what answer was the only one possible, was something more
than extraordinary. Advice of the kind which you infer me
to have received, I did receive; and had I suspected the
possibility of your being in doubt as to my position throughout
the whole course of the recent transactions, I should have
acquainted you at the time with the nature of my answer to the
theatrical management; for I can well imagine that such uncertainty on your part can hardly have furthered the progress
of the negotiations. But, as I have said, its possibility never
occurred to me.

On the 16th of July Richard Petersen wrote, informing me
that the negotiations with you had failed, and offering me, on
behalf of the Theatre, the position of " artistic director "—or
rather, to be quite correct, he represented to me that since you
*would not* accept the appointment, I *must*. Some cuttings from
the *Morgenblad,* enclosed in the letter, showed me the outward
aspect of the affair at the moment. As I was staying at
Genzano then, the letter was long in reaching me; but the
moment I received it I made my reply without hesitation. I
declined the offer—declined it absolutely—without reservation,
and without suggesting any possibility that altered circumstances might induce me to change my mind. Never, either
then or since, has it occurred to me for a moment that any
answer could have been given but an absolute refusal.[1]

[1] In the early Sixties the Christiania Theatre was in a very unsatisfactory condition. In the beginning of 1864, Björnson, who had

So you see, dear Björnson, that you have done me an injustice by harbouring such a suspicion as that indicated in your letter to Dietrichson. I will acknowledge, however, that I can understand the suspicion; and I do not lay the blame for its having arisen, so much upon you as upon myself. I know it to be a defect in me that I am incapable of entering into close and intimate relations with people who demand that one should yield one's self up entirely and unreservedly. I have something of the same feeling as the Skald in *The Pretenders*; I can never bear to strip myself completely. I am conscious, in personal intercourse, of only being able to give incorrect expression to what lies deepest in me and constitutes my real self; therefore I prefer to lock it up; and this is why we have sometimes stood, as it were, observing one another from a distance. But you yourself must have perceived this, or at least something of the kind; it cannot be otherwise, or you could not have preserved such a warm feeling of friendship for me in your heart.

I cannot account for your having been kept so long in ignorance of my answer; or rather, I prefer not to try to account to myself for it; and now, enough has been said on this subject.

Accept my thanks for all the beauty I have drunk in on my journey. It has done me good, I can assure you. My mind has received many new impressions, especially here in Rome. But I have not yet come to an understanding with ancient art; I cannot make out its connection with our own time. To me it lacks illusion, and above all, personal and individual expression, both in the work of art and on the part of the artist; nor can

---

lately returned from abroad, offered to take the post of director; but the management found it difficult to come to terms with him, because he stipulated for a freer hand than they were inclined to allow him. He was, however, when the application to Ibsen proved fruitless, elected "artistic director"; and he held the post from New Year 1865 till the summer of 1867—a brilliant, if by no means tranquil, period in the history of the theatre.

I yet help often seeing only conventions where others maintain that there are enduring laws. It seems to me as if the plastic works of antiquity, like our heroic ballads, were the product of the age in which they came into being, rather than of this or that master; consequently it also seems to me that a great many of our modern sculptors make a vital mistake in continuing to compose heroic ballads in clay and marble in these days. Michael Angelo, and Bernini and his school, I understand better; those fellows had the courage to commit a folly occasionally.

The architecture has impressed me more; but neither the antique architecture nor its descendants appeal to me so much as the Gothic style. To me the cathedral of Milan is more overpowering than anything else I can imagine in the domain of architecture. To the man capable of conceiving such a work, it might occur, in his leisure hours, to make a moon and throw it out into space.

You are sure to disapprove of many of the ideas which I have here slightly indicated; but I believe that they are in harmony with my general standpoint, and that along with it my understanding of art will develop.

Here in Rome there is blessed peace for writing. I am working at a long poem, and I have also in preparation a tragedy, *Julianus Apostata*, a labour which fills me with irrepressible joy. I believe it will be a success. I hope to have both works finished in spring, or at any rate in the course of the summer.

My wife and little boy are to join me here in the autumn. I hope that you will approve of this arrangement. Leaving more directly personal motives out of the question, I shall only remark that it will be cheaper for us to live together than for me, as hitherto, to keep up a separate household in Copenhagen. Besides, Dietrichson is leaving Rome in the beginning of next year, and I am to take his appointment, which will give me a free house and its appurtenances, and also a small salary.[1]

---

[1] The post alluded to, that of librarian to the Scandinavian Society in Rome, was never taken by Ibsen, because, from the end of 1865 onwards, he began to receive considerable sums for his works.

Four hundred specie-dollars (£90) will cover my expenses in Rome for a year. My brother-in-law in Christiania will provide my wife's travelling expenses out of what remains of my travelling grant. We expect them to be moderate, as she is coming with a lady from Copenhagen who has been here before, and is experienced in travelling economically.

By the beginning of October I shall be in need of money, as I see by your letter you are prepared to hear. Will you kindly manage to have some sent me by that time.

I congratulate you on the addition to your family, which I had no idea was expected. Give every kind message from me to your wife. And please remember me very kindly to Advokat Dunker. I should be glad if you would show him this letter, since most of what I have said to you I should also wish to say to him. I may almost assume that the same possibilities which suggested themselves to you with regard to my behaviour in the Theatre affair have also occurred to him. He has written me a few friendly words every time he has sent me money; and I shall never cease to remember with gratitude the delicate and kindly feeling which has never permitted him, in spite of the fact that I owe him so much, to hint by so much as a word that he regards me as his property while I am abroad, or to give me definite instructions of any kind. My debt of gratitude to you both is a double one; you have not only helped me much, but you have helped me with delicacy and tact.

You are mistaken in drawing the inference from my letter from Copenhagen that I do not desire to correspond. I am a poor correspondent, and have often a horror of sitting down to write; but I thirst for even the most meagre note from home.

What are you working at at present? I hope soon to hear a little from you about this, the affair of the Theatre, and other matters.

The political situation at home has grieved me very much, and embittered many a pleasure for me. So it was all nothing but lies and dreams! The influence of recent events upon me, for one, will be great. We may now consign our ancient history to oblivion; for the Norwegians of the present age have clearly no more relation to their past than the Greek pirates of to-day have to the race that sailed to Troy and were helped by the gods. I see by your letter that you do not despair. Ah, well, I hope that you are right, and may not be disappointed.[1] Farewell !—Yours,

HENRIK IBSEN.

18.

*To* BJÖRNSTJERNE BJÖRNSON

ROME, 28*th January* 1865.

DEAR BJÖRNSON,—I am very anxious and troubled. About the middle of last month I wrote acknowledging and thanking you for the cheque for 100 specie-dollars (£22, 10s.) enclosed in your letter of the 4th of October. At the same time I took advantage of your kind suggestion in that letter, that I should let you know when I needed more money, to inform you that I should be penniless towards the end of the month. In fact, my money gave out before that; for my monthly outlay comes to 40 scudi,[2] and I had been obliged to borrow, to defray my expenses from the 1st of October until the arrival of the remittance on the 16th of October.

To this last letter of mine I have received no answer; and although I can imagine many reasons for delay on your part, such as your having been away from Christiania, or your having had difficulty in procuring the money, etc. etc., I am inclined to the belief that my letter has not reached you. In spite of my being kept in such suspense I am really glad if this is the case; for I must confess to you (supposing you not to

[1] What had bitterly disappointed Ibsen was the failure of Norway (and Sweden) to come to the assistance of Denmark in the struggle with Prussia and Austria in 1864, which led to the acquisition of Schleswig and Holstein by Prussia.

[2] Equivalent to about £8, 10s.

have seen it) that the letter was written in an unamiable, bitter, and possibly too hopeless spirit, in so far as regards the affairs and the outlook of our country. I have regretted pouring out all that bitterness to you, instead of giving you bright descriptions of all the splendour here, which you have put me in a position to be ennobled and uplifted by. But I cannot keep myself from dwelling with sadness on the situation at home; nor was I able to do so during my whole journey. If I had stayed longer in Berlin, where I saw the triumphal entrance in April, with the howling rabble tumbling about among the trophies from Dybböl,[1] riding on the gun-carriages and spitting into the cannon—the cannon that received no help and yet went on shooting until they burst—I do not know how much of my reason I should have retained.

When you write, be sure to tell me what you think of the condition of our affairs? What direction are they likely to take? And what do you believe our leaders can accomplish with the present generation? It will be a comfort to me to hear. I know that you have hope and confidence, but I should like to know their basis. The possibility of our complete ruin often seems inconceivable to me, too. A state may be annihilated, but not a nation. Poland is not really a nation; it is a state. The aristocracy have their interests, the citizens theirs, and the peasants theirs—all independent of, or even antagonistic to, each other. And Poland has no literature, art, or science with any special mission for the world's advancement. If Poland is made Russian, the Polish people will cease to exist; but we Scandinavians, even if we were deprived of our apparent independence, even if our countries were conquered and our states disintegrated, should still survive as a nation. The Jews were both a state and a nation; the Jewish state is destroyed, but the nation still lives. What is best in us will, I believe, live thus—provided our national spirit has life enough to thrive in and on misfortune. But this

---

[1] The capture of Dybböl (German, Düppel) from the Danes was the most decisive event in the war of 1864.

6

is the great and decisive question. Oh, for faith and confidence; But now a truce to politics for to-day.

The beauty of the antique sculpture becomes more and more evident to me, as you predicted in your letter that it would. The perception of it comes in flashes, but such an occasional flash casts its light over vast areas. Do you remember "The Tragic Muse," which stands in the room outside of the rotunda in the Vatican? No statue that I have yet seen in Italy has taught me so much as this. I verily believe that it has revealed to me what Greek tragedy was. That indescribably great, noble, calm joy in the expression of the face, that richly wreathed head which has something supernaturally exuberant and bacchantic about it, those eyes, that look inward and yet through and far beyond the outward object they are fixed on,— such was Greek tragedy. The statue of Demosthenes in the Lateran, the faun in the Villa Borghese, and the faun (Praxiteles') in the Vatican (Bracchio Nuovo), have also given me a deep insight into Greek life and character, and have, moreover, helped me to understand what the imperishable element in beauty really is. Would that I could bring this understanding to bear upon my own work. I had not seen Michael Angelo's "Moses" in San Pietro in Vincoli when I last wrote to you, but I had read about it, and constructed in my own mind something to which the reality did not quite come up; however, I have only seen it once.

How glorious nature is down here! Both in form and colour there is an indescribable harmony. I often lie for half a day among the tombs on the Via Latina, or on the old Appian Way; and I do not think this idling can be called waste of time. The Baths of Caracalla have also a special attraction for me.

There is still something left of my travelling grant, and perhaps also a little of what was due me by the Theatre; this I have thought of spending upon a trip in the Sabine Hills, to . . . and whatever else can be had along with that. . . . I have written on the subject to my brother-in-law in Christiania, to whom I intrusted the care of these matters before my departure. I intend soon to make an application to the Scientific Society of Trondhjem, and I hope that you will allow me to send my petition through you, and that you will interest yourself in the matter.  I have been living on borrowed money since before Christmas, and must continue to do so until I receive a letter from you; so that a large part of what I receive this time will have been spent in advance.  If you can possibly send me a larger amount than last time it will be exceedingly acceptable. But you must just do what you think best and find possible. My best thanks for all that you have done for me, and for your last kind letter.  You may be quite certain that I shall join forces with you cordially in everything when I get home; for home I shall go, although I believe I said the contrary in the letter which I now wish and hope you may not have read.

My Zouave asks to be remembered to you, and sends you many thanks.[1]  Our very kindest remembrances to your wife. We are very happy and comfortable, and when the little suspense I am in now is over I shall take to my work with renewed energy; it is work that gives me great pleasure, although I expect it will be rather sombrely coloured.

I congratulate you upon your *Maria Stuart*.  Along with all the Scandinavians here, I rejoice greatly over the reception it has had.  I do not know how we are to get hold of it here.  The Norwegian papers are a month old when they reach us from the Scandinavian Society in Hamburg, so I do not know if you have accepted the directorship of the Theatre.  The management of the Theatre was guilty of a falsehood when it asserted, in its annual report, that it had entered into negotiations with me.  The appointment was offered me without any negotiations, and they received my refusal long before the report was issued Remember me most cordially and gratefully to Advokat Dunker.—Yours,

HENR. IBSEN.

---

[1] The Zouave was Ibsen's little son.  Björnson had presented him and his own eldest son with Zouave costumes.

19.

ROME, 25*th March* 1865.

To the Directors of the Royal Scientific Society
in Trondhjem.

SIRS,—A grant of 400 specie-dollars (£90) was made me
some time ago by the Government, to enable me to travel
abroad, and more particularly to visit Rome and Paris.

Partly with the aid of this grant, but mainly supported by
private assistance from Christiania, I have now resided abroad
for one year, the greater part of which has been spent in Rome.
But it is impossible to learn what Rome has to teach in so short
a time. I shall require another year if my foreign tour is
not to be almost a failure. Moreover, I have in preparation
a long dramatic work, the material for which is taken from
Roman history. This work, which I have begun here, I must
finish here. To change one's place of residence whilst engaged
in such a production is equivalent to changing one's mood and
mental point of view, a proceeding which would injure, if it did
not completely destroy, the unity of the work.

I can no longer count upon the help which till now I have
received from home, and a Government grant can only be given
again after a long interval.

Such are my reasons, gentlemen, for hereby petitioning that,
following the precedent of what has been done for scientists
and other Norwegian authors, a sum of 500 specie-dollars
may be granted me from the funds of the Society to enable
me to prolong my stay in Italy for one year, dating from the
receipt of the grant.

My friend, Björnstjerne Björnson, to whom I have confided
the care of this matter, will, I hope, enter more fully into the
arguments in favour of my petition.

It is, naturally, of great importance to me that a speedy decision should be arrived at.—Your obedient servant,

HENR. IBSEN.[1]

### 20.

*To* BJÖRNSTJERNE BJÖRNSON.

ARICCIA,[2] 12*th September* 1865.

MY DEAR BJÖRNSON,—Your letter and the cheque from Hegel came when they were wanted. Thank you, my dear, good friend, for both! But, kind and loving as your letter was—nay, for that very reason—I have read it with self-reproach, because it shows me that you have been anxious and worried on my account. Thank you for this, too! For all that is included in the one great thing — by far the most important for me and my fortunes that has ever happened—namely, my having met and really found you, I shall never be able to make any return except a devotion which neither my friends nor your enemies will be able to alter. I know that you understand me; you know that it is not Björnson the subscription-collector who is chiefly present to my thoughts. Well—more of this when we meet. I can talk to you now; I never could do so quite frankly before.

Things are going well with me now; and they have really

---

[1] This application, in spite of Björnson's eloquent arguments in its favour, was refused; but a second and more urgent one, made by Björnson on Ibsen's behalf in August of the same year, produced a contribution of 100 specie-dollars (£22, 10s.) towards the latter's expenses while completing in Rome the dramatic work with the subject taken from Roman history. It was long, however, before Ibsen set himself seriously to this work. Not till 1873 did he send the Society (from Dresden), as a sign of gratitude due to it, a copy of *Emperor and Galilean.*

[2] At Ariccia, a village eighteen miles south-east of Rome, Ibsen wrote *Brand.* Björnson was meanwhile exerting himself in every possible way to procure pecuniary assistance for him.

been doing so the whole time, except on the one or two occasions when I have been at my wit's end, not only where to turn to for money, but with regard to my work also. It would make no progress. Then one day I strolled into St. Peter's—I had gone to Rome on an errand—and there I suddenly saw in strong and clear' outlines the form for what I had to say.

I threw to the winds all that I had been unavailingly torturing myself with for a whole year, and in the middle of July began something new, which progressed as nothing has ever progressed with me before. The work is new, in the sense that I only began to write it then, but the subject and the mood have been weighing on me like a nightmare ever since the many lamentable political occurrences at home first made me examine myself and the condition of our national life, and think about things that before had passed me lightly by. It is a dramatic poem, modern in subject, serious in tone, five acts in rhymed verse (not a second *Love's Comedy*). The fourth act is now nearly finished, and the fifth I feel I can write in a week. I work both in the morning and the afternoon, a thing I have never been able to do before. It is delightfully peaceful here; we have no acquaintances; I read nothing but the Bible—it has vigour and power.

If I were asked to tell at this moment what has been the chief result of my stay abroad, I should say that it consisted in my having driven out of myself the æstheticism which had a great power over me—an isolated æstheticism with a claim to independent existence. Æstheticism of this kind seems to me now as great a curse to poetry as theology is to religion. You have never been troubled with it; you have never gone about looking at things through your hollowed hand.

Is it not an inexpressibly great gift of fortune to be able to write? But it brings with it great responsibility; and I am now sufficiently serious to realise this and to be very severe with myself. An æsthete in Copenhagen once said to me: "Christ is really the most interesting phenomenon in the world's history." The æsthete enjoyed him as the glutton does the sight of an oyster. I have always been too strong to become a creature of that type; but what the intellectual asses might have made of me if they had had me all to themselves, I know not; it was you, dear Björnson, who prevented them doing as they would with me. You are clear-sighted enough both regarding yourself and me, to see that my need lies exactly in the direction of what you have given and intended to give. I seem to have no end of things to say to you. They come rushing into my mind in a disorderly manner, and if I were to write them all down, there would be more than any postage could cover—so let me come at once to business.

You say that the Storthing *must* grant my petition. Do you really believe it will? I have an impression that my new work will not dispose the members more charitably towards me; but hang me if I can or will, on that account, suppress a single line, no matter what these "pocket-edition" souls think of it. Let me rather be a beggar all my life! If I cannot be myself in what I write, then the whole is nothing but lies and humbug; and of these our country has enough without giving special grants to get more. I will make the attempt, however. What will be my best plan? May I send the petition through you? There is time enough yet, I suppose, but I will not delay too long.

The Trondhjem people are surely making an empty excuse in asserting that my petition arrived too late. It is dated the 26th of March. If School Superintendent Müller is on the board of management, I have reason to believe that I have an enemy there. Thank you for not letting the matter drop, and also for applying in my behalf for the appointment at the University Library.[1] I do not know what appointment it is; but that is of no consequence.

The Ancker Scholarship funds are not likely, in present circumstances, to be given to "Scandinavians," either Norwegians or Danes, but if you will apply, I shall be grateful for your good offices in this matter also.[2]

[1] That of amanuensis. It was given to J. Lieblein.
[2] Björnson was informed that only Danes were eligible.

Will you kindly forward the enclosed letter to Attorney Sverdrup.[1] Before my departure he requested me to let him know if I were in want of money at any time during my absence. So far I have not made use of his offer; but my debt to Bravo[2] weighs upon me; and I cannot send the manuscript before the whole is finished, unless I make a copy for my own use during the writing of the rest, and that would delay me. I do not believe the Theatre can give me a performance—were I in the management myself, I should have to vote against it. But if you can make use of my new play, that is quite another matter. It is undoubtedly dramatic; but how far it is present- able in other respects is something you must decide for yourself.

We received your *Maria Stuart* last spring, and enjoyed it and were invigorated by it. When may we expect your comedy? What nonsense is this about a People's Theatre in Christiania?[3] Is it Krohn who is at the bottom of it? It would be just like him. Goodbye. Our love to you and yours.—Your devoted

HENR. IBSEN.

### 21.

#### *To* FREDERIK HEGEL.[4]

ROME, 25*th November* 1865.

To Councillor Hegel.

DEAR SIR,—Last night I had the honour of receiving your communication of the 18th inst., together with the second proofs

---

[1] This shows that Ibsen was already on friendly terms with Johan Sverdrup, the famous Liberal political leader.

[2] Johan Bravo, a German, was first Danish, and afterwards also Norwegian and Swedish, consul in Rome.

[3] A People's Theatre actually came into existence in August 1865. Björnson's management of the Christiania Theatre was by no means satisfactory to all concerned.

[4] Frederik Hegel (1817-1887) had, since 1850, been the head of the well-known "Gyldendalske" publishing firm in Copenhagen. Björnson, whose publisher he had been since 1861, introduced Ibsen to him. On

of the first three sheets of my poem. I hope that you received the last instalment of the manuscript on the 22nd. From the letter accompanying it, which left here on the 16th of November, you will have seen that I place the publication of the book at the time indicated by you (early in December), above all other considerations. This I can do with much more confidence now that I see, from the three sheets received, what care both compositor and proof-reader are taking. I hope, therefore, that you are allowing the printing to go on uninterruptedly. Any further sending of proofs is unnecessary. I do not return the sheets I have received, supposing that you have already had the second proofs read in Copenhagen, and that the few small mistakes have been corrected—in particular that pages 26 and 27, which are inserted in the wrong order, have been given their proper places.

I think it my duty to conform to your wishes in the matter of the spelling, at least in so far as it is possible to change it now without loss of time; but may I beg of you to limit the changes to the letters before indicated: l, k, and p. That I myself regard my spelling as the most correct, is natural. It was the accepted spelling of our old common tongue, and the more universal the rejection in Denmark and Norway of double vowels indicating the *length* of the syllables becomes, the more necessary it seems to me to indicate their *shortness* by the use of double consonants. Where a misunderstanding might arise, I must request that the doubling be retained, for instance: *egg* (sharp edge), *eg* (oak); *dugg* (dew) and *dug* (tablecloth); *en viss mand* (a certain man), and *en vis mand* (a wise man), etc To Swedish readers my spelling is of great help.

All letters to me ought still to be sent under cover to the Consul, for in that way I receive them more quickly and surely. The message to Professor Molbech shall be delivered.

the 14th of November 1865, Ibsen received a letter from Hegel, proposing terms for the publication of *Brand*. He replied the following day, accepting them with thanks, and sending the last eighty-four pages of the manuscript.

I take the liberty to ask that, when the time for payment comes, providing no difficulties stand in the way in Copenhagen, the sum sent me may be made payable in francs. These, under present circumstances, stand at a favourable rate of exchange here, whereas no rate of exchange at all is quoted for Hamburg marks.

In conclusion, allow me to express the hope that my desire to read proofs has not delayed the press work too much, and to subscribe myself, with every assurance of my high esteem,— Yours respectfully,

HENRIK IBSEN.

22.

*To* MAGDALENE THORESEN.[1]

ROME, *3rd December* 1865.

MY DEAR MOTHER-IN-LAW,—It has been my intention for long to write to you—for I can do it now. Until now I have never been quite myself in my relations with you, neither in personal intercourse nor in correspondence. My real thoughts and feelings always got expressed wrongly; and, as I felt this, I shut myself in. But a time abroad such as I am now having makes many changes in a man, and in my case they have been for the better.

---

[1] Fru Magdalene Thoresen, the authoress, who became a widow just before Ibsen's marriage with her step-daughter, had settled in Copenhagen in 1861. She wrote there under her own name; her previous works had been published anonymously. *The Story of Signe* came out in 1864, and was very soon translated into Swedish, German, English, and Dutch. She took her subjects from Norwegian peasant life; and it was her ambition, though she was of Danish birth, to be regarded as a *Norwegian* writer. In 1866 she went to live in Christiana; but after a hard struggle there for four years, was obliged, from financial considerations, to return to Denmark. In Copenhagen in the Sixties she was, we learn from reliable sources, still unable to appreciate Ibsen's gifts.

I am not going to tell you of my adventures and the sights I have seen; I could not do it satisfactorily; nor is it this that is of real importance. The eventful and significant thing for me has been that I have got far enough away from home to see the hollowness of all the lies that parade themselves in our so-called public life, and the despicability of that canting spirit that is glibly eloquent in talk about "a great cause," but has neither will nor ability nor feeling of duty when a great deed is called for. How often we hear good people in Norway talk with the heartiest self-satisfaction about Norwegian discretion, which is really nothing more than a lukewarmness of blood that makes the respectable souls incapable of committing a grand piece of folly. It is a well-drilled troop; that cannot be denied. The uniformity is in its way exemplary; step and time are the same for all. It is very different here, I can tell you! The man who has managed to retain and bring here with him a certain amount of human feeling, becomes keenly conscious that there is something better worth having than a clever head, and that is a whole soul. I know of mothers away up in Piedmont, women of Genoa, Novara, Alessandria, who took their boys of fourteen from school to send them with Garibaldi on his daring expedition to Palermo; and, remember, it was not a case of saving their country then, but of realising an idea. How many of the members of our Storthing will do the same, I wonder, when the Russians enter Finmark? With us the impossible begins as soon as the demand exceeds what is expected of us every day of our lives.

My journey down here was by no means a pleasure-trip, I assure you. I was in Berlin when the triumphal entry took place. I saw the rabble spit into the mouths of the cannon from Dybböl, and to me it seemed an omen that history will one day spit in the face of Sweden and Norway because of their behaviour then. Here, in Rome, I found all kinds of spiritual depravity among the Scandinavians. What will you think when I tell you that even Danish men and women sat among the Germans in the chapel of the Prussian Embassy on

Sundays while the war was going on, and listened devoutly to
the Prussian clergyman praying for the success of the Prussian
arms in the just war against their enemy.   But I assure you
I have stormed and raged and put things into a little better
order; for I am afraid of nothing here; at home I was afraid,
when I stood in that clammy crowd and felt its wicked smile
behind me.   What tempts you to go to Norway ?   In Denmark
there is so much that is good and beautiful even now.   My
little boy shall never, with my consent, belong to a people
whose aim it is to become Englishmen rather than human
beings.   It often seems to me hopeless to work at a time like
the present.   Unless the spiritual life of the people has an
endless future before it, it does not really matter whether the
time granted is one year or a hundred.   And my idea of
Norway and Sweden is this—we have not the will to make the
sacrifice when the time comes.   We have nothing to rally
around—no great sorrow, such as Denmark has; because our
people lack the elevation of soul which is a condition of being
able to sorrow.   The downfall of the *state* would be regarded
by our countrymen as the worst thing that could happen; but
the downfall of a *state* cannot be a reason for sorrow; and the
significance of the downfall of the nation they would not feel.
Denmark will not perish as a nation; for as long as a people
can sorrow, so long will that people live.   I do not understand
any one saying that Denmark is in a worse position than our
other two countries.   You may believe me when I say that
this is not the case.

Have you not written anything lately?   No poems?   It
seems to me you should be able to do so now.   That most
beautiful work, "The Story of Signe," we have here; when we
meet again, I can talk to you about it.   Until now there has
always seemed to be a barrier between us.   And this was
undoubtedly what you meant when you said, at parting, that
things would become different and better.   I understood you so
far even then; but you may be sure that I appreciate you now
as you deserve, and have always deserved.   But I had to get

away from the beastliness up there before I could begin to be purified. I could never lead a consistent spiritual life there; I was one man in my work and another outside of it—and for that very reason my work failed in consistency too. I am aware that my present standpoint is in all probability only a transitory one, but I do feel solid ground under my feet. I have written a long dramatic poem this summer, which will be published by Hegel at Christmas-time. A copy will be sent you at once; do write to me when you have read it, and tell me exactly what you think of it. In the enclosed letter I ask Clemens Petersen[1] to review it, and to do so promptly; the Norwegian reviewers are inefficient.

Susanna has sent you two letters, one by L. Dietrichson and another favoured by Runeberg, the sculptor. If anything in these letters made you unable to answer them, do answer now!

I see Thomas[2] did not pass in all his subjects at the examination, but I suppose he can make amends for this at Christmas What shall you decide about Axel?[2] Is he really to go back and become Norwegian again? Every one with any ability should stay in Copenhagen; for it is the real Scandinavian centre, the place where one is least trammelled by all the existing prejudices. At least it appears so from this distance.

Remember me to big Sara[3] and little Dorothea;[3] and to Axel too; I hope he is still a promising boy. So Marie[4] is away travelling. Sophie[4] is well, I hope; we have not heard from her for more than a year.

[1] Clemens Petersen, born 1834, was the chief Danish literary critic of the day. From 1857 to 1868 he wrote in *Fædrelandet*. In 1864, Hostrup the poet wrote of him that he was "one of the doctrinary æsthetes who do great injustice with their ready-made standards"; a remark the truth of which Ibsen proved when *Peer Gynt* appeared. See Letters 44 and 45.

[2] Thomas and Axel, Magdalene Thoresen's sons, step-brothers of Ibsen's wife, Susanna.

[3] Magdalene Thoresen's daughters.

[4] Magdalene Thoresen's stepdaughters, sisters of Fru Ibsen.

Of Rome it is impossible to write; one may describe it, but one always fails to convey what is best, what is unique about it. I work a great deal and stay in-doors. Susanna and Sigurd roam about the city in all directions—now among the ruins, now in the museums and galleries. Everything here is stupendous; but an indescribable peace rests over it all. No politics, no commercial spirit, no militarism, give a one-sided character to the population; they are undoubtedly people who cannot do much and do not know much, but they are indescribably beautiful, and sound, and calm. I wish you could spend some time here.

Sigurd can read now: he reads legends and fairy-tales every day; but if you could send us a small Bible history with any one coming this way, I believe you would be doing a genuine good deed.

.  .  .  .  .  .  .  .  .

Farewell!—Yours most sincerely,

HENRIK IBSEN.

### 23.

#### To BERNHARD DUNKER.

ROME, 4th March 1866.

Hr. Advokat Dunker.

DEAR MR. DUNKER,—I ought long ago to have sent you my most sincere thanks for the cheque which I received on New Year's day, and which was extremely welcome, both in itself and because it gave me renewed evidence of your goodwill towards me, a goodwill which I shall ever do all that lies in my power to deserve.

If my book has not already appeared, it will do so soon. Last autumn I gave orders to my publishers to send you a copy; and if, after reading it, you would tell me your opinion of it, without reserve, I should be more than pleased, no matter what your verdict might be.

I have gone through a great deal since I left home, more perhaps inwardly than outwardly. I believe that the comparison between what has been going on at home and what I have seen to be possible here, has perhaps had more effect on me than anything else. The book is the outcome of it all. But though I have an absolutely immovable faith that I am right, I am not at all sure that many will agree with me. I often wonder anxiously how you, especially, will receive the play; for, whilst it has been coming into being, you have been one of the few spectators whom I have always seen in imagination in the front row.

Do not be angry because in spite of my obligation to you, you only now receive thanks and a greeting from—Your ever sincerely grateful,

HENRIK IBSEN.

## 24.

*To* BJÖRNSTJERNE BJÖRNSON.[1]

ROME, 4*th March* 1866.

DEAR BJÖRNSON,—Yesterday I received from Norway a reminder so harsh and so wounding to my pride, that I neither can nor will believe but that some misunderstanding must have called it forth. Tell me, did you receive a letter from me about the middle of December, which was sent from here enclosed in a communication from Ravnkilde[2] to F. Bætzman?[3] In it I wrote that, consequent on your communication to me regarding the payment of my debt to Bravo, I had taken the liberty to

[1] It has been impossible to discover more about the money transaction to which the greater part of this letter refers, than the letter itself tells.

[2] Ravnkilde (1823-1890), a Danish musician, long resident in Rome.

[3] Frederik Bætzman had spent most of the years 1859-1863 in Italy. He had been librarian of the Scandinavian Society in Rome. From 1864 onwards he lived in Norway, following the profession of journalist. He was also amanuensis at the Christiania University Library from 1864-1869.

oblige Ravnkilde by drawing a draft on you to the amount of
25 specie-dollars, which amount I received from him and paid
to Bravo. I asked, moreover, that if, contrary to the expectation you had expressed, such a sum should not yet have been
paid to you on my account, you would kindly advance the
amount yourself, notify me of it, and accept from me a counter-
draft on Hegel, from whom I have not received anything except
what you sent me this autumn. Dear Björnson, if this has
offended you, do not leave me to be tortured by uncertainty and
all manner of painful and wearing conjectures, but write to me
and tell me frankly how my letter can have had such an effect.
Compared with all you have so generously and magnanimously
done for me at home, what I asked of you this time was surely
no more than a drop in the sea.

Yesterday, however, Ravnkilde received an extremely scornful, insolent, and, to a certain extent, inexplicable letter from
Bætzman, who returned the draft, making use of the expression, "This sort of thing won't do here"—words one might
use if one caught a swindler in the act of doing some rascally
trick which one could prevent. But such words must not
be written about me. The man who said them to me, I would
kill on the spot. Dear Björnson, if you know, tell me frankly
what reason Bætzman can have had for writing as he did. I
made a mistake, perhaps, in not at once enclosing the counter-
draft on Hegel; here it is, and now you must help me to get the
matter cleared up, for I cannot bear to be dishonoured in
Ravnkilde's estimation. Dear friend, it is of course quite within
the bounds of possibility that you may some day feel called upon to
break with me; but that the breach should come about through
an affair like this is, I am sure, impossible; you are too noble-
minded. This makes it all the more inexplicable to me that you
have not sent a few lines in answer to the many questions that
I asked in my letter. Do so now, and help me out of my state
of suspense.

In consequence of your silence on the subject, I have not sent
in any application to the Storthing or the Government; I knew

that it would only have meant fruitless humiliation. I will apply for a second travelling-grant, however, if you think it of any use. Tell me at the same time if the application sent to Trondhjem would need to be renewed.

My book will appear in a day or two, I expect.[1] . . . About my present position—waiting, worn out with anxiety and suspense—looking forward to the appearance of the book and to the possibility of its producing strife and attacks of all sorts—unable in such circumstances to begin something new, which, nevertheless, is already fully developed within me—about all this I will say no more.

Dear Björnson, it seems to me as if I were separated from both God and men by a great, an infinite void.

Last summer when I was writing my drama, I was, in spite of all that harassed and perplexed me, indescribably happy. I felt the exaltation of a Crusader, and I don't know anything I should have lacked courage to face: but there is nothing so enervating and exhausting as this hopeless waiting. I dare say this is only a transition period. I will and shall have a victory some day. If the powers that be have shown me so little favour as to place me in this world and make me what I am, the result must be accordingly. But enough of this.

Though my wishes for a happy and prosperous year for you and yours and for all your undertakings come late, I must still send them. From you, we in Rome have already received the best New Year's greeting you could have sent, namely, *Die Nygifte* (The Newly Married Couple). It has been read at A. Munch's to an assembly of Scandinavians, all of whom send you their enthusiastic thanks. Yes, that is how the drama must take shape with us now. Is it not strange—up there in the north the day is dawning, the song-birds are twittering, there are gleams of light; levers, powerful, and flower-garlanded, such as are offered to no other people, are offered to ours with which to raise themselves; but they do not rise. I have a terrible foreboding that our life as a nation will not be eternal, but definitely

[1] *Brand* was published in Copenhagen on the 15th of March 1866.

7

terminable. When I read the news from home, when I gaze upon all that respectable, estimable narrow-mindedness and worldliness, it is with the feeling of an insane man staring at one single, hopelessly dark spot.

What is going on at the Theatre, and what turn are its affairs taking? From the papers I am none the wiser as to what is of most importance, namely, the state of public feeling. And so Fru Brun is dead; that is a great loss.[1] Brun's rescue must be worth much when such a price could be paid for it—and will the price suffice? I do not believe it.

You will receive my book as soon as it is published; and you will do me a truly friendly service if you will tell me candidly what you think of it in every respect.

Dunker sent me a cheque at New Year, which came at an opportune moment. Don't forget what I asked you for in my last letter—information as to the donor or donors of the large sum you sent me last, and which came when it was most acceptable. Again my best thanks for it. A few enigmatical words accompanied it; how am I to interpret them? Also tell me whether I have anything to thank Pastor Sverdrup for; he is here, and it is awkward for me to meet him while I am uncertain as to whether or not I should express gratitude to him, which I, of course, cannot do until I am sure. Fru Munch you will find most appreciative; she is a woman of both warm and delicate feelings, a thousand times more high-minded than her husband.[2]

I will send in a report of my proceedings while abroad, with a petition for another travelling-grant, if you think it of any use; please assist and advise me in this matter. Be kind enough to give the enclosed letter to Dunker. The matter of the enclosed counter-draft concerns my honour. For God's sake settle it, and then with one of your kind letters put an end to the painful suspense I am in. You are my one and only trusted friend; you do not know what it means to have only one.

[1] Louise Brun, a well-known actress.
[2] Andreas Munch, a Norwegian poet (1811–1884), married a Danish lady.

I have written to Clemens Petersen asking him to do as much for my book as his conscience will allow. I do not look for any instructive criticism from the Norwegian reviewers; of attacks I am, of course, certain. Things will just have to take their course. I have right on my side, and nothing they can say will make me yield. Farewell! Remember me most kindly to your wife, and write soon to—Your affectionate,

HENRIK IBSEN.

*P.S.*—My dear Björnson! This time I take advantage of your suggestion that I should not prepay the postage of my letters; I do it unwillingly, but have no choice.

H. I.

Nordraak's music to *Sigurd Slembe* is regularly played at the meetings of our Society, and is the favourite piece. I know that he is, or has been, ill. Remember me to him.[1]

25.

*To* JOHN GRIEG.[2]

ROME, 22nd March 1866.

MY DEAR SIR,—I ought long ago to have written and thanked you for your kind and friendly letter; the only thing which can excuse my procrastination is my having already sent you a message by your brother.

Of course I shall be glad to have my work translated. If it proves capable of touching and elevating any one outside of our

---

[1] The Norwegian composer, Richard Nordraak, Björnson's cousin, set much of Björnson's poetry to music. He died in 1866, at the age of 24.

[2] John Grieg (1840–1901), merchant in Bergen, a brother of Edward Grieg, the composer, and himself possessed of both musical and literary talent, made a German, versified, translation of *The Pretenders*, which never found a publisher.

own country, my pleasure will be great. In our native land poetry must, unfortunately, strike into another path now. At the present moment there is no really true call or need to re-awaken our historical memories. What has occurred in the last two or three years in our country—or rather what has not occurred—sufficiently demonstrates the fact that there is no more connection between the Norwegians of to-day and those of the great days of old, than there is between the Greek pirates of modern times and those ancients who had courage and faith and strength of will, and therefore the gods also, on their side. Well, things may brighten again, but it seems to me that for the present it is of something else our fatherland stands in need.

I am convinced that you will be successful with your adaptation, and that it will be a success, in the best sense of the word, with the public for which it is intended. I have been looking through the play again, and think myself that there is a good deal in it which should awaken some response in Germany. It is strange how history repeats itself in different forms, like variations on a musical theme. In Germany at the present time they are fighting the same battle, over the question of unity or separation; the same passions and interests are at work. In a way the Germans have both their "Bishop Nicholas" and their "Earl Skule"; and Hakon is the man for whom they long and in whom they hope.

It is quite true that I have a strong dislike, not, as you rightly put it, of Germans, but of Germanism and Teutomania. When we meet, as I hope we some day shall, you will allow me to explain myself further. I cannot enter into the subject at length in a letter, and shall therefore only say that in many ways I do the fullest justice to the beauty and the goodness which exist in such abundance among these, our born enemies —for that is what they are at this moment; but the situation must and will change, for it is unnatural to the last degree. Several years ago I lived in Dresden for a period of four months, and my recollections of that time are among the pleasantest and brightest that I possess.

As to whether it is best to make the translation in iambic verse, I dare not give an opinion; I trust entirely to your judgment in this as in all else. Of course I quite agree with you that this form of translation necessarily entails a free treatment of details.

Wishing both of us success with your enterprise, and hoping that, when convenient to yourself, you will let me know how things progress,—Believe me, with kindest regards, Yours sincerely and gratefully,

HENRIK IBSEN.

## 26.

*To* KING CHARLES.

ROME, 15*th April* 1866.

To HIS MAJESTY THE KING!—I, the undersigned Henrik Ibsen, hereby most humbly petition that your Majesty will graciously be pleased to cause a proposition to be laid (through the intervention of the Norwegian Government) before the Storthing now assembled, to the effect that there may be granted to me a yearly pension of 400 specie-dollars (£90) to enable me to devote myself exclusively to my calling as a poet.

In 1862, and again in 1863, I received a Government grant of 100 specie-dollars, to enable me to travel in Norway for a couple of months in the summer. In 1863 a grant of 400 specie - dollars was voted me from the fund for enabling scientists and artists to travel abroad, whereupon, in the beginning of the year 1864, I left Norway, and have since resided chiefly in Italy.

The first-fruits of my foreign travel have now been given to the public in the form of my dramatic poem, *Brand*, which was published in Copenhagen a month ago, and has already attracted attention abroad as well as at home. But I cannot live on the expressions of gratitude I have received; and the payment made

me by my publisher, though most liberal under the circumstances, is likewise insufficient to enable me to continue to reside
abroad, or, indeed, even to provide for my immediate future.

It is in consequence of advice wired to me by my friends in
Christiania that I venture to take the unusual step of directly
addressing your Majesty.

We had hitherto believed that there would be an opportunity
next year of presenting my case, by means of a Government
proposition, to an assembled Storthing; but now it appears that
this cannot be done for three years: and so long as that I
cannot wait.

It is not for a care-free existence I am fighting, but for the
possibility of devoting myself to the task which I believe and
know has been laid upon me by God—the work which seems to
me more important and needful in Norway than any other, that
of arousing the nation and leading it to think great thoughts.

The private proposal which, as I have been told, several
members of the Storthing intend to present, has no chance of
success: the short time does not permit of an application to the
Government.

My King is therefore my one, last hope.

It remains with your Majesty to decide whether or not I
shall have to keep silence, and suffer the bitterest disappointment which can befall a human soul—the disappointment of
having to give up my life-work, of having to surrender when I
know myself to be in possession of exactly the intellectual
weapons required. And what makes surrender ten times harder
for me is that I have never given in before.

But I am full of hope; because I know that, whilst indicating, as I have here done, what is my life-work, I have at the
same time indicated myself to be a soldier fighting under your
Majesty's spiritual banner.—Your Majesty's most humble servant,

HENRIK IBSEN.[1]

---

[1] On the same day on which Ibsen wrote this letter to the King, P.
Botten-Hansen's *Illustreret Nyhedsblad* contained a fervent appeal to
the Storthing not to allow the absent poet's career to be blasted by the

27.

*To* GEORGE BRANDES.

ROME, 25*th April* 1866.

DEAR MR. BRANDES,—A letter which I had begun to write to you, I cannot send. It was written in the mood of painful depression which prevailed among all of us Scandinavians here for the first few days after David's death.[1] Now we see the affair in a different light; we feel that none of us need reproach ourselves, and therefore a different account must be given of the occurrence. I have no idea how much you know of what has happened, so I shall write as if you knew nothing.

About the middle of March, David returned from a trip to Naples and its neighbourhood. He was in perfectly good spirits, but not quite well. He complained chiefly of slight feverish symptoms, which, however, did not prevent him from going about; and neither he nor we thought them of any importance, as they are so very common here, especially in spring. After his return I often talked with him—more frequently than before. The political situation at home formed the chief topic of our conversation; and we also talked a great deal about you. The controversies in which you were engaged interested me, and here we have only casual opportunities of hearing about them. The place which David had admired most

want of means of subsistence; and two days later, twenty-eight of the most influential members of the Storthing proposed that a pension should be granted him. Several of his private friends petitioned the Government in his favour. As will be seen from later letters, the King and "Statsminister" Sibbern did their part willingly and promptly; and on the 10th of May the pension was almost unanimously voted by the Storthing.

[1] Ludvig David, the story of whose death is told in this letter, was a promising young Danish lawyer, and an intimate friend of George Brandes.

on his trip to the south was Sorrento; he thought its situation, close by the sea, charming. And when he was suffering from the heat, the feverish symptoms, and the sirocco, which was plaguing us at that time, he again and again animatedly remarked how delightful it would be to be able to jump from the rocks at Sorrento and have a nice cooling bath. (Note this!)

On Friday, the 23rd of March, I met David at the Society's rooms; he had been intimating his intention to take part in banquet which we were to give that evening to State-Councillor Bravo. He seemed well, but I saw him take some medicine; and he told me that he had consulted Dr. Erhard,[1] who had ordered him to be careful in the matter of food, and had given him this medicine. We continued talking, and touched on various serious subjects. As I was about to leave, he said: "By the way, I had a letter from George Brandes to-day; he asked to be remembered to you." I thanked him and, feeling sure that my new poem must have been published before you wrote, asked if there was nothing more in the letter for me. He replied with a decided "No." We exchanged some further remarks. He expressed his surprise that I did not know you personally, a surprise which seemed strange to me, seeing that I had expressly told him, when talking about you before, as well as shown him by asking questions about you, that no personal acquaintance existed. However, I did not think anything of this forgetfulness, for amidst the crowd of new impressions which one receives when travelling, a casual remark easily escapes one's memory. And David's mind seemed still to be much occupied with his travels.

He was not present at the banquet for Bravo; it was said that he had gone to bed. On Saturday the 24th there was the usual gathering in the evening at the Scandinavian Club, and also a concert. At half-past eight o'clock I spoke to David, who seemed to be in excellent spirits, and who now told me, with a smile, that your letter contained much more than a simple greeting for me, but that he had been so confused on

---

[1] The German doctor who attended the Scandinavians in Rome.

the previous day that he had been unable to tell me what it was. He now told me everything, and, as far as I could judge, quite correctly; at least, what he said was perfectly coherent. I requested him, of course, to give you my best thanks. Then we talked a little about my book, which I promised to lend him next morning; and, in this connection, I asked him on which floor he lived. He replied: "On the first floor"; and immediately afterwards, declaring that the music and the heat annoyed him, said he would go home and to bed. Soon after I heard from Chamberlain Wolfhagen that he had gone home.

The house in which David lived is a corner house. Its front is on the Corso, and the windows of one long side look into a narrow cross-street, the Via della Croce. This long side-building is irregular in its architecture. It was in it David lived—not, as he told me, on the first, but on the third or fourth floor (it is difficult to tell exactly which, as the floors in the different rooms are not on a level with each other.) In the part of the house fronting the Corso lives a French colonel. There is always a sentry at his door. On Palm Sunday, about four o'clock in the morning, the sentry heard a heavy fall in the Via della Croce. He went round and discovered a naked body lying lifeless on the paving-stones. It was David; the window of his room was wide open. The soldier of course at once raised an alarm, and succeeded in summoning some stretcher-bearers from the adjacent hospital of San Giacomo, to which the unfortunate man was carried immediately.

Mr. Kierkegaard was the first of us to learn what had happened, when he went in the morning to inquire after David's health. He summoned the Consul, who sealed the papers of the deceased, and gave them, together with his other belongings, into the charge of his aunt, the Princess Pignatelli.

David, on coming home at ten o'clock on Saturday night, had asked the maid-servant for some boiling water—enough for making tea and for a foot-bath as well. When she brought the water, he presented her with a scudo. Feeling a little surprised, she asked if he was going to move, to which he answered "No," thanking her, and adding that he did not want anything more. Upon this the girl went to bed.

The room next to David's was inhabited by a man-servant who takes odd jobs, and whom he sometimes employed. This man had heard nothing during the night.

In the morning the door of David's room was found half-open, and the candle was still burning. The foot-bath appeared to have been used. In the large tea-pot were the remains of some exceedingly strong tea—as black as coffee, the Consul said it was—and there was very little left. A spirit-lamp which David was in the habit of using was in its own place. According to the girl's statement, it had been out of order for several days; and, anyhow, it had not been required on the Saturday evening, because the water supplied was boiling. However, the methylated-spirit bottle was standing on the table, and beside it a wineglass which bore traces of having contained methylated spirits. Beside the bed lay David's shirt and the flannel vest which he wore underneath it. Both were still wet with perspiration.

On the writing-table lay two partly-finished letters. Both of them are evidently to David's aunt. One of them begins by telling that he has delivered the invitations for a certain dinner-party to Chamberlain Wolfhagen and a number of other persons mentioned by name; but that on account of indisposition he will be unable himself to go to see her before Wednesday. All this was quite correct; the invitations had been delivered on Saturday evening. But then come a few lines which have evidently been written later in the night; these are partly illegible, partly meaningless. The first page of the letter (which is of about the same size as the sheet I am writing on) is completed; the second and third pages have been passed over; on the fourth page he has continued, more and more confusedly. The last, almost illegible, words are: "I am dead; I am as mad as I can be"; and instead of signing his name, he has written: "I am distracted!"

The other letter, which is upon a small scrap of paper, has evidently been written between the commencement and the conclusion of the one just described; it was to have been delivered to his aunt's servant, who was in the habit of coming to the house every morning. It speaks in confused terms of the misfortune which has befallen him. He requests that the doctor may be called at once, as he is very ill; and also that his parents may be informed. They are not to be unnecessarily alarmed, but the full truth is to be told them. In this note, also, the rapidly increasing mental derangement is discernible. He concludes with the statement that he will not awaken any of the people in the house, "so that they shall not, by failing to come to his assistance, be accessory to what must happen." Both letters were open. The bed showed that he had been lying down; on the pillow were the stains of two or three large drops of blood, as if his nose had suddenly begun to bleed violently, and as suddenly ceased.

What was it that happened up there during that awful night?

The possibility of David's having committed a premeditated act is entirely precluded. Such mental aberration as is evidenced by every line of the two letters in question cannot possibly be imitated by any person in the full possession of his faculties. The disease from which David was suffering was gastric fever, which, in the climatic conditions prevailing here, may easily and speedily affect the brain. He had for several days been living exclusively on bouillon and tea. He would not admit his condition to any one, not even to the doctor. It annoyed him to be asked how he was.

On his return home that evening the disease evidently developed rapidly. The large quantity of strong tea must have been injurious; and if, in addition to this, he in his feverish condition drank methylated spirits for the purpose of inducing sleep, the violent development of the fever need surprise no one. But even in his delirium he had evidently no idea of committing suicide; for his allusions to "what must happen,"

evidently apply to a fear that the authorities will put him into
an asylum, and that the people of the house will do nothing
to prevent it.

He jumped out perfectly naked, and head foremost, as one
jumps to dive. This, I think, gives us the clue to his confused
train of thought; and my hypothesis is regarded as the correct
one by the doctor, as well as by all David's fellow-countrymen
here. Confused memories of Sorrento and the bathing there
had come into his mind; the raging, burning fever was con-
suming him, the streaming perspiration was unbearable; reality
and remembrance mingled into one — and the catastrophe
happened—there was no one there to prevent it.

Because the deceased was not a Roman Catholic, his body
could not remain at San Giacomo. His aunt was quite beside
herself, and, moreover, the law did not permit of the body being
taken to her house. So on Sunday at noon it was taken to the
Scandinavian Club, where an Italian doctor and Dr. Erhard
made a post-mortem examination on Monday, in the presence
of the police, in order to substantiate the cause of death.

I was present. The fall had caused instant death. The top
of the skull was crushed and pressed in, which shows that he
had jumped out head foremost. This is further evidenced by
the fact that the face was marked with blood, as if it had been
roughly scratched *downwards*, which is undoubtedly to be
ascribed to his having struck the projecting sill of the window
below in his fall—this being also the explanation of his being
found thrown across towards the opposite side of the street.
Arms and legs were intact, but several ribs were broken. The
lungs were torn, in consequence of which a considerable effusion
of blood had taken place. The symptoms of bad and rapidly
developed typhoid fever were observable.

Dr. Erhard declared that the deceased had deliberately concealed from him, in spite of much questioning, how ill he really
was. And the doctor added that, if anybody had been with
David, the manner of his death might certainly have been prevented, but not in any probability its occurrence in a natural

way.  We have taken comfort in this thought, and in repeating to each other that his doctor had not seen the slightest occasion for advising any particular care to be taken of him.  Others of our fellow-countrymen here were, to all appearance, much more seriously ill.  And, as already remarked, David would not allow any one to express concern for him.  Nor did it occur to his aunt, in whose house he was a daily visitor, that there was any cause for anxiety in his state of health.

On the Tuesday following his death he was buried in the pleasant Protestant cemetery.  Almost all the Scandinavians were present; and out there, in a more serious manner than usual, we brought to a close our social gatherings for the season.

I have given you a cold, matter-of-fact account, a kind of official report, of the whole tragic event.  I can look back upon it now, when necessary, in this manner; and it seems to me that it is the best way for you to receive the communication.

You were often present in the thoughts of your deceased friend during his last days.  I had not penetrated the depths of his character; but I saw that there *were* beautiful, silent depths to penetrate.

How much of the sad story has reached his parents, I do not know.  You will, therefore, be careful in imparting to them the information you have received.

Permit me to conclude by thanking you for the friendly message sent me.  I look forward with pleasure to making your personal acquaintance.  If it lies in my choice, my future place of residence will be Copenhagen; farther north I do not wish to go.

May I ask you to do me the favour of sending the enclosed note to Mr. Hegel.  If you know Clemens Petersen, please give him my kind regards and thanks for his review.  *Fœdrelandet* is the only Danish paper which we take here.  If the other papers should review my book, I shall be most grateful to you if you can, without too much trouble, send me (by the ordinary, unprepaid newspaper post) the numbers in which the notices appear—or if you will ask Mr. Hegel to do it. I have forgotten to say anything about it in the enclosed note.

Farewell, and fight on! Such blows as yours are not unneeded among us in the north.[1]—Yours very sincerely,

HENRIK IBSEN.

28.

*To* MICHAEL BIRKELAND.[2]

ROME, 4*th May* 1866.

MY DEAR AND GOOD FRIEND,—Thank you for both of your letters, the last of which I received yesterday. I have not sent in a petition for a travelling-grant, as Björnson some time ago wrote that he would do it for me. I do not know whether it has been done or not; but if the Storthing grants me a pension, I cannot expect to get the travelling-grant; and if the pension is not granted, then my work in Norway is at an end: and in that case I should not consider it right to ask for any further favours from such a quarter. I shall never forget how you splendid fellows have worked on my behalf! I applied directly to the King in a petition, which I enclosed in a letter to "Statsminister" Sibbern on the 16th of April. Of course I have not received an answer: a letter takes from ten to eleven days to reach Stockholm from here. I could not write the petition in verse. It seemed to me, however, not to lack force; and I asked Sibbern to use his influence. Björnson tells me that he has been canvassing the members of the Storthing on my behalf.

---

[1] George Brandes (b. 1842) had, in the spring of 1866, become involved in his first dispute with the representatives of the philosophic doctrines prevalent in Denmark. See Letter 43.

[2] Michael Birkeland (1830–1896) had been since 1863 Chief Keeper of the Norwegian Archives. He collected large stores of material for writing a history of Norway in modern times, but wrote comparatively little. In politics he was an ardent "Scandinavian" and a strict Conservative. He belonged to the circle of which Botten-Hansen was the central figure.

Speak to him, and see to it that his ardour does not abate even if a Royal proposition is laid before the House.

I shall, under all circumstances, send in a report on my tour in Norway.

Remember me to my good friends, Bachke, Botten-Hansen, and Lökke. If I ever return, I shall be able to thank you all better.

I did not expect my book to be so well received. Any number of greetings, congratulations, and expressions of gratitude have come to me from Denmark, some of them from such well-known people as Councillors Krieger and David, and Fru Heiberg. I have also received invitations and kind offers of various kinds. They may be useful, as Copenhagen will possibly be my home in the future.

Do me the great favour to send me as many copies as you can procure of the different Norwegian papers (except the *Morgenblad*) that contain reviews of my poem. Send them by the usual unprepaid newspaper post; they will then cost me only a trifle. And tell Hansen, please, that we are longing to know if he grants our petition for the *Nyhedsblad*. The Swedish paper has already come.

Rome is beautiful, wonderful, magical. I feel an extraordinary capacity for work, and the strength of a giant-killer. I kept struggling with my poem for a whole year before it took shape clearly; but once I had hold of it, I wrote from morning to night, and finished it in less than three months. It is impossible to write about Rome, especially for one who knows it as thoroughly as I do. Taking one district at a time, I have, with my knapsack on my back, walked through the greater part of the Papal States. The brigands are not so dangerous as we Northerners imagine.

I am not giving up *Julian*, though I see that Hauch has treated the same subject.[1]

You write that the classical scholars are cudgelling their

---

[1] The Danish poet, Carsten Hauch (1790–1872), published in 1876 a dramatic poem entitled "Julian the Apostate."

brains over "*quantum satis.*" Confound me, however, if it wasn't
good Latin in my day, though, no doubt, " doctor's Latin." Any
medical student will tell you that it is a standing formula on
prescriptions when the quantity ordered is not a certain quantity
by weight, but as much as is necessary, or a sufficient quantity.
And therefore it is the *doctor* in the play who uses the phrase
first; and it is the remembrance of this which makes Brand
repeat it.

I do not know whether "caritas" is a classical expression
or not; but it is used in modern ecclesiastical Latin (in contra-
distinction to " amor "=earthly love) to express heavenly love,
with the idea of mercy included. We have the same in the
Italian " carità."

I know you will pardon the incoherence of this letter, and
that you will be kind enough to have the enclosed notes delivered to the persons to whom they are addressed. Give my
kind remembrances to your wife, and to all whose friendship
and good opinion you know I value.

As regards the inner man, I believe that I am in some ways
very much changed; yet it seems to me that I am more myself
now than I have ever been. As regards the outer man, I have
grown thin, which I shall prove by a photograph, to be sent
with Fladager when he goes home in summer.

*5th May.*—Thus far I had got yesterday, when I quite
unexpectedly received a letter from that excellent man,
" Statsminister " Sibbern, dated the 25th of April, in which
he informs me that he has received my communication, has
delivered the appeal to the King, has been ordered by his
Majesty to forward it for approval to the Ecclesiastical
Department, and has already done so—all this having happened
on the day he writes. Quick work, is it not? It can do no
harm to make it known that the King also has thus, in a way,
taken an active step in my behalf. I wish that you would
express my gratitude to State-Councillor Stang; I will write to
him myself, later.

*The Pretenders* has been translated into German, and will probably be published immediately.[1]  The first three acts were read aloud at a literary reunion in Dresden, and met with a splendid reception.  The letter which tells me of this is conceived in such warm and flattering terms that I am unwilling to quote from it.

Hearty greetings to you, and to all of my good friends.— Yours ever,

HENRIK IBSEN.

*P.S.*—I have received another letter from Sibbern, in which he announces that the petition has arrived, and will be redespatched the same evening.  My appeal to the King is, of course, not intended to be published, and surely will not be. See to this, please.—Yours,

H. I.

## 29.

*To* BJÖRNSTJERNE BJÖRNSON.

ROME, *5th May* 1866.

MY DEAR BJÖRNSON,—Only a few words to-day.  The matter of vital importance to me which is now under discussion at home, leaves me no peace of mind, either to write or to do anything else.  But I owe it both to you and to myself to declare that I have not, and have never had, anything to do with the steps which have been taken by Birkeland and others, in their desire to help me.  I do not know, but I hope, that they consulted you before acting.  If not, then I beg of you not to see in this any evidence of my trying to keep several channels open at the same time.

I can assure you that I have done with such tactics. Birkeland has written me two letters; in the first he advises me to make a direct appeal to the King, and also to send in

---

[1] The translation by John Grieg, mentioned in Letter 25.

8

an application for a travelling-grant. In the second ne
informs me that he, along with several others, has sent in a
petition for me, as he judged from my silence that I myself
had taken no action. These letters I am only answering to-
day. I did not apply for the travelling-grant, as I had placed
this matter in your hands. My appeal to the King I enclosed
in a letter to Statsminister Sibbern, who informed me at once
that the King, on the very day on which my appeal arrived,
had sent orders to Christiania for a Royal proposition to be
drawn up. And in another letter, written the next day,
Sibbern told me that the Government recommendation had
arrived from Christiania, and would be signed by the King
that same evening. This is what has taken place, and what
I owe you an account of, as I do not know on what footing
you stand with the parties concerned.

And now to another matter, on which I wish to write in
the strictest confidence to you alone. In his last letter Birkeland casually mentions some disagreement between you and
Dunker. I sincerely trust that it is nothing of any consequence; but if it should come to a real breach between you,
then I beg of you to have confidence in me.[1] You will remember
that two years ago an attempt was made to employ me to
coerce you; and I have therefore the right to assume the
possibility of such a thing occurring again. I therefore assure
you now that I consider myself morally bound to have nothing
to do with the Theatre or anything connected with it, in any
relation whatever, unless with your consent and in accordance
with your wishes. This assurance, which is, of course, for
the present given to you alone, I give you full permission to
make public if I should ever act contrarily to what I have
here written. But what I really hope is that everything will

---

[1] Björnson and Advokat Dunker both desired to be autocrats, as
regarded the management of the Christiania Theatre; and in June
1866, Björnson made a direct demand that his authority should be
extended. This was refused, and in June 1867 he gave up his appointment of "artistic director." It was offered to Ibsen, who declined it.

come right. I should, of course, be sorry to offend Dunker, who has shown me so much real goodwill and kindness.

If time had allowed of it, I should have asked you to persuade old Rektor Holmboe[1] to assist me, either with a newspaper article or in some other way; his utterances carry weight with the Storthing. It seems to me, however, as if my prospects were fairly hopeful. Thanks to you for all your unwearied exertions!

I hear that your paper is succeeding remarkably well.[2] Bætzman will probably be sending a box of books to the Club here in the course of the summer; if you cared to take this opportunity to send us such numbers as are already published, and were to continue to bear us in mind afterwards, you would give much pleasure to all Scandinavians in Rome, those now here and those to come.

All kind messages to your wife and your little boys from me and mine.—Your sincerely affectionate,

HENRIK IBSEN.

*P.S.*—If my mother-in-law has arrived, and you happen to meet her, be sure to remember us to her.

H. I.

## 30.

### *To* FREDERIK HEGEL.

ROME, 21*st May* 1866.

DEAR COUNCILLOR HEGEL,—To-day I have had the great pleasure of receiving your letter of the 12th inst., and I hasten to answer it before the departure of the mail.

Nothing could be more welcome to me than the information

---

[1] Rektor (head-master) of the Bergen Cathedral School from 1825 to 1862, and for many years Member of the Storthing.

[2] The *Norsk Folkeblad*, the first number of which appeared in March 1866, was issued by Björnson for nearly six years.

that a new edition of my poem is required.[1] I hope that the proof-reader will see that the misprints indicated are corrected, and will prevent any new ones from slipping in. I accept with sincere gratitude the payment you offer. May I request that you will this time also send the money in the shape of a draft on Paris. I furthermore take the liberty of asking you to deduct five rix-dollars from the amount, and order them to be paid in at the office of *Fædrelandet*, for the benefit of the widow and children of Grimm, the editor, but without mentioning my name.[2]

I have heard by telegram that the Storthing has voted the yearly pension of 400 specie-dollars (£90), which the Government had proposed it should grant me. As I further learn from the Norwegian newspapers that the Scientific Society of Trondhjem has granted me 100 specie-dollars, and as I, moreover, have some ready money here, I do not for the present need to take advantage of your kind offer of an advance. But it is an offer which, I assure you, I sincerely and heartily appreciate, and for which I return my best thanks.

There is another favour, however, which I would ask of you. Will you kindly have three copies of the second edition of *Brand* handsomely bound at my expense, and have two of them sent to Stockholm, to Statsminister Sibbern, and the third copy to State-Councillor Stang in Christiania. One of the copies which go to Sibbern is intended for the King, who has warmly espoused my cause at this time. The binding I leave to your taste. On an early mail day I shall take the liberty of sending a couple of short notes, which I wish to accompany the books.

I shall be able to let you know very soon what work I am

---

[1] The second edition of *Brand* was published on the 24th of May 1866, only two months after the first.

[2] Grimm was the editor of a newspaper of Danish tendencies published at Sonderburg, and had distinguished himself as a Danish patriot. After his death his widow was forbidden by the new Government to continue the publication of the paper, and was thus deprived of the means of supporting herself and her four young children.

taking up. I feel more and more inclination to set seriously to work at *Emperor Julian*, who has been occupying my thoughts for two years. The fact that Hauch has dealt with the same subject will, of course, not deter me, as I feel quite certain that my conception of it will be in every respect essentially different from his. I do not, under the circumstances, intend to read Hauch's poem. More on this subject at another time !

Please give my kind regards to Clemens Petersen, Brandes, and Chr. Richardt. From the two last-mentioned I have received letters. Perhaps you will, when opportunity offers, kindly tell Richardt that I shall send him a contribution to the proposed collection, but that it will barely fill a sheet.[1]

I am looking forward with eagerness to Pastor Helveg's review of *Brand*. I have received intimation from Norway that V. Lyng, lecturer in philosophy, is writing a long article on the poem, intended for Professor Hamilton's new Scandinavian magazine.[2]

Thanking you for all your kindness, and wishing and hoping that the new edition may justify its publication,—I remain, Yours sincerely and respectfully,

HENRIK IBSEN.

31.

*To* GEORGE SIBBERN.[3]

ROME, *2nd June* 1866.

To His Excellency Mr. Sibbern,
    Minister of State.

SIR,—I take the liberty of sending these lines to express, with all due respect, my profound gratitude to your Excellency,

[1] The Danish poet, Christian Richardt, published in 1866, at Christmas, under the title of *Vintergrönt*, a collection of short pieces by various Scandinavian authors. Ibsen did not send the promised contribution.

[2] This article is not discoverable.

[3] G. C. Sibbern (1816–1901), Norwegian Minister of State at

and my appreciation of the good service done to my cause in the Storthing by your Excellency's friendly and influential intervention. I have learned from Christiania what I might quite well have known, that the very expeditious despatch of the necessary documents from Stockholm inclined various members of the Storthing in my favour.

No less sincerely do I appreciate the kindness and favour shown me by your Excellency in writing to me twice, with so short an interval.

The reason why I have delayed performing this my bounden duty of returning thanks is, that I wished to send your Excellency along with my letter a copy of the second edition of my new book. I humbly request that the accompanying copy may be deposited in the private library of His Majesty the King, as a small expression of my most submissive gratitude.

My future is now assured, and I can devote myself undisturbedly to my calling. I shall never forget to what an extent I am indebted for this to your Excellency.—Yours most sincerely and respectfully,

HENRIK IBSEN.

32.

*To* FREDERIK HEGEL.

FRASCATI, *9th June* 1866.

DEAR COUNCILLOR HEGEL,—My best thanks for the reviews forwarded to me! Helveg's book I have read with much interest; it corrects several mistakes made by most of the other critics. Please remember me to Brandes. I have received with pleasure the copies of the 2nd edition of *Brand*. Enclosed I send the two letters which I mentioned in my communication

Stockholm from 1858 to 1871, and Swedish and Norwegian ambassador in Paris from 1878 to 1884, was a cultivated gentleman of the old school, benevolent and helpful in both his private and his public life.

of the 21st ult. If the bound copies are ready, please forward them as before directed—one with the letter to Christiania, and two with the letter to Stockholm.

My address is still the same. I am living out here among the hills. I never see a newspaper, and know nothing of what is going on in the outside world. But it is delightful and wonderful here.—Yours most sincerely,

HENRIK IBSEN.

*P.S.*—Björnson in all probability resigns his appointment at the Theatre in summer.

To return to Helveg's book—I must, for the sake of truth, say that his assumption that it was Sören Kierkegaard I had in my mind when I wrote, is incorrect. The presentment of a life which has as its aim the realisation of ideals will always possess certain points of resemblance to the story of Kierkegaard's.[1]

H. I.

33.

*To* PAUL BOTTEN-HANSEN.[2]

FRASCATI, *22nd July* 1866.

MY DEAR FRIEND,—First of all, let me convey to you the most sincere and hearty thanks of one and all of the Roman-

---

[1] It has often been asserted that the Danish philosopher, Sören Kierkegaard (1813–1855), was the prototype of Brand; but the fact has been always denied by Ibsen himself. A spiritual kinship between them, however, undoubtedly exists; and there can also be no doubt that Kierkegaard's passionate warfare with the temporal authorities has, unknown to himself, influenced the poet's conception. It is, moreover, certain that, even before he left Grimstad, Ibsen had read some of Kierkegaard's works.

[2] P. Botten-Hansen had been Librarian of the University of Christiania since 1864. In 1866 he was still publishing the *Nyhedsblad.*

Scandinavians for your excellent paper, which we have long
been eagerly expecting, and which has now begun to come.
Photographs of the works of Scandinavian artists, together
with whatever else is likely to be useful for your paper, shall
be sent to you, accompanied by the necessary letterpress, or
by short explanatory notes, whenever we are in possession of
anything of the kind. For the moment most of the finished
works are in Stockholm, and it will be simpler for you to get
what you need from there.[1]

In the next place I have to ask you, in my official capacity
as one of the managing committee of the Scandinavian Society,
to be good enough to take charge of the enclosed application;
to send it in, of course, in the first place, and then when you
are asked for information—as you probably will be—to support
it with as strong a recommendation as your conscience will
permit.[2] I do not know whether it is made in proper form;
if it is not, we hope that both you and the Department will
excuse us, and still do your best for us.

The catalogue mentioned in the application as to be sent
later, goes along with this, which will prevent some unnecessary
correspondence. One of your assistants, Mr. Fr. Bætzman,
offered last winter, in a letter to Consul Bravo, to be of service
to our Society by endeavouring to procure donations of books
from the publishers in Christiania for his countrymen here, who
are hungering for them. I am sure that he will gladly undertake the selection, under your direction, and thus spare you
the actual work—which is important; for I know how fully
occupied your time is. By the way, I learn that the Storthing
has granted you another assistant. Accept my congratulations.

My wife wishes to be very kindly remembered to you and
your wife. We are in excellent health, but have, of course,
been obliged to leave Rome during these hot summer months,

[1] There was an Exhibition at Stockholm in the summer of 1866.

[2] The application in question was a petition to the Ecclesiastical
Department for a donation of such books as the University possessed
duplicates of.

when the poisonous sirocco is blowing over the Campagna. We are at Frascati, among the Alban Mountains, where we have rooms in an old palace, the Palazzo Gratiosi, and live most comfortably and cheaply.

Frascati lies close to the ancient Tusculum, where, as you remember, Cicero had his magnificent villa, and where he wrote his Tusculan Disputations; the ruins of the villa are still to be seen. His small theatre, which is presumably what he called his schola, where he used to deliver speeches to a select audience of guests, is almost uninjured. It is indescribably delightful to sit up here of an evening, 2000 feet above the sea, enjoying the magnificent view of the Mediterranean, the Campagna, and Rome. The mountainous Sabine country, with the Apennines, lies to the east; and to the south rise the Volscian Mountains, on the Neapolitan frontier. From the windows of my study I see in the extreme distance Mons Soracte rising, isolated and beautiful, from the level of the immense plain; in short, wherever you turn you seem to be looking at the battlefield where the chief engagement in the world's history took place.

I shall soon be starting to write in good earnest. I am still wrestling with my subject, but I know that I shall get the upper hand of the brute before long, and then everything will go smoothly.

Thank you for your able assistance in the matter of the pension. Remember me to all my good friends. Please convey my thanks to Lökke for his welcome letter, which I have not yet answered; and ask him to send me his Grammar, according to promise, at the earliest opportunity.[1]

I do not know when I shall return. I feel very much at home here now; but back to Norway I must go, some time or other. I can live on my pension here, because everything is extraordinarily cheap; and the climate suits us all well.

There is still much about which I should like to write, but

---

[1] J. Lökke, a master at the Cathedral School in Christiania, published, in 1865, a school-grammar, which was for many years almost the only one used in the Norwegian schools.

time will not allow of it, for I have a chance of sending this to Rome to-morrow. We dare not trust to the local post.

Dear friend, answer this letter, and answer it soon; it would give me unspeakable pleasure to hear from you direct. Thank you for your review of *Brand.* By the way, what can be the meaning of its not having been reviewed in the Swedish *Aftenblad*?[1]

My conscience tells me that my behaviour towards the good Swedes down here has not been all that it ought to have been. I wonder whether the silence of the newspaper is in any way connected with this; it has also taken no notice whatever of a pension having been granted me.

There has no doubt been some addition to your family. I want to know about this. With the heartiest greetings to yourself and all our mutual friends, and begging you to send me a few lines now and then,—I am, Yours most sincerely,

HENRIK IBSEN.

*P.S.*—I have kept the manuscript of *Brand* for you, as I suppose you are still collecting curiosities.

### 34.

*To* FREDERIK HEGEL.

FRASCATI, 22*nd August* 1866.

DEAR COUNCILLOR HEGEL,—I have had the pleasure of receiving your friendly communication of the 5th of August. I suppose that by this time the third edition is already in the market.[2] Allow me to assure you that I am, and ever shall be, fully alive to the fact that the success of my book is very

---

[1] Bætzman, Botten-Hansen's amanuensis, had reviewed it for the *Aftenblad*, but the review had escaped Ibsen's notice.

[2] The third edition of *Brand* came out in August 1866, three months after the second.

largely due to its connection with your deservedly esteemed name. I only hope that our literary relations may yield you in the time to come a small measure of the same satisfaction which they have already given me.

I have been so neglectful as not yet to have acknowledged the receipt of the payment made me for the second edition which came to hand in the month of June in the form of a bill of exchange for 400 francs. I herewith return my best thanks for it.

I hope that the third edition also has undergone careful proof-reading. The fact that so large a portion of it has been disposed of in Denmark, confirms me more and more in the opinion which I have long held—that it is in Copenhagen that our Scandinavian literary activity must be concentrated.

At present I am in doubt as to whether my new work will be finished by autumn. But I have a proposal to make, namely, that you should publish *Love's Comedy* as a Christmas book. It came out at New Year, 1863, as a supplement to the *Illustreret Nyhedsblad*—a New Year's gift to its subscribers— and cannot possibly be well known in Denmark.[1] The book may be regarded as a forerunner of *Brand*, and it will find a public in Denmark. Some of the language must be altered; in fact, there are various corrections to make; and the new edition should be accompanied by a few prefatory words. I have a copy here which I will send you, revised and corrected, if you, who are in a better position to judge, agree to my proposal. I venture to expect a few lines from you soon in regard to it.

I hope that my letter of the middle of June with the enclosed communications to Statsminister Sibbern at Stockholm and State-Councillor Stang has arrived, and that the bound copies have been sent to the said gentlemen. I have heard nothing from either of them. I learn from the Norwegian newspapers that the Government has, without any

---

[1] *Love's Comedy* had been reviewed by C. Rosenberg in the *Dansk Maanedsskrift* at the time of its appearance in Norway; but it had made no impression and had had no sale in Denmark. Hegel published it at Copenhagen in May 1867.

application on my part, granted me, in addition to my pension, 350 specie-dollars from the fund for artists' and scientists' foreign travel. This makes it possible that I may take a trip to Greece next summer.

I do not remember if I have already asked you to give my kind regards to Brandes, and to thank him for his most friendly and appreciative criticism. I hear that he also has received a travelling-grant. It would give me great pleasure if we could meet somewhere here in the south; but he has probably other plans.

*24th August.*—A careful re-reading of *Love's Comedy* has fully confirmed me in my belief that it may be republished with advantage. I have begun making corrections and altera-tions, and have already planned a preface; but this is not to influence you; I leave the decision entirely in your hands. I will only add that I have seen an article in the *Illustreret Nyhedsblad,* in which the editor mentions that eminent Danes who have recently made acquaintance with the book, have expressed their surprise that it has not been circulated in Denmark.

Kindly oblige me by sending the enclosed note to Mr. Grieg, whose address in Copenhagen I do not know.[1]

Expecting a few lines from you very soon,—I remain, Yours respectfully and sincerely,

HENRIK IBSEN.

## 35.

### *To* MICHAEL BIRKELAND.

ROME, *5th October* 1866.

DEAR FRIEND,—First of all I must thank you for what I believe I largely owe to you, namely, the new travelling-grant

[1] Edward Grieg, the composer, who had been in Rome in 1866–67, was now in Copenhagen, on his way back to Norway.

which I have received.  My brother-in-law writes that it is the result of a petition sent in by him; but your remark in a previous letter that an application ought to be made for me for 750 specie-dollars, the sum resulting from the addition of this grant to my pension, and your general activity on my behalf, lead me to conclude that you (and perhaps other good friends) have assisted in this matter also.  Therefore, again my heartfelt thanks!

I wrote a letter of thanks to State-Councillor Stang in summer.

And now there is another matter which you must manage for me.  Hegel is going to publish a new, revised, and corrected edition of *Love's Comedy*.  The money which it brings me I intend to spend next summer on a trip to Paris and a tour in Greece.  But Hegel makes the condition that the copies of the first edition which have not been sold shall be taken out of the market.  There cannot be many of these.  I sold the first edition, as you know, to be used as a New Year's gift for the subscribers to the *Nyhedsblad*.  A few more copies were printed than were needed; these I permitted Jonas Lie to take, and they are now most probably in Dybwad's possession.[1]  Please see him (or any others concerned) and use your most persuasive eloquence.  Take others with you, if necessary.  Make him understand — what he is likely to know already — that the Norwegian edition is as good as valueless; tell him that the matter is one of great importance to an exiled poet; show him that by destroying the remaining copies he will run no risk of loss—for he will have the new and revised edition to sell—and will do me a great service.

Taking the matter from the legal point of view, I probably have a claim on Jonas Lie, who must surely see that the ridiculously insignificant price paid gave him no right except that of supplying copies to the subscribers to the *Nyhedsblad* of

[1] Jonas Lie owned and published the *Nyhedsblad* in 1862 – 63; Dybwad, a bookseller and publisher in Christiania, owned it at the time this letter was written.

that year. But to make good this claim would require time; and time is precious, seeing that the book must be completed and despatched to Norway by November. Get hold of Bachke, Lökke, Botten-Hansen, Sars, Daae, and other friends. Go in a body to the gentleman in question, and do not leave him until the matter is settled. As soon as it is, please let Hegel know the result; he is waiting for this information before beginning to print.

But keep the affair a secret from Björnson and others; if you do not, I fear, between you and me, that there will be counter-moves.

As you see, dear Birkeland, I am drawing heavy drafts on your time and friendship. But this matter is a very important one to me; if nothing comes of it, then no tour in Greece for me! Do not keep Hegel waiting longer than is absolutely necessary; he has already received the revised and corrected copy of the book.

Thank Lökke very much indeed for his letter, and ask him to remember the Grammar whenever there is an opportunity.

We have been in the mountains all summer, and only returned to Rome in the beginning of October. If everything goes well, my wife will remain at Sorrento next summer while I go off on my tour. There is no news here, but much disturbance and expectation. The Empress of Mexico arrived lately, and has since become insane. The Foreign Legion has entered Rome, and it is said that the French are to leave before Christmas. If there is a revolution, we intend to lay in provisions for some days, and lock ourselves in until the worst is over; the Papal power will not make any long resistance.

Give my kind regards to your wife, and to all our mutual acquaintances.

I quite expect you will be successful with my commission, and I hope you will forgive me for having burdened you with it. Good-bye for to-day. Accept the warmest thanks of—Yours most sincerely,

HENRIK IBSEN.

## 36.

#### *To* FREDERIK HEGEL.

ROME, *5th October* 1866.

DEAR COUNCILLOR HEGEL,—I have the pleasure of herewith sending you the revised and corrected copy of *Love's Comedy*. The reason for its not coming earlier is that I dared not trust to the mail service in the mountains. A careful reading of the proof will be necessary. Please give orders for the correction of any inconsistencies. I accept with gratitude the terms offered. The size of the edition is to be determined by you. If, to diminish the risk, you should prefer to issue it in two, smaller, editions, I shall, of course, regard the two as *one* edition, and make no demand for any further payment.

For the sake of appearance, I wish the notes relating to the characters to be printed *under* their names, as in the Norwegian edition.

The first edition was sold by me to the *Illus. Nyhedsblad*, to serve as a New Year's gift for its subscribers. I permitted the gentleman who owned the paper at that time to keep the extra copies printed; it is these which are still in the market. I have written to one of my friends in Christiania, the librarian of the University, P. Botten-Hansen, requesting him to ask Mr. Dybwad to withdraw the said copies. He is to inform you of the result of his application. Knowing Mr. Dybwad, I have no doubt of its success. And in any case the few remaining copies of the Norwegian edition must be almost valueless. Therefore it is hardly necessary to wait for the information. If necessary, I shall buy up the remaining copies of the book; but I am certain this will not be required of me.

I shall send the preface for the second edition in a few days; it will be short, from half a page to a page.

I am sorry not to be able to keep my promise of a contribution to Chr. Richardt's Christmas Miscellany.[1] I have some small things by me, but I do not consider any of them good enough to send; though they may pass muster in some future collection of my own poems. Will you be good enough to give Richardt my kindest regards, along with an apology, and with thanks for his flattering offer.

To yourself my thanks are due for the draft for 400 francs, enclosed in your letter of the 12th of September. When the payment for *Love's Comedy* falls due, please do not send me it, but let it stand to my account until next summer or some other future time; I do not wish to have more money than necessary in my possession here.

I have a favour to ask of you, if the granting of it does not involve too much trouble. Will you advance the money, and order to be purchased for me, a lottery-ticket (either one whole ticket or two half tickets or four quarter tickets) in the Copenhagen "Class-Lottery." I cannot say that I expect to win anything, but there is an excitement about a lottery which appeals to me. Forgive me for presuming to ask you to do this.

It will be both an honour and a pleasure to me to send you my photograph whenever I get one that is worth sending. Is it too much to ask that I may have the pleasure of receiving yours in return ?

I hope soon to send a few lines to Clemens Petersen.

I was pleased to receive, through Dr. Salomonsen, the two handsome and beautiful copies of the third edition of *Brand*. It is a real edition-de-luxe, and I sincerely trust there will be a sale for it.

The present package I am prepaying only as far as the frontier. Please charge the additional postage to my account.

As already said, in a few days you shall have the preface, and hear again from—Yours respectfully and sincerely,

HENRIK IBSEN.

P.S.—Any errors of punctuation that may not have been

---

[1] See Letter 30.

corrected in the accompanying book are commended to the attention of the proof-reader. And I should wish the compositor's attention to be drawn to the fact that the lines begin as in *Brand*, with small letters—except, of course, after a period, or when the first word in the line is a noun, or in any other self-evident case.

## 37.

*To* BJÖRNSTJERNE BJÖRNSON.

[ROME, *October* 1866.]

DEAR BJÖRNSON,—Along with my official reply I must write a few lines to thank you for your last letter, which I have not yet answered. The correspondence had, indeed, taken such a turn that a speedy communication from me might seem called for; but I took it for granted that you did not see in our little encounter anything more than a mere passing disagreement; moreover, it was not with you, directly, that I was annoyed. No, my dear good Björnson, I know for certain that nothing will ever have the power so to come between us as to separate me really from you and all that is yours. But you will admit that it must have been an indescribably disagreeable communication for me to receive. I did not bewail the loss of the furniture, and things of that kind; but to think that my private letters, and literary and other papers, were in goodness knows whose hands, annoyed me excessively, as did also the loss of many things the value of which to me was not their money-value.

You were not told the truth when you were told that the auction was held because I had not given my address. It was held because Nandrup, immediately after my departure, was treated at Dunker's office in a high-handed and irritating manner, of which I shall not give any detailed description.[1] Let the whole affair be forgotten !

[1] J. Nandrup, attorney in Christiania, had advanced Ibsen money in the spring of 1862, and had also redeemed some of his distrained

Give my kind regards to Dunker (I hope that the relations between you are very friendly), and say to him that I shall send him a few good photographs, as I promised. Tell him, at the same time, that I took the little red fragment which I sent him in spring from the recently excavated villa of Cicero at Tusculum.

Thank you for your kind proposal that I should write something for your paper; if I write anything of a journalistic nature while I am here, I shall send it to you. There have been some articles in the *Nyhedsblad* on the palaces of Rome, and that sort of thing; I have no share in the authorship or anything to do with them.

You would give great pleasure to the Scandinavian Society if you would (beginning from the New Year) send it regularly a copy of your paper; the postage would, of course, be paid here. Tell me what you say to this suggestion, as your determination will influence the general meeting in its orders for papers for the coming year.[1] I am looking forward eagerly to your new story.

Give our kindest remembrances to your wife, and also to my mother-in-law, from whom I have not heard a word since her arrival in Norway. If you should meet my sister-in-law, Marie, ask her not to mention the auction, or anything of that sort, in her letters to my wife. I know it would grieve her very much; and I hope to be able to recover everything.

I suppose you are now autocratic manager of the Theatre; but do you think you will find this the best arrangement in the long run?[2] Do not infer from my question that I desire to have

---

effects. Nandrup had applied for payment to Dunker, who had charged himself to a certain extent with the management of Ibsen's money-matters; and Dunker had told him curtly to sell certain effects of Ibsen's which were stored at the Theatre. The proceeds of the auction did not fully cover the debt, which was, however, in course of time completely discharged.

[1] In the spring of 1866, Björnson had become editor of the *Norsk Folkeblad*. Ibsen never wrote in it.

[2] Björnson's demand for unlimited power had been refused in August 1866.

anything to do with these matters—quite the contrary! I expect to go North again in a year, or perhaps two; but probably not farther than Copenhagen; an occasional summer trip to Norway, is, I imagine, what will suit me best.

Now a few private words about the performance of the Fourth Act of *Brand*. I should have liked very much if your letter had contained some indication of your own opinion on the subject; but as it did not, I have returned such an answer as leaves you full liberty of action. I feel sure that you will manage in the best possible manner.[1]

Write to me as soon as you can.—Your attached,

HENRIK IBSEN.

*P.S.*—To put an end to the Bætzman affair, I have repaid the amount in cash to Ravnkilde. So that matter is now settled. H. I.

38.

*To* FREDERIK HEGEL.

ROME, *2nd November* 1866.

DEAR COUNCILLOR HEGEL,—It was indeed an extremely pleasant surprise to me to learn, by means of your friendly communication of the 17th ult., that a fourth edition of *Brand* is needed. That it should be called for so soon surpasses my expectations.[2] I shall never forget how much of this unusual success I owe to you.

Pray be good enough to keep the money due me, for which I thank you most sincerely in advance, until spring, or such time as I request you to send me it.

---

[1] The Fourth Act of *Brand* was played on the occasion of an actor's benefit in June 1866. From the 20th of September of the same year it formed part of the regular repertory of the Christiania Theatre.

[2] The fourth edition of *Brand* was published on the 14th of December 1866, four months after the third.

I quite understand that, under the circumstances, the publication of the second edition of *Love's Comedy* will have to be postponed until next spring, as you indicate in your letter. In all such matters I trust entirely to your discretion.

It grieves me, truly grieves me, that I am unable to contribute to Richardt's Miscellany; and you must believe that when, in spite of the flattering reminder sent me, I find myself unable to redeem my promise, my refusal is the result of mature consideration. Please convey my very kindest regards to Richardt. I sincerely trust that neither he nor you will consider me deserving of blame in this matter; it is I myself who suffer most.

I am exceedingly grateful to you for the promise of new works by Dunker, Dietrichson, and Listov. I am looking forward with special pleasure to Listov's book.[1] I do hope that your endeavour to bring our ancient Danish - Norwegian literature to honour again may also bear pecuniary fruits. It is pleasant to think that some day, when the idea of unity has taken a stronger hold of the two peoples, you will reap the gratitude of both; but this is not sufficient.

I am very much indebted to you for the photograph you sent me. I enclose my own, the best I have at present; I shall take the liberty of sending you another later.

I see from your letter that a little misunderstanding prevails regarding a proposed work of mine which I have mentioned. It will not deal with the youth of Christian IV., though the subject belongs to that period.[2] I am not yet certain, however, that this work will be the first I shall finish. I am revolving one or two other themes in my mind; and this division of interest shows that no one of them is sufficiently matured. I feel certain, however, that one or other will be so soon; and I hope to be able to send you a finished manuscript in the course of the summer.

[1] A vocabulary of the words employed in Norwegian literature since 1842.

[2] This work was never written.

I have now received from Statsminister Sibbern (which means practically also from King Charles) an exceedingly kind letter. Sibbern has been absent from Stockholm, and consequently did not receive the books till last month.

My best thanks for your readiness to take the trouble about my lottery-ticket. Would that it were in my power to show you in some practical way my gratitude for all your kindness!

You will in all probability soon receive a satisfactory answer regarding the remaining copies of the Norwegian edition of *Love's Comedy*, either from P. Botten-Hansen or another of my friends, Mr. Birkeland, Keeper of the National Archives, to whom I also wrote on the subject.

I will send you the few prefatory lines soon; they are costing me a good deal of trouble, for they must contain neither too much nor too little.

I hope that Dr. Salomonsen has conveyed my greeting to you. I am longing for Professor Clausen's arrival. There are very few Scandinavians in Rome at present; the condition of public affairs is far from attractive, and there is no prospect of improvement in the near future. With kindest regards, I remain—
Your respectfully devoted, HENRIK IBSEN.

39.

*To* FREDERIK HEGEL.

ROME, *5th January* 1867.

DEAR COUNCILLOR HEGEL,—I have the pleasure of sending you herewith the preface for *Love's Comedy*. These few lines have taxed my brain more than the whole poem. I have written and rewritten them times without number, and in the end have used my first draft. If you do not like the preface, you have my permission to dispense with it; but in that case, something to the effect of what it contains ought to be inserted in one of the most widely circulated newspapers, as an explanation to

Danish readers. It would please me best if my own lines appeared at the beginning of the book; but I leave the matter to your decision.[1]

Permit me to wish you and your family a very happy New Year. Please accept my best thanks for the valuable present of books which you sent me by the Bruns. I have read all the volumes with interest. The maturity to which Dietrichson has attained as a writer delights and surprises me. One reads his book[2] with real pleasure; and I think that I may predict a wide circulation for it in Norway, as well as in Denmark. Listov's *Vocabulary* has also interested me much, chiefly because it shows me that a great many of the so-called New-Norwegian forms of words are to be found in the Danish dialects, and that it is therefore only their adoption into the literary language which is new.

I do not know if you read the Norwegian newspapers; if you do, you will have noticed that in them, and more particularly in the *Morgenblad*, the *Nyhedsblad*, and the *Aftenblad*, an entire literature on the subject of *Brand* has sprung up. The articles in the *Morgenblad* of the 1st and 4th December contain, in my opinion, the best Norwegian criticism of the poem which has yet appeared. I do not know who is their author. Please give my kind regards to Clemens Petersen. I shall, as in duty bound, write to him soon.

I have heard nothing about the remaining copies of *Love's Comedy*; but as the owner of them is an old friend of mine, I regard the matter as settled.

And now I must tell you that my new work is well under way, and will, if nothing untoward happens, be finished early in the summer. It is to be a long dramatic poem, having as its chief figure one of those half-mythical, fanciful characters existing in the annals of the Norwegian peasantry of *modern*

---

[1] Ibsen's short preface to *Love's Comedy* was printed in the second edition of the poem and is also to be found in his *Samlede værker*, vol. x. pp. 501, 502.

[2] *Outlines of the History of Norwegian Poetry.*

times. It will have no resemblance to *Brand*, will contain no direct polemic, etc. I have long had the subject in my thoughts; now the entire plan is worked out and written down, and the First Act begun.[1] The thing grows as I work at it, and I am certain that you will be satisfied with it. But I must ask you to observe secrecy in the matter at present.

With sincere thanks for the old, and repeated good wishes for the new, year,—Believe me, Yours most respectfully and sincerely,

HENRIK IBSEN.

### 40.

*To* FREDERIK HEGEL.

ROME, *8th March* 1867.

DEAR COUNCILLOR HEGEL,—My principal purpose in writing to-day is to ask you to have the two enclosed notes delivered. Goldschmidt, with whom I am not personally acquainted, has written me a most admirable and cordial letter.[2]

For the annual account, duly received, I owe you thanks in more ways than one. I have searched it in vain for various items, more particularly for the cost of the three specially-bound copies of *Brand* sent to Stockholm and Christiania. This omission I venture to regard as a fresh proof of that great liberality of which I have already had so many; and I thank you most sincerely for it.

I have received the two numbers of the *Illustreret Tidende*, and am much obliged to you for the trouble taken. But who is the biographer? None of the Danes here know him. The tactlessness with which he treats private, irrelevant matters would incline me to the supposition that he is a Norwegian; and yet that is hardly possible. In many respects his criticism

---

[1] This new poem was *Peer Gynt.*

[2] M. Goldschmidt (1789–1887), a well-known Danish poet and political writer.

is kindly and appreciative. He is, however, guilty of several inaccuracies, as, for instance, in his account of Councillor Riddervold's attitude at the time of the granting of my pension. He is also wrong in saying that I have made a thorough study of Heine. I have only once read through the *Buch der Lieder* and one volume of the *Reisebilder*. Of Kierkegaard also I have read little, and understood less.—It would interest me, however, to know who the man is.[1]

My new dramatic poem has now advanced to the middle of the Second Act. There will be five acts, and, as far as I am able to judge now, the book will run to about 250 pages. If you wish it, I shall be able to send you the manuscript in July.

I learn from Ravnkilde that my draft of 100 rix-dollars has been presented and honoured. May I ask you to be good enough to send me some time during this month a cheque for the balance of the payment due me for the fourth edition of *Brand*? The lottery speculation has certainly begun well— if only it does not give you too much trouble.

I have read several times with much pleasure the review of Listov's *Vocabulary* in *Fædrelandet*, signed A. L. No- thing so good or so correct has hitherto been written about the modern Norwegian language. If you should happen to know the author, may I ask you to add my thanks to the many expressions of gratitude which he must undoubtedly have received. Professor Clausen has arrived here with his family. A. Hage has also come; and Orla Lehmann is expected.

Björnson writes me that he intends to give up his appoint- ment at the Theatre this summer. I think he is quite right. He is not writing anything at the present time, he says; and I fear that his newspaper, the *Norsk Folkeblad*, is stealing more of his energy than is desirable.

Let us hope that the new edition of *Love's Comedy* will

[1] The author of the short biography of Ibsen in the *Illustreret Tidende* was Axel Falkmann, a Danish journalist.

be a success! The reviewers of the first edition are hardly likely to criticise the book again; still, I hope it will be taken notice of.—With kindest regards, Yours respectfully and sincerely,

HENRIK IBSEN.

### 41.

*To* FREDERIK HEGEL.

VILLA PISANI, CASAMICCIOLA, ISCHIA,
*8th August* 1867.

DEAR COUNCILLOR HEGEL,—After having long neglected my duty, I at last beg to acknowledge, and thank you for, your esteemed letter with the enclosed 600 francs, which I received on the 9th of May.

To-day I am sending you, through Consul - General Danchertsen of Naples, the manuscript of the first three acts of my new work, the title of which is: *Peer Gynt, a dramatic poem.* I hope that you will receive the parcel about the same time as these lines. What I have sent will run, in print, to about 120 pages, and there is about the same quantity to come. I hope to be able to send you the Fourth Act towards the end of this month, and the rest not very long afterwards.

I am curious to hear how you like *the poem.* I am very hopeful myself. It may interest you to know that Peer Gynt is a real person, who lived in Gudbrandsdal, probably at the end of last, or the beginning of this, century. His name is still well-known among the peasants there; but of his exploits not much more is known than is to be found in Asbjörnsen's *Norwegian Fairy-Tale Book,* in the section, " Pictures from the Mountains." Thus I have not had very much to build upon, but so much the more liberty has been left me. It would interest me to know what Clemens Petersen thinks of the work.

Assuming you to be satisfied with it, the next question is:

Do you wish to bring out the book at Christmas? This would be what I should like, but I leave myself in your hands.[1]

And now I am going to avail myself of the kind offer you made me some time ago, and ask for an advance of 200 rix-dollars, which sum, together with the small amount due me, I should be glad to receive in the form of a draft on Paris, in a registered letter, addressed: Cavaliere D. Danchertsen, Console-Generale di Danimarca, Vico Calanzione, Pizzofalcone, Napoli. If I may calculate on finding such a letter at Naples towards the end of the month, I shall be exceedingly obliged to you. I am going about that time to Sorrento, there to put the finishing touches to my work.

We have been living in Ischia since the middle of May. The thermometer has sometimes risen to 30° Réaumur, and to keep on working in good spirits in such heat one must be strong, which, thank God, I am.

How is *Love's Comedy* selling? I hope its publication is not to be an altogether disadvantageous transaction for you. I often think about this.

V. Bergsöe, who is also here with his family, sends a manuscript in the same parcel with mine.[2] Please divide the cost of carriage as fairly as possible between us, and charge my share to my account.

Remember me kindly to Molbech, G. Brandes, and Clemens Petersen. Hoping soon to receive a few lines from you,—I remain, Yours respectfully and sincerely,

HENRIK IBSEN.

---

[1] *Peer Gynt* was published in Copenhagen on the 14th of November 1867, Ibsen having sent the remainder of the manuscript from Sorrento in October. In the letter accompanying it he wrote to Hegel: "I am very curious to know how the book will be received; but the matter causes me no disquietude: I wrote after mature reflection." More particulars and legends regarding the hero have since been collected. See an article by Per Aasmundstad in the Norwegian periodical, *Syn og Segn*, 1903, pp. 119–130.

[2] Vilhelm Bergsöe (born 1835), a Danish poet.

## 42.

*To* MAGDALENE THORESEN.

SORRENTO, 15*th October* 1867.

MY DEAR MOTHER-IN-LAW,—I shall make no attempt to justify my long silence; all I can do is to ask you to forgive it. Week after week I have resolved to write you a long letter, and, as with all my other correspondence, never got beyond the resolution.

I congratulate you most heartily upon Sara's marriage.[1] Please give her my best wishes. I am really glad on her account that her home is to be in Copenhagen, as I do not think her particularly fitted for the conditions of life in Norway. If there is any disparagement in this remark, it applies to the conditions, and not to her. I often wonder how you can endure them yourself. Life there, as it presents itself to me now, has something indescribably wearisome about it; it wearies the soul out of one, wearies the strength out of one's will. That is the accursed thing about small surroundings —they make the soul small.

It will not be long, I imagine, before Dorothea,[1] too, leaves home; and then you will not be so tied down. You ought to, and must, see Italy; and you must not make a rush through the country, but a considerable stay in it. Get a travelling-grant. Do not petition for it; demand it, insist upon getting it; it is the only way. Set pens and mouths going. Such methods ought not to be necessary; but it is impossible to get anything done without them at home—or perhaps anywhere else.[2]

I cannot tell very much about my travels in a letter. We

---

[1] Sara and Dorothea, daughters of Magdalene Thoresen, and step-sisters of Fru Ibsen.

[2] Magdalene Thoresen made various applications for travelling-grants between the years 1869 and 1873—all unsuccessful.

went to Ischia about the middle of May, and stayed there until the middle of August; since then we have been moving from one place to another on the southern side of the bay, manœuvring to escape cholera, etc. At the end of this month we go back to Rome. The Papal States are, as you probably know, in revolt, and we should like to see a little of what is going on.

I have completed a new dramatic poem, which is to be published at Christmas; it will greatly interest me to know what you think of it. It is called *Peer Gynt*, after the chief character, about whom a little is told in Asbjörnsen's book of fairy-tales. I had not much to build upon, but have consequently been able to deal the more freely with the subject, according to my own requirements.

I learn from Hegel that your new book is not to be published until spring, and that it will be a big one. This is all that we know about it; but I am looking forward to it with pleasureable eagerness.[1] One advantage, at least, we reap from living abroad—the national life comes to us from home purged and in extract; we are spared what goes on in the streets and lanes, and are gainers thereby. We have not seen any Norwegian newspapers of later date than the beginning of May.

How is Thomas getting on? Has he kept to his purpose of becoming an actor? If so, has he made his first appearance? The outlook for a scenic artist in Norway is not very tempting, but if his real calling is in that direction, there is nothing to be said. Axel is a clever boy, I hear. Will not his time at school soon be over?

I was very much surprised to be asked by Tönsberg, the publisher, for a contribution to a book which he intends to publish. When I left Norway, Tönsberg was supporting himself partly by the publication of a scurrilous newspaper in which I, along with many others, was frequently defamed, in

---

[1] The book in question, *The Sun of Siljedal*, did not appear till December 1868.

the manner common to such papers. I do not know if he still continues this publication. But I do not intend to buy over my enemies, and Mr. Tönsberg will never receive a line written by me.

I hope that Susanna's letter from Ischia reached you. She and Sigurd are well. One or two slight attacks of fever passed over in a few days. Both of them are a great deal out on the hills whilst I work.

Now we have only to see Pompeii and the Naples Museum, and then we hope to go back to dear Rome. I should be sorry if politics and humbug were to find their way there too; but sooner or later I suppose it must happen.

May you have good health whilst you are writing your book! How you can work when you are sick and suffering, is incomprehensible to me.

You must not be angry with me for what I am now going to say, namely: Be careful of the language in your new book. In *The Story of Signe*, and in your other tales, there are many words and expressions which in Norwegian mean something entirely different from what you have meant by them; and there are still more which are not and never have been Norwegian. Provincialisms which have no root in the ancient language are inadmissible. Ask advice when you are not quite certain. And do not take it amiss that I call your attention to this. It is better to be told privately in a letter than publicly in a review; and sooner or later some one is certain to attack you on this subject, which is, as you know, much under debate at the present time. We must not put weapons into our enemies' hands.—Best wishes to all from—Your affectionate,

HENRIK IBSEN.

43.

*To* Jonas Collin.[1]

Sorrento, 21*st October* 1867.

Dear Mr. Collin,—It really is quite inexcusable of me not to have answered your friendly letter before now; but a literary work of considerable length has entirely occupied my time during the past few months, and put a stop to any little correspondence which I carry on with friends at home.

In spite of my protracted silence, I can assure you that you have often, very often, been in my thoughts. We frequently talk about you; and our short sojourn together in Rome will ever be one of the pleasantest and most cherished memories of my foreign tour.

My best thanks for the pleasure you have given me by sending me your portrait!

Bergsöe has, I hope, meanwhile delivered a greeting from me. I asked him to do so, and he promised.

I received your letter the day before we left Rome. Most of our time since then has been divided between Ischia and Sorrento. Here in Sorrento I have completed my new work, a dramatic poem, which I presume will be published next month. I have, according to promise, preserved the manuscript for your father's collection; and I shall take the first opportunity of sending you the parcel.

I hope that you have long ago completely recovered from your illness. I cannot sufficiently thank you for your kind letter. I am a poor letter-writer, and shall postpone entering upon many subjects until we meet again.

We and the Bergsöe family have followed each other about all summer. Of course he and I often meet; but we are not the

---

[1] Jonas Collin (born 1840), a geologist by profession, has travelled much in the south. He belongs to a Danish family with a reputation for literary interests.

least likely ever to become close, intimate friends. We are both to blame for this. I shall not discuss the question of what the hindrance is on my side. In Bergsöe's nature there is much that is good; but I do not think it would do him any harm to be possessed of a little more character, conviction, and independence. And what he needs above all else is to be able to defend himself against outward influences. He has had a tolerably disturbed summer—in Ischia the earthquake fright, cholera in Naples, brigands at Sorrento, and now war with Garibaldians here, and wrecked railways in the Papal States!

In spite of the disturbed state of the country, however, we go next week *viâ* Pompeii and Naples to Rome, to spend the winter there. It is not easy to predict what will be the result of the political events, but a settlement must certainly come soon.

If, in spite of my negligence, you should care to send me a few lines when opportunity offers, you would give me great pleasure. My wife desires to be very kindly remembered to you. Of the Scandinavians in Rome we have no news. You have probably heard the sad news of Schou's death in Florence; it is indeed a loss. Schou was an unusually promising artist.

Enclosed is a note from V. Bergsöe. He tells me that there is a greeting for me in a letter which he received from your father yesterday. Will you greet Mr. Collin respectfully from me in return.

I see from the *Dagblad* that a pen-and-ink war has broken out between the philosophers and the theologians. I do not understand the matter well enough to form any opinion on it; but I must confess that there is unusual strength and energy of conviction in George Brandes's behaviour. I do not know whether you are his friend or his opponent; but to me it is clear that this man will play a prominent part in the intellectual life of Scandinavia. In saying this I am not, of course, giving expression to my personal view of his stand-point.[1]

---

[1] In 1866 George Brandes made his first attack on Rasmus Nielsen's philosophy, with its attempt to reconcile religion and science. Rudolf

And now good-bye for to-day, dear Collin. The warmest of greetings to yourself from—Your attached,

HENRIK IBSEN.

44.

*To* BJÖRNSTJERNE BJÖRNSON.

ROME, *9th December* 1867.

DEAR BJÖRNSON,—What sort of infernal nonsense is it that comes between us at every turn ? One might almost believe that the devil himself was casting his shadow between us. I had received your letter. In the man who writes as you write there, there is no guile. There are things which it is impossible to counterfeit. I, too, had written from a full and grateful heart, in answer. One cannot return thanks for being praised; but being understood—that makes one inexpressibly grateful. But now I can't send my letter. I have torn it to pieces. An hour ago I read Mr. Clemens Petersen's review in *Fædrelandet*. If I am to answer your letter now, I must begin in another way; I must acknowledge the receipt of your esteemed communication of such and such a date with the enclosed criticism from a certain paper.[1]

Schmidt's (anonymous) defence of Nielsen was subjected by Brandes to a severe criticism in the *Dagblad* (September 1867), in which he opposed the doctrines of positivism to those of religious philosophy, and called on the youth of Denmark to widen their horizon. He declared that Nielsen and his allies were fighting against progress—making a vain endeavour to prevent what was true in the new ideas from prevailing. This article produced a short but sharp controversy, in which Björnson (also anonymously) took part against Brandes.

[1] The first edition of *Peer Gynt* was published in Copenhagen on the 14th of November 1867, and the second edition only a fortnight later. Björnson reviewed the book in a letter from Copenhagen to the *Norsk Folkeblad*. A week later it was reviewed in *Fædrelandet* by Clemens Petersen. Petersen declared that the work is not " real poetry," because " in its transpositions from reality to art it neither completely fulfils the requirements of art nor those of reality." It is, in his opinion " full of

If I were in Copenhagen, and some one there was as great a friend of mine as Clemens Petersen is of yours, I would have thrashed the life out of him before I would have permitted him to commit such an intentional crime against truth and justice. There is a lie involved in Clemens Petersen's article—not in what he says, but in what he refrains from saying. And he intentionally refrains from saying a great deal. You are quite at liberty to show him this letter. As surely as I know that he has a profound, ardent apprehension of what really makes this life worth living, so surely do I know that this article will come to burn and scathe his soul; for the lie involved in keeping silence is as much a lie as the positive assertion. And on Clemens Petersen there rests a great responsibility, for God has entrusted him with a great task.

Do not believe that I am a blind, conceited fool! I can assure you that in my quiet moments I sound and probe and dissect my own inward parts—and where it hurts most, too.

My book *is* poetry; and if it is not, then it will be. The conception of poetry in our country, in Norway, shall be made to conform to the book. There is no stability in the world of ideas. The Scandinavians of this century are not Greeks. He says that the Strange Passenger is symbolic of terror. Supposing that I had been about to be executed, and that such an explanation would have saved my life, it would never have occurred to me. I never thought of such a thing. I stuck in the scene as a mere caprice. And tell me now, is Peer Gynt himself not a personality, complete and individual? *I* know that he is. And the mother, is she not? There are many things to be learned from Clemens Petersen, and I have learned much from him; but there is something that it might do him good to learn, and in which I, even though I cannot teach it to him, have the advantage of him—and that is what you in your letter call "loyalty."

fallacious ideas " and of " riddles which are insoluble because there is nothing in them at all." He assigns it to the domain of polemical journalism.

Yes, that is just the word! Not loyalty to a friend, a purpose, or the like, but to something infinitely higher.

However, I am glad of the injustice that has been done me. There has been something of the God-send, of the providential dispensation in it; for I feel that this anger is invigorating all my powers. If it is to be war, then let it be war! If I am no poet, then I have nothing to lose. I shall try my luck as a photographer. My contemporaries in the North I shall take in hand, one after the other, as I have already taken the nationalist language reformers.[1] I will not spare the child in the mother's womb, nor the thought or feeling that lies under the word of any living soul that deserves the honour of my notice.

Dear Björnson, you are a good, warm-hearted soul; you have given me more of what is great and fine than I can ever repay you; but there is something in your nature that may easily cause your good fortune—yes, that more than anything else— to be a curse to you. I have a right to tell you this; for I know that, underneath the crust of folly and frowardness, I have taken life very seriously. Do you know that I have entirely separated myself from my own parents, from my whole family, because a position of half-understanding was unendurable to me?

What I have written is somewhat incoherent, but, put together, it amounts to this: I will not be an antiquarian nor a geographer; I will not cultivate my talent for the Monrad philosophy; in short, I will not follow good advice. But one thing I will do, even though the powers without and the powers within drive me to pull the roof down upon my head—I will always, so help me God, continue to be—Your faithfully and sincerely devoted,

HENRIK IBSEN.

---

[1] In the figure "Huhu" in the Fourth Act of *Peer Gynt*, Ibsen aims at the "Maalstrævere," the would-be nationalisers of the Norwegian language.

*10th December.*—I have slept upon the above lines, and have now read them in cold blood. They are the expression of my mood of yesterday, but still they shall be sent.

I will now tell you, calmly and after due consideration, what will be the result of Mr. Clemens Petersen's article.

I have no intention of yielding, and Mr. Clemens Petersen cannot oust me; it is too late for that. He may possibly oblige me to withdraw from Denmark; but in that case I intend to change more than my publisher. Do not under-estimate my friends and my adherents in Norway. The party whose newspaper has opened its columns to calumnies about me, will be made to feel that I do not stand alone. When things go beyond a certain point, I know no consideration; and if I am only careful to do what I am quite capable of, namely, combine this relentlessness of mind with deliberateness in the choice of means, my enemies shall be made to feel that if I cannot build up, I am, at least, able to pull down.

This, however, concerns only the future. Now I will tell you something of present moment.

I am carrying on no correspondence with any one at home; nevertheless I can give you a piece of home intelligence. Do you know what they are saying just now in Norway, wherever Carl Ploug's paper is read? They are saying: "It is evident from Clemens Petersen's review that Björnson is in Copenhagen."

If you have reviewed *Peer Gynt* in the *Norsk Folkeblad*, they are saying: "Diplomatic, but not clever enough." Some will say it in all good faith; others from vindictiveness and resentment. The critics will divide into parties, for or against. You will see that I am right.

They will call Clemens Petersen's review a return for favours received. A man unknown to me wrote some articles in the *Morgenblad* lately, in which he unmercifully disparaged Mr. Petersen's literary work; I was favourably mentioned in them. These combinations will be recalled. I know the way the fellows reason.

Dear Björnson, do let us try to hold together. Our friends have often enough made life miserable for us, and the struggle more onerous than it need be.

You see, from the very fact that I write all this to you, that I harbour no suspicion of you in this matter. I neither am nor ever shall be on the side of my adherents when they are opposed to you. When the opposition is to your friends, that is another matter.

Mr. Petersen's article—to return to that again—will not do me any harm. The absentee has always a great advantage in the very fact of his being absent. But to write the article in such a style, was imprudent. In his review of *Brand*, he treated me with respect, and the public will not find anything in the intervening years which renders me deserving of contempt. The public will not permit Mr. Petersen to dispose of me as summarily as he has attempted to do. He ought to leave such attempts to those of his colleagues who live *by* their critical labours. Until now I believed that Mr. Petersen lived *for* his.

All I reproach you with is inaction. It was not kind of you to permit, through negligence, such an attempt to be made to place my literary reputation under the auctioneer's hammer in my absence.

There! I have written myself into a good temper again. Now do you abuse me like a pickpocket. I shall be glad if you find it necessary to do so in a long letter.

Accept in a friendly spirit a friendly greeting from us all. Do not show your wife this letter; but give her our best wishes for Christmas and New Year, and, most particularly, for the approaching third great event.—Yours,

HENRIK IBSEN.

## 45

*To* BJÖRNSTJERNE BJÖRNSON.

ROME, 28*th December* 1867.

DEAR BJÖRNSON,—Nothing in the wide world could have been more welcome than the greeting which your letter, received on Christmas morning, brought me.

The thought of the cargo of nonsense which I shipped to you in my last epistle had not left me at peace with myself for an hour in the interval. The worst that a man can do to himself is to do injustice to others. Thank you, noble-minded man that you are, for taking the matter as you have done. I could see nothing before me but dispeace and bitterness for a long time to come; and yet now it appears to me as only what might have been expected of you, that you should take it just as you did, and in no other way. I read your letter over and over again, every day, and read myself free from the tormenting thought that I have hurt you.

Do not understand what I said in my former letter to mean that my conception of what is essential in poetry is entirely different from Clemens Petersen's. On the contrary, I understand and am entirely in accord with him. But I contend that I have fulfilled the requirements. He says: No.

He writes of our over-reflective age, which makes the witches in Macbeth symbolise something which takes place in Macbeth himself; yet in the very same article he himself makes a distracted passenger on board a ship symbolise "terror"! Why, proceeding in this manner, I will undertake to turn your works and those of every other poet into allegories, from beginning to end. Take *Götz von Berlichingen.* Say that Götz himself represents the ferment of the idea of liberty in the nation, that the Emperor represents the idea of the state, etc. etc.; and what result do you arrive at? Why, that it is not poetry!

As for my "paroxysms," do not worry about them; there is

nothing unhealthy in them, either one way or another. I shall
very probably take your advice and write a comedy for the
stage; the idea had been occupying my own mind. It is possible that we shall go to Northern Italy for the summer, but
where we shall spend next winter I do not know. I only know
that it will not be in Norway. ¶ Were I to go home now, one
of two things would happen: I should either within a month
make an enemy of every one there; or else I should sneak
myself into favour again in all manner of disguises, and thus
become a lie, both to myself and others.

Dear Björnson, are you really going back to the theatre
again? There is work for you there, undoubtedly; but you
have a task calling to you, much nearer at hand, in your
authorship. If your taking up theatrical work meant merely
a loss of time, meant merely that all the visions, moods, and
imaginings of the poet were put aside, to make their appearance
later, it would not matter so much. But such is not the case.
Others come, but the intervening ones die unborn. For a poet,
the toil of a theatre is equivalent to a daily fœticide. The
civil laws make this a punishable crime; I do not know if God
is more lenient. Think it over, dear Björnson! A man's gifts
are not a property; they are a duty.[1]

No, go abroad, carissimo! Both because distance gives a
wider range of vision, and because much more value is set
upon the man who is out of sight. I am certain that the good
people of Weimar were Gœthe's worst public.

It would be glorious if we could meet down here. But I
have a feeling that this will not happen. I am longing for
*The Fisher Maiden* like a thirsty man for water—yes, it is
true.[2] I roam about by myself, and am very unsociable in the

---

[1] In June 1867, Björnson had given up the managership of the
Christiania Theatre; but before many months had passed, negotiations
were being carried on with the view of his becoming "artistic director."
They were unsuccessful; he would not accept the conditions offered.

[2] Björnson's tale, *The Fisher Maiden*, came out in April 1868. Ibsen
wrote of it to Hegel: "I think the first half excellent; but the rest

large circle of Scandinavian Romans. By and by I may perhaps send you something on the subject of my travels for the *Norsk Folkeblad*; a few sketches from Italy you shall certainly have. Thank you for what you have written about me. Hegel has promised to send me the numbers of the newspaper. Thank you in advance for the biography, too![1]

My sincere conviction obliges me to disagree entirely with you in what you write on the subject of "decorations." We live under a monarchy, and not under a republic. I, for my part, am not partial to a republic. "The resemblance to Bravo"[2] already exists; for we, as well as he, accept a salary from the state. From the Government of the day we accept money; royalty gives us a decoration because it respects a popular feeling of which it acknowledges the existence. Why reject the one, when we have not rejected the other form of expression for the same thing? Let us examine ourselves carefully! Is it our intention henceforth to be ascetics? Do we intend to decline every kindly-meant festivity offered us, every toast, etc.? If not then of what avail is the rejection of this one particular thing; Orla Lehmann has declaimed against decorations and titles; but, tell me truly, do you know a vainer man than he is? August Blanche has spoken sarcastically about such matters; but does he not permit himself to be starred and be-ribboned all over by popular favour in the "Operakällar" and other places? For my part, I feel that by declining I should make myself guilty of a lie to myself and others. If I had had any real desire for such finery, I should certainly have refrained from playing the part of "state-satirist." But if the finery comes my way—why, then, no ado about it![3]

is not properly worked out, and, moreover, in it he is attempting something which lies beyond the range of his powers."

[1] A biography of Ibsen appeared in Björnson's newspaper, the *Norsk Folkeblad*, in 1869, Nos. 3 and 4.

[2] Consul Bravo in Rome (see Letter 23) was noted for his vanity in the matter of titles and orders.

[3] Björnson has always been an enemy of orders and decorations. Ibsen has accepted several.

I will soon write you another long letter; this one is by no means what it should be. As to my "friends of the *Morgenblad*," you may feel quite easy—they will never be able to harm me. I know no more who these writing friends are, than I know who writes in the newspapers of the South Sea Islands. I have no correspondence with Norway except an exchange of a letter with my brother-in-law every three months.

And now I wish you a happy New Year! Write when you can—and may the burden of your letter be that all is well! Remember us all to your wife and the little boys.—Your devoted,                    HENRIK IBSEN.

*P.S.*—Remember me to Hegel, please; also to Clemens Petersen and any others who will accept a greeting. It is a triumphal progress you have started on, the Danes here tell me. And you deserve that it should be. If only it does not take too much of the time and composure of mind claimed by your work!—Yours,                    H. I.

46.

*To* FREDERIK HEGEL.

ROME, 24*th February* 1868.

DEAR COUNCILLOR HEGEL,—I beg of you once again to have forbearance with my negligence as a correspondent, and to pardon my not replying until to-day to your esteemed and friendly letter of the 12th of December last. I thank you most sincerely for the enclosed draft for 700 francs.

The corrections in *Brand* which you write about shall be attended to and sent in a few days.[1]

What have you to tell me about *Peer Gynt*? In Sweden it has, as far as I can judge from the newspaper reviews, been very well received; but are the sales correspondingly good?

[1] The fifth edition of *Brand* was published in August 1868.

I learn that the book created much excitement in Norway. This does not trouble me in the least; but both there and in Denmark they have discovered much more satire in it than was intended by me. Why can they not read the book as a poem? For as such I wrote it. The satirical passages are tolerably isolated. But if the Norwegians of the present time recognise themselves, as it would appear they do, in the character of Peer Gynt, that is the good people's own affair.

I am very much obliged to you for the many reviews which you have been kind enough to send me. The *Morgenblad* is the only Norwegian paper which is taken here. If you could, at your convenience, procure for me the articles by Björnson in the *Norsk Folkeblad*, you would give me much pleasure.

My next work will probably be a play for the theatre, and I hope it will not be long before I begin to work at it seriously.

I am tormented by the thought that I have not yet written to Mr. G. Brandes on the subject of his article in the *Dansk Maanedsskrift*; but it shall be done now. Please give him my kind regards when opportunity offers.[1]

I am sincerely sorry to hear that the publication of P. Hjort's Letters has caused you unpleasantness; but it seems to me that what falls to your part should be easy to bear, since it is evident that all the responsibility lies with the editor.[2]

[1] George Brandes wrote an essay on Ibsen in the *Dansk Maanedsskrift* (1867, ii.). Ibsen, who had heard of his intention to do this, wrote to Hegel: "I am very glad to hear that Brandes intends to write about my works. Will you thank him from me, and say to him that I am eager for his criticism, but that I wish very much that he would include *Peer Gynt* among the works on which it is based; if he does, several of his opinions will be modified; he himself will tell which." Brandes added an appendix on the subject of *Peer Gynt* to this essay; but the poem did not at that time find favour in his sight. He judged it differently afterwards.

[2] The Danish author, Peder Hjort (1793–1871), published in 1867 the first volume of *A Selection of Letters from Men and Women to P. Hjort*, a book which, by reason of numerous indiscretions, aroused great indignation.

Neither need you much mind the howls of the nationalist language reformers over *Peer Gynt's* not arriving in better time at Bergen. To judge by what has since occurred, it seems as if the fellows had got it early enough.

Yes, I have had thoughts of making a collection of my scattered and unpublished poems; but it cannot be done down here; for they must be hunted up in a variety of newspapers, etc. Some time I shall have to go north again, and then I shall probably pay a visit to Christiania, on which occasion the undertaking might be set agoing. Thank you for having broached the subject. With a hearty, though somewhat late, New Year's greeting, and with thanks, no less warm, for the past year, I am—Yours most respectfully and sincerely,

HENRIK IBSEN.

*P.S.*—Dare I add one more to the many calls I have made on your kindness? If you permit it, then I shall ask you to purchase and place to my account a geography, a universal history, a history of Scandinavia, a book of natural history, an arithmetic, and the first books used in religious instruction— all suitable for a child of eight, who, however, is not entirely a beginner. My little boy has read a great deal, especially general and Bible history, but hitherto quite unsystematically: and he must not go on in this way. If it is not too expensive to send the books as goods or by post, I should prefer to have them sent thus; but if it is not practicable, then perhaps some traveller coming this way will find room for them in his trunk. Please do not be annoyed by this request; it is a matter of importance to me.—Yours,

H. I.

## 47.

*To* MAGDALENE THORESEN.

ROME, 31*st March* 1868.

DEAR MOTHER-IN-LAW,—Will you kindly accept a few lines, even though they come from such a bad correspondent as I am. I feel as though there were no end to the things I could say to you, but in writing they never come to anything. Let us hope that it would be better if we could talk! I not only hope, but believe that it would; though I am well aware that only when alone with my thoughts am I myself.

I can hardly imagine how it will be possible to live out of Italy—and in Christiania of all places! But it will have to be done.[1] I feel, however, that one must isolate one's self up there —at least I must, if I do not want to make an enemy of every second person. I can put up with everything else, but the coquetry with the Swedes I cannot stand. The Swedes are, by reason of what forms the foundation of their civilisation, our intellectual antagonists; and yet it is thought possible to patch together what is antagonistic by means of mutual complaisance, or something of the kind. It is lucky for the fellows who are charging themselves with this task that our press is in such a condition that no honest man can have anything to do with it without putting on gloves. With them on, one cannot fight well. And whom would one have on one's side? Not a single person. It is often evident to me that there is nothing left in our country for any one gifted with mind and heart to do, but to retreat, like the wounded deer, into the thicket, to die in solitude and silence. The best thing that could befall our country would be a great national disaster. If we could not stand that, we should have no right to exist. I have been a witness here to sacrifices which enable me to institute com-

---

[1] Ibsen left Italy in the spring of 1868, but did not then return to Norway. He lived in Germany for a number of years.

parisons—and the result of them is not creditable to our country.

Allow me to congratulate you upon your readings.[1] I was certain they would be a success. We get almost no home news. No Norwegian newspapers have been sent us this year. This, too, is significant. While the Danish and Swedish newspaper-proprietors, out of regard for their countrymen here, not only present us with their papers gratis, but pay the postage of them to the frontiers of the Papal States, the owner of the *Morgenblad*, Dr. de Besche, the physician-in-ordinary to the King, has stopped sending his paper because the postage of it was not paid *in advance* at New Year by the Scandinavian Society. There is something exceedingly exasperating in having to feel ashamed before foreigners of one's own countrymen.

Thomas is now in Stockholm, I presume? I hope he will get on well. You will no doubt soon have the pleasure of seeing Axel a bright young student. Remember me to all the family. Every good wish for yourself from — Yours affectionately, HENRIK IBSEN.

*P.S.*—What all the above talk amounts to is this: Try to get away! Go abroad! Do it whether it is possible or impossible. But nothing is impossible that one desires with an indomitable will.

H. I.

### 48.

*To* FREDERIK HEGEL.

MUNICH, 22*nd September* 1868.

DEAR COUNCILLOR HEGEL,—My best thanks for your last kind letter, containing the necessary information concerning the Theatre management. As soon as I reach Dresden I

---

[1] In December 1867, Magdalene Thoresen began to give public readings from her own works.

shall take advantage of your offer, and send you a revised copy of *The Pretenders* for the purpose named. It was no surprise to me to be told that the time for a new edition has not come yet; for the first edition was a very large one. I am certain that for such sale and circulation as it has had, I have chiefly to thank you, who have put me in touch with the Danish public. Norway alone cannot support an author.

In Dresden I shall write my new play, about which more in course of time. I hope that it will be finished by Christmas; but as the time for publication and performance this season will then be over, it will have to wait. I shall have it copied out for you, and, when you have read it, we shall come to an agreement as to further proceedings. This new, *peaceable* work is giving me pleasure.

All the time here we have been living under a glorious Italian sky, enjoying the true art treasures of the town and the Prussophobia of its inhabitants, of which no one at home has any conception.

We shall probably go direct from Munich to Dresden on the 1st or 2nd of October. Though I am not actually in want of money, I take the liberty, in view of possible emergencies, to ask you kindly to send me 200 rix-dollars, either in Prussian notes or in the form of a draft. My address is: c/o Frau C. Bauer, Maximiliansplatz 13, III.

Thank you again and again for the newspapers sent me. The package of books from Turin has not yet made its appearance; thereby hangs a long and curious tale, which I shall tell you when I write from Dresden.[1]—Yours most sincerely,

HENRIK IBSEN.[2]

[1] The books in question were the school books, which Hegel had sent off from Copenhagen in March. They did not reach Ibsen till the following spring.

[2] Ibsen left Rome on the 13th of May 1868; spent some time in Florence; June, July, and August at Berchtesgaden in Southern Bavaria; and September in Munich. It was his intention to return to Norway after a winter in Dresden. At Berchtesgaden he had already been planning his new play, *The League of Youth*.

49.

*To* FREDERIK HEGEL.

DRESDEN, 31*st October* 1868.

DEAR COUNCILLOR HEGEL, — The regular arrival of the newspaper shows me that you have received my last note, with the address, etc. I rather think I promised in it to write soon at greater length. You give us real and great pleasure by sending us the *Dagblad,* and I only wish it were in my power to show you my gratitude in more than mere words.

My new work is making rapid progress. I have been mentally wrestling with it all summer, but without really writing anything. Now the whole outline is finished and written down. The First Act is completed, the second will be in the course of a week, and by the end of the year I hope to have the play ready. It will be in prose, and in every way adapted for the stage. The title is: *The League of Youth,* or *The Almighty & Co.*: a comedy in five acts.[1] It deals with the frictions and tendencies of modern life, and will, though the action takes place in Norway, be just as well adapted for Denmark. I am in a reconciled and happy frame of mind, and write accordingly; this time that dear and excellent man, G. Brandes, shall have no cause for complaining of illicit intercourse with the muses. By the bye, will you kindly send me a copy of Brandes's *Æsthetical Studies,* and charge it to my account. Before we left Rome I heard that he was writing an Essay on the Comic, a subject upon which, viewed theoreti-

---

[1] *The League of Youth* was published without the second title. Hegel wrote at once proposing that it should be omitted. To this Ibsen willingly agreed. "I had half thought of suppressing it myself," he wrote; "though it could have given offence to no one *who had read the play.* . . . The work is more artistically elaborated than any I have yet written; and I do not believe there is a single expression in it so peculiarly Norwegian as to be unsuitable on the Copenhagen stage."

cally, I must confess that I have no very distinct ideas, and which I shall be particularly glad to have elucidated for me by Brandes.[1]

The package of books from Turin is, in the meantime, lost, and seems likely to remain so; and this under what appear to me suspicious circumstances. I have made a last attempt to get hold of it, and as soon as a letter which I am expecting from Rome arrives, I shall write to you and send you the whole correspondence.

Do you not know any Danes who intend to winter in Dresden? I am longing greatly for the society of Scandinavians. Possibly there are some here already, but I have not met any and the Consul knows of none.

Dresden is a very pleasant and a very cheap place of residence. But as we have made preparations for remaining here six months, various payments have had to be made in advance, and I have consequently run short of money. I therefore take advantage of your kind offer made me some time ago, and request you to be good enough to send me 200 rix-dollars. Now you are not to be alarmed, and at once come to the conclusion, remembering the handsome amounts for which I have drawn on you this summer already, that I have become a "Verschwender" here in Germany. The case is rather the reverse. I have been so fortunate this year as to be able to save my Norwegian pension, and I am unwilling to draw any of it from the Christiania Kreditkasse, in which it is deposited.

Thank you very much for the copy sent me of the fifth edition of *Brand*. I hope the sale will be brisk.

[1] In the letter already quoted, Ibsen thanks Hegel for sending him Brandes's *Æsthetical Studies*, " a book," he writes, " which has been a real gold-mine for me—especially the Essays on the Comic. Brandes has a truly remarkable power of seeing clearly, penetratingly, and connectedly; and I should be inclined to say that, if it were possible, his power of making himself clear to the reader, and above all making himself so impressive as to be remembered, is still greater."

What I have written regarding the title of my new play is between ourselves; that I am engaged on the work is, of course, no secret. I shall keep *The Pretenders* by me in the meantime, so as not to send in two plays at the same time.

I have been requested by Mr. Rudolf Schmidt to contribute to a new periodical; but for the moment I have nothing to send. I am going to write to him to-day.

The weather is raw and stormy, but good when regarded as working weather; and we are comfortably situated in every respect.

I go a great deal to the theatre; it is one of the best in Germany. In matters of taste and art it ranks far, far below the Copenhagen Theatre. And the remark applies to the German theatres generally.

Pray forgive me for troubling you as I do, and believe me to be—Yours most sincerely,

HENRIK IBSEN.

*P.S.*—How is V. Bergsöe's long new novel succeeding?

H. I.

50.

*To* RUDOLF SCHMIDT.

DRESDEN, 31*st October* 1868.

DEAR SIR,—I beg to acknowledge the receipt of your esteemed letter of the 11th inst., and to return my best thanks for your kind and flattering proposal. It is, however, at present impossible for me to accept it. I cannot attach to any of the short poems at my disposal (all of them written in times long past and from abandoned standpoints) such value or importance as would, in my opinion, justify their publication—and least of all in the first numbers of a new periodical. Besides, I have left all such manuscripts in Rome, and do not expect to receive them until spring. Should I, on re-reading them then, form a more favourable opinion of one or other of the compositions, I shall be most happy to send it to you—and shall not be the least offended if it is rejected.

I dare not promise any new short things, as at present my whole attention is devoted to a long work, a five-act comedy. You mention as your colleagues in the editorship, Professor R. Nielsen and Mr. Clemens Petersen. I know Mr. C. Petersen, and I do not know Professor Nielsen. Taking both of these circumstances into account, I imagine that I am not making a mistake in addressing my thanks for the proposal to you alone.—Yours respectfully,

HENRIK IBSEN.

*P.S.*—If, at a future period, you should want a few small articles about Italy—brief character or travel sketches, without any claim to artistic value—I have sufficient material, and have no doubt I should be able to put it into shape. But, I again repeat, this is for a future season.[1]

H. I.

51.

*To* RUDOLF SCHMIDT.

DRESDEN, 26*th January* 1869.

DEAR SIR,—In reply to your esteemed letter of the 16th inst., I find myself obliged to inform you that I do not wish to

---

[1] The Danish philosopher, Professor Rasmus Nielsen (1809–1884), and Rudolf Schmidt, the author (1836–1899), assisted first by Clemens Petersen and afterwards by Björnson, published a monthly magazine, entitled *For Ide og Virkelighed*, from April 1869 to July 1873. Ibsen never wrote in it.

be named as a future contributor to the proposed periodical, since I do not see my way to taking advantage of your flattering offer.

The explanation of my decision is that I cannot prevail on myself to collaborate with men of whom I have the impression, produced by experience, that, at the first opportunity, they will use their respective newspapers and pens against me. In a letter from Copenhagen to the Norwegian *Morgenblad*, I find Mr. Björnstjerne Björnson named as probable joint-editor of *For Ide og Virkelighed* (For Idea and Reality). This circumstance would in itself decide me against accepting your proposal, even if other motives were not present in abundance.

I feel certain of your concurrence when I assert that a clear understanding is the first requisite in all relations; and I therefore confidently hope you will not take it amiss that it is with a refusal I subscribe myself—Yours respectfully,

HENRIK IBSEN.


## 52.

*To* FREDERIK HEGEL.

DRESDEN, 20*th February* 1869.

DEAR COUNCILLOR HEGEL,—Accept a few lines in reply to your last two letters, of the 22nd of January and the 2nd of February. It is not impossible that I may come to Copenhagen this summer; but if I do, it will be only for a short time, and to return here again.

I am exceedingly obliged to you for the *Dagblad*. The *Morgenblad* contains nothing of interest, only never-ending disputes about trifles, and a great deal of stupidity.

Thank you very much for the copy of *The Sun of Siljedal*.[1] The book has its good points, but it seems to me confused in construction, and as regards language, extraordinarily bad. I

[1] Magdalene Thoresen's new book.

have never seen a language so maltreated in print before, not even in the late Reiser's *Fyrgterlige ildebrandsgeschichte* (Terrible Story of a Fire).[1] If you wish, in a literary sense, to save the authoress, then advise her to stop writing peasant-tales. Björnson and I employ words and expressions belonging to the language of the peasantry, because we know and understand which are legitimate, as being derived from the ancient language, and which are corrupt and uncouth colloquialisms. But Mrs. Thoresen is not able to distinguish between these, and her language has consequently become a conglomeration which is not, never has been, and never will be, Norwegian. I have myself written to her on this subject, just as frankly as I here write to you, but have as yet received no answer.

I cannot expect to have my new dramatic work performed this season. It is now almost finished; then the copying-out will begin, after which I hope to be able to send you an act every week. I hope and believe that you will be pleased with this peaceable play, which is as well adapted to Danish and Swedish, as to Norwegian, conditions. If it could be sent in to the theatres in May, then it would be possible to have it performed in September, and have it in the book-shops by October. It will fill about two hundred printed pages.

For the annual statement received I am, as usual, grateful to you, and that in every respect.

The parcel of books will be brought to me from Rome by some one coming. It is not of such pressing importance now, as I sent my son at New Year to a school here specially intended for foreign children, where the instruction is given orally, in French and German.

We have had hardly any winter here; ten to twelve degrees of heat are quite common, and in many places the grass is beginning to grow.

---

[1] C. F. Reiser was a Danish doctor of German extraction. He wrote the book referred to in such bad Danish that he exposed himself to much ridicule.

Who is Mr. Chr. Thorkildsen? Can he possibly be a Norwegian pocket-book and portfolio manufacturer of that name who was living in Christiania a few years ago, and had always some new and remarkable project on hand? He has asked me to contribute to a grand book which he is bringing out; but I have refused. I have received some peculiar letters from Mr. Rudolf Schmidt. He continues to ask me for contributions, telling me at the same time that his magazine "needs to beg from no one"; he writes that the said magazine "is to focus all the intellect of the north," and declares that he "will regard me as a man who shirks his duty" if I do not write in it. An odd way of putting things, is it not?

And now no more to-day, except my very kind regards. If there is any objection to the time which I have indicated for the publication of my play, or anything else concerning it which you would wish arranged differently, please let me hear from you.—Yours most sincerely and respectfully,

HENRIK IBSEN.

### 53.

#### *To* FREDERIK HEGEL.

DRESDEN, 14*th March* 1869.

DEAR COUNCILLOR HEGEL,—I have the pleasure of sending you herewith the first quarter of the manuscript; a similar consignment will follow every week, so that you will have the whole in three weeks. As far as I am concerned, the printing may begin at once.

I have confidence in your proof-reader, and in my own manuscript, which I believe to be free from any slips of the pen. I shall be glad if the book is printed immediately, for I cannot change or correct anything.

Accept my best thanks for the 150 Prussian thalers; also for Richardt's new book of poems, the *Illustreret Tidende*.

Hamilton's magazine, etc. R.'s collection of poems is a particularly fine one. I see that the Christiania correspondent of
the *Nordisk Tidskrift* fears that a prolonged stay abroad will
be injurious to me. I hope that my new work will prove the
contrary. This correspondent's own letters are such extremely
awkward, tasteless productions, that one might almost believe
them to be from the pen of G. A. Krohg.[1]

A German, Mr. Siebold, writes to me that he has translated
*Brand*, and is arranging for its publication here. Do you know
him? I must confess that I have a want of confidence in the
undertaking.[2] It is, however, my desire to have my works
circulated in Germany. It ought to be from Leipzig, I imagine.
To whom should I apply there? This is, of course, not a
matter of immediate importance.

From the papers I learn to my surprise that my countrymen
meditate having a students' gathering this summer. I thought
that the fellows had done enough now in the way of feigning
Scandinavian patriotism. Will such an invitation really be
accepted by the Danes?[3]

Kindest regards from—Your sincerely obliged,

HENRIK IBSEN.

[1] Ibsen's conjecture was correct. The letters in question were
written by G. A. Krohg, who was notorious for his affected, primitive-
Scandinavian style.

[2] P. F. Siebold, a Cassel commercial traveller, was the first German
who attempted to make Ibsen's poetry accessible to his countrymen.
His travels in the Scandinavian countries had awakened in him an
interest in their literature. His translation of *Brand* was published in
1872. It is very unfavourably criticised by Lindner; but Siebold
himself maintained that much of it has been made use of in the third
German translation of the poem, that by A. von Wolzogen.

[3] In February 1869 the Norwegian Students' Union issued invitations for a gathering of Scandinavian students at Christiania; and the
assembly was actually held at the appointed time; but it did not par-
take of the political character of the students' assemblies of former
days.

54.

*To* LORENTZ DIETRICHSON.[1]

DRESDEN, 28th May 1869.

HO, CARISSIMO!—I hope that, in spite of the professorship and all other dignities, I may be allowed to use our old Roman salutation.[2]

So you are a professor now! Dear friend, accept my most sincere congratulations. I take it for granted that it is not simply an honorary title, but that a considerable income goes along with it. And as you are also Curator of the National Museum, I hope the meaning of it all is that you are comfortably settled in Stockholm for a long time. Please give me full information.

There were two reasons for my not answering your friendly letter of last autumn. The first was, that I felt unable to decide in regard to *The Pretenders*; the second, simply that I am a perfect wretch in the matter of correspondence. During the winter I wrote a new dramatic work, a comedy in five acts, entitled *The League of Youth*, which is now in the press, and which I wished to offer to the Theatre before *The Pretenders*; I shall send it to you in about a month, trusting that you will do the best you can for it.

I imagine I was not mistaken in thinking that I recognised your friendly pen in Swedish reviews of *Brand* and *Peer Gynt*.

---

[1] Lorentz Dietrichson (born in 1834), a Norwegian writer on literature and art. He resided in Italy from 1862–1865. Ibsen, who had known him in Christiania, called on him at once in Rome in 1864. From this year onwards the friendship was an intimate one, and, in spite of one serious quarrel, it has been a lasting one. On the 1st of January 1904, Dietrichson's seventieth birthday, Ibsen sent the heartiest good wishes to his "dear old friend."

[2] In February 1869, Dietrichson was appointed "Extraordinary Professor" of art-history in the Stockholm Academy of Art, an appointment which he held till 1875, when he was made Professor at the University of Christiania.

For them, as well as for much else, I hope to be able to thank you personally in a not too distant future.

I have a special reason for doing my bounden duty to-day in the matter of writing to you. I wish to draw a draft on your friendship.

Let me explain.—A German literary man, P. F. Siebold of Cassel, has translated *Brand,* and his book is to be published at Leipzig in autumn. He, or his publisher, or both of them, are, however, of opinion that the public ought to be prepared for it; they therefore intend as soon as possible to publish my portrait in a German magazine, most likely the *Illustrirte Zeitung,* along with a short biography, containing information as to my position in Scandinavian literature, my personal circumstances, etc. They have applied to me for such information; but I do not care to give it myself; and Mr. Siebold is of course not sufficiently acquainted with the facts of the case. You can understand that the matter is one of considerable interest to me. Therefore it is that I come to you, as my old friend. String some facts together, dear old fellow, in a manner that will suit the Germans. Write as favourably as your conscience will permit. The starving poet business is no good nowadays; tell about my pension from the Government and the Storthing; tell that I am travelling, that I am for the time being "in dem grossen Vaterland," etc.

Is it too much to ask you to do all this? Or will you help me? If you do write, write briefly and concisely, and send your article either to me or to "Herr P. F. Siebold in Cassel." That is all the address necessary; he will translate it into German. I know no one better fitted than you to whom I could apply; hence I trouble you. Reply to me at all events. From the 8th of June my address will be: Königsbrückerstrasse 33, 1 Etage.[1]

---

[1] In the autumn of 1869, Dietrichson published a biography of Ibsen in the Swedish *Ny Illustrerad Tidning.* P. F. Siebold based upon it a German biography, which appeared in the *Illustrirte Zeitung* of March 19, 1870.

I have not time to give you an account of my travels since
we parted. I am living a comfortable and care-free life, and
purpose tackling *Julian* in autumn. Please remember us very
kindly to Mrs. Dietrichson and your little daughter. I think of
coming to Stockholm next year; but more of this another time.

I see by the papers that you are to lecture at Gothenburg.
I do not know where you are at the present moment, and therefore send this letter through Hegel.

When is the next volume of your history of Norwegian
literature to appear? I cannot sufficiently thank you for the
volume already in print; it has given us great pleasure; and I
may truthfully say that it is the only book, except *Holberg's
Comedies*, which I never tire of reading. My wife knows it
almost by heart. It is indeed a book that does you honour.[1]
With this, dear friend, I shall take leave of you for to-day. If
you can help me in the above-mentioned matter, I know that
you will do it. Remember me to all mutual friends.—Yours
most sincerely,

HENRIK IBSEN.

55.

*To* FREDERIK HEGEL.

DRESDEN, 10*th June* 1869.

DEAR COUNCILLOR HEGEL,—The explanation of my not yet
having answered your kind letter of the 21st of last month is,
that I have been busy moving. We are now in the house
which we intend to occupy for the summer, and my address is,
Königsbrückerstrasse 33, 1 Etage.

I will send you the letters to the three Theatre-managements
in good time. If the play is accepted in Copenhagen, there can
be no question of waiting for the performance there—the book

---

[1] The second, and last, volume of Dietrichson's *Outlines of the
History of Norwegian Poetry* appeared in the autumn of 1869.

must, of course, come out in the autumn; and I am quite prepared to be paid less by the Theatre in consequence of this.[1]

May I ask you to tell Mr. H. Scharling that at present I
have nothing suitable for the *Dansk Tidsskrift*. If I should
have something at a future time, it will give me pleasure to
send it to him.

I have been requested by the Norwegian committee of
management of the Students' Gathering to write a song of
welcome; this, however, I have declined to do.

At last I am going to embark on the long, and long-planned
work, *Emperor Julian*; my conception of it has now become
sufficiently distinct, and, when I once begin, things will go at
a rattling pace. In this connection I must ask you to do
me a great service. In the spring of 1866 there appeared in
*Fædrelandet* an excellent article in three parts by Listov, which
gives a concise account of Julian's life. If it is at all possible
for you to procure this for me, I shall be exceedingly grateful.

One thing more. I see that G. Brandes has received a
travelling-grant. Do you happen to know where he is going?
I should very much like to meet him; and if he is in Germany
I should willingly go some distance for that purpose.

And now, last of all — will you kindly advance me, in
addition to what I have already had, 100 rix-dollars, either in
the form of a draft or in Prussian notes? The moving has
led to my having to pay various things in advance, otherwise
I should not have had to ask this favour.

The *Dagblad* has come to hand regularly, in spite of my
change of address.—Yours most sincerely,

HENRIK IBSEN.

[1] *The League of Youth* was published on the 30th of September
1869. It was acted for the first time at the Christiania Theatre on
the 18th of October, at the Dramatiske Teater of Stockholm on the
11th of December 1869, and at the Theatre Royal of Copenhagen on
the 16th of February 1870.

## 56.

*To* P. F. SIEBOLD.

DRESDEN, 15*th June* 1869.

DEAR SIR,—I have had the pleasure of receiving your friendly letter and the accompanying manuscript. The latter I will read as quickly as possible. I have some difficulty in deciphering your handwriting, but I hope to master it. I have a copy of the original.

If Professor Dietrichson has not already sent you the biographical sketch, you will probably receive it soon; he writes that almost simultaneously with my request came one to exactly the same effect from the *Ny Illustrerad Tidning*, and that he will do his best.

I shall permit myself to write to you more fully next week. Many passages in your translation seem to me to be surprisingly well rendered. I think a couple of speeches which I noticed in glancing over the pages might possibly gain by condensation; but how far this is possible in German, is a matter in which I dare not oppose my opinion to yours.

I hope that things will go well with you in your temporary bachelorhood. It is not impossible that I may take the liberty of calling upon you in Cassel some time during the summer.— Yours sincerely and indebtedly,

HENRIK IBSEN.

## 57.

*To* FREDERIK HEGEL.

DRESDEN, 16*th June* 1869.

DEAR COUNCILLOR HEGEL,—Enclosed you will find my letter to the Direction of the Christiania Theatre. Instead of writing to the Direction of the Stockholm Theatre, I am giving Mr.

Dietrichson authority to act on my behalf. May I therefore request of you to send the Stockholm copy of the play to him. Everything else I will attend to from here.

I see that Björnson's *Folkeblad* is in a bad way; but I cannot help feeling that in reality the best thing that can happen to him is that he should be restricted to his calling of author. The article in the *Morgenblad,* which I make no doubt you have seen, is malicious and brimming over with hatred; but Björnson is not entirely blameless.[1]

The Storthing has refused to increase my mother-in-law's pension; and now I hope that she will return to Copenhagen. Looking at the matter from every point of view, it is the only right thing for her to do. She ought never to have gone to Christiania. It is not the place for an author to live in unless he is able coldly to turn his back on all parties and take up a position for himself; but this she does not do. As for me, I am glad and happy to be able to keep outside of all the plotting and intriguing which goes on up there, and which is unavoidable where the conditions of life are pettily small. Kindest regards from—Yours most sincerely and respectfully,

HENRIK IBSEN.

## 58.

*To* LORENTZ DIETRICHSON.

DRESDEN, 19*th June* 1869.

CARISSIMO!—My best thanks for your kind letter, and also, in advance, for your biographical labours.

---

[1] The *Norsk Folkeblad* was, pecuniarily, so unsuccessful that it failed in 1869. Thereupon Björnson bought it and published it on his own account.

The *Morgenblad* had charged the *Norsk Folkeblad* with dishonesty. The latter paper had, at a time when its deficit amounted to several thousand dollars, averred, for the purpose of advertisement, that its surplus funds were to be devoted to the pensioning of teachers.

I enclose the requested portrait of my ugly visage. I do not know if you, who knew me in my bearded period, will recognise me. They say here, and I believe myself, that it is a good likeness.

I hope that you have by this time received a copy of *The League of Youth*. I give you liberty to do exactly what you choose with it; pray do the best you can. I do not reckon on receiving payment for it; and fortunately that is not what is of most consequence to me.

As you will see, the play is a simple comedy, and nothing more. It will, perhaps, be said in Norway that I have portrayed actual persons and conditions. This, however, is not the case. I have, of course, used models—which are just as necessary for the comedy-writer as for the painter or sculptor.

It seems to me that the play ought to be suitable for Sweden too—that is to say, the Sweden of real life. How far it may be suitable for the stage in that country, is what you will have to decide. It is, at any rate, easy to play, and requires no outlay in the way of properties; in fact, no outlay at all but a payment to the translator—so, dear old friend, do your utmost to have it performed.

If we are successful in this matter, I shall probably pay a visit to Stockholm; but we need not think of this yet. Let me hear from you as soon as you can. Give me your opinion of the play. It will not appear in print until autumn.

A hearty greeting from us to you all! And now, good-bye. People who have so much to communicate to each other as we have, cannot write long letters; it must all wait until we meet. —Your devoted friend,

HENRIK IBSEN.

*P.S.*—Give my kind regards to H. Wieselgren (I believe he is in Norway now);[1] and to all other friends and acquaintances.

[1] Harald Wieselgren, a Swedish author—from 1866 to 1879 editor of the *Ny Illustrerad Tidning*.

59.

*To* GEORGE BRANDES.

DRESDEN, 26*th June* 1869.

DEAR MR. BRANDES,—It has greatly eased my mind to receive your friendly lines; for I had good reason to fear that you must think me very ungrateful—not writing you so much as a word, after you had thrown such light upon my work as no one else has done. But indeed I am not ungrateful. For most assuredly the important thing is, not to be blindly admired, but to be understood.[1]

The reason why I did not write was that my answer grew in my mind to a whole article on æsthetics. And as I found that this must begin with the question: What is poetry? you will admit that the letter threatened to become rather lengthy, and that the subject is more fitted to be discussed on the occasion of a personal interview.

*Brand* has been misconstrued, at least as regards my intention (to which you may answer that the critic is not concerned with the intention). The misconstruction has evidently arisen from the fact of Brand's being a priest, and from the problem being of a religious nature. But both these circumstances are entirely unimportant. I could have constructed the same syllogism just as easily on the subject of a sculptor or a politician, as of a priest. I could have found an equally satisfactory vent for the mood which impelled me to create, if, instead of Brand, I had written, say, of Galileo—making him, of course, hold his ground, and not admit that the earth stands still. Indeed, who knows but that I might, had I been born a hundred years later, have dealt just as well with you and your battle with Rasmus Nielsen's philosophy. On the whole, there is a great deal more of masked objectivity in *Brand* than any one has so far perceived; and of this, *qua* poet, I feel quite proud.

[1] This letter refers to Brandes's essay on Ibsen in *Æsthetic Studies*.

In my new comedy you will find the common order of
things—no strong emotions, no deep feelings, and, more particularly, no isolated thoughts. Your deserved condemnation of
the unelaborated "remarks by the author" which occur in *The
Pretenders* has had its effect. Your article—and remember, it
would be impossible for me to say more in the way of thanks
—has been to me what Mons. Wingaard's Chronicles were to
Jacob v. Thybo; I have read it sixteen times, and sixteen times
more, and hope to make it of use "in sundry wars."

But now I am very anxious to hear what you have to say
about my new work. It is written in prose, which gives it a
strong realistic colouring. I have paid particular attention to
form, and among other things I have accomplished the feat of
doing without a single monologue, in fact, without a single
"aside." However, all this of course proves nothing; and
therefore I earnestly beseech you, if you have a leisure moment,
to do me the kindness to read it, and let me hear your verdict.
Whatever it may be, you will confer a real benefit on me in
my loneliness here, by expressing your opinion. The book
will not be published until autumn, and that is a long time
to wait.

Please remember me to two of our mutual friends, Jonas
Collin and Julius Lange; the latter can hardly have received
a very favourable impression of me from our meeting in Rome;
but at that time I was feeling more like a wild beast than
anything else, and not without cause.[1]

I regret, on my own account, that in all probability we shall
not meet during your intended tour; but for you I am heartily

[1] Julius Lange (1838–1896), a Danish art historian. Lange wrote
from Rome in 1868 to a Danish friend: "If you meet Ibsen in
Florence, remember me to him. I was present at a farewell entertain-
ment given in his honour at a tavern, at which he was very witty and
amiable. If there were not a bit of the devil in that man he would
be much better than he is. If it were my affair to cure him, I should
order Greek literature or art—first in small doses, so that he should
not spit them out; then ever larger and larger, until his sense for
proportion and form came right."

glad, since it means that you are going to the South. It is inexpressibly great good fortune to be going there for the first time.

Accept my hearty thanks for your letter, and for everything.—Yours most sincerely,

HENRIK IBSEN.

*P.S.*—You are, I know, personally acquainted with Goldschmidt. If he is in Copenhagen at present, then please remember me most kindly to him also.

### 60.

*To* GEORGE BRANDES.

DRESDEN, 15*th July* 1869.

DEAR MR. BRANDES,—What you tell me about Björnson has not surprised me.[1] For him there exist only two kinds of people: those from whom he can derive some benefit, and those who may be a hindrance to him. Moreover, B.'s cleverness as a psychologist, when dealing with his own created personages, is quite equalled by his inability to calculate where real people are concerned.

I am beginning to suspect that perhaps I ought not to have asked you to read my new comedy. Further reflection has led me to the conclusion that the things which really interest you in poetry are the tragedies and comedies enacted in the inner life of the individual, and that you care little or nothing about actually existing outward conditions—political, or any other. If this be the case, you may ask in regard to my play: What's Hecuba to me? But this time I did not wish to convey anything but exactly what the work contains; and it must be

[1] Björnson, who had heretofore been very hostile to Brandes, had now written inviting him to accompany him on a trip to Nordland. He desired Brandes's friendship and collaboration. Brandes refused the invitation.

judged accordingly. Moreover, you are not entirely without responsibility in the matter yourself, as you, in a sense, impelled me in this direction by a remark made in your æsthetical writings. More about this by word of mouth.[1]

You are mistaken in imputing to me the belief that you do not love strong emotions or deep feelings. I believe nothing of the kind; I only wished to warn you against expecting what you would not find.

I cannot agree with you regarding the parts of *Peer Gynt* referred to. Of course I bow before the laws of beauty: but I have no regard for its conventions. You name Michael Angelo. In my opinion no one has sinned more against the established conventions of beauty than he; nevertheless everything which he has created is beautiful, because it is full of character. Raphael's art has never really warmed me; his personages belong to a period before the fall of man. Besides, the Southerner's æsthetic principles are quite different from ours; he wants absolute beauty; while to us conventional ugliness may be beautiful by virtue of its inherent truth. But concerning this there is no use in disputing with pen and ink—we must meet.

What I said about *Brand* I must adhere to. You surely will not blame me because the book may have given pietism something to lean on. You might just as well reproach Luther with having introduced philistinism into the world; it was certainly not his intention to do so, and he must therefore be held blameless.

But whatever we may disagree about, thanks for your letter; and thanks a thousand times for having met me in friendship; it is a great blessing to have found a complete personality.

---

[1] Somewhat later Brandes, by Ibsen's own desire, reviewed *The League of Youth* (in the *Illustreret Tidende*). Ibsen wrote from Stockholm to Hegel, asking him to prevail on Brandes to do it: "There is no one who can do it as he can; and I feel that he is a true friend to me."

On Thursday I leave for Stockholm, my family remaining here. In autumn, when I rejoin them, I shall probably travel by way of Copenhagen, so as to talk with you—not only of all the literary matters on which we disagree, but also on many human topics, upon which I believe we are much more closely in accord.[1]—Yours most sincerely,

HENRIK IBSEN.

*P.S.*—When opportunity offers, give my kindest regards to Councillor Hegel.

## 61.

*To* HEDVIG STOUSLAND.[2]

STOCKHOLM, 26th September 1869.

DEAR HEDVIG,—Months have passed since I received your kind letter—and only now do I answer it. But so much stands between and separates us, separates me from home. Understand this, please, and do not think that it is indifference which has kept me silent all these long years, and even this summer. I cannot write letters; I must be near in person and give myself wholly and entirely. But you, on the other hand—you can

---

[1] A travelling-grant from the Norwegian Government enabled Ibsen to take this journey to Stockholm. He attended the Congress of Orthographists, and studied Swedish art and Swedish educational methods. His stay, of which he wrote that it was one great fête, lasted for two months. It was his intention to have remained longer, but in the end of September he accepted an invitation from the Khedive of Egypt to be present at the opening of the Suez Canal.

[2] Hedvig Stousland (born 1832) is Henrik Ibsen's only sister—married to H. J. Stousland of Skien, a captain in the merchant service. She belongs to a religious sect founded in 1856 by G. A. Lammers, a well-known clergyman (one of the models for Brand). On a photograph which Ibsen sent her he wrote: "I believe that there has always been a close tie between us, and that there always will be."

write. Do so! Write often! I will answer with at least a loving greeting, with a message which I trust will not grieve you.

I look into myself; there is where I fight my battles, now conquering, now suffering defeat. But about all this one cannot write in a letter. Make no attempts at conversion. I will be honest; what is to happen, will happen.

So our dear old Mother is dead. I thank you for having so lovingly fulfilled the duties which were incumbent on us all. You are certainly the best!

I do a great deal of wandering about the world. Who knows but that I may come to Norway next summer; then I must see the old home to which I still cling with so many roots. Give Father my love; explain to him about me—all that you understand so well, and that he perhaps does not.

I have been here in Stockholm since the middle of July; now I am going, by way of Dresden and Paris, to Egypt, where, as you have possibly learned from the newspapers, I am to be the Khedive's guest. By the middle of December I expect to be back in Dresden, where my wife is, and where my little boy goes to school. I have only the one.

Enclosed I send you my photograph; if you have any of yourself and your family, send us them in return. I wish you knew my wife; she is the very wife for me. She asks to be remembered to you. Our address in Dresden is Königsbrücker-strasse, No. 33.

This letter is short, and I have made no allusion to what you perhaps wished most that I should write about. It cannot be otherwise at present; but do not think that I lack the warmth of heart which is the first requisite where a true and vigorous spiritual life is to thrive.

     *     *     *     *     *     *     *

## 62.

*To* FREDERIK HEGEL.

DRESDEN, 14*th December* 1869.

DEAR COUNCILLOR HEGEL,—At last I have returned from my two months of travel in Egypt, and I hasten to thank you for your friendly letter to my wife, as well as for the reviews received, which have been supplemented by others from Norway. The reception which *The League of Youth* has received pleases me very much; for the disapprobation I was prepared, and it would have been a disappointment to me if there had been none. But what I was not prepared for was that Björnson should feel himself attacked by the play, as rumour says he does. Is this really the case? He must surely see that it is not himself I have had in mind, but his pernicious and "lie-steeped" clique, who have served me as models. However, I will write to him to-day or to-morrow, and I hope that the affair, in spite of all differences, will end in a reconciliation. That a second edition should already have been published is quite beyond anything I had expected; I am now only anxious to see in how far the play may prove suitable for the Copenhagen Theatre.[1]

[1] The first edition of *The League of Youth* came out on the 30th of September, and the second on the 4th of November, 1869. It was hissed by adherents of the Liberal party at its first performance at the Christiania Theatre. They felt themselves attacked in it. Björnson gave expression to his anger at the attempted "assassination," in his poem to Johan Sverdrup, written in November of the same year. And in 1881, in an article in the *Dagblad*, he explained: "What I called 'assassination' was not the representation of actual circumstances and prominent personages in Norway; it was the attempt of *The League of Youth* to make of our young party of liberty a troop of ambitious, phrasemongering speculators, whose patriotism lay in their phraseology; and more particularly this—that certain characters, after being made recognisable as well-known personages, were given false hearts and bad characters, and placed in positions which they never occupied." In 1870, Ibsen himself wrote (in a letter to Jonas Collin): "They are

May I take the liberty to ask you to send me, either by draft or in Prussian money, an amount equal to 200 Danish rix-dollars? It would also be very agreeable to me to receive one or two copies of the book; and may I ask you to send a copy to my brother-in-law in Christiania: Cand. Jur. Johan Herman Thoresen, Chief Clerk in the Dept. of Justice.

I have abundant material for sketches of travel, as I kept my diary carefully all the time I was away. I promise you a contribution to the *Dansk Tidsskrift* without fail, as soon as I have kept an earlier promise to the *Morgenblad*.[1]

Please remember me to G. Brandes; I will write to him ere long. There is something both in his praise and in his censure that does me an indescribable amount of good; and that something is—that I am understood.

I am pondering the plan for a new, serious modern drama in three acts; and I shall probably begin to write it very soon.[2]

I have had a delightful trip. I was as far as Nubia, and then at the Red Sea. I had many adventures, and made the acquaintance of many interesting people. But what is better than anything else is to sit quietly here at home and look back upon it all. Of Danes I met P. Hansen, and Robert Watt; we lay in tents in the desert, and read Danish newspapers.

In case I do not write to you again before Christmas, permit me now to wish you and yours all the best wishes of the season.—Ever yours most sincerely,

HENRIK IBSEN.

judging my work from the political, instead of the æsthetic, standpoint. From the attacks which I have read, one would conclude that phrase-mongering, hollowness, and roguery are regarded in Norway as national characteristics, which must not be meddled with."

[1] Ibsen never wrote any actual description of his travels in Egypt, but in December 1870 he gave his general impressions in the poem, "Ballonbrev til en svensk Dame" (Balloon Letter to a Swedish Lady).

[2] The modern drama alluded to in this and the following letter was not written.

## 63.

*To* FREDERIK HEGEL.

DRESDEN, 25*th January* 1870.

DEAR COUNCILLOR HEGEL,—I beg to acknowledge the receipt of the 150 thalers enclosed in your esteemed letter of the 16th of December, and at the same time to thank you for the great pleasure you have given us by your present of books It also gave me pleasure to hear that *The League of Youth* continues to be in demand. I hope that the performance at the Theatre Royal will still further increase the interest of the public in the play.

Mr. R. Schmidt has again written to me; this time to request that I will publish in his periodical a protest against an alleged rumour that I meant "Stensgaard" to be a portrait of Björnson. However, I have sent him such a decided answer that I hope to be spared any further correspondence with him.

I was exceedingly pleased to learn that the right of publication of *The Pretenders* has passed into your hands.

But the work ought to be revised, and if, when convenient, you will send me a copy, I will do what is needed in a very short time.

I have myself been thinking of publishing a volume of my poems; and several of my Norwegian friends have been urging me to do so; more particularly Mr. Lökke, the schoolmaster, who quite lately offered to collect what I have written in the various newspapers and periodicals. I have accepted his offer, and told him that I will come to Christiania this summer and put the finishing touch to the work. I shall have to get hold of various poems which are not in print; and a preface must be written. Of course I shall go by way of Copenhagen, and I shall take the opportunity then to talk the matter over with you. I especially desire to know your opinion (and this concerns *The Pretenders* also) of the rules of orthography adopted by the Orthographists'

Congress (Sprogkongress) in Stockholm last summer. We must also come to some decision as to the time of publication; for, if the new edition of *The Pretenders* comes out in spring, and my new play, as I hope, in October, it might be too much to issue a collection of poems in the same year. The one book might damage the other. But of course I leave all this to your better judgment; and we have plenty of time before us.

I am very much obliged to you for the annual settlement enclosed in your letter of the 21st of January. I am now busy arranging the notes of my travels in Egypt; when this is done I shall begin my drama.

I am glad to be far away from the squabbling that is going on in Norway; if I have lost a few friends there for the present, I have won many more to make up for them. With thanks and kindest regards,—Yours respectfully and sincerely,

HENRIK IBSEN.

### 64.

#### *To* GEORGE BRANDES.

DRESDEN, 6*th March* 1870.

DEAR MR. BRANDES,—The reason why I am only answering your friendly note to-day is (along with the fact that it was belated—probably by the freezing of the Belt) that I have been for several days debating with myself whether I ought not at once to go to Copenhagen.

Upon due consideration, however, I have come to the conclusion that it would be a foolish proceeding, since I should be obliged to go in summer, too. Besides, I suppose that the preparations for your journey occupy you so completely that you have no thought for anything else.

At present I have no opportunity of seeing the Danish papers. But by now you are doctor, of course? Accept my heartiest congratulations.

You say that you have no friends at home. That is what I have fancied for a long time. When a man stands, as you do, in an intimately personal relationship to his life-work, he cannot really expect to keep his "friends." But I believe that it is better for you that you go without leaving friends at home. Friends are an expensive luxury; and when a man's whole capital is invested in a calling and a mission in life, he cannot afford to keep them. The costliness of keeping friends does not lie in what one does for them, but in what one, out of consideration for them, refrains from doing. This means the crushing of many an intellectual germ. I have had personal experience of it; and there are, consequently, many years behind me during which it was not possible for me to be myself.

And now I will stop for the present. My thoughts are often occupied with you; I have formed for myself a picture of you both in the present and in the future; for, little as I know you personally, you are closely associated with that which I spiritually possess, live upon, and make poetry of.

I have many other things to say to you; but they must wait. Thank you for your review of *The League of Youth*, and thank you for your letter! I hope you will thoroughly enjoy all the loveliness that awaits you. Write to me from the sunshine.

Dear friend, you must believe me—I do not require the kind of unanimity upon which the preservation of a friendship usually depends.—Yours most sincerely,

HENRIK IBSEN.

## 65.

### *To* FREDERIK HEGEL.

DRESDEN, 11*th April* 1870.

DEAR COUNCILLOR HEGEL,—I hope the revised copy of *The Pretenders* has reached you; I sent it on Saturday. There are few corrections; for I must say I found the dialogue so firmly constructed—the speeches following so logically one upon the other—that it was not in my power to condense or improve. n accordance with our agreement, I have taken the decisions of the Orthographists' Congress as a standard for the orthography;[1] but my corrections in the book are incomplete. I have, for instance, done nothing in the matter of the capital letters or of the å's, except in the list of *dramatis personæ*. I refer you to J. Lökke's report of the decisions of the Orthographists' Congress, which was published by Gad in Copenhagen. And I rely confidently upon your excellent proof-reader, who is himself a good judge in these matters. I am afraid I have made wrong changes in a few places. It is my opinion, for instance, that the silent h in the words "thi" and "thing" ought to be retained; and I suppose that the proper way of writing the following words is: "sees," "seet," "gået," etc. If, without delaying the printing too long, I could have a corrected proof of the first sheet for inspection, it would be very satisfactory to me. "Bagler," "Birkebejner," etc., ought to be written with capitals. I suppose you agree with me that the musical supplement should be omitted.[2] I can think of nothing else to mention at present —except that I should very much like to have the book printed in somewhat larger type.

I have received your three friendly letters, dated 18th March, 21st March, and 2nd April. I cannot remember if I have thanked you for Brandes's book; if not, then I do so now.

In the meantime I only wish tickets for the first six lottery drawings.

I have heard nothing from Dahl. I am much pleased that the matter has been settled. Thank you for your offer regarding the new edition; I accept it with pleasure.

---

[1] The Congress aimed in its decisions at introducing, as far as possible, common rules of spelling for the Scandinavian languages.

[2] The first edition of *The Pretenders*, published by Dahl of Christiania, had a musical supplement, namely, a setting of Margrethe's Cradle Song, by Emma Dahl, wife of the publisher.

As yet all that is ready of my new play is the outline; and the period for arranging my notes of travel is still in the far future.

It is my intention to submit *The Pretenders* to the Danish Theatre Royal as soon as the new edition is ready. If it is accepted, as I hope it will be, it can be played in the beginning of next season. This should promote the circulation of the book.

Please forgive me for letting you wait so long for an answer. One thing I must ask. Has *A Wealthy Match* been played at the Theatre Royal? It is written by my mother-in-law—anonymously—but you are, of course, in the secret. She is thinking of leaving Christiania, and in this she is right. I have heard nothing from Björnson; he is, presumably, taken up with the approaching " expedition to Iceland."[1]  I am very sorry for the breach between us; I hope, however, that it will not be lasting. If I knew that you had nothing against it, or that you did not, for reasons unknown to me, consider it unadvisable, I should be almost inclined to dedicate the new edition of *The Pretenders* to him—possibly in a couple of verses. If you approve, I should be glad if you would ask him about this when opportunity offers, as direct diplomatic relations are broken off between us.—With kindest regards, I am, Yours respectfully and sincerely,

HENRIK IBSEN.

[1] Björnson's " expedition to Iceland " (felttog til Island) began with an article in the *Norsk Folkeblad* for March 5, 1870, in which he argued that Iceland should be united to Norway, instead of Denmark. Subsequent numbers of the paper contained a series of articles from his own pen and that of a scientific collaborator, further developing the argument.

## 66.

*To* FREDERIK HEGEL.

DRESDEN, 13*th April* 1870.

DEAR COUNCILLOR HEGEL,—I have received information from Christiania to-day which obliges me to withdraw the request made in my last letter, that you would put a certain question to Björnson.

Hoping that this recall may arrive in time, — I remain, Yours respectfully and sincerely,

HENRIK IBSEN.

## 67.

*To* FREDERIK HEGEL.

DRESDEN, 6*th May* 1870.

DEAR COUNCILLOR HEGEL,—I beg herewith to return the proof-sheet of *The Pretenders*, together with the list of doubtful words. Of the principles regulating the spelling of these I cannot in every instance approve; but I entirely agree with the majority of the Norwegian members of the Orthographists' Congress in maintaining that we must not separate ourselves too much from the Danes, or go farther than you are disposed to accompany us.

I think the new type and spelling look very well indeed, and are easy to read.

My unwillingness to dedicate the book to Björnson is not occasioned by his attitude towards me, although this is anything but friendly. My reasoning runs thus: his behaviour as a publicist threatens to bring about real disaster in Norway; and as a result of this a party has been formed against him, so strong, especially among the book-buying public, that a dedication to him at present would be unjustifiable on my part, in view of your interests as publisher.[1] But there is nothing I desire more than a reconciliation; and I should be very much pleased if you could find an opportunity to tell him that the rumour which he believes, and is spreading, namely, that I intend to take the appointment of Director of the Christiania Theatre, is absolutely false. The appointment was offered to me; and I embraced the opportunity to support his cause— at the same time advocating the retention of M. Brun as stage-manager; this being what I regard as in every way the most advantageous arrangement.[2]

Thank you very much for depositing the 1000 rix-dollars in the Savings Bank; also for your excellent suggestion that a composer should be found for *The Pretenders*. I have an acquaintance with P. Heise, dating from Rome, and shall write to him to-morrow about the matter.

It is, I find, an open secret in Norway too, that my mother-in-law is the authoress of *A Wealthy Match*. She has herself to thank for its being known. I am very anxious to hear how it is received in Copenhagen. I think *The Pretenders* ought to be sent to the management as soon as the new edition is ready.

With kindest regards, I am, Yours respectfully and sincerely,

HENRIK IBSEN.

[1] During the winter of 1869–70, Björnson came ever more to the front in party warfare as a spokesman of the growing democratic opposition.

[2] In 1868 there were again unsuccessful negotiations between Björnson and the Christiania Theatre on the subject of the director-ship. For three years, from 1868, M. W. Brun held the appointment of "artistic director"; but he gave so little satisfaction that the post was offered to Ibsen in 1870—M. W. Brun to act as his stage-manager. Ibsen replied by indicating Björnson as the proper director. But the management did not wish Björnson. In February 1870 many of the best actors gave up their appointments, in order to start a new theatre, under Björnson's superintendence, in autumn.

68.

*To* FREDERIK HEGEL.

DRESDEN, 25*th May* 1870.

DEAR COUNCILLOR HEGEL,—My best thanks for the copy of
*A Wealthy Match*. I had been eagerly looking forward to it.
The book is really interesting; it is cleverly written—the
dialogue perhaps a little too cleverly; whether the character-
drawing is quite natural is another question. The style of
thing reminds me a good deal of Alfred de Musset's *Proverbes*,
and still more of Björnson's *Newly Married Couple*. Have
none of the Danish reviewers made the same observation? I
take it for granted that the play has been splendidly acted,
and hope that this will enable it to hold the stage. In any
case, I regard it as fortunate for the authoress that she has
given up the peasant-tale, which was unmistakably leading
her into more and more affectation and eccentricity — a fact
which I mentioned to her very plainly. Unfortunately, she
places most reliance on those who do her most harm.

The chief object of my letter to-day is to ask you to be so
very good as to send me 200 Danish rix-dollars, in Prussian
notes or in the form of a draft, whichever is most convenient.

*The Pretenders* has, as you probably know already, been
definitely accepted for production at the Theatre Royal; it
will, Councillor Berner writes me, be played in the beginning
of next season.[1] Mr. Heise has willingly undertaken to compose the necessary music. I am sending him the words for the
choruses; but these ought not to be printed in the book; they
would only impede and confuse the reader, being quite unnecessary to an understanding of the action.

I have to thank you, too, for the number of the *Dansk
Tidsskrift* which you sent me. Who can be the author of the

[1] It was acted for the first time at the Theatre Royal, Copenhagen,
on the 11th of January 1871.

letter from Norway? I guess him to be my old friend, G. A. Krohg.

The time for my trip to Denmark is as yet undecided; I should like to take it at the finest season of the year; and down here, at least, the weather is still rather changeable. I have many literary plans and projects in my mind; but as yet nothing definite has come of them. If you have heard anything of the proposed cast for *The Pretenders*, a little information on the subject, when you have an opportunity, would interest me exceedingly.

From Norway I hear of nothing but dissension and disturbance in all directions.

Björnson seems to have entirely put aside his work as an author, in order to devote himself to other things; but I hope for his sake that it will not be for long.—With kindest regards, I remain, Yours respectfully and sincerely,

HENRIK IBSEN.

## 69.

### *To* MAGDALENE THORESEN,

DRESDEN, 29*th May* 1870.

DEAR MOTHER-IN-LAW,—In the hope that these lines may reach you on the 3rd of June, I write now to send you my double congratulations—on the occasion of the day, of which I hope you will celebrate many, many returns in a bright and happy future—and on the new play, the publication and performance of which in Denmark and Norway must have been an unalloyed triumph for you. Hegel has sent me a copy of the play; I have read it over and over again, and have not done with it yet. In it you have truly given to the world a work which only you could have written. It did not come as a surprise to me, because I knew with absolute certainty that in this particular domain of literature you possessed powers which I have long and deeply deplored that you were disinclined to turn to account. Now, however, the first step is taken; and it may be safely assumed that many other productions of the same nature will follow. All the qualifications demanded for such production are yours; you have warm and sympathetic feeling, experience, stores of observation both of characters and of situations, a superabundance of cleverness, and the ideal vision which elevates reality into the sphere of the innermost, highest truth, a transfer in which the real genesis of poetry is to be found.

What the critics have said, I do not know. If they have been finding fault, then to the devil with them! Most critical fault-finding, when reduced to its essentials, simply amounts to reproach of the author because he is himself—thinks, feels, sees, and creates, as himself, instead of seeing and creating in the way the critic would have done—if he had been able. The great thing, therefore, is to hedge about what is one's own—to keep it free and clear from everything outside that has no connection with it; and, furthermore, to be extremely careful in discriminating between what one has observed and what one has experienced; because only this last can be the theme for creative work. If we attend strictly to this, no everyday, commonplace subject will be too prosaic to be sublimated into poetry.

. . . . . . .

—Yours,

HENRIK IBSEN.

70.

*To* MAGDALENE THORESEN.

DRESDEN, *5th June* 1870.

DEAR MOTHER-IN-LAW,—

·   ·   ·   ·   ·   ·   ·   ·

Just as I was about to send off the above lines, I received your letter, and will therefore add something more.

I see, and am not surprised to see, that we two are completely at variance in our view of the Theatre question.[1]  I am entirely on the side of the Management as opposed to the rebels.  I cannot share this sentimental sympathy with all kinds of disloyalty to duty ; the Management of a theatre cannot adopt the Bible standpoint, according to which the lost sheep is all in all, and the rest of the flock nothing.  The carrying of such theories into practice results in nothing but chaos and wrangling and confusion, as in the days when Lamartine tried to govern France.  I myself have been manager of a theatre ; I know that in ninety-nine cases out of a hundred the actors are indisputably in the wrong, and the Management is right. " Vae victis ! " they said in ancient times ; and the same should be said to-day.  It would be acting most unpardonably towards the institution not to put a check on the spirit of rebellion on such an occasion as the present.  An actor stands in a different position from other artists.  He is not complete in himself ; he belongs to a complicated machine, in the working of which he is bound by law to take part ; and if he has chosen the position, he must bear the consequences of the position.  This theory is not the outcome of hard-heartedness, but of salutary experience.

I do not consider the realism of the Management so very reprehensible, seeing that what is proposed is a second-class

[1] The quarrel between the actors and the management of the Christiania Theatre.  See Letter 67.

theatre, without state-aid, in a third-class city. It is, of course, another matter if Mr. Isachsen, Mrs. Gundersen and her husband, and others endowed with the noble artist-nature, prefer to draw an ideal salary; but in my day the people with the artist-natures were realistic enough in the matter of salary. I know, indeed, that Mr. Björnson managed the theatre so ideally that had he been permitted to manage it one year more he would have "raised" the whole concern out of the realm of reality; but I cannot agree with those who think this praiseworthy. It is also my opinion that Mr. M. Brun's proper position in the Theatre is a subordinate one; and I repeat what I wrote in a former letter, that I have done my best to bring about Mr. Björnson's reinstatement, with a proper limitation of his power.

·     ·     ·     ·     ·     ·     ·     ·     ·

HENRIK IBSEN.

## 71.

### *To* LAURA KIELER.[1]

DRESDEN, 11*th June* 1870.

DEAR MISS LAURA PETERSEN,—For the compliment you have paid me by dedicating your book to me, I beg you to accept my sincerest thanks. If I were asked to express any opinion in regard to the work itself, I should be, in a way, in a difficulty. You desire to have the book regarded as a religious work, and of that kind of literature I am no judge. What has appealed to and interested me in reading it is the description of character —in combination with your unmistakable imaginative gift. Whether you regard such praise as a compliment or not, I have no idea.

---

[1] In 1869 there appeared, as a continuation of *Brand*, a story called *Brand's Daughters*, by "Lili." The lady who wrote under this pseudonym was Laura Petersen, daughter of a sheriff (Foged) in the Trondhjem district. In 1873 she married the Danish schoolmaster, V. Kieler. See Letter 205.

The impression conveyed to me is that you would probably be horrified by the idea that you had written " a novel." If such be the case, then we two do not understand each other. *Brand* is an æsthetic work, pure and simple. What it may have demolished or built up is a matter of absolute indifference to me. It came into being as the result of something which I had, not observed, but experienced; it was a necessity for me to free myself from something which my inner man had done with, by giving poetic form to it; and when by this means I had got rid of it, my book had no longer any interest for me.

It is not quite clear to me in what light you regard this kind of secular work. That you have the natural qualifications for authorship in this secular domain, I am quite certain. But it is not possible to combine two things that have no connection with each other. And perhaps you have not yet clearly realised what art and poetry really are; in which case, pray believe meanwhile that they are not of the evil one!

What continued to occupy me as a problem long after reading *Brand's Daughters* was the personality of its authoress —was your inner, psychical relation to your book. It is possible that if one got to the root of this, one would, despite your protest, find that the book, after all, came into being as an æsthetical work, or whatever bad name is usually given to such a production. All that is in the book, simply for the sake of your religious purpose, may be taken away without injuring the organism as a whole.

Is it your intention to pursue the career of an author? For this, something else and more is required than talent. One must have something to create from, some life-experience. The author who has not that, does not create; he only writes books. Now I know very well that a life led in solitude is not a life devoid of experiences. The human being is, however, in the spiritual sense, a long-sighted creature; we see most clearly at a distance; the details confuse; we must get away from what we desire to judge; one describes summer best on a winter day.

I had a thousand things to say; but in a letter one can only

13

indicate them. It is always a risky thing to give advice; and, moreover, you have not asked for it. The great thing is to become honest and truthful in dealing with one's self—not to determine to do this or determine to do that, but to do what one *must* do because one is one's self. All the rest simply leads to falsehood.

Sooner or later I intend to visit Norway, and perhaps I shall then have an opportunity of seeing you, as my tour will include the north. You must not believe that I am so unkindly disposed towards my countrymen as many accuse me of being. But, let this be as it may, I can at least assure you that I am not kinder to myself than to others.—With best wishes, I am, Yours respectfully,

HENRIK IBSEN.

72.

*To* FREDERIK HEGEL.

DRESDEN, 2nd July 1870.

DEAR COUNCILLOR HEGEL,—I send you a few lines to-day in the hope that I am not making a miscalculation in assuming that they will reach you on Monday.

At New Year time, when I was examining the books which you were so kind as to send me then, I discovered in the stamp of the firm the date 1770. This year, then, is the hundredth of the "Gyldendalske Boghandel's" existence; and, as I hear from a trustworthy source in Norway, the anniversary of its foundation is the 4th July. If I am mistaken in this, the fault is not mine; but I presume that I am right.

It would have given me the greatest pleasure to congratulate you in person; but circumstances positively oblige me to remain in Dresden, at all events until the middle of the month. My family are to spend the school holidays, which begin at that time, at one of the Bohemian watering-places; and I cannot leave until I have seen them settled there.

So there is nothing left for me but by means of a letter to join the many who will offer you their hearty congratulations on the day.

In the first place, I beg of you to accept my sincerest thanks for all that I personally owe to you. My becoming connected with you as my publisher was a turning-point in my career as an author, as well as in my private circumstances. The introduction and spread of my works in Denmark, effected by you, has reacted upon the feeling towards me in Norway, and largely contributed to securing for me the solid vantage-ground which is peculiarly necessary in the case of an author like myself, who, in consequence of his general tendency, must venture not a little.

In the second place, I thank you as a Norwegian for what you have done for Norwegian literature generally. I shall, in this connection, only mention the large edition of the works of Welhaven, which, without you, would certainly never have seen the light of day. All this is, in my opinion, a national debt, which Norway certainly cannot repay, but which I hope will be recognised in the right quarter when opportunity offers.

And now, in conclusion, I wish you success and everything that is good for many years to come. I hope that your name may be connected for many generations with the " Gyldendalske Boghandel"; it assuredly will be connected for all time with the prosperity and development of the Danish-Norwegian literature.

My kindest regards to your son.[1] In our little circle here we shall drink the toast of the day.—Yours most sincerely,

HENRIK IBSEN.

[1] Frederik Hegel's son, Jacob (born 1851), became a partner in his father's business in 1857, and carried it on alone from 1887 to 1903.

### 73.

*To* FREDERIK HEGEL.

DRESDEN, 10*th October* 1870.

DEAR MR. HEGEL,—Here I am, settled once again in my home in this foreign land, where I have found everything as usual in our own circle, but where the general condition of affairs is anything but pleasant. The city is full of sick and wounded. One is certain, whenever one goes out, to meet military funerals or patients being conveyed to the hospitals. There are several thousand French prisoners in the town; they are allowed much freedom, are kindly treated, and seem to thrive. There is not the slightest evidence of enthusiasm for the war here: what one reads on this subject in the papers is pure invention. The country is suffering terribly; work—enterprise of every kind—is almost at a stand-still; half-grown boys and middle-aged heads of families are called out and sent to France; nearly every family is in mourning; many have lost *all* of their relatives who were sent to the front. And the list of casualties for the last six weeks is still to come. As already remarked, life here is not pleasant.

When I recall my stay in Copenhagen this summer, the contrast is great.[1] I cannot be sufficiently grateful for all the kindness and friendship I met with there; and I need hardly add that you are among those to whom I am most deeply indebted. My best thanks for all your kind attentions. Remember me most kindly to your son, and to all whom I met at your house.

I have written to Mr. Lökke about my poems, and am daily expecting his answer and the copied verses; they shall be sent to you at once in a corrected and improved shape.

I should very much like to have two quarter-tickets for the approaching lottery, if it is not too late to trouble you in the

---

[1] Ibsen was in Copenhagen from July to October 1870.

matter. The first drawing takes place, I think, on the 14th instant.

My new work, a play in three acts, has now developed so far in my mind that I shall presently begin to write it.

What I hear from Copenhagen about Holm-Hansen's acting in *Axel and Valborg* makes me anxious in regard to *The Pretenders*. I shall write on this subject to Mrs. Heiberg or Councillor Berner. After the new edition comes out, it would interest me very much to see what the newspapers have to say to it. I received a letter from P. Hansen yesterday with a request for biographical data. This shall be attended to immediately.

Again begging you to accept my best thanks and best wishes, —I am, Yours most sincerely,

HENRIK IBSEN.

74

*To* PETER HANSEN.

DRESDEN, 28th October 1870.

MY DEAR FRIEND,—It was with the best of intentions that, one Sunday afternoon, I received and read your letter. " Within three days he shall have my answer," I thought—and now nearly three weeks have passed. One advantage, however, is gained by the delay, namely, that haste now compels me to be briefer than I at first intended. I believe this is better for you, as it leaves you a freer hand.

Since we parted I have often regretted that we did not manage to talk over these matters; writing is so much more difficult. But never mind.[1]

The biographical data you will find in the least distorted

---

[1] P. Hansen had requested information for a biography of Ibsen to be inserted in his anthology, *Norwegian Poets of our Century*, which was published at Christmas 1870.

hape in a biography written by P. Botten-Hansen, in the *Illustreret Nyhedsblad* for the year 1862, if I remember rightly.

But it is really more the story of my intellectual development that you want. Here it is, then.

Everything which I have created as a poet has had its origin in a frame of mind and a situation in life; I never wrote because I had, as they say, "found a good subject."

Now I shall confess chronologically.

*Catilina* was written in a little provincial town, where it was impossible for me to give expression to all that fermented in me except by mad, riotous pranks, which brought down upon me the ill-will of all the respectable citizens, who could not enter into that world which I was wrestling with alone.

*Lady Inger of Östraat* is the result of a love-affair — hastily entered into and violently broken off—to which several smaller poems may also be attributed, such as "Markblomster og potteplanter" (Field-flowers and pot-plants), "Fuglevise" (A Bird Song), etc., which were printed in the *Nyhedsblad* (and to which I take this opportunity of calling your attention).[1]

*The Vikings at Helgeland* I wrote whilst I was engaged to be married. For Hjördis I had the same model as I took afterwards for Svanhild in *Love's Comedy*.

Not until I was married did more serious interests take possession of my life. The first outcome of this change was a long poem—"Paa Vidderne" (On the Heights). The desire for emancipation which pervades this poem did not, however, receive its full expression until I wrote *Love's Comedy*, a book which gave rise to much talk in Norway. People mixed up my personal affairs in the discussion, and I fell greatly in public estimation. The only person at that time who approved of

[1] *The Feast at Solhaug* is a study which I now disown; but for this work also there was a personal cause.

the book was my wife. Hers is exactly the character desider-
ated by a man of mind—she is illogical, but has a strong
poetic instinct, a broad and liberal mind, and an almost violent
antipathy to all petty considerations. All this my countrymen
did not understand, and I did not choose to make them my
father-confessors. So they excommunicated me. All were
against me.

The fact that all were against me—that there was no longer
any one outside my own family circle of whom I could say:
" He believes in me "— must, as you can easily see, have aroused
a mood which found its outlet in *The Pretenders*. But enough
on this subject.

Exactly at the time when *The Pretenders* came out,
Frederick VII. died, and the war began. I wrote a poem, " En
broder i nöd " (A Brother in Need). The Norwegian American-
ism which had driven me back at every point, rendered it
ineffectual. Then I went into exile!

About the time of my arrival at Copenhagen, the Danes
were defeated at Dybböl. In Berlin I saw King William's
triumphal entry with trophies and booty. During those days
*Brand* began to grow within me like an embryo. When I
arrived in Italy, the work of unification there had already been
completed by means of a spirit of self-sacrifice which
knew no bounds. Add to this, Rome with its ideal peace,
association with the care-free artist community, an existence
in an atmosphere which can be compared only with that
of Shakespeare's *As You Like It*—and you have the conditions
productive of *Brand*. It is a great mistake to suppose that I
have depicted the life and career of Sören Kierkegaard. (I
have read very little of S. K., and understood even less.) That
Brand is a clergyman is really immaterial; the demand, " All
or nothing," is made in all domains of life—in love, in art, etc
Brand is myself in my best moments—just as certainly as it is
certain that by self-analysis I brought to light many of both
Peer Gynt's and Stensgaard's qualities.

During the time I was writing *Brand* I had on my desk

a glass with a scorpion in it. From time to time the little animal was ill. Then I used to give it a piece of soft fruit, upon which it fell furiously and emptied its poison into it—after which it was well again.

Does not something of the same kind happen with us poets? The laws of nature regulate the spiritual world also.

After *Brand* came *Peer Gynt*, as though of itself. It was written in Southern Italy, in the Island of Ischia and at Sorrento. So far away from one's future readers, one becomes reckless. This poem contains much that is reminiscent of my own youth; for Aase my own mother — with necessary exaggerations—served as model (as she also did for Inga in *The Pretenders.*)

Environment has a great influence upon the forms in which the imagination creates. Can not I, in the style of Christoff in *Jakob v. Tyboe*, point at *Brand* and *Peer Gynt*, and say, "See, wine did this"? And is there not something in *The League of Youth* which reminds one of sausage and beer? I do not intend by this to place the last-mentioned play on a lower level. I only mean that my point of view has changed, because here I am in a community well ordered, even to weariness. Whatever will happen when I reach home! I must seek salvation in remoteness of subject, so I mean then to begin *Emperor Julian*.

The choice of the poems to be used I prefer to leave to you, in whose judgment I have the greatest confidence, in this matter as in many other respects. Most of the small pieces in question are to be found in the *Illustreret Nyhedsblad* for the years 1858-64.

And now I have provided you with the required skeleton; it is for you to clothe it with flesh and inspire it with life. Use these notes as you please; regard them as a meagre musical theme on which you may freely extemporise. I am sure that you will make out of it all that can be made; use whatever instruments you fancy. . . .

Thank you for helping to make my stay in Copenhagen

a pleasant one. I have returned as from a rejuvenating bath. Give my thanks for this to all our mutual friends. Remember me especially to Mr. and Mrs. Bille, to whom I will write later myself; also to Professor Höedt. — Your affectionate,

HENRIK IBSEN.

## 75.

*To* FREDERIK HEGEL.

DRESDEN, 6th November 1870.

DEAR MR. HEGEL,—A few words in haste, in answer to your last kind letter.

I shall be satisfied with whatever you buy in the way of lottery-tickets, whether you take two quarters, two halves, or a whole ticket. I hope for luck! The next drawing is on the 11th.

It was a great comfort to me to learn of the change in the cast for *The Pretenders*. The unfortunate thing about it is, that perhaps the performance will be somewhat delayed now.

I entirely agree with you in the advisability of postponing the publication of my poems until spring.

In these stirring times I cannot concentrate my thoughts on anything very deep. What I have taken a great fancy to do is to write the libretto for an opera for Heise. The subject I have in my mind is " Sigurd Jorsalafar." [1] But I have not the necessary books of reference here. So I am going to beg something of yon.

You hold the largest stock of Munch's great *History of Norway*. Are there, by any chance, defective sets in the edition of which single volumes are sold? If so, would you let me have the volume in which the Saga of Sigurd is treated?

---

[1] Nothing came of this plan.

If you have no defective set, then I can order Snorre
Sturlason from Norway; but he gives far fewer details.

When you can find time, you will, I am sure, let me hear
from you in regard to this matter.

Kindest regards to you and your son from—Yours most
sincerely,                  HENRIK IBSEN.


## 76.

### *To* JOHAN HERMAN THORESEN.

DRESDEN, 21*st November* 1870.

DEAR BROTHER-IN-LAW,—To be business-like I must not
neglect to acknowledge the receipt of your last letter, together
with the enclosed draft. I wrote to Mr. Lökke in the beginning
of October, but up to the present I have received no answer; if
you should meet him, you will perhaps be kind enough to ask
if he has received my letter.

The political sky is now beginning to look threatening in
the East also. What will the end be? The feeling here is very
despondent, and even the surrender of Metz did not arouse the
slightest enthusiasm. Dresden has, according to official reports,
fifteen thousand prisoners to provide for; and now a new contingent of four thousand is announced. Two thousand sick and
wounded lie in the hospitals. Great barracks have been built
quite near our house for the Imperial Guard; and we see them
pass every day, taking the walk prescribed for their health.
They show no signs of having suffered any hardships at Metz.
They are dressed as if for parade. The sick and wounded
Saxons ordered home look as if they had gone through much
more. The Frenchmen are very well treated, and bear their
captivity with incredible indifference; it strikes me that many
of them are pleased to have got out of their difficulties so easily.
In the ale-houses the non-commissioned officers lay down the
law, rail against the Emperor, against the generals, against

everything possible except themselves. The situation in France does not seem to trouble them. All this, however, is perfectly natural in men belonging to a revolutionary nation, which lacks proper discipline and control. We Norwegians ought to take a lesson from this; for it is in the direction of exactly such internal disintegration that fellows like Jaabæk, Johan Sverdrup, etc., are trying to draw our nation.

Will you be so kind as to renew my subscription to the *Morgenblad* when the time comes. It will be a favour if you can pay it for me, repaying yourself at New Year out of the interest on my money in the Kreditkasse. I hope you keep an accurate account of your disbursements, postages among the rest. I do not wish, besides giving you all the trouble, to cause you loss of money as well.

The new edition of *The Pretenders* has now appeared, and the play is to be given in Copenhagen on the 1st of January. In Christiania, I suppose, the two theatres are working out their own destruction.[1] The division of our few artistic forces cannot lead to anything else.

If, contrary to my intention, I should not write again before New Year, you will, I trust, nevertheless remember to send me the usual cheque at the usual time. Kindest remembrances from us all.—Yours ever,

HENRIK IBSEN.

[1] See Letters 67 and 70. On the 8th of September 1870 the actors and actresses who had left the Christiania Theatre (with Björnson as their manager), started the "Möllergadens Teater"; a year and a half later, however, most of them returned to the Christiania Theatre.

## 77.

*To* GEORGE BRANDES.[1]

DRESDEN, *20th December* 1870.

DEAR GEORGE BRANDES,—You have been in my thoughts every day lately. I had heard of your illness from Councillor Hegel, and read of it in the Norwegian papers; but, fearing that you might still be too weak to receive letters, I did not write. Your kind note received yesterday has, however, quite reassured me. Very many thanks for thinking of me!

You ask what you ought to undertake in the future. That I can tell you. In the immediate future you must undertake nothing at all. You must give both imagination and thought holiday for an indefinite period; you must lie still and be ennobled; for that is the blessing of such illnesses—the condition in which one comes out of them! A glorious time awaits you when you begin to regain your strength. I know this from personal experience: all evil thoughts had gone from me; even in the matter of eating and drinking I would touch nothing but what was light and delicate; coarse things, it seemed to me, would soil me. It is an indescribable state of thankfulness and well-being.

And when you have grown strong and fit again, what shall you do then? Why, then you will do what you must do. A nature such as yours has no choice.

I am not going to write a long letter, as that would not be good for you. And you had better not write to me for some time yet.

Last summer I was in Copenhagen. You have many, many friends and adherents there; more, perhaps, than you yourself believe. If you are away for a time, so much the better; one always gains by allowing one's self to be missed.

At last they have taken Rome away from us human beings,

[1] Brandes was at this time ill in Rome.

and given it to the politicians. Where shall we take refuge now? Rome was the one sanctuary in Europe; the only place that enjoyed true liberty—freedom from the political liberty-tyranny. I do not think I shall visit it again after what has happened. All that is delightful—the unconsciousness, the dirt —will now disappear; for every statesman that makes his appearance there, an artist will be ruined. And then the glorious aspiration after liberty—that is at an end now. Yes— I must confess that the only thing I love about liberty is the struggle for it; I care nothing for the possession of it.

One morning, some time ago, my new work became strikingly clear to me; and in the over-welling joy of the moment I wrote you a letter. It was not sent; for the mood did not last long; and when it was over, the letter was useless.

The great events of the day occupy my thoughts much at present. The old, illusory France has collapsed; and as soon as the new, real Prussia does the same, we shall be with one bound in a new age. How ideas will then come tumbling about our ears! And it is high time they did. Up till now we have been living on nothing but the crumbs from the revolutionary table of last century, a food out of which all nutriment has long been chewed. The old terms require to have a new meaning infused into them. Liberty, equality, and fraternity are no longer the things they were in the days of the late-lamented guillotine. This is what the politicians will not understand; and therefore I hate them. They want only their own special revolutions— revolutions in externals, in politics, etc. But all this is mere trifling. What is all-important is the revolution of the spirit of man; and in this you will be one of those who lead. But the first thing to do is to get rid of your fever.—Your devoted friend,

HENRIK IBSEN.

78.

*To* FREDERIK HEGEL.

DRESDEN, 10*th January* 1871.

DEAR MR. HEGEL,—Please accept my best thanks for the 75 Thalers received. I beg a thousand pardons for having inconvenienced you in the middle of your busiest time.

Your assumption that *Julian* is so far advanced that the printing may begin next month, is based on a misunderstanding. The First Part is finished; I am working at the Second Part; but the Third Part is not even begun. This Third Part will, however, be done comparatively quickly; allowing myself plenty of time, I expect that the whole will be in your hands in June. The Roman type will suit the antique subject capitally; and it will, I believe, be very suitable for my other books too.[1]

It was a great and pleasant surprise to me to learn that the second edition of *The Pretenders* is already sold out. I should be much pleased to see the new edition in the above-mentioned type. I will go carefully through my copy of the play; and if, contrary to my expectation, there should be anything to correct, I shall trouble you with another communication.

Professor Rovsing's book on the orthographical reform is particularly well written; but it will be absolutely impossible for him, or any one else, to stay the stream. The influence of the new spelling on the development of the Danish-Norwegian bookmarket in Sweden will soon make itself apparent; in nearly every letter I receive from there, expression is given in various forms to the feeling that our books in their new dress are read

[1] On the 31st of January 1871, Ibsen wrote to Hegel: "I am quite in love with the large Roman type; I have seen nothing prettier for a book of poems; and, what is of chief importance, it seems to be exactly suited to the character of my poems. Printed in this type they will be as good again."

as easily as if they were written in Swedish, And what is the alteration really ? Nothing but an elimination of the corruptions which have crept in in course of time, and a return to the original and correct usage. By the way, if you meet Professor Rovsing, please remember me kindly to him and his family, and say that I still think with pleasure of the time spent in his company in Rome.

Mrs. Collett [1] is still staying here, and is spending the time in fretting ; she intends to go to Italy ; but when she will go, if she goes at all, I do not know. She is a very gifted woman, with a most unhappy temperament.

Best wishes to you and your son from—Yours ever sincerely,

HENRIK IBSEN.

## 79.

### To GEORGE BRANDES.

DRESDEN, 17th *February* 1871.

DEAR BRANDES,—I suspected that my long silence would make you angry ; but I confidently trust that our relations are such that they will stand the strain. In fact, I have a decided feeling that a brisk correspondence would be a much more dangerous thing. Once we have actually met, many things will assume another aspect ; much will be cleared up on both sides. Until then I really run the danger of exhibiting myself to you, by means of my casual remarks, in quite a wrong light. You philosophers can reason black into white — and I have no desire to allow myself to be reduced, per correspondence, to a stone or a cock—even with the possibility in view of being restored, after an oral explanation, to the rank of a human being.[2]

---

[1] The well-known Norwegian authoress, Camilla Collett (1813–1895).

[2] The philosophical "reduction to a stone or a cock " is to be found in Holberg's comedy, *Erasmus Montanus*.

In your previous letter, you ironically admire my undisturbed
mental equilibrium under the present conditions.   There we
have the stone!   And now in your last friendly (?) note, you
make me out a hater of liberty.   The cock!   The fact is that my
mind is calm because I regard France's present misfortune as the
greatest good fortune that could befall her.   As to liberty, I take
it that our dispute is a mere dispute about words.   I shall never
agree to making liberty synonymous with political liberty.
What you call liberty, I call liberties; and what I call the
struggle for liberty is nothing but the constant, living assimilation of the idea of freedom.   He who possesses liberty otherwise
than as a thing to be striven for, possesses it dead and soulless;
for the idea of liberty has undoubtedly this characteristic,
that it develops steadily during its assimilation.   So that a man
who stops in the midst of the struggle and says: "Now I have
it"—thereby shows that he has lost it.   It is, however, exactly
this dead maintenance of a certain given standpoint of liberty
that is characteristic of the communities which go by the name
of states—and this it is that I have called worthless.

Yes, to be sure, it is a benefit to possess the franchise, the
right of self-taxation, etc., but for whom is it a benefit?   For
the citizen, not for the individual.   Now there is absolutely
no reasonable necessity for the individual to be a citizen.
On the contrary — the state is the curse of the individual.
With what is the strength of Prussia as a state bought?
With the merging of the individual in the political and
geographical concept.   The waiter makes the best soldier.
Now, turn to the Jewish nation, the nobility of the human
race.   How has it preserved itself—isolated, poetical—despite
all the barbarity from without?   Because it had no state to
burden it.   Had the Jewish nation remained in Palestine, it
would long since have been ruined in the process of construction,
like all the other nations.   The state must be abolished!   In
that revolution I will take part.   Undermine the idea of the
state; make willingness and spiritual kinship the only essentials
in the case of a union—and you have the beginning of a liberty

that is of some value. The changing of forms of government is mere toying with degrees—a little more or a little less—folly, the whole of it.

Yes, dear friend, the great thing is not to allow one's self to be frightened by the venerableness of the institution. The state has its root in Time: it will have its culmination in Time. Greater things than it will fall; all religion will fall. Neither the conceptions of morality nor those of art are eternal. To how much are we really obliged to pin our faith? Who will vouch for it that two and two do not make five up in Jupiter?

These suggestions I cannot and will not enlarge upon in writing. My best thanks for your poem! It is not the last you will write; for the (poet's) calling proclaims itself in every line. That you over-estimate me, I set down to the account of our friendship; and I thank you. Keep me ever so in your thoughts; I shall not fail you![1]

And now get strong again; and come to Dresden on two sound legs! That leg business—did you not feel as if there was a nemesis in it? You were once so furious with another philosopher because he stood on *two* legs. Thank God that you did not have to demonstrate the possibility of a philosopher's being able to do with *one*. I take it for granted that all danger is past, otherwise I should most certainly not jest on the subject.

I have as yet received only the First Part of *Criticisms and Portraits* from Hegel; but even if I had received the whole, I should have confined myself to thanking you heartily for the book.[2] I am an exceedingly poor critic. Concerning certain works I am unable to express myself; and what my general conception of you, as a complete personality, is, you already know.

---

[1] From the hospital in Rome, on the night between the 9th and 10th of January 1871, Brandes had sent his poem, "To Henrik Ibsen," as an answer to the concluding words of Ibsen's letter of the 20th of December 1870.

[2] Part First of Brandes's book, *Criticisms and Portraits*, was published in February 1870 ; Part Second, in April of the same year.

I have been occupied almost night and day since Christmas, preparing for the publication of my collected poems. It has been an accursed business, having to go over all the many points of view which I had long ago done with. However, taken together, they make something like a whole; and I am very anxious to hear what you will say about the book.

The thousand and one things which your letter might give occasion for writing about, I shall at present leave untouched. I must first learn if I may expect to see you here soon. Then we shall discuss both "Bishop Arius and the Seven Electors"; you shall see that it is not for nothing I have lived two years in the vicinity of Gert Westphaler's native land.[1]

Sincerest wishes for restored health and all that is good, from —Yours most sincerely,

HENRIK IBSEN.

P.S.—As soon as I come into possession of a fairly respectable photograph of myself, I will send you one; meanwhile accept the enclosed. I hope you will send one in return.

### 80.

*To* LORENTZ DIETRICHSON.

DRESDEN, *2nd March* 1871.

DEAR OLD FRIEND,—It was, in more ways than one, a great pleasure and a surprise to me to receive your kind letter, which, of course, I intended to answer at once—an intention which, equally of course, was not carried out. But to-day you shall really hear from me.

In the first place, let me congratulate you heartily upon the

---

[1] "Arius and the Seven Electors" were among the stock subjects of conversation of Gert Westphaler, the hero of the comedy of Holberg, to which he gives his name.

success you have had this winter as a play-writer. It was, however, only what I had always expected; and I predict more to come if you continue in the field.

You are, of course, writing a book on your travels in the East? I hope I am right in taking it for granted that the trip has had the intended effect on your health. And I conclude, from what I have heard from various sources, that your life in Stockholm is a very pleasant one. You have many friends and great influence—neither of them things to be despised.

As for me, I have been working this winter at my own poems, of which a complete edition is now in the press, and will be published in a short time. It is a huge edition, and I am receiving a big price for it. I have various plans for dramatic works; but these infernal war disturbances have a distracting effect upon me, as you can well imagine.

Be so good as to give my kind regards to the Limnell family at the first opportunity, and to thank Mrs. Limnell for her letter, which I will answer soon.[1]

Please also to convey my sincerest thanks to His Excellency, Mr. Sibbern. What you sent me from him was indeed a surprise. I am thankful that they have no idea of what once happened in Rome. That was in our " Sturm- und Drangperiode," carissimo! Now we are both past that stage. But it was a necessary one in our development; I wish nothing undone.[2]

Remember me to all other good friends, and assure them that their kindness is still fresh in my memory. Don't forget the " Hofmarskalk " and others connected with the theatre.

[1] Mrs. Limnell was the Swedish lady to whom (in December 1870) Ibsen had addressed his " Ballonbrev " (Balloon Letter).

[2] Statsminister Sibbern had transmitted to Ibsen a letter from Count Ludvig Manderström (Swedish and Norwegian Minister of Foreign Affairs from 1858 to 1868), who had been delighted with the " Balloon Letter."—One day in Rome during the winter of 1864–65, Ibsen had made an addition in pencil to a portrait of Count Manderström, in the shape of a rope round his neck. This performance led to a quarrel between Ibsen and Manderström's nephew, Carl Snoilsky, the poet. And the story of this affair had found its way to Norway.

I must return to Stockholm, that is certain. I am planning a trip to Norway this summer, if everything goes well; and I might manage Stockholm then, too. If this plan is carried out, we shall be able to talk over our respective "journeys from Haderslev to Kiel,"[1] carissimo! We have both been tolerably far afield since we camped in Stockholm. In Egypt I was, as perhaps you know, one of the party on the big twenty-four days' expedition up the Nile, right into Nubia; I was also one of those who made their way to the Red Sea; the majority turned back at Ismailia. But I did not manage to see old Rome again! However, I have not given up hope of going back some day. Perhaps we shall meet there. I assume that you still privately cherish a hope of being able to settle there in a certain official capacity.

If I did not know that in the matter of letter-writing you are exactly like myself, I should ask you to tell me a little about people and things in your parts. What is the Gambetta of the Rigsdag about? He interests me very much; remember me to him.[2] Has Malmström finished his great "Braavalla" painting?[3] And old Kjellberg?[4] I suppose he, too, is sighing for the flesh-pots of Rome? I understand that Carl Snoilsky published his poems last Christmas. Did they meet with such a reception as to encourage him to write more? He is a lyric poet of very high rank.[5] If you should meet Captain R. V. Koch, ask him if he received my letter. Be sure to remember me to the Stjernström family.

My ladies send their best thanks for the pleasure of your company in Dresden. Your messages, the declaration of love

[1] The "journey from Haderslev to Kiel" was another of the stock subjects of conversation of Holberg's "Gert Westphaler."

[2] The "Swedish Gambetta" was the young Liberal politician, Adolf Hedin.

[3] August Malmström (1829–1901), a Swedish historical painter.

[4] J. K. Kjellberg (1836–1885), a Swedish sculptor.

[5] Carl Snoilsky (1841–1903), a famous Swedish lyric poet. Ibsen had made friends with him in Rome; and they met again in Stockholm in 1869.

included, have been received with great satisfaction. In return, give many kind messages to your wife from us, and to your little daughter, too; I did not see her at all in Stockholm.

Whether we meet again sooner or later, personally or only by letter, do not in the meantime forget—Your affectionate friend,

HENRIK IBSEN.

### 81.

*To* GEORGE BRANDES.

DRESDEN, 18*th May* 1871.

DEAR BRANDES,—I hope that you received a greeting from me lately through our old Consul; at all events, I sent you one. I heard with great pleasure from Copenhagen that you were out of danger long ago, and are now well again. As for the danger, I never really believed in it; one does not die in the first act; the great world-dramaturge needs you for a leading part in the "Haupt- und Statsaction," for the performance of which before a highly-esteemed public he is doubtless now preparing.

Many thanks for the photograph! It has been of great assistance to me in my endeavour to understand your character, or rather to familiarise myself with it. No doubt it reveals itself distinctly in your works; but I always like to have a personal form with which I can connect my idea. And therefore I shall not be satisfied until I have met you. I think it will then become apparent that we agree in more than a partiality for velvet coats.

During this rather long interval I have not been able to persuade myself to write to you. From your last letter I gathered that you were rather annoyed with me; and as my *Poems* were then about to be published, I did not want to make any advances that might look like an attempt to conciliate you before you had read them.[1] I am well aware that your judg-ment does not allow itself to be corrupted; but tact bade me avoid any appearance of having imagined such a thing to be possible. Dear friend, you will understand this.

I hope Hegel sent you the book long ago. There is both new and old in it, and much which I regard as of no great importance; yet it is all part of the story of my development. Let me know your verdict; I attach the greatest importance to it.

And with what are you occupying yourself in beautiful, warm Italy? One benefit you will perhaps reap from your illness — that of spending a summer there. I think of you every day; now I picture you at Frascati, now at Albano or Ariccia. Tell me which supposition is right? And what is being prepared there for our intellectual future? For sure I am that something has grown into maturity during your long illness. It is one of the blessings of such an illness that it gives distinctness and the opportunity of growth to so much which otherwise would have no chance of unfolding itself. I have only once been really ill; but for that very reason, perhaps, I have never been really well. *Chi lo sa!*

Is it not shameful of the Commune in Paris to have gone and spoiled my excellent state-theory—or rather non-state-theory? The idea is ruined for many a day; I cannot in decency even proclaim it in verse. But there is a sound kernel in it—that I see very clearly; and some day it will be put into practice, without any caricature.

I have often thought of what you once wrote—that I had not made the present scientific standpoint mine. What oppor-tunity have I had of doing so? And yet, is not each generation in a manner born with the qualifications of its age? Have you never noticed in a collection of portraits of some past century a curious family resemblance between persons of the same period? It is the same in spiritual matters. What we, the uninitiated do not possess as knowledge, we possess, I believe, to a certain

[1] Ibsen's *Poems* were published on the 3rd of May 1871.

degree, as intuition or instinct. But, let this be as it may, the poet's essential task is to see, not to reflect. For me in particular, there would be danger in too much reflection.

Dear Brandes, it is always a relief to me to talk to you, and a great, great pleasure to hear you talk, even though it is only on paper.—Yours most sincerely,

HENRIK IBSEN.

## 82.

### To FREDERIK HEGEL.

DRESDEN, 12th July 1871.

DEAR MR. HEGEL,—On looking at your last kind letter, I see, to my horror, that it is quite two months old, and as yet unanswered! I hope, however, that in the meantime you have received two signs of life from me, namely, the revised copy of *Brand*, and a greeting sent by Mr. R. Kaufmann, who took back with him the books borrowed from Mr. Gundorph, the Librarian. Will you be good enough to convey my very best thanks to Mr. Gundorph.

I am most grateful to you, dear Mr. Hegel, for the papers containing reviews of my *Poems* which you have sent me at different times. On the whole, I may be satisfied with the criticism they have received; I only hope that the book will have a quick sale.

And now the reason for my long silence: I am hard at work on *Emperor Julian*. This book will be my chief work, and it is engrossing all my thoughts and all my time. That positive theory of life which the critics have demanded of me so long, they will get in it. But now I have a request to make of you. In the spring of 1866, Pastor Listov wrote an article on the life of Julian, which ran through three numbers of the *Fædreland*. If it were possible for you to procure a loan of these three numbers for me, you would do me a great service. But this is not all. Does there exist in Danish any other historical treatment of this subject, in which the *facts* are at all thoroughly entered into? If so, will you buy it for me and send it at my expense. I have Neander's German works on the subject; also D. Strauss's; but the latter's book contains only argumentative folly, and that I can furnish myself. Facts are what I need. Do not be annoyed with me for troubling you with this matter!

I shall be exceedingly obliged if you will buy me 2000 rix-dollars' worth of Government Bonds, as you kindly suggested in your last letter.

If Jonas Lie should pass through Copenhagen on his way south, tell him that he must be sure to travel to Italy *viâ* Dresden, as I wish to scold him and to give him good advice —to communicate much to him, in fact, which can only be done by word of mouth.

Hitherto we have had horrible summer weather here; I hope that it has been better in Denmark.

Kindest regards to you and your son.—Yours most sincerely,

HENRIK IBSEN.

### 83.

#### *To* HANS JACOB JENSEN.

DRESDEN, 17*th September* 1871.

SIR,—The impudent effrontery displayed in the letter which I have received from you to-day has caused me extreme astonishment. You inform me that you intend to issue a new edition of my dramatic works, *Lady Inger of Östraat* and *The Vikings at Helgeland.* I naturally make a vigorous protest against this attempt to rob me. You have not the slightest right of ownership in the said works, which were sold by me solely for publication in the *Illustreret Nyhedsblad.* Allow me to inform you that both books are to be published by the

"Gyldendalske Boghandel" in a completely revised form, and that the public will immediately be informed of this, so that from your contemplated fraud you will reap nothing but disgrace and loss. Moreover, I have to-day put the matter into the hands of a lawyer; and if you dare to persist in your intention I shall show you, both in the columns of the newspapers and in open court, what the consequences of such rascality are. The package sent me, I return unopened.

HENRIK IBSEN.[1]

84.

*To* GEORGE BRANDES.

DRESDEN, 24*th September* 1871.

DEAR BRANDES,—It is always with a strangely mixed feeling that I read your letters. They are more like poems than letters. What you write comes to me like a cry of distress from one who has been left the sole survivor in some great tract where all other life is extinct. And I cannot but rejoice, and thank you, that you direct this cry to me. But then, again, I become most anxious, when I ask myself: "To what will such a mood lead?" And I have nothing to comfort myself with but the hope that it is only a transition. You seem to me to be passing through the same crisis which I passed through in the days when I began to write *Brand*; and I am certain that you, too, will find the remedy which drives whatever is the cause of

---

[1] Hans Jacob Jensen (1824–1890), printer in Christiania, published in the autumn of 1871 a "second edition" of *The Vikings at Helgeland*, which he had printed and published in 1858 as a supplement to the *Illustreret Nyhedsblad*; and at the same time he announced a new edition of *Lady Inger of Östraat*, which had appeared in the *Nyhedsblad* in 1857. Ibsen immediately published a protest in the Danish *Dagblad*, and his friend, L. Daae, inserted one in the Norwegian *Morgenblad*. The dispute was taken to court. Jensen had to pay a fine and compensation, and his whole stock of the two plays was confiscated and destroyed.

the disease out of the body. Energetic productivity is a capital specific.

What I chiefly desire for you is a genuine, full-blooded egoism, which shall force you for a time to regard what concerns you yourself as the only thing of any consequence, and everything else as non-existent. Now don't take this wish as an evidence of something brutal in my nature! There is no way in which you can benefit society more than by coining the metal you have in yourself. I have never really had any very firm belief in solidarity; in fact, I have only accepted it as a kind of traditional dogma. If one had the courage to throw it overboard altogether, it is possible that one would be rid of the ballast which weighs down one's personality most heavily.— There are actually moments when the whole history of the world appears to me like one great shipwreck, and the only important thing seems to be to save one's self.

From special reforms I expect nothing. The whole race is on the wrong track; that is the trouble. Or is there really anything tenable in the present situation—with its unattainable ideals, etc.? The whole succession of human generations remind me of a young shoemaker who has forsaken his last and gone on the stage. We have made a fiasco both in the heroic and the lover rôles. The only parts in which we have shown a little talent, are the naïvely comic; but with our more highly developed self-consciousness we shall no longer be fitted even for that. I do not believe that things are better in other countries than in our own; the masses, both at home and abroad, are without all understanding of higher things.

And so I ought to raise a banner, ought I? Alas, dear friend! that would be much the same kind of performance as Louis Napoleon's landing at Boulogne with an eagle on his head. Later, when the hour of his destiny struck, he needed no eagle. In the course of my occupation with *Julian*, I have in a way become a fatalist; and yet this play will be a kind of banner. Do not fear, however, any underlying purpose; I study the characters, the conflicting plans, the *history*, and do not concern myself with the *moral* of the whole—always assuming that by the moral of history you do not mean its philosophy; for that *that* will clearly shine forth, as the final verdict on the struggle and the victory, is a matter of course. But all this can only be made intelligible by practical application.

Your last letter on this subject did not cause me any uneasiness—in the first place, because I was prepared for such misgivings on your part; in the second, because I am not handling the subject in the way you assume.

I have received your book; and all I can say is that I never tire of reading it.

It is incomprehensible to me, my dear, good Brandes, that you can be despondent—you whose spiritual calling is unmistakable in a degree vouchsafed to few. What is the use of being despondent? Have you any right to be so? But do not think that I do not understand you perfectly.

Oblige me by forwarding enclosed visiting cards to Dr. Fr. Knudtzon, Amalie Street; and should you happen to meet him, remember me to him; I have in many ways a very high opinion of him—and I may add that he has an enthusiastic and unbounded admiration for you.

And now, in conclusion, accept my best thanks for your visit to Dresden; those were festive hours for me. Best wishes for health, courage, happiness—everything good!—Yours most sincerely, HENRIK IBSEN.[1]

86.

*To* MICHAEL BIRKELAND.

DRESDEN, 10*th October* 1871.

DEAR BIRKELAND,—A thousand thanks for your letter, which shows me that your friendship is unchanged. I am

---

[1] On his way back to Denmark, in July 1871, Brandes paid a visit to Ibsen in Dresden. This was their first meeting.

quite pleased that my article has been kept back. The thought of engaging in an altercation with a fellow like Jensen, the printer, has been most repugnant to me. It is much better for an outsider to do it. My request to you is this: either, after consultation with Thoresen, to remodel the article in such a way that it will produce its effect without injuring me, or—what I should prefer—to take what is useful in it, and write an article on the subject yourself.

I must make a few observations on your letter, however. You write as though it might be doubtful which of us is in the right. Does barbarism actually prevail to that extent in the Norwegian book-world? Is a contribution to a paper the property of the publisher? If so, how was I permitted, unmolested, to publish a second edition of *Love's Comedy*? How was it possible for me to publish my collected poems, if the "Balloon Letter" and many other pieces belonged to Dr. de Besche and the *Illustreret Nyhedsblad*? How could Björnson (in his *Short Pieces*) reprint "Between the Battles" and "A Happy Boy," works of which the one, according to Norwegian ideas, belonged to the *Christiania Post*, and the other to the *Aftenblad*? Throughout the whole civilised world there is no doubt on this subject; and it pains me to think that my native land should form the solitary exception to the rule. Supposing I am mistaken, and my letter to Botten-Hansen about *Lady Inger* still exists, it will amply prove that the *Nyhedsblad* acquired only a certain limited right; in any other case, there would have been no sense in stipulating about the size of the edition.

It would be another most extraordinary thing if that piratical publisher, H. J. Jensen, were able to make capital out of my private letter. There are only two strong expressions in it—my qualification of his enterprise as "a fraud," and my declaration that, "if he persists in his intention, I shall show him, both in the columns of the newspapers and in open court, what the consequences of such rascality are." If Jensen owns the copyright, then he is practising rascally tricks on his creditors; if he does not own it, then he is practising them on me. In either case his speculation is, according to European standards, a dishonest speculation. Is it possible that it can be dangerous at home to say this? Yes—I understand why it is dangerous; the danger is connected with that "state of affairs and of public feeling" to which you allude. If Jensen were a State Councillor, or any kind of Government official, or even simply a private individual of education and refinement, there would be no danger; but a dirty scoundrel, who, by virtue of his dirtiness, belongs to "the people," must on no account be dismissed with scorn. I will not subscribe to such principles as long as I live! I confess, however, that this private quarrel does not provide the most favourable opportunity for stigmatising barbarism and its idolaters. But how can the man dare to think of an action for libel, when we have the whole story of his bankruptcy to hold over him?

Thank L. Daae from me for his valuable assistance, and beg him not to desert me. This matter is one of serious importance to me; for if this dishonest speculation of Jensen's really obtains sympathy and support at home, it is my intention, come what may, to sever all ties with Norway, and never set foot on her soil again.

I was working in happy tranquillity of mind at my new book. From Sweden, from Denmark, and from Germany, I hear nothing but what gives me pleasure; it is from Norway that everything bad comes upon me. What do the people want? Am I not far enough away?

Something occurs to me. Could not parts of my article be used as extracts from a private letter from me? Do whatever you and Thoresen think proper; but prevent the fatal possibility of the reprint of my books seeing the light of day.

Once more, thank you for your letter. A cordial greeting to your wife. I intend, if I get out of this despicable affair successfully, to come home this summer, in order to take part in the celebration of the thousandth anniversary of our country's existence as a Kingdom. Nothing deters me except the thought of our demagogic political millennialists.—Yours ever, HENRIK IBSEN.

*P.S.*—I am writing to Thoresen to-day.

### 86.

*To* FREDERIK HEGEL.

DRESDEN, 27*th December* 1871.

DEAR MR. HEGEL,—Allow me to offer you our very best thanks for the beautiful and valuable gift which has contributed so much towards making our Christmas a pleasant one. Mrs. Dunker's book is sure to find a large circle of readers, especially in Norway, where I know it has been eagerly looked forward to.[1]

My new work progresses steadily. Part First: *Julian and the Philosophers*, in three acts, lies finished—the fair-copy of it. It makes exactly one hundred pages; but I shall not send you any of it, as I presume you wish the whole before beginning to print. I am now working industriously at Part Second, and this will progress more rapidly and be considerably shorter. Part Third, on the other hand, will be somewhat longer. The whole work will probably run to between two hundred and eighty and three hundred pages, all of it in prose. In style it bears most resemblance to *The Pretenders*.

I have lately been involved in a German controversy. The periodical *Im neuen Reich*, published in Leipzig and edited by Alfred Dove and Gustav Freytag, attacked me on account of some references to the Germans in my poems.[2] The war spread

---

[1] *Gamle Dage* (Old Days), capitally written reminiscences by Fru Conradine Dunker, mother of Advokat Bernhard Dunker.

[2] Ibsen's assailant wrote: "As a German reader I cannot but feel exceedingly hurt and indignant when he (Ibsen) permits himself, with

to the *Constitutionelle Zeitung*, and several other papers of less importance. I was, of course, obliged to defend myself, and have done so in a manner which will, I hope, render my position here tenable, for some time at least.

May I ask you to be good enough to send me 36 Thalers Prussian? I am afraid of running short of money before the usual quarterly remittance from Christiania arrives.

I trust you have received the books belonging to the University Library? I have been uneasy in regard to this, because a Post-Office official here told me that they were not sufficiently well packed. If any damage should thereby have been caused to the binding or the books generally, I shall, of course, make it good; that the parcel has arrived I know, from the fact that I have been refunded an over-charge for postage which had been noticed at the Copenhagen Post-Office.

Mrs. C. Collett is staying here at present. She talks of going on to Rome; but I doubt her doing it, she is such a bad traveller.

If you should see G. Brandes, please remember me to him; I will write to him soon.

Accept my thanks for all your kindness in the past year, and our best wishes for you and your son, for the coming one. I hope and expect that our mutual enterprises in 1872 will have results satisfactory to us both.—Yours most sincerely,

HENRIK IBSEN.

a cynicism to which we are accustomed only in the learned and literary men of Copenhagen, to apply the ugliest epithets of derision and scorn to Germany. And a German feels this the more because Ibsen has for some years been enjoying German hospitality in Dresden, and only ventures to behave as he does, because he assumes that no one there can read and understand his poems." In evidence of his accusation, the writer quotes some expressions from the "Balloon Letter," and the poem "On the Death of Abraham Lincoln." The editors of the periodical expressed the opinion that such "lyric effusions," being of no practical importance, ought not to be taken so seriously. Ibsen's reply was inserted.

## 87.

*To* THE NORWEGIAN ECCLESIASTICAL DEPARTMENT.

.     .     ,     .     .     .     .     .

After the aforesaid grant had, in part, been voted me, I went to Sweden, where I carefully inspected the public museums and art institutions — more particularly those of Stockholm. I was, moreover, enabled, by the great courtesy of the authorities, to acquire a very thorough understanding of the Swedish educational system—its standpoint, its principles, and its whole outward and inward relation to the character and history of the nation.

In the month of September I received an official invitation to be present at the opening of the Suez Canal: and, although I had not completed my study of Swedish conditions and institutions, I considered it unwarrantable, and contrary to the general plan of my foreign travel, to allow such an opportunity of acquiring knowledge—an opportunity which could never occur again — to pass unimproved. I therefore proceeded immediately, *via* Dresden and Paris, to Egypt, where I arrived about the middle of October, and took part in the Nile expedition arranged by the Khedive for about sixty European gentlemen. We went some distance into Nubia.

The Khedive's aim in arranging this expedition was to direct the attention of the different European nations, through us, their representatives, both to the ancient monuments of the country, and to the great undertakings by which the present Government is endeavouring to improve the condition of the land and its inhabitants. It was planned by one of the Khedive's Conservators of the national art treasures, Mariette Bey,[1] and conducted by the most eminent Egyptologists. I had thus the best possible opportunity of acquiring a groundwork for those studies of Greek and Roman architecture and sculpture

---

[1] A. F. F. Mariette (1821–1881), an eminent French Egyptologist.

to which I had applied myself with ardour during my four years' residence in Italy.

In the middle of November the expedition returned to Cairo. From there we went to Port Said, took part in the ceremonies at the opening of the Canal, sailed through it to the Red Sea, then returned to Cairo, and thence, *via* Alexandria, to Europe. I stopped in Paris to make acquaintance with the art collections there, but returned to Dresden before the winter was over.

This tour I made, as already mentioned, in the character of an invited guest; but it nevertheless, as a matter of course, entailed very considerable outlay on my part. Every one who knows the East knows that presents, in money and other forms, on all possible occasions, are demanded of one to an extent utterly unknown in Europe. The company in which I travelled, the society abroad with which I came in contact, and the fact that I and the fellow-countryman who travelled with me were regarded as the representatives of our native land, obliged me, moreover, to behave more in the style of a rich man than of one of my means.

.    .    .    .    .    .    .    .

Although my Egyptian tour has been of incalculable value in furthering my development (it has, in particular, given me a clearer idea of the progress of civilisation throughout the ages), the full intellectual benefit obtainable from it will not be derived unless I am enabled, by means of a thorough course of study at the Berlin Egyptological Museum, to acquire the supplementary knowledge necessary to give me a complete understanding of Egyptian architecture and sculpture, and their relation to the corresponding antique forms of art in Europe.

Family considerations will oblige me to return to Norway next year. I had expected to be able to set out on the homeward journey this year; but a new, lengthy work makes this impossible.

The disturbance of mind which would be unavoidably

15

entailed by a change of residence and a return to surroundings which, after my eight years' absence, are strange to me, could not but leave its marks on an incompleted work, the inner structure of which requires in a very special degree to be of one material and one casting.

. . . . . . . .[1]

## 88.

### *To* FREDERIK HEGEL.

DRESDEN, *2nd March* 1872.

DEAR MR. HEGEL,—Pardon me for troubling you with a few words to-day. I should be very much obliged to you if, one of these days, you could send me 100 rix-dollars, either in Prussian paper-money or, if it gives less trouble, in post-office orders.

The action against Jensen the printer—and pirate, is in full swing. It is being conducted on my behalf by Mr. Stang, Advocate at the Supreme Court, a son of State-Councillor Stang. He is delighted to have this opportunity of attacking Jensen. Jensen, as you are perhaps aware, is the publisher of the *Dagblad*, which paper has for some time been making rancorous assaults on the Stang Ministry. Dybwad and

[1] This petition to the Ecclesiastical Department for another travelling-grant, of which only fragments are in existence, had no result. On the occasion of his visit to Egypt, Ibsen received one of his first decorations (see Letter 45), being made Commander of the Medjidie Order. He wrote to Hegel in May 1871 : "When I was invited to Egypt, it was believed in Norway that I had received the invitation because I had laid part of the scene of *Peer Gynt* in the regions of the Nile; if I alone had been decorated, it would at once have been supposed that my 'Balloon Letter' had been translated into Egyptian. The orders were really conferred in return for a number of Swedish and Norwegian decorations sent to Egyptian dignitaries, of which we were the bearers."

Cammermeyer, the booksellers, were also prosecuted for having exposed for sale copies of the reprint; but as it was proved that they had not sold any, and as they bound themselves to have nothing more to do with the Jensen affair, the prosecution was withdrawn.

Everything is as usual here. I work every day at *Emperor Julian.* I hear that *Brand* has appeared in German; as yet I have not read the translation.

Kindest regards to you and your son from—Yours ever sincerely,

HENRIK IBSEN.

89.

*To* FREDRIK GJERTSEN.[1]

DRESDEN, 21*st March* 1872.

DEAR MR. GJERTSEN,—Some little time ago I was pleasantly surprised by receiving, direct from yourself, your translation of Horace's *Ars Poetica.* The pleasure was a double one. I was delighted to receive tangible evidence of the fitness of our language, when properly used, to reproduce the substance and form of antique thought—and it gave me no less pleasure to learn that you had preserved a friendly remembrance of me all this time.

To translate well is a difficult matter. It is not simply a question of rendering the meaning, but also, to a certain extent, of remodelling the expression and the metaphors, of accommodating the outward form to the structure and re-quirements of the language into which one is translating. For instance, I am very much in doubt as to whether Molbech, in his translation of the *Divina Commedia,* has

---

[1] Fredrik Gjertsen (1831–1904), master of a private school in Christiania, is known as a good translator, especially of Greek and Latin classic authors. He also wrote well-turned occasional poems.

done wisely in using only feminine rhymes. If the Italian language had contained masculine rhymes, Dante would, naturally, have employed them in their turn; and I do not see that it is right, in a translation into Danish, to burden the translation with a defect from which the Danish language does not suffer.

It may be asserted, and quite truthfully, that the soft terminal rhymes give a sort of Italian colouring to the Danish version; but this is only of consequence to the few who are acquainted with the original, or, at any rate, know Italian. It is my opinion that a poem should be translated in the style in which the author would have written it himself had he belonged to the nation who are to read him in the translation.

From this point of view it seems to me that you have been extraordinarily successful; and a large measure of the success is due to the judgment which you have shown in choosing the metre. The hexameter is unsuited to our Scandinavian languages. Both Meisling and Wilster have, in their otherwise meritorious translations, sufficiently proved this. In this foreign metre, the meaning becomes obscure; the foreign effect which it produces on the language acts like a disturbing melody coming between the reader and the sense of what he is reading. The same seems to me to be the case with the German original poems which are written in hexameters. In *Hermann und Dorothea*, both the characters and the situations have been conventionalised by the metre in a degree observable nowhere else in Goethe, and incompatible with the demand of our age for realistic representation.

I have often wondered why you have not attempted to translate Byron. Judging by the specimens which you published some time ago in the *Nyhedsblad*, it seems to me that you ought to be the very person to do it. A knowledge of the English language is very general among us, it is true; but chiefly in the classes amongst whom one cannot assume the existence of any particular interest in poetry. I have not read very much of Byron, but I have a feeling that his works, translated into our language, would be of great assistance in freeing our æsthetics from many moral prejudices—which would be a great gain. There is a great lack of freedom in our public opinion; the different spiritual spheres are mixed up with each other. What will not pass muster when tried by our conventional national standard of morality, is at once condemned as not fulfilling the requirements of the æsthetic standard either. But a foreign authority carries weight. It is acknowledged here that German literature required Byron's assistance to enable it to reach its present standpoint; and I maintain that *we* need him to free us from ours.

What astonishes me, however, most of all is that you have not seriously taken to original writing. I cannot understand how ability can exist without a corresponding impulse to employ it; and I imagine that a search of your secret hiding-places would bring to light documents which would amply confirm me in my theory. I hope that it will not be long before you decide to publish. When you do, I can be of use to you, as I have still in my possession a sonnet which you wrote to me in 1851, on returning an eye-glass which you borrowed from me one evening at the Students' Club It was to the late George Krohn that our slight acquaintance at that time was due. I wonder if you remember this. Afterwards, when I was groping and struggling towards a new conception of life, much was revealed in me that could not but raise a barrier between us. During my absence I have won the favour of many of our best men. I count you among these, and I trust that I am no longer likely to forfeit, in personal intercourse, what my exile has won for me.

There is a little circle at home which I must always think of in connection with you. Some of its members I knew well, others less intimately. Please remember me to them all. I have not many friends; I am quite ready to increase their number—it would be running no risk. There is no danger of my soon having, out of regard for myself and my own peace of mind, to surrender my fundamental principle in every field and domain—that the minority is always in the right. Farewell! and thank you for thinking of me.—Cordially yours,

HENRIK IBSEN.

90.

*To* EDMUND GOSSE.[1]

DRESDEN, *2nd April* 1872.

HONOURED SIR,—A few days ago I had the great pleasure of receiving your very flattering letter, together with your kind review in *The Spectator*.

My knowledge of the English language is, unfortunately, not so thorough that I can venture to write in English; and I hope you will forgive me for employing my native tongue to express my most sincere and grateful thanks for the favour which you show to my literary labours.

I could not wish a better or more laudatory introduction to a foreign nation than you have given me in your excellent review; nor is there any nation to whose reading public I should feel it a greater honour to be made known than yours. If it can be done through your friendly and capable intervention, I shall be everlastingly indebted to you.

Your esteemed letter does not make it quite clear to me,

---

[1] The first article in the English language on Ibsen was a review of his *Poems* by Mr. Gosse, published in the *Spectator* of April 22nd, 1872. Mr. Gosse translated fragments of *Love's Comedy* and *Peer Gynt*, and collaborated with William Archer in the translation of *Hedda Gabler* and of *Bygmester Solness*; but it was especially in his capacity of critic that he endeavoured to make his countrymen acquainted with Ibsen's works.

however, whether you intend yourself to translate my writings, or whether you will confine yourself to drawing attention to them in England by means of reviews. If the former is the case it will, of course, be an honour and a pleasure to me to place my books at your disposal, as I feel assured that I could not place them in better hands. I should be particularly glad of information on this subject.

I very much regret that circumstances do not permit of my visiting Scandinavia this summer, and that I shall thereby, unfortunately, miss a pleasant and much-desired opportunity of personally expressing my sincere gratitude for the important step which you have already taken towards realising one of my fondest literary dreams. The English people are very closely related to us Scandinavians; and it has consequently been a special grief to me to think that language should form a barrier between my work and the whole of this great kindred world. So you can imagine what pleasure you gave me by holding out the prospect of this barrier being demolished.

Several editions of my works are being prepared here in Germany. A translation of *Brand* has appeared in Cassel; but it is one which does not satisfy me. Another translation of the same work is announced from Berlin. *The Pretenders* and *The League of Youth* have also been published in Berlin, in an excellent German rendering by Dr. Adolf Strodtmann, the clever translator of Byron and Tennyson. At present Dr. Strodtmann is busy translating my minor poems.[1]

To have my works presented to the English reading public is, however, the matter of chief importance to me; and the sooner it can be done, the better I shall be pleased. Should you think of honouring and gratifying me with a letter on this subject, my direct address is, and will be, at least until the end of June—

[1] Adolf Strodtmann (1829–1879), a native of Flensborg, who knew Danish from his youth, did much, by his translations, for the spread of Scandinavian literature in Germany.

Dippoldiswalder-Strasse No. 7, Dresden.

If you should happen to come to Dresden in the course of your summer tour, it would give me great pleasure to have a talk with you.

Allow me to give expression once again to my sincere appreciation of the cordiality and sympathy which you display towards me and the literature of my country generally. And believe me to be—Yours very respectfully and gratefully,

HENRIK IBSEN.

## 91.

### To GEORGE BRANDES.[1]

DRESDEN, *4th April* 1872.

DEAR BRANDES, — I have just received your letter, and answer it immediately.

What manner of incredible things are these that you write! And I, meanwhile, have been picturing you to myself joyful and triumphant! Nevertheless, I am certain that you have a host behind you. Remember that they are recruits whom

---

[1] On the 3rd of November 1871, George Brandes began a series of lectures at the University of Copenhagen on "Main Currents in Nineteenth Century Literature." The first volume of these, *The Emigrant Literature*, was published in February 1872. The lectures created a great sensation and gave rise to violent discussions. Not one of the Copenhagen newspapers took Brandes's side. In the beginning of 1872 he wrote, in *Nyt Dansk Maanedsskrift*, the story of "a little free thought," which had been eaten up by the wolf, "the old opposition press," which had previously eaten up Liberty. C. Ploug, of the *Fœdreland*, chose to feel himself personally insulted by this, and made a violent attack on Brandes. To secure the insertion in the *Dagblad* of his answer to Ploug, Brandes was obliged to pay for it as an advertisement; henceforth, for several years, the press was closed to him. [The whole series of Lectures on "Main Currents in Nineteenth Century Literature" are published in English, in six volumes, by Heinemann, London.]

you are leading into the fire; the first time they retreat, the second time they hold their ground, and after that they follow you to assault and victory.

The Liberal press is closed to you? Why, of course! I once expressed my contempt for political liberty. You contradicted me at the time. Your fairy-tale of "Red Ridinghood" shows me that you have had certain experiences. Dear friend, the Liberals are freedom's worst enemies. Freedom of thought and spirit thrive best under absolutism; this was shown in France, afterwards in Germany, and now we see it in Russia.

But I must turn to what has lately been constantly in my thoughts, and has even disturbed my sleep. I have read your Lectures.

No more dangerous book could fall into the hands of a pregnant poet. It is one of those works which place a yawning gulf between yesterday and to-day. After I had been in Italy, I could not understand how I had been able to exist before I had been there. In twenty years, one will not be able to comprehend how spiritual existence at home was possible before these lectures. I have no clear conception of what it was that Steffens accomplished in his day; but I presume that it was the giving of a new form to the conventional æstheticism.[1] Your book is not a history of literature according to the old idea, nor is it a history of civilisation. I will not trouble to find a name for what it really is. It reminds me of the goldfields of California when they were first discovered, which either made millionaires of men or ruined them. Is the spiritual constitution in the north robust enough? I do not know; but this cannot be taken into account—what cannot bear the ideas of the times must succumb.

You say that every voice in the philosophical faculty is against you. Dear Brandes, would you wish it otherwise? Is it not the philosophy of the faculty that you are opposing? A

---

[1] By his lectures in Copenhagen in 1802, Steffens had prepared the way for the Romantic movement in Denmark.

war such as yours must not be conducted by a government functionary. If they did not lock you out, it would show that they did not fear you.[1]

As regards the agitation against you, the lies, calumnies, etc., I will give you a piece of advice which I know from personal experience to be the best possible. Be dignified. Dignity is the only weapon against such assaults. Look straight ahead; never reply in the newspapers; if in your writings you become polemical, do not direct your arguments against this or that particular attack; never show that what your antagonists have said has had any effect upon you; in short, behave as though you had no idea that you had any antagonists. How much vitality do you imagine there is in these assaults? In the old days, when I read an attack on myself in the morning, I thought: I am ruined; my reputation will never survive this. But it did survive it; and now no one remembers what was written—even I myself have long ago forgotten it. Therefore, do not demean yourself by bandying words with this, that, or the other person. Begin, imperturbable and unmoved, a new series of lectures; and display a cheerful indifference and contempt for whatever may collapse to the right or the left of you. Do you believe that what is worm-eaten has any real power of resistance?

What will be the outcome of this mortal combat between two epochs, I do not know; but, anything rather than the existing state of affairs—so say I. I do not promise myself that any permanent improvement will result from the victory; all development hitherto has been nothing more than a stumbling from one error into another. But the struggle is good, wholesome, and invigorating; to me your revolt is a great, shattering and emancipating outbreak of genius. When the men of the old school raise the cry of blasphemy, they ought to bear in

---

[1] Immediately before beginning his lectures, Brandes had applied for the post of interim professor (Docent) during the absence of Professor Hauch, the lecturer on Æsthetics. But it was thirty years before he received any University appointment.

mind that they also are blasphemers; the Great One in question has surely had a purpose in creating you.

I hear you have organised a society. Do not rely implicitly upon every one who joins you; with an adherent everything depends upon his reasons for adherence. Whether you may be strengthening your position or not, I cannot tell; to me it appears that the man who stands alone is the strongest. But then I am sitting here under cover, and you are standing there in the midst of the storm; that makes a great difference.

Farewell, dear Brandes! Give a friendly thought to me and mine when you can spare it from that which must henceforth be of supreme, sole importance to you, because in spirit and in truth it is your own.

Excuse haste and incoherence!—Yours ever,

HENRIK IBSEN.

## 92.

### *To* FREDERIK HEGEL.

DRESDEN, 24*th April* 1872.

DEAR MR. HEGEL,—My best thanks for the 75 Thalers enclosed in your kind letter of the 4th of March. I have also to thank you for the beautiful edition of *The Pretenders* which I received last Sunday.

This play, and *The League of Youth*, have been translated into German by Adolf Strodtmann, and I hear that they have already been accepted for production by the theatres of Breslau and Prague; I also understand that both books have been received with favour by the reading public.

I wonder if you happen to have read a review of my poems in the English weekly paper, *The Spectator*, which has been reprinted in part in the *Morgenblad*. Similar reviews of my other works are to be published, to prepare the way for a translation of them which it is proposed to issue in England and

America. The leader in this undertaking is Mr. Edmund Gosse, an official (librarian or something of the kind) in the British Museum in London. This gentleman has requested me to send him copies of *Love's Comedy*, *Peer Gynt*, and *The League of Youth*. Will you do me the great favour of despatching them—charging them to my account. No letter need be sent; I have myself written all that is necessary. The full address is: Edmund W. Gosse, Esq., British Museum, Great Russell Street Bloomsbury, London.

And you would oblige me very much by paying (through a business correspondent, or in any other way that may be convenient to you) 9 rix-dollars Danish (18 rix-dollars Swedish) for me to Chr. Hammer, Picture Dealer, Fredsgatan, Stockholm.

I have almost finished the 2nd part of *Julian*. The 3rd and last part will be mere play. Spring has come here, and the warm season is my best season for working.

We have had the pleasure of seeing quite a number of Danish tourists; H. C. Andersen is here at present.

I must give up my intended visit to Copenhagen at the time of the Exhibition, because, as soon as *Julian* is finished, I intend to begin revising *Lady Inger of Östraat*, which I think of offering to the Theatre Royal.

I am very grateful to you for the books by G. Brandes, His Lectures seem to me exceedingly fine; but I can well understand that they have given great offence in many quarters. One thing, however, is certain—he will have the future on his side; many of his opponents will have injured their own renown in the days to come by the manner in which they have behaved to him. I wrote to him last week. With kindest regards to you and your son, believe me — Yours most sincerely,

HENRIK IBSEN.

93.

*To* EDMUND GOSSE.

DRESDEN, 30*th April* 1872.

HONOURED SIR,—Will you forgive me for not answering your friendly letter sooner. I shall consider myself most fortunate if you decide to translate one or more of my books; but I shall, of course, be equally indebted to you if you continue to draw attention to my works by means of articles in the English papers. I presume this would contribute in no small degree to removing the difficulties of finding a publisher. There can be no question of beginning a translation without some assurance of a reasonable compensation for the time and trouble spent on it. I leave the matter in your hands with the greatest confidence, convinced that you will choose the surest and most advantageous way of attaining our aim.

Last week I wrote to my publisher in Copenhagen, requesting him to send you *Love's Comedy*, a play in three acts, along with the two books for which you asked. *Love's Comedy* should really be regarded as a forerunner of *Brand,* for in it I have represented the contrast, in our present state of society, between the actual and the ideal in all that relates to love and marriage. The book aroused a storm of anger in Norway when it appeared—the reason for which you will find explained in my preface to the second edition, which is the one sent you. *Peer Gynt* is the antithesis of *Brand*; many consider it my best book. I do not know how you will like it. It is wild and formless, written without regard to consequences—as I only dare to write far away from home; it came into being during my stay on the island of Ischia and in Sorrento in the summer of 1867.

You ask for some information about recent Norwegian literature. I should with pleasure have told you what I know about it, if I had not been fortunate enough to find an abler substitute. A friend of mine, one of the masters at the Cathedral School in Christiania, Jakob Lökke, is staying in London at present. I have written requesting him to call on you and give you the desired information. Mr. Lökke has a thorough acquaintance with our literature, and is a competent judge of it; I know no one to whom I could entrust the task with more confidence. Your article in *The Spectator* on my *Poems* has been translated in the Scandinavian papers; and I am certain that my many friends at home share my feeling of gratitude to you for the friendly and flattering manner in which you have written in your own country of me and my work.

Hoping that the books sent you from Copenhagen will not lessen your regard for me, I remain, dear Sir—Yours respectfully and gratefully,     HENRIK IBSEN.

94.

*To* GEORGE BRANDES.

DRESDEN, 31st *May* 1872.

DEAR BRANDES,—Thank you for your note. I have read your *Explanation and Vindication* with great interest; but I cannot free myself from the impression to which I gave utterance before I knew that such a book was to appear, namely, that you do the majority of your opponents far too much honour by condescending to make a reply.[1] Your cause is the cause of the future, and will defend itself, if we only give it time.

Last time I wrote in such haste, and was so taken up by the one great subject, that I entirely forgot to thank you for your review of my *Poems.* It came to me like a letter from a friend, and as such I should have answered it. Now it is too late, and I shall say nothing until we meet.

But how and where will it be possible for us to meet this

[1] In the spring of 1872 Brandes published a polemical pamphlet entitled: *Explanation and Vindication : Criticism Criticised.*

summer? I cannot come to Copenhagen; in fact it will hardly be possible for me to leave Dresden. But have you no intention of coming south and establishing connections in Germany? Do you not think of translating your Lectures? In a letter which I received a few days ago, Adolf Strodtmann calls you "den geistvollsten aller modernen Kritiker." I believe and know that you are not merely this, but also something much greater; and therefore I know, too, that you have not been sent into the world to work for Scandinavia alone. Come to Germany if you can!

It surprises me that you have not thought of giving lectures in Sweden. In certain respects the Swedes are a stage behind the other two Scandinavian nations in development; but this only results in their being nearer than us to what is coming; we have gone ahead of them, but it has been in a wrong direction.

I go on wrestling with *Julian.* I have the greatest desire to open myself to you on the subject of this play; but I feel that I cannot do so without running the risk of being misunderstood.

I hope my last letter has reached you. Is it your intention to have your new Lectures printed at once?

I have many things to write about; but as long as I have some hope of meeting you soon, I shall let them wait. Write soon!—Yours ever,

HENRIK IBSEN.

## 95.

### *To* MICHAEL BIRKELAND.

DRESDEN, 30*th June* 1872.

DEAR FRIEND,—Please accept my thanks for your last letters, and pardon me for not having answered them sooner. To-day only a few words.

I sent my poem to the Festival Committee on the 27th. I

hope there is nothing in it likely to give offence. I shall be very grateful to you if you will see to the proof-reading being perfectly done. If time permitted I should very much like to see a revised proof; but I know it is impossible. I rely upon you.

I am glad that Mr. M. Beyer has been chosen to read the poem at Haugesund; I am personally acquainted with him, and know that he has the necessary qualifications for the task. They will surely be able to find a capable man in Christiania also—not an actor, for any sake![1]

You must yourself decide between which speeches the poem is to be read. I do not think there is anything in it to make the placing of it a difficult matter. I agree with you that it ought previously to be submitted to Prince Oscar.

I am not at all surprised by the way in which the grants have been distributed. I originally applied for the Schäffer Bequest, but afterwards asked that my application might also be considered at the time of the distribution of the funds for enabling artists and scientists to travel abroad.[2] You may rest assured that I do not feel my honour affected in the least; it is not in the power of the Norwegian Ecclesiastical Department to dishonour me. But I cannot agree with you in thinking that the reason I have been left out is that I have been so long abroad already. One of my more fortunate fellow-applicants, Mr. Stenersen (a near relative of Statsraad Riddervold), has also lived abroad for a long time, and has already had at least one grant. Mr. Jonas Lie has, in the course of a little over a year, received four different grants, amounting in all to 1050 specie-dollars. The explanation is quite simple: Mr. Lie belongs

[1] For the celebration of the thousandth anniversary of Norway's existence as a united kingdom, Ibsen wrote a poem, which was read at the festival at Haugesund (July 18, 1872), not, indeed, at the unveiling of the memorial statue by Prince Oscar (the present King of Sweden) but at the banquet afterwards. At the celebrations in Christiania on the same day it was not read aloud at all, but copies of it were distributed. It contained too many sentiments unacceptable to the party aiming at national independence.

[2] For Ibsen's application, see Letter 87.

to the party which must not be offended, and I to the party for which one must not do anything "for fear of rousing ill-feeling." I should like very much to write publicly about the mean behaviour of our Government; but as I regard Statsraad Riddervold as my personal enemy, I must, of course, as a matter of honour, refrain from doing so.

You would do me a great service if you could procure a copy of *Lady Inger of Östraat* and send it to me by post. But, for certain reasons, let no one know about this.

The school holidays begin on the 20th of July, and about that time we leave here, to spend six weeks at Gastein or some other watering-place in the Tyrol. My literary work will not suffer; I take all my paraphernalia with me; and the trip is nothing but a pleasure trip. I have quite determined to come home next year. Kindest remembrances to your family.— Yours ever, HENRIK IBSEN.

## 96.

### *To* GEORGE BRANDES.

BERCHTESGADEN, BAVARIA, 23rd *July* 1872.

DEAR BRANDES,—When you know the reason of it, you will not take my long silence amiss; this time, for once, I am really blameless.

The fact is, I have been roaming about in Bohemia and other parts of Austria. We are settling down at last here in the Bavarian Highlands, where I have taken quarters for four or five weeks. Here I found your letter.

Nothing you wrote in previous letters had suggested to me the possibility of your coming to Dresden in summer; otherwise you may be sure I should have arranged my plans differently. But the summer is long down here, and, if you come in September, you will be certain to see me, and will be received with open arms.

16

Far from feeling alarmed at the idea of contributing to your periodical, I have already made a list of various subjects connected with present-day politics, literature, etc., on which I have a desire to express my opinions. I think of doing so in the form of rhymed letters, which I imagine would suit your purpose. They would, in a manner, form my confession of faith. They would be no direct assistance to you and your cause; but, dear Brandes, it is the only way in which I can collaborate. I must confine myself to that which is my own, to that around which all my thoughts circle. My domain is not an extensive one, but within it I do my best. Now don't be discovering egoism in this, I beg of you.

I do not know as yet how soon I can begin to these letters; that monster, *Julian*, still has such a grip of me that I cannot escape from him. But we can enter into further particulars later—best of all, when we meet. I do not shrink in the least from being regarded as a partisan. I do not really understand how it comes that I am considered to belong to no party.

I have long thought that you would need an organ of your own; but it would never have occurred to me that you could need it, as you say you do, "to live by." Is it possible that Denmark has no vacant place for you? One cannot find fault with the old gentlemen for wanting to keep you out. But who is there that would dare to take the appointment when you have been passed over? Who could exhibit himself as the favoured one without sinking into the earth with shame at the thought of the comparison? This is what I cannot understand.

I am glad to hear that your Lectures are to be published in German. The extracts from them which have already been translated in *Ueber Land und Meer* have roused much attention. I heard them discussed in the Literary Society of Dresden. Come to Germany! It is abroad that we Scandinavians must win our battles; a victory in Germany, and you will have the upper-hand at home.—Hoping to see you again soon, I am, Yours ever, HENRIK IBSEN.

97.

*To* FREDERIK HEGEL.

BERCHTESGADEN, IN BAVARIA, 8*th August* 1872

DEAR MR. HEGEL,—I do not remember if I told you in my last letter that I was to be off soon to the Tyrol? At all events, we are now here, in this lovely district, where we spent the summer of 1868 on our way from Italy. We intend to stay until the end of this month.

I write to you to-day because I am beginning to run short of money. Will you be so very kind as to send me 150 Thalers Prussian. As we have difficulty in changing large notes here, it will be a favour if you can let me have small ones—10 to 20 Thalers at most. I left my account-book in Dresden, so I am not certain that I have any right to draw on you for so large an amount; but I know you will oblige me and, at any rate, our account will soon be balanced again.

I am glad to be able to tell you that I have finished the second part of the trilogy. Part First, *Julian and the Philosophers*, a play in three acts, will come to about one hundred printed pages; Part Second (of which I am now making a fair-copy), *Julian's Apostasy*, a play in three acts, is about the same length. The third play, *Julian on the Imperial Throne*, will be in five acts. I have done so much in preparation for it, that I shall be able to write it much faster than the others. What is already finished forms a complete work in itself, and could well be published separately; but for the sake of the general impression I think it advisable that all three plays should appear at the same time. If you should think differently, I trust to your letting me know.

I wonder if you have read a series of essays published by Adolf Strodtmann in the *Hamburger Correspondenz*, on modern Danish-Norwegian literature. Literary people in Germany have told me that the Danish papers (the *Fædreland* was the particular one named) have made reply to these friendly and flattering articles, declaring them to be incorrect and misleading. Unless my informants were mistaken, I should be exceedingly obliged to you if you could, *when convenient*, procure for me the Danish newspapers in which the criticisms appeared.

I have had a long letter from my old friend, Jonas Lie; but he does not tell me if he is engaged on any new work. I wrote a poem on the occasion of our thousandth anniversary. At the request of the Committee, I placed it at their disposal; but in the end, the cowardly fellows dared not have it read! Worthy descendants of the old hero-king!

I suppose the Exhibition is at its best now, and Copenhagen overcrowded with strangers? If you have the opportunity, I wish you would remember me to Brandes; also to P. Hansen, and all other good friends. Kindest regards to you and your son,—Ever yours sincerely,

HENRIK IBSEN.

*P.S.*—My address is as above, simply: Berchtesgaden, in Bavaria.

98

*To* JOHAN HERMAN THORESEN.

DRESDEN, 27th September 1872.

DEAR BROTHER-IN-LAW,—Thank you for the last remittance sent. I am, as usual, late in sending an acknowledgment. From my Government pay for the third quarter, please deduct what you have kindly laid out for me; and send me a post-office order for the rest.

Our holiday in the Tyrol this summer was a particularly pleasant one in every respect. Since our return we have been unusually sociable, as so many Scandinavians have been in

Dresden.  Goldschmidt and G. Brandes came on purpose to see us.  The motive of the majority of the Norwegians who call on us, I suspect to be curiosity.  I cannot reckon on any true sympathy from my countrymen when I think of the typical Norwegian inconsiderateness with which I was treated last summer by the "Harald" Committee.

They ask me to write a poem to be read at Haugesund.  I write the poem.  They omit it from the Festival programme, and sell it like a hawker's ballad, without having as yet considered it necessary to offer me the slightest explanation of the remarkable proceeding.  If the reason for their rejection of the poem is that reference is made in it to the separatists of our day, then all I can say is that the cause of order, culture, and progress is at present in the hands of men who are incapable of furthering it and ensuring its victory.  And I shall regard it as my first duty, in my capacity of state-satirist, to represent this party in all its wretched weakness, with all its lack of courage and determination, and its absurdly naïve belief in the possibility of a peevish, passive resistance accomplishing anything at all in the face of a well-organised, reckless, antagonistic party.  In short, I should consider that I was doing a public service if I could make all those concerned ashamed of themselves.  I imagine that you do not entirely disagree with me; I take for granted that you will admit that the present situation at home is not so much the result of any great ability in the leaders of the Opposition, as of an absolutely indefensible cowardice, compliance, and spirit of compromise in nearly all of those whose task it ought to be to defend the foundations of our society.  This lack of inclination in individuals to place themselves personally in the breach, is our country's misfortune; they retreat foot by foot, they lose ground bit by bit.  This is what has brought us to the position we are in now; and it would require a superhuman effort of self-denial to let such material for epigrams and comedies slip through one's fingers.

In the meantime, however, I am too busy with *Emperor Julian*, which will probably be finished about Christmas.  Nor do I imagine there is any call for hurry in carrying out the above-mentioned plans; the conditions are hardly likely to improve very soon—if they did, that would be better than anything else. I often wonder what we may expect from our new King. A determined and fearless man in his position could accomplish a great deal; but it seems uncertain if he owns these qualifications. This much is certain, however, that if he is to accomplish anything useful, it will not be by the help of the present royal advisers. People who permit Jaabæk and Björnson to be at large, deserve to be shut up themselves.

We often think of Marie. I still consider that she acted inadvisedly in leaving Dresden. I do hope she will be successful in finding a tolerably satisfactory situation.[1]

The Falsens are well. I hear from them that the plan of making a soldier of Axel has come to nothing. This is only what might have been expected. So he stands now just where he did when he left Heyerdahl's factory—only that several hundreds have been uselessly thrown away.

And now I must stop for the present. Susanna and Sigurd send you their love.—Yours ever,

HENRIK IBSEN.

## 99.

### *To* EDMUND GOSSE.

DRESDEN, 14th October 1872.

DEAR MR. GOSSE,—It was to a new house in Dresden we came back from our summer outing in the Tyrol, and it has taken me a little time to settle down; but I must no longer postpone what is always a pleasant duty to me, namely, to write to you—especially as I have to thank you, which I now

---

[1] Marie Thoresen, Fru Ibsen's sister, had been for several years an inmate of Ibsen's house in Dresden. For the Falsens and Axel Thoresen, see Letter 22.

do heartily and sincerely, for fresh proofs of your interest in me, received at different times during these last months.

At Berchtesgaden I had the pleasure of receiving your friendly letter of the 1st of August, together with *The Spectator* containing your review of *Peer Gynt*. A better, clearer, and more sympathetic interpretation of my poem I could not desire. I only wish that the praise which you give it were fully merited. For your fault-finding I have no doubt there is reason ; I see some of the defects of the work myself now. In the long interval which has elapsed since I wrote it, I have got so far away from it that I am able to look back upon it as upon the work of a stranger.

I have also to thank you for the copy of *The Academy* containing the review of *The Pretenders*. The remarks which I have permitted myself to make on the review of *Peer Gynt* are equally applicable to your criticism of *The Pretenders*. One small correction, however, I must make: A. Munch's drama, *Duke Skule*, did not appear at the same time as *The Pretenders*, but a little later. And *The Pretenders* has all along enjoyed, both on the stage and with the reading public, a far greater measure of favour than *Duke Skule*. This, however, is a matter of no importance.

Then I had the pleasure, a few days ago, of receiving your excellent article on Norwegian poetry in *Fraser's Magazine*. Just as you have laid me personally under a great obligation by the two reviews, you have now, by this longer article, placed the whole Norwegian people under a debt of gratitude to you. I am certain that the Scandinavian press will understand and publicly recognise this; perhaps it has already done so.

I was glad to learn from your letter that you had enjoyed your stay in Copenhagen. I hope that your visit to Christiania has been an equally pleasant one, although it was not made at the most favourable season of the year. In the middle of summer many people whose acquaintance it might have interested you to make are out of town. I hope, however, that you saw our mutual friend, Mr. Lökke. I regret very much, on my own account, that circumstances forbade my visiting home this summer, and thus deprived me of the much-desired opportunity of making your acquaintance.

I work every day at *Julianus Apostata,* and hope to have the whole work finished by the end of the present year. As soon as the book is printed, I shall take the liberty of sending it to you. I hope that it may meet with your approval. It is a part of my own spiritual life which I am putting into this book; what I depict I have, under different conditions, gone through myself; and the historical subject chosen has a much more intimate connection with the movements of our own time than one might at first imagine. The establishment of such a connection I regard as imperative in any modern poetical treatment of such a remote subject, if it is to arouse interest at all.

And now, once again assuring you of my sincere and hearty gratitude, I must say farewell. Always, dear Mr. Gosse—Yours truly,

HENRIK IBSEN.

*P.S.*—I have forgotten to thank you more especially for your translation of the little poem in *Brand,* which seems to me most beautifully done.

### 100.

*To* LUDVIG DAAE.

DRESDEN, *4th February* 1873.

DEAR FRIEND,—In the certain hope that, in spite of my nine years' absence abroad, you have preserved a kindly remembrance of me, I am writing to draw a draft on the helpfulness which I have never failed to find among my old fellow-"Dutchmen."

It is, as you may suppose, your scholarship by which I wish

to benefit. My new large work is now so far advanced that within a fortnight I shall begin to make the fair-copy. Being, as you are aware, not much of a Greek scholar, I have, in drawing information from the original sources, only been able to make use of works written in Latin. But in these there exists a great confusion with regard to the manner of writing the Greek names. I wish, where it is possible, to use the Greek forms. Therefore allow me to ask you—

1. What are the Greek terminations of the names of persons which the Latin authors write with the terminations *us*, *eus*, and *ius*? Is there any regular rule by which I can tell how names ending thus in Latin were written in Greek?

2. Were the Greeks in the habit of Grecianising Latin names? And if so, according to what rules?

For instance: Did the Greeks write Basilios, Basileos, or Basileus? Is the name Cæsarius the same as Cæsarion? I particularly want to know whether the Grecians used to Grecianise the name Maximus? And if so, how? How is Libanius written in Greek? In short, dear friend, I want, if possible, a rule to go by.

Then I would like to know the farthest extreme to which I may go in the use of *k* for *c*. For instance, is it permissible to write *Kappadokia*, in the manner of those who have lately taken to writing *Kirke* for *Circe*, *Kybele*, etc.

These are very easy questions for you to answer; but now comes something more difficult. There exists a work by a certain Eunapius (Eunapios, eos?) on Maximus, the mystic. Neander quotes this book under the title, *Vita Maximi*, from which one might conclude that it was written in Latin. But this is not the case; it is written in Greek; and I have been unable to procure a translation. Can you give me a short account of the contents of the book, which I know is not a classical work? What I especially want are facts relating to the life and career of Maximus. Ammianus does not give many, and there are no other sources available to me.

Can you and will you help me in this matter? If so, please

let me hear from you soon. Within a fortnight, as I have already mentioned, I shall begin to despatch the fair-copy to Hegel. I will not say anything about my work now, except that I am confident that it will be my "Hauptwerk." It consists of two separate dramas, each in five acts, and makes a book of over four hundred pages.

Forgive me for troubling you with these questions. Time does not permit me to write about many other things which I should like to discuss with you. No more to-day, except a greeting to all my friends; I hope I may be permitted to count Mrs. Daae among them. If you should see Principal Gjertsen, remember me cordially to him, and tell him that I will soon write to him. Remember me also to Lökke, Birkeland, Bachke, Tygh, and all other good "Dutchmen."—Your sincere friend,

HENRIK IBSEN.

My address is Wettiner-Strasse No. 22, 2 Etage.


### 101.

*To* FREDERIK HEGEL.

DRESDEN, *6th February* 1873.

DEAR MR. HEGEL,—I have the great pleasure of being able to inform you that my long work is finished—and more to my satisfaction than any of my earlier works. The title of the book is, *Emperor and Galilean: a World-Drama in Two Parts*. Part First is *Cæsar's Apostasy*, a play in five acts (170 pages); Part Second is *Emperor Julian*, a play in five acts (252 pages). Do not let the title "World-Drama" alarm you! In form it is an imitation of "folkedrama, familjedrama, nationaldrama," etc. And the play's range of subject entitles it to the appellation.

Owing to the manner in which my idea has developed

during the process of composition, I shall be obliged to re-copy the first play. It will be no longer, however, than it is now; on the contrary, I hope to shorten it by about twenty pages, so that the whole will come to four hundred. (Each of my pages is equivalent to about one printed page).

In a week from now I shall begin the re-copying. Thereafter I shall send you an instalment of forty-eight pages every week; this is at the rate of seven pages per day, which I ought to be able to accomplish. The second play could quite well go into the hands of the printers as it is; but if you are in no hurry to publish, I will, to make certain, copy it also.

This drama has been a Herculean labour—not the writing of it—that has been easy, but because of the trouble it has cost me to revivify in my own mind an age so remote from our own and so little akin to it. I am very glad to see, from the letter before your last, that there is the prospect of a good sale; for several years of my life have been given to this book. I venture to predict that it is one from which both of us will derive satisfaction.

Please decide the time of publication yourself. The reason why I do not at once begin re-copying, is that I have had to consult a learned friend in Christiania as to the proper manner of writing certain Greek names. I only found out a few days ago that these have been corrupted in the Latin works from which I have drawn my facts.

My best thanks for the 150 Thalers enclosed in your letter of the 26th of November; also for the very valuable package of books received at Christmas.

It was a great and unexpected pleasure to learn that new editions of *Brand* and *Love's Comedy* are called for. The former may be issued unchanged; in the latter, I am correcting the orthography and a few details. I devote my evenings to this. During the summer I shall re-write *Lady Inger of Östraat* entirely; it will then be one of my best books. If you can let me have a copy of it, I shall be very much obliged to you. *The Pretenders* does not require many alterations. I think that these two books may be issued to advantage in the wake of the big new work.[1']

I have still a favour to ask. I have, in the Savings Bank and with you, about 49 Rix-dollars. Will you advance what is needed to make up 150 Thalers Prussian, and send that sum to me? From the Christiania Theatre having postponed the production of *Love's Comedy*, I have not received money which I expected, and of which I am in want. Do not take my asking this amiss! It is a case of necessity. With kindest regards to your son and yourself,—Yours most sincerely,

HENRIK IBSEN.

102.

*To* EDMUND GOSSE.

DRESDEN, 20*th February* 1873.

DEAR MR. GOSSE,—You no doubt expected, and with good reason, that, after receiving not only a kind, friendly letter, but the most welcome and valuable New-Year's gift you could have sent me, I would immediately have written you at least a few lines.

There are various reasons for my not having done so. To begin with, I wanted to send you, not a few lines, but a long letter. I had, however, literally not a spare hour between the 21st of November and the 16th of February. During that period I completed my new dramatic work, which is now going to press, and which will appear in May.

The whole work will make a book of over four hundred

---

[1] The third edition of *Love's Comedy* was published in June 1873. It was acted for the first time at the Christiania Theatre in November of the same year. The second edition of *The Pretenders* was published at Copenhagen in December 1873, the seventh edition of *Brand* in April 1874, and the second (revised) edition of *Lady Inger* in December 1874.

pages. It is called *Emperor and Galilean: a World-Drama*, and is in two parts: I. *Cæsar's Apostasy*, a play in five acts; II. *Emperor Julian*, a play in five acts. It is on the latter play that I have been engaged uninterruptedly during the above-mentioned period. Now I am working busily every day at the fair-copy. I am supposed to send off three printed sheets every week to Copenhagen, and, as I submit the language to very strict criticism, my time is well filled up. I am writing this late at night, so kindly excuse any confusedness.

When the book is ready, it shall be sent to you at once. No one shall read it before you!—In my facts I have adhered strictly to history. I have seen everything happen, as it were, before my own eyes; and I have represented it as I saw it. And yet there is a great deal of self-analysis in the book.

It is very natural that I should send it first to you, for I value your criticism more than that of any of my other friends—and this because of the real, intimate, poetic under-standing revealed in everything that you have been good enough to write about me.

How can I sufficiently thank you for your last exhaustive article! I shall not attempt to do so; I will only say to you that it made me very happy. The translations from *Love's Comedy* and *Peer Gynt* are excellent; I do not know of any-thing in them that I could wish different.

I have to thank you, too, and that very heartily, for the photograph you sent me. I shall have much pleasure in sending you mine in return. At the present moment I do not possess one, but as soon as I have a morning hour to spare, I shall employ it in paying a visit to my photographer. One of the reasons why I have so long put off writing to you is that I have not as yet been able to do this.

I should like to tell you more about my work, but time does not permit of my doing so at present. I hope and trust, how-ever, that the book will not in any way tend to alter the good opinion you are kind enough to entertain of me.

Begging you to continue, in spite of my remissness, to show me the same favour as heretofore,—I remain, Yours most sincerely,　　　　　　　　　　　　　　　　HENRIK IBSEN.


### 103.

#### To LUDVIG DAAE.

DRESDEN, 23rd *February* 1873.

DEAR FRIEND,—I felt certain that I was applying to the right man when I applied to you; and the promptitude and carefulness with which you answered my questions showed that I had been right.

I myself, however, had not been explicit enough. I forgot to mention something important. I certainly did wish to know the correct Greek forms of the names, only it was not for the purpose of employing these forms, but to help me to decide how far I may lawfully proceed in "Scandinavising" them. I am aiming at a certain conformity, at preventing any awkward clashing of names. As I am using the abridged, naturalised Scandinavian forms, Julian, Gregor, etc., I cannot employ the pure Greek form, Basileios. Since the Romans changed this name into Basilius, may not I change it into Basilios? What makes this the more desirable is that the name (in the play) is constantly in juxtaposition with the name of the man's birthplace: Cæsaræa, a word with the spelling of which I dare not tamper, because the Roman title Cæsar occurs so often in the book.

And now, dear friend, you know what my standpoint is; from the philological point of view it may be a wrong one, but it is, I believe, justified by my purpose. What I wish to avoid, as something too unfamiliar, are the Greek diphthongs, *ai*, *ei* and *oi*. For instance, I should like to write Ædesios, Basilios, Œdipos.

May I write *Cæsarios*, or was the man (a brother of Gregory of Nazianz) called *Cæsarion*? The letter C in this name I dare not change to K, because of the reasons given above. May I write: Emperor *Konstanzios*? Was the city called *Pergamon*? Was the Dog-Star called *Sirios*? Is *Hilarion* the proper Greek form?

If in the above there should be anything too absurdly barbarous, then do me the kindness to send Hegel the necessary corrections; but no more, please, than *are* necessary; for I consider it of great importance to hold fast to my principle, providing it is possible to justify it by subtle arguments.

So Eunapios wrote his book in Latin, after all. My bookseller assured me that it was a Greek book. I am glad to see that the biography contains nothing that conflicts with what I had read before, and made use of.

The work which I am now bringing out will be my chief work. It is entitled *Emperor and Galilean*, and consists of: 1. *Cæsar's Apostasy*, 2. *Emperor Julian*. Each of these parts is a long, five-act drama. The play deals with a struggle between two irreconcilable powers in the life of the world—a struggle which will always repeat itself; and because of this universality, I call the book "A World-Drama." In the character of Julian, however, as in most of what I have written in my riper years, there is much more of my own inner life than I care to acknowledge to the public. But at the same time the work is an entirely realistic work. I have seen the characters before my eyes in the light of their age—and I hope that my readers will do the same.

Many thanks for the little work on Holberg. It has been a great delight to us to read it; and we shall read it over and over again. I need hardly tell you that we have read all your articles in the *Morgenblad* with eagerness and pleasure.

I hope that my message of thanks for your help in the Jensen matter reached you through the person to whom it was entrusted.

I am writing this late at night, as my whole day is taken up with copying. Good-bye! I shall never forget your readiness to help me in this matter.—Your faithful friend,

HENRIK IBSEN.

104.

*To* GEORGE BRANDES.

DRESDEN, 30*th April* 1873.

DEAR BRANDES,—You certainly have good cause to complain of my negligence in letter-writing; but the fact is that my pen has scarcely been out of my hand since we saw each other last, except whilst I have eaten and slept. This must serve as my excuse.

My best thanks for the books. I have read *Ladislaus Bolski* with great interest, although I must say that the description you gave me of the contents of the book made even more impression upon me than the reading of the book itself.[1]

But now as to Stuart Mill's book![2] I do not know whether I ought to express my opinion on a subject in which I am not an expert. Yet, when I remember that there are authors who write on philosophy without knowing Hegel, or without even a general knowledge of German scholarship, many things seem to me permissible. I must honestly confess that I cannot in the least conceive of any advancement or any future in the Stuart Mill direction. I cannot understand your taking the trouble to translate this work, the sage-like philistinism of which suggests Cicero and Seneca. I am convinced that you could have written a ten times better book yourself in half of the time the translation must have taken you. I also believe that you do Stuart Mill gross injustice when you doubt the truth of his assertion that he got all his ideas from his wife.

You once remarked, when we were talking on the subject, that whereas German philosophy set itself the task of defining the meaning of things, English philosophy concerned itself with

[1] The book here referred to is a Danish translation of Victor Cherbuliez's *L'aventure de Ladislas Bolski*, published in 1872, with a preface by George Brandes.

[2] Brandes published, in 1872, a translation of John Stuart Mill's *Utilitarianism*.

showing the laws of things. This remark made me desirous of reading something of what the English philosophers have written; but it does not seem to me that Stuart Mill has accomplished what, according to you, was his task. "Things" are surely not all kinds of fortuitous occurrences. A great deal of acumen may be contained in such a work; but if this is science, then *The Ethics of Christianity*[1] is also a scientific work.

I dare not enter into this subject further in writing; but some day, in conversation, I hope to defend my opinion.

I am looking forward with great pleasure to your book on the German Romantic School,[2] and with no less to meeting you again. But where are we to meet? I cannot possibly go to Munich this summer. Can you not travel *viâ* Dresden? About the middle of June I go to Vienna, to remain there until the end of July. If you can arrange your plans to fit in with this, I trust you will do so.

Our mutual friend, Adolf Strodtmann, has taken my poem, "The Signals of the North," amiss. In the preface to his book he called it a "Hohngedicht" (poem of scorn) directed against Germany. I wrote to him on the subject; but as he chose to remark, in his answer to my letter, that he had not imagined I wished them to remain ignorant in Germany of what I wrote in the Danish papers, I have had nothing further to say to him. Of course I have nothing against their knowing in Germany what I write in Denmark; but what I must protest against is the false interpretation of what I write. The poem is scornful, that is true; but it is not directed against Germany. There is too much in our own countries deserving of scorn and derision for me to go out of my way to deride the Germans. Now, no more to-day on the subject of Strodtmann's book, though I shall have a good deal to say to you about it when we meet.

Come soon! I look forward with joy to having you here

---

[1] *Den christelige Ethik*, a work by H. L. Martensen, a Danish bishop.

[2] *The Romantic School in Germany*, vol. ii. of "Main Currents in Nineteenth Century Literature."

in spite of all our differences of opinion. At all events, let me hear from you. I promise you to be more punctual in answering, since I have now much more time at my disposal.

With kindest regards from my wife and myself,—Yours ever,

HENRIK IBSEN.

### 105.

### *To* FREDERIK HEGEL.

PILLNITZ, near DRESDEN, 8*th August* 1873.

DEAR MR. HEGEL,—Do not take it amiss that I have put off acknowledging the receipt of your kind letter of the 14th of last month, with its enclosure of 75 Thalers, until my return from Vienna. I have also to thank you for your kindness in sending me the beautiful ribbon of my Order. I am certain I could not have got anything like it here. My being made a Knight of St. Olaf at the time of the coronation was a great surprise to me, as I had not written anything for the occasion, or been asked to do so. This mark of attention shown me by the King and the Government would have been very much more acceptable to me if Björnson had received the same; but, as you know, he himself has made anything of the kind impossible, at least for the present.

I am very glad indeed to hear that you were pleased with your stay in Norway. I hope that you will see more of the country next time; you do not make acquaintance with what is magnificent in Norwegian scenery until you find your way to the high mountains and the country to the west of these.

I have followed the proceedings of the Publishers' Congress with interest in the newspapers; I agree with you in thinking that no particularly valuable determination has been arrived at; but I also believe, like you, that the personal intercourse of the members must have been beneficial in many ways.[1]

[1] The third Congress of Scandinavian Publishers met in Christiania in July 1873.

My work as a juror at the Vienna Exhibition was extremely fatiguing, although very interesting; I came home more exhausted than I have ever felt before, and did not recover until we came out here to the fresh forest air. What gave me great pleasure in Vienna was that I was able to be of some service to Denmark. The Danish juror, Theophil Hansen, devoted his whole attention to the architecture section, of which he was the president, but in which Denmark had no exhibitors. He did not even attend the jury meetings of the painting and sculpture sections. Therefore the Danish General Commissioner appointed me to represent Denmark also in these sections; and I was fortunate enough to secure nine medals for the Danish artists. I need not assure you that I took as great pleasure in these as in the nine Norwegian medals.

We shall probably remain here in Pillnitz, an hour by steamer from Dresden, till the end of this month, or until the epidemic of cholera in Dresden is at an end. I am going to set myself seriously to the task of re-writing *Lady Inger*. It would interest me to know if you heard anything when you were in Norway about the law-suit regarding this play and *The Pretenders*. I have heard nothing myself for a long time; but there cannot possibly be any doubt as to the result.

I am glad that the printing of the new book progresses rapidly. We shall not have to wait many weeks for it, I hope. With kindest regards to yourself and your son, believe me—Yours most sincerely,

HENRIK IBSEN.

106.

To THE EDITOR OF THE "MORGENBLAD."

VIENNA, 23rd *August* 1873.

. . . . . . . .

Official information regarding the awards of prizes will probably reach you about the same time as this letter. It

is not conceivable that the decisions arrived at by our jury
should have been altered by the Council of Presidents. This
council, according to Article No. 76, § XII. has only the power
to decide in regard to *diplômes d'honneur*, and, according to
the same Article, § XI. the jury has the right of final decision
as regards all other awards.

. . . . . . . .

Of the medals awarded for painting, Austria received 81,
Germany 152, Hungary 14, France 138, Switzerland 26,
Belgium 76, Holland 24, Denmark 9, Norway 9, Sweden 9,
Spain 14, Greece 2, America 2, Italy 48, England 29, Russia 29.
The countries are mentioned in the order in which their exhibits
were considered.

I could easily produce a variety of statistics for purposes of
comparison, but no comparison of figures would give any real
insight into the international art-situation. It is of no use
doing what several newspaper correspondents have done, that
is, comparing the number of medals awarded to the various
countries with the number of pictures exhibited by each
country; for, while the painters of some countries are, generally
speaking, represented by one picture each, other countries have
sent several pictures by each painter exhibiting; but only one
medal is obtainable by each artist, however many pictures
he shows. Nor would a comparison of the medals with the
number of painters of each country exhibiting, give a correct
idea of the comparative artistic level on which the different
countries at present stand. Many other circumstances have to
be taken into consideration. For instance, some countries have
debarred their best artists from competing by appointing them
jurors, whilst the jurors of other countries have been selected
exclusively from non-artistic professions. And there is another
important consideration. One of the rules provided that medals
were to be awarded only to living artists, and to them only for
pictures painted since 1863. Now, some countries, and notably
England, paid no attention to this rule; and the result as regards
the English exhibit was that, in spite of its being composed

almost entirely of masterpieces, it was awarded only a comparatively small number of medals.

We must also take into account the varying degree of strictness shown by the committees at home in accepting paintings offered for exhibition. In some countries they seem to have accepted almost everything that was offered, whilst in others, especially in Russia and Belgium, they took only works which they believed had some chance of receiving prizes. In a combination of these circumstances we must seek the explanation of the fact that Belgium, for instance, received, in proportion to the number of its exhibits, 50 per cent. more medals than France. That the comparative statistics do not represent the true relative position of the two countries as regards art, will be apparent to every one acquainted with the matter.

In spite of these incongruities, which were to some extent inevitable, it is certain that the present International Art Exhibition in Vienna offers very great advantages for the study of the civilisation of the present age. It will, more especially, be of great assistance in correcting certain erroneous opinions, and removing certain prejudices, which have been in force up to the present. I refer, in the first instance, to the prevalent belief that the Slavonic race is taking little or no part in the great common work of civilisation. The acquaintance which Europe has made during these last years with the literature of Russia should have invalidated such a theory, but, supposing this not to have yet happened, I am certain that the Vienna Exhibition will create a very different and more correct impression. It teaches us that in every domain of pictorial art, Russia comes up to the highest standard of the period. Refreshingly and vigorously national in their conceptions, her best artists are unsurpassed in the technical qualities of their work; and I am not allowing myself to be led astray by the striking effect of the unusual subjects, when I maintain that Russia has a school of painting equal to that of Germany, France, or any other country.

Something to the same effect may be safely maintained of

Hungary, in as far, at least, as figure-painting is concerned. The Hungarian painters have fortunately been able to resist the temptation presented to able colourists by a showy national costume. Nowhere in the Hungarian section does one come upon pictures that have been painted with the object of effectively grouping contrasting colours in dress materials, ornaments, and the like.

I have dwelt chiefly on the painting department, because it is the one of most interest to us. I believe we are worthily represented in it, even though some of our exhibitors have not sent their best pictures. Our younger painters, able as they may be, would learn a great deal by a visit to Vienna; and it would be doing a great and valuable service to the art of our country if by some means or other we could enable one or two of them to go there. As far as I know, there are at present no grants available; but it has occurred to me that it might be possible for the art societies in Christiania and other towns to help by ordering pictures and paying for them in advance, with the stipulation that at least a part of the money should be used by the artists in visiting Vienna. Who knows but that, if this suggestion were made public, some of our rich men might offer assistance ?

## 107.

### To George Brandes.

Dresden, *8th September* 1873.

Dear Brandes,—It is exactly a year since we were going about together here in Dresden; and now that I have moved into my winter quarters again, after a rambling, restless summer, I think every day of the time last year when you brought life and variety into our solitude. So, as I am thinking of you, I will write you a few lines, to find out at least where and how you are, for I am ignorant on both these points.

First of all, I must clear up a misunderstanding, or whatever it ought to be called. In the month of July you were here with your brother and sister-in-law. Your sister-in-law was kind enough to call upon us, with Mrs. Falsen; afterwards, according to Mrs. Falsen, you expressed surprise that my wife "*would not receive*" you! My wife requests me to tell you that such a supposition on your part must be the result of a misunderstanding. She expected both you and your brother, but you did not come. I do not know what you may have been told; but the whole affair is not inexplicable to me; for, during the latter part of your previous visit to Dresden, some one here was evidently anxiously on the watch lest you should be too much with us, and we should have too much undisturbed, intimate intercourse. You are rather free-spoken, dear Brandes, and it really looks as if some one dreaded this propensity of yours; I shall not say for what reason.

I write all this because I want you to know that you have been misled; and because in us you have real friends, not mere acquaintances of the kind who are cordial or cold according to the circumstances.

I spent several months in Vienna this summer as a member of the Art Jury. Afterwards I was for some weeks in the country near here. Neither in Vienna nor in the country had I the opportunity of reading our newspapers at all regularly, and my correspondence with Denmark and Norway was purely on matters of business. So I have no idea what you are doing or where you are. Tell me, first of all, if anything is to come of your plan of a lengthy stay in Germany. There are no end of things I wish to discuss with you; but if it is to be done exhaustively, we must talk, not write. It seems to me as if many signs indicate that something new is in process of evolution. Or how else do you explain the craze in Renan's France for pilgrimages? Concerning this and much else I will not, however, write more, for fear of being misunderstood.

I expect my new book to come any day now. I am very anxious to know your opinion of it. I hear from Norway that

Björnson, though he cannot know anything about the book, has spoken of it as " atheism," adding that it was inevitable it should come to that with me. What the book is or is not, I have no desire to inquire into; I only know that I saw a fragment of the history of humanity plainly before my eyes, and that I tried to reproduce what I saw.

I hope that this letter will find you, wherever you may happen to be; if it does, please let me hear from you soon, unless you can and will give me the still greater pleasure of coming to see me.

Farewell for the present. I should like—if I may be per-mitted—to send my very kind regards to your brother.—Yours ever, HENRIK IBSEN.

*P.S.*—Please remember me also to Mr. Drachmann. He half thought of returning here. I should be glad if he made a long stay; for many reasons it would be agreeable to me to see more of him, and under less disturbed conditions than last time.

H. I.

### 108.

### *To* EDMUND GOSSE.

DRESDEN, 15th *October* 1873.

DEAR MR. GOSSE,—During this long interval, not a week has passed without my thinking of writing to you; but until to-day various reasons have prevented my carrying my intention into effect.

There have really been many hindrances. In the middle of June I had to go to Vienna, to act as the Norwegian represen-tative in the international art-jury of the Exhibition. This was extremely fatiguing work; it was not finished before the end of August; and since then, the publication of my new book has claimed all my time and all my thoughts.

This book is now finished; on Friday, the 17th inst., it will appear in all the Scandinavian countries. I have requested my publisher in Copenhagen to send you a copy immediately. It ought to reach you in a few days from now; please accept it in remembrance of one who will always think of you with gratitude and sincere attachment. I am very anxious to know what you think of the work. I will not say anything more about it myself; but it will be of great interest to me to hear your verdict.

Our mutual friend, Mr. Lökke, wrote to me in summer that you were ill then, or at least indisposed. I trust, however, that you have now quite recovered, and that you have once more resumed your duties at the British Museum.

I take the liberty of enclosing my photograph, as a slight return for the pleasure you gave me by sending me yours.

I trust that you will send me a few words before very long, to show me that you have not taken my long silence amiss. Many literary projects occupy my thoughts, but none of them have quite matured as yet. I shall, in all probability, go next summer to Norway, where I have not been for ten years. It will then be seen whether or not I can suit myself to the conditions of life at home. If not, then I shall go back to Rome again, probably for good. It often occurs to me that you, too, may perhaps be planning to revisit the Scandinavian countries, where you now have so many friends, and where there might be a possibility of our meeting.

Let the friendly feeling for me, which I hope you will always preserve, prompt you to send a few lines soon to—Yours most sincerely,

HENRIK IBSEN.

109.

*To* GEORGE BRANDES.

DRESDEN, 16*th October* 1873.

DEAR BRANDES,—In your last letter you express surprise **at** my not having written a single word about the second volume of your Lectures [*The Romantic School in Germany*], which you were kind enough to send me this summer. My answer is simply this, that when I heard I had not written about it, I was as surprised as you, for I was completely under the impression that I had done so, and that at length, shortly before my departure for Vienna. It appears that I must have forgotten to do it after all, and I entreat you to forgive my carelessness.

You seem to be in some uncertainty as to what impression the book has made upon me. Dear Brandes, if I had not been absolutely certain that you did not mean this seriously, I should have answered by return of post. I never doubted your being aware that the second volume must make the same impression upon me as the first. You know very well that I regard your work as epoch-making in our philosophy of life; and I feel certain that this will be generally acknowledged at home, even though a few years must pass before it is. You say that the papers in Denmark have killed the book with silence; but other Danes tell a different story. It may be the case that the papers have kept silent, but it is not the case that they have succeeded in killing the book by doing so. I can quite well understand that the second volume has not aroused the same storm as the first, for there is no such direct revolt in it against what is peculiarly our own; but this fact, if fact it be, gives no indication of the depth of the impression the book has made. There is no need, however, that an outsider should tell you all this; you are a sufficiently able critic to know it yourself. I have, to be quite honest, not felt that there was any necessity to address words of comfort to you. I can well understand your becoming despondent at times, surrounded as you are at home by all kinds of miserable narrow-mindedness; but then, I also know that there come great and beautiful moments, when you see with joyful certainty where right lies, and what is certain to come in time.

This is all I have to say to you. I do not feel myself called on to offer any criticism; criticism lies outside of my sphere; and mine would be valueless to you. You have in me a glad and grateful reader; that is all.

Proceed confidently with your work! It seems to me that the time is propitious. When we look back upon the history of Scandinavian development, it becomes apparent that we do not go forward simultaneously, and abreast, with the other European nations. These every now and then take a step forward without our discovering it. Europe comes upon us occasionally as a surprise. One of these surprises cannot now be far off. Then every one at home will see your book in the right light—and insist upon it that they have done so all along. The reaction will be instantaneous; the book will be accepted without probation.

When you receive these lines, *Emperor and Galilean* will probably be in your hands. The direction public affairs are taking abroad makes this work a more seasonable one than I myself had thought possible.

May I ask you to thank your brother for his purpose of calling on me in Vienna; I am very sorry that I did not meet him. It would be a great pleasure to me to see you or him here in Dresden.

Every good wish, dear friend, from — Your sincerely attached

HENRIK IBSEN.

### 110.

*To* EDMUND GOSSE.

DRESDEN, 15*th January* 1874.

DEAR MR. GOSSE,—You must think it very ungrateful of me to keep silence for so long, after receiving such a gift as you sent me towards the end of last year.   But I beg you to believe that you have been in my thoughts every day since.   The reason why I have not written sooner is, that I wanted to read your book first—and not merely read it through, but study it and assimilate its contents and spirit as completely as possible.[1]   This has taken time; for I have but an imperfect knowledge of the English language, which I have taught myself without assistance.

Allow me, now, to congratulate you upon the book in question, which will surely win a place of honour for you among the lyric poets of our day.   Only in the work of a very few of those now writing do I find anything resembling the refinement and beauty which distinguish these poems. And it seems to me that these are qualities which ought to be specially appreciated by the English, whose characteristic practical ability is blended in such a remarkable manner with a purity and nobility of the emotional nature and a generosity of sentiment which make the whole nation a nation of aristocrats—in the best sense of the word.

And allow me, in the second place, to thank you heartily for the friendly and flattering attention which you have shown me by inserting a special greeting to me among your poems. Would that I might soon have an opportunity of thanking you for this personally, and more warmly and satisfactorily than I can by writing.

I am greatly obliged to you for your kind review of my new drama.   There is only one remark in it about which I must say a word or two.   You are of opinion that the drama

---

[1] In 1873, Edmund Gosse published a collection of his poems, under the title, *On Viol and Flute*.

ought to have been written in verse, and that it would have gained by this. Here I must differ from you. The play is, as you must have observed, conceived in the most realistic style; the illusion I wished to produce was that of reality. I wished to produce the impression on the reader that what he was reading was something that had really happened. If I had employed verse, I should have counteracted my own intention and prevented the accomplishment of the task I had set myself. The many ordinary, insignificant characters whom I have intentionally introduced into the play would have become indistinct, and indistinguishable from one another, if I had allowed all of them to speak in one and the same rhythmical measure. We are no longer living in the days of Shakespeare. Among sculptors there is already talk of painting statues in the natural colours. Much can be said both for and against this. I have no desire to see the Venus of Milo painted, but I would rather see the head of a negro executed in black than in white marble. Speaking generally, the style must conform to the degree of ideality which pervades the representation. My new drama is no tragedy in the ancient acceptation; what I desired to depict were human beings, and therefore I would not let them talk the "language of the Gods."

I have a great deal more to say to you, both about this and other things; but I am always hoping for an opportunity of doing it by word of mouth. I shall, therefore, stop for to-day. Thanking you again most heartily, I remain—Yours very sincerely, HENRIK IBSEN.

## 111.

### *To* EDWARD GRIEG.

DRESDEN, 23rd *January* 1874.

DEAR MR. GRIEG,—My object in writing to you is to ask if you would care to co-operate with me in a certain undertaking.

It is my intention to arrange *Peer Gynt*—of which the

third edition is soon to appear—for performance on the stage. Will you compose the music which will be required? I will briefly indicate to you how I think of arranging the play.

The First Act is to be retained in full, with only a few abridgments of the dialogue. Peer Gynt's monologue on pages 23, 24, and 25, I wish to have treated either melodramatically, or in part as a recitative. The wedding-scene in the house (page 28) must, by means of a ballet, be made into something more than is in the book. For this purpose a special dance-melody will have to be composed, which is to be continued softly to the end of the Act.

In the Second Act, the musical treatment of the scene with the three Sæter girls, pages 57 to 60, must be left to the discretion of the composer—but there must be devilry in it! The monologue on pages 60–62 should, I think, be accompanied by chords, in melodramatic style, as also the scene between Peer and the Green-clad One, pages 63–66. There must also be some kind of accompaniment to the episodes in the Hall of the Old Man of the Dovrë; here, however, the speeches are to be considerably shortened. The scene with the Boyg, which is to be given in full, must also be accompanied by music; the Bird-Cries are to be sung; bell-ringing and psalm-singing are heard in the distance.

In the Third Act I need chords, but not many, for the scene between Peer, the Woman, and the Ugly Brat, pages 96–100; and I imagine that a soft accompaniment would be appropriate from the beginning of page 109 to the foot of page 112.

Almost the whole of the Fourth Act is to be omitted at the performance. In place of it I think there should be a great musical tone-picture, suggesting Peer Gynt's wandering all over the world; American, English, and French airs might occur as alternating and disappearing motives. The chorus of Anitra and the Girls, pages 144 and 145, is to be heard behind the curtain, in combination with the orchestra. During this music the curtain is raised, and there is seen, like a distant dream-picture, the scene described at the foot of page 164, in which Solveig, now a middle-aged woman, sits in the sunshine outside her house. After her song the curtain is again slowly lowered, the music continuing, but changing into a suggestion of the storm at sea with which the Fifth Act opens.

This Fifth Act, which at the performance will be called the Fourth Act or the Epilogue, must be considerably shortened. A musical accompaniment is needed from pages 195 to 199. The scenes on the capsized boat and in the churchyard are omitted. On page 221 Solveig sings, and the music continues, accompanying Peer Gynt's speeches, and changing into that required for the choruses, pages 222–225. The scenes with the Button-Moulder and the Old Man of the Dovrë are to be shortened. On page 254, the people on their way to church sing on the forest path; bell-ringing and distant psalm-singing are suggested in the music played during what follows. Then Solveig's song ends the play; and whilst the curtain is falling, the psalm-singing is heard again, nearer and stronger.

These are my ideas. Will you let me know if you are willing to undertake the task? If I receive a favourable answer from you, I shall at once write to the Management of the Christiania Theatre, sending along with my letter the revised and abridged text, to make sure, before we go any further, that our play will be performed. I intend to ask 400 specie-dollars for it, to be divided equally between us. I am certain that we may also count upon the play being produced in Copenhagen and Stockholm. But I shall be obliged by your keeping the matter secret at present. Please reply as soon as possible.—Yours most sincerely,

HENRIK IBSEN.

*P.S.*—My address here in Dresden is: Wettiner-Strasse, 22, 2. Etage.[1]

---

[1] *Peer Gynt*, with Grieg's music, was performed at the Christiania Theatre for the first time on the 24th of February 1876. The abridgment was carried out, in some respects, on a different plan from that proposed by Ibsen.

112.

*To* LUDVIG JOSEPHSON.

DRESDEN, *6th February* 1874

DEAR MR. JOSEPHSON,—In view of the circumstance that my dramatic poem, *Peer Gynt,* is shortly to appear in a third edition, I have been occupying myself with it during the winter. I have made an *adaptation* of it, shorter than the original, which will be suitable for performance on the stage. This is arranged as a musical drama, and the necessary music will be composed by Mr. Edward Grieg, to whom I have written on the subject. I have explained to Mr. Grieg the plan by which I have been guided in making the adaptation, and he will, at my request, make this known to you.

Before I approach the Stockholm and Copenhagen Theatres in the matter, I wish to ask if the Christiania Theatre would care to make use of the play, and if, in that event, you would attach any importance to your theatre being the first to produce it?

I trust to your kindly sending me a provisional answer after you have talked with Mr. Grieg. Should this be favourable, I shall then send you a revised and abridged copy of the play. The music will be composed in the course of the summer; in the meantime the Theatre might be making the necessary scenic arrangements, and the play would thus be ready to appear at the most suitable moment of the coming theatrical season.

I am convinced that, under your skilful management, it will be very effective on the stage, especially when it is accompanied by good music. As, however, it is of importance to both Mr. Grieg and myself to know for what theatre, in the first instance, we are working, I trust to your communicating with me as soon as you have sufficiently looked into the matter. If the idea as a whole appeals to you, details can be arranged afterwards; I. shall be pleased to pay attention to any suggestion you may make.—Yours most sincerely,

HENRIK IBSEN.[1]

*P.S.*—It gave me much pleasure to receive the friendly note you sent me by your nephew in autumn; I hope he delivered my message of thanks for it. Unfortunately I was suffering from a severe cold at the time he was here, so that it was absolutely impossible for me to be of any use to him. Of the other young artist about whom he spoke to me, and who, I believe, was also the bearer of a letter from you to me, I have heard nothing. My kindest regards, please, to the other Directors.

H. I.

113.

*To* GEORGE BRANDES.

DRESDEN, 20*th April* 1874.

DEAR BRANDES,—I certainly did not deserve to be remembered by you on my birthday and to be rejoiced by a kind letter, for which I thank you with all my heart. Rest assured that my thoughts are with you more frequently than you would suppose from my negligence in the matter of letter-writing.

The reason why I did not answer your previous letter, on the subject of the proposed periodical, was that I put off too much

---

[1] Ludvig Josephson (1832–1899), a Swedish theatrical manager and play-writer, had, in spite of the opposition of the Norwegian National party, been appointed "artistic director" of the Christiania Theatre in 1873. Hartvig Lassen (1824–1897), a well-known Norwegian literary man, had been "Æstetisk Consulent" since 1872. Josephson's production of *Love's Comedy* in 1873 had been a great success, and this encouraged Ibsen to propose the production of *Peer Gynt*, which was even more successful. In 1876, the year of its first appearance on the stage, it was performed thirty-seven times.

18

time considering what and how I should answer. You see, it
became more and more evident to me that it was not a mere
question of "yes" or "no"; if I was to be honest—and such
was my intention—I had much more to say; but it seemed to
me that it could be done best by word of mouth, and therefore I
waited, in the hope of seeing you soon again here. As it now
seems unlikely that this hope is to be realised, I shall delay no
longer in expressing my views on the subject. Please do not
take my frankness amiss!

It was your and your brother's plan to publish a " magazine."
But what kind—a *Danish* or a *Scandinavian* magazine? The
Danish literary men like to have subscribers and readers in all
the Scandinavian countries; but they live and move, and feel
only in the atmosphere of Copenhagen. All the discussions
in your periodicals and daily press refer to what is going on
*with you*; only your own, indeed, strictly speaking only the
Copenhagen disputes in matters of philosophy, politics, etc., seem
to you to be of any importance; in fact, you really know about
no other, as far as Scandinavia is concerned—though you are
remarkably well-informed as regards foreign countries. The
Danes regard it as almost an act of grace to acknowledge that
what is peculiarly Norwegian has the right to express itself in
literature; if they are in a friendly mood, they make excuses; if in
a hostile, they sneer; but the supposition always is that Denmark
sets the standard. What do the Copenhagen people know about
our domestic affairs, about our politics, and about our politicians?
Nothing. We Norwegians, and a certain proportion of the
Swedes, know all about your matters; you hardly know anything of what is going on with us. The Copenhagen ignorance
of matters Scandinavian is so great that it can be compared with
nothing but the Copenhagen arrogance.

This is (compressed into a thousandth part of what I have to
say) the reason why the Copenhagen periodicals are unsuccessful.
Your population of two millions cannot support a periodical; if
it is to succeed, you must not, in your Copenhagen superiority,
overlook the four million Swedes, the two million Norwegians,

the one million of Finns, and the almost equally large Scandinavian population in America. This makes a public of about ten millions in all. Give up your Copenhagen particularism. Write for them all. Then I will join you. But, to tell the truth, I do not consider it worth while to address myself in literary style to the people who live within the ramparts and in the suburbs of Copenhagen.

I am quite aware that you yourself are on many points openly antagonistic to this "Copenhagenism"; nevertheless you are unconsciously affected by it; the whole first volume of your *Main Currents in Nineteenth Century Literature* is more an attack upon Copenhagen narrow-mindedness than upon the narrow-mindedness of Scandinavia generally; they are the Copenhagen theories in literature, philosophy, and art, which you assail; and it is this limitation of the range of his warfare which, it seems to me, an author with us, as elsewhere, must avoid, if he is to succeed.

All this, dear Brandes, I beg you to regard in the light of a friendly invitation to come down here, in order that we may make our war-plans together. You must not give up the idea of the periodical; but it is absolutely necessary that it should be established on a wider basis than former Danish periodicals, if it is to spread your ideas as widely as they deserve to be spread, and to secure you a care-free existence.

I shall not enter upon the many other things to-day; but think over what I have said, and write soon to—Your faithful friend,

HENRIK IBSEN.[1]

[1] George Brandes spent a few days with Ibsen in Dresden in June 1874.

114.

*To* FREDERIK HEGEL.

DRESDEN, 23*rd November* 1874.

DEAR MR. HEGEL,—In the first place I have to offer you my wife's and my own most sincere thanks for all your friendly attentions to her during her last sad visit to Copenhagen, and for the honour you showed us and our deceased relative by attending the funeral.[1]

Then I have to acknowledge and thank you for the 150 Thalers enclosed in your kind letter of October 25th, and for the sum given to my wife in Copenhagen.

I am obliged again to request you to send me 150 Thalers.

My wife brought me pleasant news from you with regard to *The League of Youth* and *Lady Inger*. Is it really true that the greater part of the new editions have already been sold in advance? The time of publication is favourable. I only hope that the needful supply of paper will not be too long in arriving. Of course the publication of *Lady Inger* must not be delayed until the play has been performed. The sooner it can be put on the market the better. I shall take the liberty of sending to you at the proper time the letters for the different theatrical managements.[2]

I was glad to learn that you have no objection to the book of *Poems* being enlarged to the extent of some thirty pages. Everything that you have to receive from me for this purpose will be ready and despatched about the end of February, or, if possible, still earlier.[3]

---

[1] Marie Thoresen, Fru Ibsen's sister, died at Copenhagen in 1874.

[2] The third edition of *The League of Youth* appeared in December 1874, at the same time as the new edition of *Lady Inger*.

[3] The second, enlarged, edition of the *Poems* appeared in December 1875.

But now I have another proposal to offer for your consideration. Next year will be the twenty-fifth anniversary of my matriculation and of my entrance on the career of an author. In the month of March 1850, appeared *Catilina, a Drama in Three Acts*, which was the first work of mine to be printed. This play contains some good, as well as some immature, writing. Of late years the critics have often remarked upon it as characteristic of me, that I made my début with this work; and I myself agree with them, for I feel now that it has a close connection with my life at that time, and that it contains the germs of a good deal which has since come to light in my poetry. My idea is to give some explanation of this, and various other things, in a Preface to a new and revised edition of the book. I should make no change in the thoughts and ideas, only in the language in which they are expressed; the verse is, as Brandes has remarked, bad—one reason of this being that the book was printed from my first rough, uncorrected draft.

I myself am of opinion that the work would be received with considerable interest, and that it would be bought by those who possess my other works. The book is now known to the public only by hearsay, because at the time it was published not more than from 60 to 100 copies were circulated; I myself saw the remainder of the issue converted into waste paper.

Will you give me your candid opinion in regard to this project? If you doubt the advisability of it, please tell me so. If you agree with me, I shall be exceedingly obliged if you will, as soon as possible, procure me a copy of the book; for, on account of the many corrections and alterations which I propose making, it will be necessary to re-write the whole play for the printers; and it would be well that the new edition should appear at the same time of year as the first one did. The borrowed copy shall be returned undamaged; I imagine that it will be possible to obtain the loan from one of the large libraries.

Hoping soon to hear your opinion on this matter, I remain with kindest regards to yourself and your family,—Yours most sincerely, HENRIK IBSEN.

115.

*To* GEORGE BRANDES.

DRESDEN, 30*th January* 1875.

DEAR BRANDES,—In order to convince you—though I don't believe you really doubt it—that you enjoy the special favour of the Gods, I shall to-day lay everything else aside in order to answer your letter received the day before yester-day.

My best thanks for the numbers of the periodical published by yourself and your brother. I have found much in them of great interest; but I still cannot help thinking that the periodical is far too exclusively a Danish, or, rather, a Copenhagen periodical. Your aim should most undoubtedly be to make it a Scandinavian one. No one dreams here in Germany of starting a periodical for Baden, or for Hesse-Cassel; and Denmark alone is just as little able to support one. Have you not thought of enlisting Professor Sars, or O. Skavlan, or F. R. Bætzman, as Norwegian contributors? And in Sweden you should be able to count upon even more than in Norway. I see you have already received one contri-bution from Sweden; and no stronger proof is required of the exclusively Danish character of the periodical, than the fact that you have seen fit to print the Swedish article in a Danish translation! Why? Do you not hope that your magazine will find readers in Sweden? And do you Copenhagen people believe that the Swedes will read original Swedish articles in a Danish translation? Are the Danes really still so ignorant of the Swedish language that communications from that country cannot be understood unless they are translated? If so, the outlook for the most important of all our causes is very bad. I have the feeling, dear Brandes, that there is not very much room to spare in your heart for this cause; as for me, I could not have lived so long in Germany without having my eyes opened to the truth that this one thing is the chief thing, and that the other aims are relatively subordinate.

Why do you and all of us whose standpoint is a European one, occupy such an isolated position at home ? Because what we belong to is not an entire, coherent state-organism; because the people at home think parochially, feel parochially, and regard everything from a parochial and not from a national or Scandinavian point of view. I do not set very much value on political organisation, but all the more upon the welding together of our national ideas. You call your periodical *The Nineteenth Century* —but how different the physiognomy of this century is at the present time in Denmark, in Sweden, in Norway! And do you believe that the fraction of Europeanism which each branch of the Scandinavian people has assimilated, provides a sufficient foundation for all that it is your desire to forward ? Only entire nations can join in great intellectual movements. A change in the theory of life and of the world is not a parochial matter; and we Scandinavians, as compared with the other European nations, have not yet got beyond the parish-council standpoint. And do you ever find a parish-council looking for, and preparing the way for "the third kingdom"? [1]

Having said enough on this subject, I will now proceed to give a direct answer to your letter.

It is quite true that I promised Councillor Hegel to send some poems as my contribution to the periodical; but, in the first place, these poems treat of specifically Norwegian matters, which leads me to fear that, as far as their subjects are concerned, they will be almost "Swedish" to the Copenhagen people; in the second place, they have not yet been elaborated, but are still in the crude, formless shape of first drafts. There is, therefore, more than "revisal" to be done; but I must admit

[1] *Det nittende Aarhundrede* (The Nineteenth Century), a magazine published by George and Edward Brandes, never had any Norwegian contributor except Ibsen; and any Swedish contributions were always translated into Danish. The first number appeared in October 1874, the last in the autumn of 1877.

that I have not thought of making them "unimprovable"; this would, moreover, be an unnecessary proceeding, for my experience is that people in Denmark, as elsewhere, are generally kind enough to put the best construction on what they do not understand. You shall have the poems, however; but, to prevent disappointment, I shall accept your utmost time-limit, and say, "in April or May."

I am unaware of having given occasion for your remark that it would not in any way compromise me to contribute to your periodical. Besides, it would be difficult for you, or for any one except myself, to decide whether I should consider it more compromising to collaborate with Bishop Martensen[1] or with the late David Strauss.

It is incomprehensible to me how you could take offence at my observing that the periodical, under given conditions, would secure you a care-free existence. I, who remember your letters quite as well as you seem to remember mine, can assure you that the observation was made in direct answer to something you had yourself written to me. And I do not understand how any one in our days can feel hurt by its being taken for granted that he expects to be able to live *by* what he lives *for*.

Accept my best thanks for having found a place in your magazine for *Emperor and Galilean*. There are several points in your review of it which I wish to discuss with you; but in writing I must limit myself to observing that it seems to me as if your condemnation of the determinism contained in my book were contradicted by your approval of something similar in P. Heyse's *Children of the World*. For in my opinion it comes to much the same thing whether I say, in writing of a person's character, "it runs in his blood," or, "he is free—subject to the laws of necessity."[2]

---

[1] H. L. Martensen (1808–1884), a bishop of the Danish Church from 1854, was a well-known orthodox theologian. His chief work is *Den christelige Ethik*.

[2] George Brandes contributed to the first number of *Det nittende Aarhundrede* both a long article on *Emperor and Galilean* and the first

In April I go to Munich, to settle there. Do you not think of taking a trip abroad soon? It seems to me that it would be easier for you to edit the periodical from abroad than at home. Everything else that I have to say must wait until some other time. Write soon to—Yours ever,

HENRIK IBSEN.

## 116.

### *To* LUDVIG DAAE.

DRESDEN, *4th February* 1875.

DEAR FRIEND,—I can no longer delay thanking you and all the other friends for the New Year's telegram which I had the great pleasure of receiving on New Year's Eve, in an almost unmutilated form, but, I regret to say, too late to permit of a return telegram from me reaching you before the turn of the year—especially as I did not know at which friend's house the gathering of the signers was being held, nor, consequently, where the answer should be addressed to find you assembled. From the language employed in the telegram I think I am pretty safe in concluding that you are the author of the message, and therefore I send my thanks to all, and my best and heartiest wishes for all, to you, requesting you duly to communicate with the other dear friends.[1]

Then I have a request to make of you, the granting of which may entail some trouble. I wish a good Norwegian translation of *The King's Mirror*,[2] of the *Sagas of the Kings*, and of a work

part of an essay on the German author, Paul Heyse. He considered that the effect of Ibsen's drama was weakened by its "thoroughgoing determinism." He also drew attention to Heyse's determinism, but expressed no actual approval of it, merely indicated it as being a characteristic feature in Heyse's writings.

[1] The telegram was in Latin.

[2] *Kongespeilet* or *Speculum Regale* is a didactic philosophic work, written in Norway towards the close of the twelfth century.

which is, I believe, ascribed to King Sverre, and is in some way connected with *The King's Mirror*—and this is all I know about it. Could you order these books, bound copies if possible, to be sent to me from some bookseller or other? The bill will be paid by my brother-in-law, Mr. Thoresen, who takes charge of my affairs, but who has no experience in making purchases of this kind.

I must tell you about a new literary undertaking. On 20th March next, my birthday, I shall have been for twenty-five years an author. *Catilina* was published on or about that day of the year 1850. During the winter I have corrected and improved this juvenile production of mine. A second, revised edition of it is now in the press, supplied with a Preface which throws light on the circumstances under which the first edition came into being; and the intention is to have it ready for publication in the month of March.

About the middle of April I leave Dresden, to settle in Munich for a time. The private school which Sigurd attends here has discontinued its two highest classes, and the arrangements and methods of the public schools do not seem to me to be suitable for foreign pupils. Besides, the roving spirit has taken possession of me again; and the number of strangers in Dresden has been steadily decreasing this last year. It is a pity that at Munich I shall be farther away from home; but to make up for this I shall be nearer to Italy, and I shall also have the advantage of living among Catholics, who, in Germany, are decidedly to be preferred to the Protestants.

And now, with repeated thanks, and with very kind remembrances to your family, I must stop for to-day. I am very often in thought among the "Dutchmen," recalling both old times and later days.—Ever yours faithfully,

HENRIK IBSEN.

117.

DRESDEN, *7th February* 1875.

DEAR MR. JOSEPHSON,—My best thanks for your kind and interesting letter. I specially appreciate your having written at such length at this season, when I know that you must be overburdened with business.

I can well understand that you are dissatisfied with all the obstruction, but I should consider it extremely regrettable if you were seriously thinking of leaving the Christiania Theatre. After all that you have accomplished there—not the least of your services being the organisation of the opera—it seems to me that you ought to be in a position to make any requisitions as to the ordering of business that you consider desirable. If the managers inconvenience you by interfering in what they do not understand, you must insist on this stopping; for it is you, and no one else, who will always be held responsible by the public. And you must keep in mind that a better time is coming for the Theatre; as to this there can be no doubt. In a few years a new and larger building will be called for; and then there will be an improvement of all the conditions under which you work. It stands to reason that you need help, but I do not consider that Thomas Thoresen is capable of giving the assistance required; he is in poor health and not fit for much work; and he is, moreover, immature, ignorant of literature, and without any thorough understanding of art and its processes. He has still much to learn.

[1] During his visit to Christiania in the summer of 1874, Ibsen had frequently met Mr. Josephson. As Director of the Christiania Theatre, Josephson—partly from the fact of his being a Swede—had many difficulties. His introduction of performances of opera as a regular part of the theatrical programme met with much opposition, and this in the end led to his resigning his post in 1877.

Will you be good enough to convey my thanks to the Management for their acceptance of *Lady Inger*? My thanks to yourself for speeding the arrangements for the performance of the play. I should be much pleased if it could be given on the 20th of March, which is my birthday, and also the 25th anniversary of my début as an author. The "Gyldendalske Boghandel" in Copenhagen is preparing a new edition of *Catilina* for the occasion—the first edition having appeared in the month of March 1850. But this matter of the performance I leave entirely to you.[1]

I intend in the month of April to change my place of residence to Munich, and am looking forward with pleasure to the possibility of your coming in that direction in summer; it would be exceedingly agreeable to me if we could take an excursion together to the Tyrol or its neighbourhood. In the meantime I hope that you will let me hear from you occasionally, when you have a little time to spare. My wife sends you her kindest regards.—Ever yours most sincerely,

HENRIK IBSEN.

### 118.

#### *To* JOHAN VIBE.

DRESDEN, *3rd March* 1875.

DEAR MR. VIBE,—In answer to your esteemed letter, I have pleasure in repeating what I said to you, when we met in Christiania, about your story, *The Recollections of Alexander Möller*—namely, that I read it with great interest at the time of its publication, and thought it an entertaining, and in several respects an able and promising work. I believe it would be well received if it were made accessible to a wider circle of readers than that reached by a serial in a daily paper.

---

[1] *Lady Inger* was performed at the Christiania Theatre for the first time on the 20th of March 1875. The public did not receive it with any enthusiasm.

What you tell me about the difficulty of finding a publisher at home, I know from personal experience to be true. I cannot help being astonished that our publishers have not learned wisdom from their losses. Because they did not, at the proper time, offer them any encouragement to remain at home, one after another of our authors has left them and found a publisher in Copenhagen. If your work had been a drama, I could have understood their unwillingness to accept it, for the readers of plays are comparatively few; but a new story must, leaving the private purchaser out of account, be bought by the circulating libraries; and these alone would almost exhaust an edition of ordinary size. All this extreme caution on the part of the publishers bears evidence to their want of foresight. They ought to prepare the way for our younger authors, ought to do all that is possible to circulate their books; they would soon reap advantage from it themselves.

I shall be very glad if you succeed in finding a publisher who shares my opinions and who looks a little further ahead than most of the Norwegian ones do. You ought to address yourself to some of the younger men; among them I believe there are now several who are both capable and enterprising. Wishing you all success, I remain—Yours very sincerely,

HENRIK IBSEN.[1]

[1] Johann Vibe (1840–1897), a Norwegian journalist and author. *The Recollections of Alexander Möller* was published by Cammermeyer in 1875. The above letter was of assistance in procuring a travelling-grant for Vibe in 1877.

119.

*To* KONRAD MAURER.

DRESDEN, 29*th March* 1875.

To Professor Konrad Maurer.

HONOURED SIR,—Although I have not the privilege of knowing you personally, I take the liberty, relying not only on the professional interest which you have shown in my country, but also on the kindly feeling towards it of which my compatriots have received so many proofs, to address a question to you, the answer to which is of considerable importance to me.

Allow me, in the first place, to give some explanations.

I have been away from Norway for eleven years. The last six of these I have spent here in Dresden, where my son has attended a "Gymnasium." He passed out of the Upper Third class last Easter, and left the "Gymnasium" for good, because the two higher classes have been discontinued by the new Principal. I am consequently obliged to find a new school for him; and, as I have long desired to become better acquainted with Munich, I have decided to remove there in the beginning of April.

On two points I am in uncertainty. In the first place, I do not know whether the class-arrangements of the South German Schools are so similar to those of the North German Schools that a pupil can pass from one of the latter to one of the former without risk of losing time by being placed in a lower class than that to which he has gained the right of entrance in the school he has been attending.

In the second place, may I ask if there is in Munich any "Gymnasium" (preferably a private one) which is particularly to be recommended for foreigners; and if so, in what part of the city it is located? Knowing this, I should be able on my arrival to look out at once for a house not too far from the school. I consider it of particular importance that the instruction in the modern foreign languages, French and English, should be imparted by Frenchmen and Englishmen. The creed taught in the school is not a matter of great moment.

Should you be able and willing to give me a little information on these points, I should be very grateful to you. I hope you will permit me, when I come to Munich, to offer you my thanks in person, along with my excuses for having ventured to trouble you in this matter.—Yours most respectfully,

HENRIK IBSEN,
Norwegian Author.[1]

*P.S.*—My address is Wettiner-Strasse, 22.

## 120.

### *To* GEORGE BRANDES.

MUNICH, *2nd May* 1875.

DEAR BRANDES,—As usual, I have allowed you to wait an unduly long time for an answer; but since the middle of last month I have not had a pen in my hand; and to-day you are the first to whom I write. We have been moving to Munich; and it was only yesterday that we got into the house which is to be our home; so you must be satisfied to-day with a word or two.

I did not, and, with this change of residence in prospect,

---

[1] This letter is written by Ibsen in German.

Konrad von Maurer (1823–1902) was Professor of the History of Law at the University of Munich. He occupied himself much with investigations into Norwegian-Icelandic law and history. He lectured in 1876 at the University of Christiania. In Munich he showed great hospitality to all Scandinavians. In reply to the above letter he sent full information regarding the Munich "Gymnasiums." During his stay in Munich, Ibsen called from time to time on Professor Maurer, but they never became very intimate.

could not promise to send you a contribution for the April or May number of your magazine; but I promised to send you a contribution in April or May, and this promise I shall keep.

My plan is now made, and on the point of being carried out. I will not send you something old, that has no connection with your undertaking; I shall address to you a series of rhymed letters, treating, in an easy style, of the intellectual movements of the day and the impression they make on me. I shall write unreservedly, as one friend writes to the other, and I think you will find out that we agree upon more points than you now seem to imagine.

This will be my exclusive occupation for some time to come, and I am looking forward with much pleasure to it; but I shall write no more about it to-day.[1]

I have a great desire to make Paul Heyse's acquaintance; and yet I hesitate, when I remember how, on two occasions at least, Copenhagen influence was exerted to injure me in Adolf Strodtmann's estimation. If you write to Dr. Heyse, please say a kind word or two for me. I left my card on him, but without giving my address; consequently I have not met him yet.[2]

Are you not soon coming South again? My address is: Schönfeld-Strasse, 17, 3 Eingang parterre. How glad we should be to see you cross our threshold!—Yours always,

HENRIK IBSEN.

---

[1] On the 8th of June 1875, Ibsen sent for insertion in *Det nittende Aarhundrede* the rhymed letter entitled, "Langt borte" (Far away). Later, in the same summer, he sent one on the subject of "Liget i lasten" (The Corpse in the Hold). This was his last contribution to the periodical.

[2] Through Brandes, Ibsen made Heyse's acquaintance; but, though they saw a good deal of each other, they never became very intimate friends. Ibsen's later plays were antipathetic to Heyse. He called hem "hospital literature."

## 121.

*To* HARTVIG LASSEN.

KITZBÜHEL, TYROL, 16*th August* 1875.

DEAR LASSEN,—It was not until yesterday that your kind letter reached me here among the mountains, where I am spending the summer. I hasten to answer it.

Of course it is impossible to stage *Peer Gynt* except in an abbreviated form. The first time I wrote to Grieg with reference to the music, I explained to him my idea of substituting for the Fourth Act a tone-picture suggesting the contents, accompanied by one or two tableaux vivants representing the situations most suited for such in the Act omitted—for instance, Peer Gynt and the Arab girls, Solveig waiting near her cottage, etc. This plan I communicated to Mr. Josephson, but he did not agree with me; he submitted to me a proposal for cutting the speeches; the cuttings seemed to me to have been made with great judgment, and I gave my assent to them.

I dare not decide here at a distance which of the two plans it will be best to adopt. I prefer that you and Mr. Josephson should discuss and decide the matter. He assures me that if his suggestion is carried out, the piece will become a popular favourite and draw large houses. I prefer not to interfere in the matter. I shall be satisfied so long as the piece is reduced to a proper length; not to do this would spoil everything. I therefore beg the Theatre authorities to act as seems best to them; there are reasons in favour of both of the alternatives mentioned; in order to decide between them one must be on the spot, must know the capabilities of the actors, the resources of the theatre in the matter of decorations, machinery, etc.

I shall permit myself to indicate only one wish, namely, that the first performance shall be before Christmas—indeed, as

19

early in the season as possible.   One cannot expect the public
to take much interest in plays which are not staged until
spring; and the reception of a play during its first year is all-
important for its future vitality.   And now, dear friend, I have
said all I have to say on this subject.

If your guest, Professor Molbech, is still with you, please
remember me kindly to him.

My best thanks to your amiable young niece for her
kind message; I permit myself to send her a very friendly
greeting in return.  My wife sends you kindest remembrances.
—Yours ever,

HENRIK IBSEN.

122.

*To* GEORGE BRANDES.

KITZBÜHEL, 16*th September* 1875.

DEAR BRANDES,—Excuse my not having written to you
sooner. I received your two post-cards yesterday. It is
impossible for me to send you any contribution for the October
number; my thoughts are concentrated, to the exclusion of everything else, on a new, long, dramatic work.   Towards the end of
the month I return to Munich and begin to write in earnest.
I will try, if possible, to do something for you "between the
acts"; but you have no idea how long it takes me to produce
these little contributions.  The transferring of the thing to
paper is, of course, a mere nothing; but I may safely say that
the last poem which I sent formed my exclusive occupation for
a month.   At present I can devote only the pauses to such
work.   But later on you shall certainly get something from
me.   I assure you that it is a pleasure to me to write for and
with you.   No more to-day, except kindest regards from my
wife and myself.—Yours ever,

HENRIK IBSEN.

123.

*To* FREDERIK HEGEL.

MUNICH, *23rd October* 1875.

DEAR MR. HEGEL,—I find myself obliged, owing to the unexpected delay in the production of *Peer Gynt* at the Christiania Theatre, to ask you to advance me 675 Marks; I trust you will not take this amiss.

My new work is progressing rapidly; in a few days I shall have the First Act ready; and that is always to me the most difficult part of a play. The title of the book will be: *The Pillars of Society*, a Drama in Five Acts. This work may, in a manner, be regarded as the counterpart of *The League of Youth*; it will enter pretty thoroughly into several of the more important questions of the day. This is, however, for the present, between ourselves; I have no objection to its becoming known when the play is further advanced, as I think that some talk among the public beforehand is of advantage to the sale of a work.[1]

I hope you duly received my letter regarding the new edition of the Poems; the work is in progress. On the title-page there ought, I think, to be printed: "Second and enlarged edition."

With kindest regards to yourself and your family,— I remain, Yours most sincerely,

HENRIK IBSEN.

[1] Ibsen was unable to send Hegel the complete manuscript of *The Pillars of Society* before July 1877.

124.

*To* FREDERIK HEGEL.

MUNICH, 25*th November* 1875.

DEAR MR. HEGEL,—I am sorry to be obliged to add to my thanks for the 675 Marks enclosed in your kind letter of the 25th ult., a request that you will be so good as to advance me 675 more, to prevent my being in difficulties at the beginning of next month. My previous request, that you would kindly invest in Government Bonds the last instalment due me by the Theatre Royal for *The Vikings*, I herewith recall, and ask you, instead, to employ the money in question in reducing the sum of the advance payments you have made me. I hope it will not be long before the Theatre Royal is in a position to perform the play again.

I avail myself of this opportunity to mention that I am not satisfied with Councillor Berner's style of remuneration. Plays which are offered in manuscript and accepted are, according to the regulations, paid with a certain percentage of the receipts. Now, both *The Pretenders* and *The Vikings* were offered in manuscript; and *The League of Youth*, too, was offered before it was published. If the procedure adopted in my case becomes general, the regulations will become deceptive; the Management can make a practice of first refusing all the manuscripts sent in, and thereby compel the authors to have their plays printed— after which they can be had for performance at a much lower price. But this is not as it should be; and I have no objection at all to Mr. Berner being told, when opportunity offers, what my opinion is.[1]

But now to the matter which is more particularly the subject of my letter to-day. Quite lately I subscribed for ten shares,

---

[1] *The Vikings* had been refused by the Theatre Royal of Copenhagen in 1858; but between February 1875 and the spring of 1877 it was performed at that theatre twenty-nine times.

price 1000 specie-dollars, in the recently reconstructed "Bergens Kreditbank," formerly a branch of the "Kreditkasse" of Christiania. On these shares 360 specie-dollars fall to be paid in the course of December. I have also subscribed for shares in the new passenger steamship *Dronningen* to the amount of 500 specie-dollars, of which 250 must be paid *at once* to H. J. Preus in Christiansand, for whom I enclose a letter. Therefore I require in all 610 specie-dollars. What I want to ask you is: Can I borrow this amount for a few months, say six, from some money-lending institution in Copenhagen, at a reasonable rate of interest, on the security of the bonds and shares which I already own, the vouchers for which are in your possession?

To procure the money in any other way would take too long; I have put off until now, hoping that the production of *Peer Gynt* in Christiania and of *The Vikings* in Stockholm would provide me with the necessary sum. Please do not be annoyed with me for giving you trouble in this matter too. If, as I hope, things can be arranged in Copenhagen, will you be good enough to send the letter to H. J. Preus as soon as possible; and the amount due for the "Kreditbank" shares some time in the course of the month of December to Mr. Lund, bookseller in Christiania, who has my instructions?[1]

The First Act of my new drama is ready — the fair-copy written; I am now working at Act Second.

What do you say to this move of Stjernström's? I have heard nothing from him since last summer. The news of the performance took me entirely by surprise.[2] With kindest regards to yourself and your family,—Yours most sincerely,

HENRIK IBSEN.

---

[1] Hegel himself lent the money required. Ibsen, in his letter of thanks, promised that such an untoward incident should never occur again, and also assured Hegel that this arrangement of the matter had never occurred to him.

[2] E. Stjernström, founder and manager of the "Nya Teater" in Stockholm, was performing *The Vikings* there.

125.

*To* LUDVIG JOSEPHSON.

MUNICH, 14*th June* 1876.

DEAR MR. JOSEPHSON,—The long letter which, in spite of many business cares, you found time to write to me, was a welcome and unmistakable sign of your friendship. My best thanks for it.

What you tell me about the troubles and annoyances connected with your post at the Theatre does not really surprise me; with the present organisation, it could hardly be otherwise. But there must and shall be a change in the system of management; and I intend in the course of the summer to do my share in bringing it about by writing some articles on the subject, which I think of sending to Hjelm's (Winterhjelm's) *Illustreret Tidende.*[1]

I have read your drama with great interest; but I fear that the same objections which have hitherto prevented the Management from producing *The Pretenders* here, will be offered to your play when it is taken into consideration. Under these uncertain conditions, there might be some difficulty in finding a translator who would be willing to expose himself to the risk of having worked in vain and without compensation. You would further your cause best by coming here yourself; then we should join forces and see what could be done.[2]

I have spoken to Dr. Grandaur with reference to your receiving free admission to the Bayreuth Festival; but he says that you have no chance at all except by applying personally to Richard Wagner. He expects, however, that an endless number of similar requests will be received, and has not much hope as to the result. The price of a ticket for the four performances is 300 Marks.

[1] This intention Ibsen did not carry out.
[2] Josephson's five-act drama, *Thord Hassle*, has never been acted.

At the beginning of this month I went to Berlin, to be present at the first performance of *The Pretenders*, which was splendidly staged by the Court Theatrical Company of the Duke of Meiningen. The play was received with great applause, and I was called before the curtain several times. I do not think that this was very agreeable to the Berlin critics, most of whom are themselves dramatic authors. The play, nevertheless, had a run of nine nights, and would have run longer if the season of the Meiningen Company had not been almost at an end; it closes on the 15th.

After the first performance I was invited by the Duke to visit him at his castle of Liebenstein, near Meiningen, where I stayed until the day before yesterday. On my departure he decorated me with the Cross of the First Class of the "Sächsisch-Ernestinische Hausorden." *The Pretenders* is now to be played at Schwerin, and *The Vikings* has been accepted at the Burg Theatre in Vienna, where Charlotte Wolter is to play Hjördis. If our mutual friend, Winterhjelm, would care for these particulars for his paper, please let him have them. And come soon! We remain at Munich till the 1st of August.

With kindest regards from my wife and myself,—I remain, Yours very sincerely,

HENRIK IBSEN.

126.

*To* FREDERIK HEGEL.

KALTERN, BY BOZEN, TYROL, 15*th September* 1876.

DEAR MR. HEGEL,—After having given no sign of life for almost four months, I shall to-day send you a few lines, chiefly because I do not trust to the Scandinavian papers being as particular in publishing good and reliable news about me as they are in spreading distorted accounts of anything unfavourable. They hastened to tell that, at the rehearsal in Meiningen, *The Pretenders* did not take the fancy of the public; but perhaps they have been in no hurry to report that, in Berlin, the same play was received for nine nights in succession with a tempest of applause—author and actors being repeatedly recalled. And this happened in spite of the fact that many of the journalists were, for obvious reasons, not well disposed towards me. After this victory the Duke of Meiningen invited me to visit him at his castle of Liebenstein. I had a delightful time there, and received on my departure the insignia of the "Sächsisch-Ernestinische Hausorden." In winter I am to visit the Duke again at Meiningen. In October, *The Vikings* is to be produced at the Burg Theatre in Vienna; I have received an official invitation to be present; and am also invited to Schwerin, where *The Pretenders* is to be played in November. In the course of a week or two they will be performing *The Vikings* at the Court Theatre in Dresden; and it is also being prepared for production at the City Theatre of Leipzig, and is having a very successful second run in Munich. From each one of the theatres named I receive ten per cent. of the gross receipts from all representations; and my heirs will receive the same percentage for fifteen years after my decease. These are undeniably more advantageous terms than Mr. Berner sees fit to offer me; and no one can be surprised that I am devoting my chief attention to making my works profitable here. A German original edition of *Lady Inger* is already prepared in manuscript, and will be played at Meiningen and Munich.

Whilst engaged in attending to all these matters, I have been obliged to neglect my new play; but after my return to Munich, at the beginning of next month, I intend to put the completing touch to it, although there is certainly little inducement to write for the theatres at home. How is *The Vikings* succeeding in Copenhagen? According to our agreement, I am to receive 500 Kroner more after the twentieth performance. Is it really Mr. Berner's intention on account of this to put aside the play after the nineteenth performance, as was done last year? One very characteristic trait of the said gentleman I have not yet mentioned to you. In the letter in which he begins negotiations with me on the subject of *The Vikings*, he writes that the Theatre can only pay me so and so much, " because the play is too short to occupy a whole evening." Yet I learn afterwards that it has been given every time as the sole performance of the evening on which it has been acted. But about this Mr. Berner has not said a single word to me. I should like, if opportunity offered, thàt his attention should be drawn to the fact; for tricks of this kind are really beneath the dignity of the manager of a Royal Theatre.

I have long been expecting to see the new edition of *Peer Gynt* advertised; I hope that it will be out soon. And possibly a new issue of one or more of my other books may be required before Christmas. I should be very glad if this were the case, for I am in need of money. The Theatres here pay only every quarter or half-year. Dare I, therefore, in spite of my debt to you, ask you to send me 450 Marks, to the address given at the beginning of my letter? It will be a very great favour. And I have every hope that it will not be long before our account is properly balanced again.

The scenery is wonderfully beautiful here on the borders of Italy; and one could not wish for a more delightful climate. A Danish and a Finnish lady, and the young author, John Paulsen, of Bergen, are the people we see most of. We hear very little from home. Young Paulsen has, however, told us a good deal about his stay in Copenhagen; he is delighted with everything. From what he tells, we conclude that all is well with you and yours; but we should be very glad to be confirmed in this idea by yourself.

Please do not see in my long silence a sign of decreasing interest in things and persons at home. Trusting that it has not occurred to you to do so,—I remain, with kindest regards to you and your family, Yours most sincerely,

HENRIK IBSEN.

### 127.

To THE NORWEGIAN GOVERNMENT DEPARTMENT FOR
ECCLESIASTICAL AND EDUCATIONAL MATTERS.

MUNICH, 7th April 1877.

IN the name and on behalf of Mr. John Paulsen, author,
I, the undersigned, hereby address a respectful appeal to the
Department, that, from the moneys voted for the purpose of
assisting scientific men and artists to visit foreign countries,
a sum of 1600 Kroner may be granted him, to enable him to
continue the studies which the career he has chosen renders
indispensable.

John Paulsen is a native of Bergen, the son of poor parents.
He is now in his 25th year. Though he has not passed through
any secondary school, he has been well taught, and has, besides,
by independent study, acquired considerable knowledge of
literary history, and of both Norwegian and foreign literature.
He is also tolerably proficient in modern languages, especially
German, French, and English Until about a year ago he was
a clerk in the Portuguese Consulate at Bergen; this situation he
gave up in order to devote himself exclusively to literary work.

About a year and a half ago his first book appeared, published by Malling; it was a collection of stories, entitled:
*Sketches of Town Life*. He next brought out, through the
same publisher, a collection of poems; and last Christmas the
" Gyldendalske Boghandel " in Copenhagen published a novel
for him, *The Sea Queen*. He has, besides, written some short
plays, several of which have been produced in Bergen; but none
of these are as yet in print. And for various newspapers and
magazines he has written letters, sketches of travel, poems, and
criticisms.

On his first public appearance John Paulsen met with
an unusually cordial reception, both from the general
public and the reviewers; and the favour and hopefulness

with which they continue to regard him, I consider fully justified.

Last year about this time he left Norway, for the purpose of improving his mind by foreign travel. After a stay of some months in Copenhagen, he came to Germany, and stayed here, in Munich, till a short time before Christmas, when he went to Rome, with the intention of remaining there for a considerable time. Daily intercourse with him during a period of several months gave me every opportunity to become acquainted with him. And I have familiarised myself with his works. It is my firm conviction that not one of our younger writers has a stronger claim to be taken into consideration in the distribution of the grants in question. His future as an author will be dependent upon the opportunities offered him for developing and cultivating his natural gifts; and his refined and ardent poetic mind, his noble nature, and his pure and in every respect exemplary morals, are, in my opinion, guarantees of a very considerable potentiality of development. I must repeat that he has no private means; up to the present time he has defrayed his travelling expenses with the income derived from his writings; but this is already proving insufficient to supply his needs. Paulsen is not a man of a strong constitution; his lungs, though not actually affected, are weak; hence I consider it possible that a prolonged sojourn in the South may be for him in a double sense a vital matter.

I therefore earnestly commend the future of this gifted young man to the care of the honourable Department, venturing at the same time respectfully and urgently to entreat that the amount applied for should not be reduced; a smaller sum will yield disproportionately small results.—Your obedient servant,

HENRIK IBSEN.[1]

---

[1] This appeal was unsuccessful; but a second, made by Ibsen in much the same terms in the following year, resulted in Paulsen's receiving a grant of 1400 Kroner.

128.

*To* LORENTZ DIETRICHSON.

MUNICH, 29*th April* 1877.

MY DEAR OLD FRIEND,—Having now in my possession two unanswered letters of yours, I dare no longer yield to my habit of procrastination in the matter of letter-writing, but must send you at least a few words of thanks and greeting. The letter from Professor Nyblom I, of course, answered at once, and to what effect I do not need to tell you. I look forward with great pleasure to our appearing together at the approaching festival and ceremony; we have kept pace with each other on the path of honour-receiving; and our paths generally, have often and for long periods run side by side.[1]

The publication of your own translation of *A Workman* is, I take it, quite out of the question. When the play is performed in Germany, which I hope it will be, Mr. Jonas will reap the benefit; you will get nothing.[2] It seems to me that you should take advantage of being at home to make a public protest against the existing lawless conditions from which we Norwegian men of letters suffer. I am delighted that you had so little trouble in finding a good publisher for the German edition of your great work, and I consider it very wise of you to bring out a Norwegian edition at the same time; for, as things are now, you would probably not have been able to prevent one or other of our literary pirates from doing it on his own account. Now do rage properly at these barbaric conditions!

[1] In 1877 the University of Upsala celebrated the four hundredth anniversary of its foundation. On this occasion L. Dietrichson and Henrik Ibsen received the honorary degree of Doctor of Philosophy.

[2] Dietrichson's drama, *En Arbejder*, was published in Swedish in 1872, and in Norwegian in 1875. An unauthorised German translation by Emil Jonas was published in Berlin in 1877, and performed in the National Theatre there in 1881.

I have decided to write something about the position of matters at the Theatre,—either a memorandum to the Board of Managers or a newspaper article. But I cannot believe that these people have actually been foolish enough to part with Josephson, a practical expert whom it would be impossible to replace.

We have now moved into our new house, Schelling Strasse 30, second floor, where we are most comfortable, and where I hope soon to complete my new work. I do not see Dr. Schmidt every day just now, but pretty often. Yesterday, Saturday, I was with him, Heyse, and Carriere, at the Achatz restaurant; so I was able to deliver your message without any great delay. I am to greet you from them in return. You have left sincere and faithful friends behind you here.[1] Whether Heyse seriously thinks of going to Upsala or not, I cannot say; I broached the subject yesterday; he seems inclined, but he always comes back to the question, how his weak nerves and the strong Swedish punch will agree. I, of course, maintained that the question could only be answered by a practical experiment. We shall see what he decides; you may trust me to do my best.

At the "Crocodile Club" they always ask for news of you.[2] Dr. Grandaur wants a piece of literary information from you, for his history of the Theatre. What is *Hermann von Unna*? The name is familiar to me, but nothing more. I thought it was a German "chivalry drama"; but Grandaur maintains that it is Swedish, and has been translated into German by Abbé Vogler. Please tell me briefly all that you

[1] Dietrichson, elected Professor of the History of Art at the University of Christiania in 1875, spent most of the year 1876 at Munich, where he and Ibsen were much together. They drank their " Frühschoppen " regularly at the Achatz restaurant in the Maximilians-platz in company with the Munich professor Moriz Carriere, Paul Heyse the author, and his friend Dr. Oswald Schmidt.

[2] To the weekly meetings of the " Crocodile Club " came the most noted literary men of Munich—Heyse, Geibel, Bodenstedt, Dahn, etc.

can find out about it; I promised him to write to you on the subject.[1]

During the week of our moving we have seen nothing of those whom you left behind in the Garten Strasse; we hope that they are well, and expect to see them to-night. Mrs. Collett has returned from Rome. Wergeland is exhibiting a good picture—a lady dressed in black, in a church pew. Kronberg is going to Italy; otherwise everything much as usual.

Goodbye for to-day, dear friend. I hope we shall meet at Upsala, if not before.—Yours ever,

HENRIK IBSEN.

## 129.

### To FREDERIK HEGEL.

MUNICH, 23rd August 1877.

DEAR MR. HEGEL,—Enclosed you will find the letters which are to be sent along with the play to the Theatre Royal and the Gothenburg Theatre. With the Stockholm theatres I shall communicate when there. The book must not be sent to the Bergen Theatre until the time approaches when it will be exposed for sale; I have a regular contract with that Theatre; and by sending a copy as early as this, we run the risk of its being circulated among those for whom it is not intended, which would injure the sale in that locality.[2] To the Christiania Theatre I do not at present intend to offer the play. The new Manager is an absolutely incompetent man; and as soon as my

[1] *Hermann von Unna* is a play by the Swedish author, A. F. Skjöldebrand (1757–1834). The German composer, Abbé G. J. Vogler, who was Kapellmeister at Stockholm from 1786 to 1799, wrote music for it.

[2] *The Pillars of Society* was published on the 11th of October 1877. It was played in Copenhagen on the 18th of November, in Bergen on the 30th of November, and in Stockholm on the 13th of December of the same year—at Gothenburg in February 1878.

play is on the market I intend to intimate in a Norwegian paper that I have broken off all connection with the Theatre for the period of his managership. I have reason to believe that Björnson will do the same. From my knowledge of the position, I feel pretty certain that this procedure, far from injuring the sale of the book, will rather cause it to be more extensively read and bought. And I am also persuaded that united action on the part of Björnson and myself will go far towards compelling the new Manager to resign very soon.[1]

The book should, in my opinion, be published with as little delay as possible, and simultaneously in all three countries. I foresee that it will create a good deal of excitement; and, if we get it out at the right time, it is not impossible that, in spite of the size of the first issue, another will be called for before Christmas.[2] It is this, I think, that we must chiefly keep in mind; the terms which we come to with any single theatre cannot be compared in importance with the good or bad sale of the book.

From the letters for the theatres you will see that I have for the time being confined myself to the question of acceptance or non-acceptance. This I consider to be the best plan. The terms can be discussed after this first question has been decided.

I am exceedingly busy with the preparations for my journey to Upsala. I look forward with pleasure to seeing you on the return journey.

With kindest regards to all your family,—I remain, Yours most sincerely,

HENRIK IBSEN.

[1] Johan Vibe, Josephson's successor, was Director of the Christiania Theatre from 1877 to 1879. *The Pillars of Society* was played in this theatre before the end of his term of office.

[2] The second edition was published in November 1877. Ibsen was, therefore, right in his prediction of a great demand for the book; but it occasioned less excitement than he expected. It attracted immediate attention abroad. After February 1878 it was acted in many of the theatres of Germany; and it was the play with which Ibsen made his first appearance (in 1880) on the English stage.

### 130.

*To* Markus Grönvold.[1]

Rydberg's Hotel, Stockholm, *3rd September* 1877.

Dear Mr. Grönvold,—It is with very great reluctance that I permit myself to take advantage of your well-known obliging-ness at this time, when you are occupied in completing your great picture, and naturally desire peace and quietness. But, should you happen one of these days to be passing the Court Theatre, you would do me a very great favour if you would get hold of Mr. Jenke, the stage-manager, and ask him from me to alter an expression in *The League of Youth* about which he and I have already had a little conversation. You will probably remember that Aslaksen in the play often speaks of "de lokale forhold"; this Strodtmann has translated literally, "lokale Verhältnisse"—which is wrong, because no suggestion of comicality or narrow-mindedness is conveyed by this German expression. The rendering ought to be "unsere berechtigten Eigentümlichkeiten," an expression which conveys the same meaning to Germans as the Norwegian one does to us Scandinavians.[2]

If the first performance takes place on the 15th, as at present intended, it will hardly be possible for me to be present; so if you would send me a line or two, addressed to care of Hegel, Copenhagen, to let me know how things go, I shall be doubly

---

[1] The Norwegian painter, Markus Grönvold (born 1845), saw a great deal of Ibsen during the summer of 1877, while the latter's wife and son were absent from Munich. He writes: "I was much impressed by the intense application with which Ibsen worked; and yet he would sit up late at night, unreservedly and lavishly communicating to us, in his practical, clear, impressive manner, his opinions on politics, social questions (which at that time interested him much), literature, the theatre, art, and men."

[2] Ibsen was mistaken in this correction of his; the literal translation conveys the meaning of the Norwegian expression.

obliged to you. I write to-day in haste, because to-morrow, according to the programme, the demon of conviviality begins to run riot—that is to say, we start for Upsala; for some days after that there will be no peace for letter-writing. I shall not be sorry to be back in Munich again, for this sort of thing gives me no real pleasure.

With thanks in advance and very kind regards, believe me —Yours most sincerely,

HENRIK IBSEN.

### 131.

### *To* EDWARD FALLESEN.[1]

MUNICH, *3rd October* 1877.

HONOURED SIR,—In my answer to your telegram I was obliged to confine myself to signifying briefly that it was impossible to delay the publication of my new play until 30th November. I now permit myself to indicate the reasons which made the refusal obligatory.

As the Theatre Royal does not see its way to allowing me a certain percentage of the receipts, I am compelled to make the sale of the book my chief source of profit. A very large edition of the play has been printed, and for this first issue Mr. Hegel has paid me a considerable sum. Taking into account, besides this payment, his expenses for printing, paper, etc., it is evident that his outlay has been anything but trifling. I therefore owe it to him as well as to myself not to make arrangements opposed to our common interests. In our Scandinavian countries, as you are aware, the last two months of the year are the book-selling season; and in order that a book, published in Copenhagen, may be available at the proper time in the more remote districts of Sweden and Norway, not to mention Finland and America,

---

[1] Edward Fallesen (1817–1894) was appointed Director of the Theatre Royal, Copenhagen, in 1876. In 1872 the title of Kammerherre (Chamberlain) was conferred on him.

20

where a good many copies of my plays go, it is imperative that
it should be sent off not later than the middle of October. If
this is not done, there is no chance of the edition being sold out
during the Christmas book-market, and the author must wait
for a whole year before a new edition is called for. I dare not
and cannot expose myself to the risk of such a pecuniary loss,
—a loss for which such a payment as the Theatre Royal offers
would be no compensation. Besides, numerous orders have come
in from the booksellers throughout Scandinavia, and promises
have been made that the book will be delivered at a certain
time. And there is yet another consideration. We understand
that this book is looked forward to by the public with considerable expectation; and it is always impolitic on the part of an
author to strain such expectation beyond a reasonable time; if
he does, the interest is apt to dwindle before the book appears.

Regarding the matter from another side, I consider it injurious to a dramatic work that it should be made accessible
to the public in the first instance by means of a stage performance. I believe that the regulation of the Theatre Royal to this
effect has acted repressively on dramatic production in Denmark.
It is, at all events, a fact that such production has shown no
tendency to increase since the regulation in question was passed.
This is only natural; as things are now, a new play can never be
considered and judged apart from its surroundings, purely and
simply as a literary work. The judgment will always comprehend both the play and its performance; these two entirely
different things are mixed up together; and the chief attention
of the public is, as a rule, attracted more by the acting and the
actors than by the play itself.

I feel that I owe it to myself to give this explanation; for
it would grieve me if my refusal were regarded as a proof of
disobligingness. Nothing would have pleased me more than
to accede to the request, if it had been possible. I can hardly
believe that my enforced refusal will injure the Theatre; when
it becomes known that the play is to be given as early as
November, the consequence will merely be that a large propor-

tion of the Copenhagen public will give up the idea of buying the book beforehand.

Allow me, for the sake of order, to return you the pass issued to me, with my sincere and hearty thanks for the enjoyable evenings which it procured me.

Hoping that the approaching production of *The Pillars of Society* will be to the satisfaction of all parties concerned,— I remain, honoured Sir, yours sincerely,

HENRIK IBSEN.

132.

*To* CHRISTIAN K. F. MOLBECH.

MUNICH, 30*th October* 1877.

DEAR FRIEND,—From your last letter, which I received yesterday, I see that you have returned, after all, to your original intention of bringing your dispute with the Director of the Theatre before the public.[1] It is impossible for me at

[1] In the beginning of October, Molbech had sent Ibsen a long letter full of complaints of Chamberlain Fallesen, who had shelved his play, *Ambrosius*, for the sake of performing *The Pillars of Society* and two Danish tragedies before it. Ibsen answered this letter the day he received it, begging Molbech not to act hastily, and assuring him that he, Ibsen, had no desire to have his play performed at once—that he would, in fact, be better pleased if it were not. Ibsen's letter concludes thus: "Dear Friend, it is now nearly eleven years since we met, in Rome, for the first time—at the period when I was just beginning to overcome many of my difficulties. You were the first perfectly mature and independent personage who held out a friendly hand to me. We have met more than once since then, both at home and abroad; and each time our relations have been more intimate and confidential. You, your name, your whole individuality, are inseparably connected with the best period of my life. And now comes this! But let it, at all events, be quite clear, to ourselves and to others, that the quarrel is not between you and me. I am ready to do everything that can contribute to settle it; and, as you know from what I have already written, it is no sacrifice I am called on to make; on the contrary, my interests are served by what serves yours."

this distance to form any decided opinion as to the advisability
of such a step; but what is quite clear to me is, that your
drawing analogous cases into the dispute will not in any way
help to enlighten and guide public opinion. The subject of
contention is solely and alone your play *Ambrosius*, which has
been set aside for another work, accepted later. This is a
simple and easily comprehensible situation. If you introduce
the two tragedy-writers and myself into the discussion, it at
once becomes more complicated. I believe that the more con-
cretely and individually the case is treated, the more effective
will your representation be. This I request you to take into
consideration before you plan your line of action on such a
broad base as is suggested in your letter. A protest against the
injury done to yourself, and an attack on the system prevailing
at the Theatre, are two different things; and I do not think
that it will be to the advantage of either to mix them up.

As regards myself personally, I am most unwilling to
interfere in the matter, not at all because I dread any unpleasantness which might arise, but because I feel that I have
no right to complain. I voluntarily accepted the Director's
conditions as to payment, and have consequently no right
to make complaints afterwards. It is true that the Director
proposed that I should do what was not in our contract, namely,
delay the publication of the play; but to this proposal I refused
to agree. He has, besides, without my knowledge, requested
the editors of the newspapers to hold back all reviews until the
play has been produced. But can I with any fairness attack
him because of this, unless I at the same time attack the editors
who comply with the request? It seems to me that in this
particular matter it is the press which ought to be denounced.
But would it be at all good policy, as far as you are concerned,
that I should attack the press at the very moment when you
most desire its goodwill, sympathy, and assistance? It seems
to me that I should be doing you a very poor service, if I were
to make a public accusation of this kind at the present moment.

Think the matter over more carefully. The answer of the

Ministry has not come yet, so you have still time to deliberate and choose your plan of action. I think that you are wrong in determining to make the affair one of greater and more general import than the single case at issue renders necessary. I tell you this frankly, because I know that, along with what is most characteristic and best in your nature, goes a propensity to rashness, which you only recognise as such afterwards, when it is too late. Do not be annoyed with me for writing thus: I have the feeling that I may speak quite frankly to you. Please think things over again, and choose such a mode of action as will give you nothing to regret afterwards.

I have read *Ambrosius* with great pleasure; it is a fine, spirited work, but in its present form not adapted for the German public, whose taste nowadays lies in an entirely different direction. Besides, the necessary previous acquaintance with the historical subject is lacking here. No one knows anything about Ambrosius Stubb. To give the play any chance of success in Germany, it would have to be completely recast; much would have to be cut away, and new matter would have to be added. All this you would, of course, have to do yourself before offering the work to the theatres; whether you can and will bring yourself to do it, I have no idea; nor can I in a letter enter into particulars as to what, judging by my knowledge of the German public, ought to be changed. But I should like very much to have an opportunity of discussing the matter with you.[1] Is there no probability of your taking a foreign trip next summer? I hope to hear from you soon again. I am very anxious to learn what turn the theatrical matter takes. If you disapprove of anything I have written, please do not refrain from saying so.

My wife joins with me in kindest regards to you and yours. —Ever yours sincerely,

HENRIK IBSEN.

---

[1] *Ambrosius* was translated into German by Strodtmann in 1878, and was subsequently performed with much success in many German theatres, some of which still retain it on their repertory.

## 133.

*To* HARTVIG LASSEN.

MUNICH, *2nd December* 1877.

DEAR LASSEN,—I have of late been so overburdened with business which would allow of no delay, that I could not even think of answering your letter. But now most of the business is disposed of, and I shall therefore send you a few words to-day.

I did not say to Mr. Vibe that the Management had tied Josephson's hands; what I said was that the Board of Management as an *institution* was a hindrance and a burden to him. I also said that the Board would have acted more in the interests of the Theatre if, instead of doing away with the Director and the opera, it had done away with itself. The Theatre will never be successful so long as it is managed by a Board. This, as a general principle, is acknowledged throughout the whole world; the theatrical Boards of Management have been done away with everywhere except in Norway; no wonder that things go on there as they do.

The opera might have been of incalculable value in developing our dramatic art; it has a disciplinary influence, and no theatre but a Norwegian one would thus carelessly and unreasonably have done away with it. Had they no feeling of responsibility towards the talented singers of our country who have now no opportunity of getting on?

What you say about Josephson's faults and deficiencies I quite understand; but these very faults and deficiencies are real advantages when it is a theatre like that of Christiania which has to be managed; the Christiania Theatre neither is nor will be for some time to come an art institution; both the money and the public necessary to make it that are lacking.

You say that it was largely owing to you that Josephson had to leave. In your place I would not have incurred such a responsibility; I should have preferred to leave myself. A theatre of no higher artistic rank than that of Christiania could far more easily have borne the loss of its "Æstetisk Consulent" than of its technically expert manager.

Dear Lassen, you are one of the few in your parts who know how to read aright, and therefore I feel convinced that you will not find a trace of depreciation or rudeness in this remark of mine. I assure you that I appreciate you thoroughly; but I think that the Christiania Theatre neither occupies nor can occupy the artistic position which renders that special kind of ability that you represent an absolute requirement. If we had a national theatre with a large annual allowance from the State Treasury, that would be a different matter; then you would be the man.

And what kind of man have you chosen as a successor to the deposed Josephson? We had him here in Munich last summer, and he talked like a child of five about the post he was presently to fill. How long do you imagine that things can go on under the management of this sadly incompetent person? Not to the end of the season.

Upon what I have personally lost by the abolishment of technical expert knowledge at the Christiania Theatre, I shall not dwell. I shall only mention that Josephson had some big projects; it was his intention to stage both *Brand* (in an abbreviated form) and the First Part of *Emperor and Galilean*. Who among you, now that you have got rid of Josephson's unrefined taste, would think of such extravagances, extravagances which to J. L. Heiberg would have been "an abomination"? And even if any one thought of them, who would put the idea into effect? Would *Peer Gynt* ever have been produced if Josephson had not put it on the stage by main force?[1]

---

[1] Josephson succeeded in producing *Brand* in Stockholm in 1885, at the "Nya Teater"; the drama was not played in Norwegian till the 14th of September 1904, when it was produced at the National Theatre, Christiania. *Emperor and Galilean* was not performed at all till 1896, when it was given in Leipzig; it was not played in Christiania till 1903.

All this I have chosen to say to you quite frankly; for it seems to me that we two ought to be able to say what we think to each other without injuring the good understanding which, I, for my part, am most anxious to preserve. I give you free permission to retaliate in kind, if you write again to—Yours very sincerely,

HENRIK IBSEN.

134.

*To* CHRISTIAN PAUS.[1]

MUNICH, 18*th November* 1877.

DEAR UNCLE CHRISTIAN,—In spite of my being one of your nearest relatives, I fear, and with good reason, that when you receive these lines which I am writing to you in this distant country, you will think of me as almost a stranger. To out-siders it may, indeed, seem as if I had of set intention made myself a stranger to my family, or, at least, quite separated myself from them; but I believe I may say with truth that we were at first chiefly separated by unalterable circumstances and causes.

The occasion of my writing you to-day you will, dear Uncle, easily guess. The foreign papers and a letter from Hedvig have informed me of my old Father's death; and I feel impelled to express my heartfelt thanks to all those of the family whose affectionate assistance has made life easier for him for so many years, and who have, therefore, done in my behalf or in my

---

[1] Christian Paus (1800–1879) was a younger half-brother of Henrik Ibsen's father, Knut Ibsen (who died in 1877), and a cousin of his mother, Cornelia Ibsen (who died in 1869). He left Skien in 1822, but returned to that town in 1848 in the capacity of Byfoged (town magistrate), a post which he held till 1873. He was a man of most upright character, with a strong sense of duty and a passionate temper. His being twice elected to represent Skien in the Storthing is a proof of the esteem in which he was held by his fellow-citizens.

stead what until quite lately I have not been in a position
to do.

From my fourteenth year I was thrown upon my own
resources; it has been by a long, hard struggle that I have won
my way to where I stand now. My chief reason for writing
home so very seldom during all these years of struggle was
that I could offer no assistance of any kind to my parents; it
seemed to me idle to write, when I could not act. I went on
hoping that my circumstances would improve; but the improvement was very long in coming; it is of perfectly recent date.

It has been a great consolation to me to know that my
parents were surrounded by attached relatives; and the
thanks that I now offer for all the kind assistance rendered
to those who are gone, are also due for the assistance thereby
rendered myself. Yes, dear Uncle, let me tell you, and ask you
in turn to tell the others, that your and their fulfilment, out of
affection for my parents, of what was my bounden duty, has
been a great support to me during my toils and endeavours, and
has furthered the accomplishment of my work in this world.

During my last stay in Norway I felt a strong inclination
to visit Skien and my family; but I at the same time felt
a strong disinclination to come into contact with certain
tendencies prevailing there, tendencies with which I do not
sympathise, and a collision with which might have caused
unpleasantness, or at least a disagreeable feeling which I
preferred to avoid. But I have by no means given up the idea
of seeing the home of my childhood once again. In a year my
son will have finished his school education here, and we shall
be able to live wherever we choose. Probably we shall first go
to Italy for a short time, and then take up our residence in
Christiania; although I fear that I shall not be able to live or
work permanently in Norway. The conditions here are far
more favourable; they are the conditions of the great world—
liberty of thought and a wide view of things. These conditions,
however, demand considerable sacrifices, of various kinds.

I enclose my photograph. It is twenty-seven years since

we saw each other, and I am sure you will not recognise me; but I hope the day is coming when the family will have an opportunity of satisfying themselves whether the picture resembles the original or not.

And now, dear Uncle, I shall conclude. Please remember me kindly to all the different members of the family, and believe me to be—Your grateful and affectionate nephew,

HENRIK IBSEN.

## 135.

### To CHRISTIAN K. F. MOLBECH.

MUNICH, 18th December 1877.

DEAR FRIEND,—It is a very long time since anything has given me so much pleasure, and at the same time affected me so deeply, as the discovery, made when I received your new book some days ago, that you had prefixed to it a visible memorial of our old friendship. A thousand thanks for doing it; and a thousand more because you did it under the present circumstances. It was a most delicate inspiration on your part; and now that I have had time for reflection, I no longer feel surprised; for such an action is in perfect keeping with the character both of this new work and of your writings generally.

But may I not also venture to gather from your friendly dedication that the Theatre affair has been arranged in a manner satisfactory to you? It is difficult for me to understand how it can have been done; but as nothing on the subject has, so far as I am aware, appeared in the newspapers, and as your play has been published, I presume a new agreement with the Theatre must have been substituted for the old one.

However this may be, it seems to me that what has happened should furnish us with an opportunity for submitting a petition to our Governments to add to the laws regulating literary matters, one providing mutual international protection in the three Scandinavian countries. The existing conditions are unjust, and most unfair to the authors. It is, on the one hand, palpably unjust to Danish authors that a play by me may, because I am a Norwegian, take precedence of Danish original works; and, on the other hand, I consider it inequitable that my works, in spite of the fact that they are published in Denmark, do not enjoy protection, but are played, without payment to the author, anywhere in that country except Copenhagen. Danish authors are, of course, treated in the same manner in Norway; and in Sweden the state of matters is, as you are aware, the same. Recently, however, a convention has been concluded between Sweden and Norway, to take effect from 1st January 1878, according to which Norwegian authors are to enjoy full protection in Sweden, and *vice versâ*. It seems to me that Denmark ought also to be included in this convention, and that the necessary steps to ensure this inclusion should be taken as soon as possible.

Think over this matter, which I have not been able to do more than indicate. It would certainly be of importance to you if the drama on which you are now engaged could enjoy the benefits of such a convention. I do not believe that either the Danish or the Swedish-Norwegian Government would raise difficulties; but it is necessary to direct their attention to the matter.[1]

I wish you all success with *Ambrosius*; it seems to me that such a work must inevitably win approbation both among the reading public and on the stage.[2] Once more, my hearty thanks! We all wish you and your family a happy Christmas. —Yours most sincerely,

HENRIK IBSEN.

[1] Denmark was included in the convention in November 1879.

[2] Molbech's *Ambrosius*, dedicated to the author's "old friend, Dr. Henrik Ibsen, the poet," was published before Christmas 1877. Although its performance was postponed till May, the worst month of the theatrical season, it had an immense success. The twelfth edition of the book was published in 1900.

## 136.

*To* MARKUS GRÖNVOLD.

ROME, *22nd January* 1879.[1]

DEAR MR. GRÖNVOLD,—To-day I write with a double purpose. In the first place, I wish to thank you for your friendly letter of the 9th inst. and the other things which you have sent me by post; in the second, taking advantage of your kind offer, to send you the enclosed receipted account for the Munich Court Theatre. If you will be good enough to deliver this to the head cashier, the amount will be paid to you. In regard to its employment I have written you already, and have nothing to add except a request that you will not forget to reimburse yourself for all the outlay you have had on my behalf.

There are a great many of our countrymen in Rome this winter, as well as in Munich; but, like you, I see little of most of them. We live quietly. Our dinner is brought ready-cooked to the house, and the landlady provides us with breakfast and supper. Everything is much cheaper here than in Munich; wine, in particular, is to be had this winter at a ridiculously low price; in the Sabine towns an excellent wine is sold at 3 soldi a litre! I do not remember if I have already told you that I am availing myself of opportunities to buy old paintings; I have already secured eleven, all good and valuable, at comparatively low prices. I intend to purchase more, in order to decorate my future home at Munich entirely with works of art. The next thing will be to find the home; I shall very likely come to Munich before the others, to look out for a house; this will give me a chance of seeing the Art Exhibition, to which I look forward with great pleasure.

Now, enough for to-day. Please remember me to your brother and other friends and acquaintances.—Yours most sincerely,

HENRIK IBSEN.

[1] Ibsen went to Rome in the autumn of 1878. He remained in Italy for about a year.

137.

*To* MARKUS GRÖNVOLD.

ROME, *9th March* 1879.

DEAR MR. GRÖNVOLD,—Please excuse my not writing until to-day to thank you for the draft enclosed in your letter of 29th January. Both came to hand at the proper time; and almost every day since I have had the good intention of writing you a few lines, but something or other has invariably come in the way.

Except for a few short spells of fine weather, the winter here has been colder and more unpleasant than it usually is in Rome. We have not had snow or ice; but snow is still lying far down on the whole chain of the Apennines and on the Sabine mountains; and they present a magnificent spectacle. We are now enjoying the most glorious summer weather any one could desire; the almond blossom is already over, the cherry trees are in full bloom, and all the fields are covered with fresh green grass and violets. I often wish that you were here; we should take excursions together. I have not much intercourse with the Scandinavians who are here this winter. Kronberg went off in the beginning of November to Tunis and Egypt, and only returned a few days ago. Nyström is in full activity; but his undertakings are more of an industrial than of an artistic nature; he employs several marble-cutters, and furnishes copies from antiques, sepulchral monuments, etc. The other Swedish artists here you hardly know; the Danish artist, Bredal, has several times spoken to me of you; of Danes there are here (besides Bredal) Olrik, Helsted, Rosenstand, and some younger ones.

·    ·    ·    ·    ·    ·    ·    ·

As regards ourselves, we are getting on well; perhaps we shall spend the whole summer in Italy, somewhere in the mountains; but at the beginning of October at latest we shall return to Munich, if nothing unforeseen occurs to prevent our doing so.

I must confess that I have several times thought of sending

Sigurd back to Munich alone, to continue his studies; but for various reasons I wish to get into closer contact again with German literary life. Here one is too entirely out of touch with the movements of the day. But enough of this for the present. With our kindest regards to yourself, your brother, and all other good friends, in particular Prof. Maurer and his family,—I remain, Yours most sincerely,

HENRIK IBSEN.

### 138.

#### *To* LORENTZ DIETRICHSON.

ROME, 18th April 1879.

MY DEAR OLD FRIEND,—You will, no doubt, be surprised to receive a letter from these parts from the undersigned, who is generally anything but a good correspondent. It is, however, not on my own account that I am writing to you, but on behalf of some one else.

To proceed at once to business: Miss Mathilde Smith, the artist, who is at present, as you are perhaps aware, residing in Munich, is applying this year for a grant from the Schäffer Bequest. She has not hitherto received any grant whatever, and it is only at my instigation that she is again making application; but she will, of course, as on previous occasions, be passed by for the sake of others, unless some influential person on the spot advocates her cause. This is why I appeal to you on her behalf. I do not know if you have anything to do officially with the distribution of the grants in question, but I have no doubt that you can be of assistance to her if you choose.

Miss Smith's gifts are not of the greatest, but she has a very fair amount of talent, quite as much as many of those whose claims receive consideration at the distribution of grants. Nothing has ever been done in Norway to help and encourage her; the Art Association of Christiania has, as far as I know, never bought a picture from her. She supports herself principally by the sale of her paintings in Germany; the Munich Art Association buys one of them almost every year; other German associations do the same; and the German art-critics always appraise her work favourably. But what she now stands much in need of, in order that she may be able to introduce more variety into her pictures, is the opportunity to make new studies· The grant which she is applying for would provide this; and it seems to me that it would be heartless on the part of the authorities at home if they were again to refuse her assistance. Miss Smith is undoubtedly no longer a beginner; but the Bequest is not intended to assist such only; old Calmeyer has for a number of years been receiving a pension from it. As regards Miss Smith's personal character, it is in every respect irreproachable; she is thoroughly deserving of assistance. I am convinced that it would be doing a good deed to grant her application; and I feel certain that it will be granted if you take the matter into your hands; so I recommend it warmly to you.

We have been here since the middle of September, and do not return to Munich till October. Sigurd, who left school last year (he passed his final examination with the highest marks in every subject, and honourable mention), is now studying at the University here. In autumn he will enter the University of Munich, and take the general law classes for a year or so, until it is necessary for him to go to Christiania to study Norwegian law. Whether or not we shall accompany him and settle down there for some time, is still undecided. I have no great inclination to do it. We are all well and happy here. I may confide to you privately that I am preparing to write a new dramatic work this summer. Another piece of news is that I have taken to buying old paintings; I hope to bring a dozen or so of excellent ones back to Munich with me.

Although there is nothing particular to answer in this letter, I shall, of course, be delighted to hear from you. Should you write, please address your letter to " Consolato di Danimarca," as there is no Swedish-Norwegian Consul here for the time being. With kindest remembrances from all of us to Mrs. Dietrichson and to Honoria, who is now, I suppose, a grown-up young lady,—I remain, Your sincere friend,

HENRIK IBSEN.[1]

139.

*To* MARKUS GRÖNVOLD.

ROME, 27*th June* 1879.

DEAR MR. GRÖNVOLD,—Allow me, although it is rather late, to offer you my best thanks for the friendly telegram received on my birthday. And may I request you to convey my thanks to the other signers of the telegram, Mr. and Mrs. Nielsen, and also to your brother and Mr. Trom, who were good enough to send me a telegram on the same occasion. I am, I regret to say, myself so negligent in the matter of such courtesies, that I have no right whatever to expect them from others; I am consequently doubly pleased and surprised to be so kindly remembered.

It is now rather hot in Rome, so in about a week we are going to Amalfi, which, being close to the sea, is cooler, and offers opportunity for bathing. I intend to complete there a new dramatic work on which I am now engaged.

Will you kindly, after receipt of this, keep for me, instead of forwarding, the little weekly paper which comes regularly from Leipzig. Letters you will be good enough to continue forwarding, addressed as at present; at the Danish Consulate here they will always know where I am.

In the beginning of October we intend to return to Munich. For a year Sigurd will be able to study there; then he must go to Christiania. It is still undecided whether or not we are to

[1] Mathilde Smith (1835–1882), a Norwegian artist, studied at Düsseldorf under Hans Gude. She did not receive the grant from the Schäffer Bequest which she applied for in 1879.

accompany him and stay in Christiania as long as he is at the University; it is probable, however, that we shall do so. But I will stay no longer than is necessary; I have the feeling beforehand that I shall have to go off again. Then I shall, in all probability, settle once more in Munich, which offers me so many advantages, and where I feel as if I were in my own spiritual home.

I have bought a number of old paintings here—twenty or so, some of them fairly large, all valuable, and one or two of them particularly good. These, with the pictures which I have at Munich, will suffice to decorate three spacious rooms in the manner which is most to my taste.[1] We have a great mind to furnish the rooms ourselves, so as to have everything as we like it, and in one style; but the possibility of soon going to Christiania prevents our deciding.

Mrs. Maurer also did me the great and undeserved favour of writing to me on my birthday. May I ask you to convey to her a first instalment of thanks, along with very kind remembrances to the whole family. Kind regards to all other friends. We are enjoying life here, but there are often times when I wish that I could be in Munich for a little; especially in this enervating heat I often think with a sigh of all that delicious " Bock " which you are revelling in there, and which I must do without. Well, we cannot have everything at once; and a change is good for people.

Good-bye for to-day. Again many thanks from—Your sincere friend,

HENRIK IBSEN.

[1] Writing to Hegel in November 1876 on the subject of these same pictures, Ibsen remarks: " You would hardly believe what bargains are to be had in Italy in this line when one is lucky ; and I have been lucky. I am certain that if I should ever be obliged to part with these pictures, I could sell them here, or elsewhere in Germany, for two or three times what I paid for them. But I hope to be able to keep them, even though they represent so and so much unemployed capital, and therefore with each year cost me more."

140.

*To* JOHN PAULSEN.

AMALFI, 20*th September* 1879.

DEAR MR. PAULSEN,—A new dramatic work, which I have just completed, has occupied so much of my time during these last months that I have had absolutely none to spare for answering letters.[1] This is the reason why you have not heard from me sooner in reference to your letter of 9th August.

It was impossible for me, while I was so busy, to read your manuscript and give a well-considered opinion about it; it would have taken much more of my time than, with every wish to oblige, I could spare. Nor is it possible for me even now to be of service to you in this matter. We are leaving here immediately. Our first destination is still uncertain, but we are due in Munich early in October.

I must also tell you that I have been obliged to make it a fixed rule not to act as intermediary between Hegel and authors who wish to have their works published by him. It was so much the easier to come to this determination as experience has proved to me that such intervention is absolutely useless. Hegel has himself a very sure instinct as to what it will, and what it will not, serve his purpose to publish; and that I should request him to take other considerations into account is, I am certain, not your intention; nor could I do so.

But, dear Mr. Paulsen, is it of advantage for your training and development generally to remain so long in Paris? I cannot believe that it is. French literature you can study just as well elsewhere; and many other studies which are imperative, if you are to make your way in the profession you have chosen, can be pursued with much more advantage in Germany. You ought to go to Munich, and work hard there for a whole year,

[1] *A Doll's House* was written in Rome and at Amalfi in the summer of 1879.

or even two—attending lectures at the University according to a fixed, well-considered plan. Nothing contributes so much to mature a man's mind as acquiring a thorough knowledge of some one subject. History would be the most suitable subject for you. You ought to make a thorough study of the history of civilisation, of the history of literature, and of the history of art; and there are particularly good professors in Munich in these branches. An extensive knowledge of history is indispensable to an author; without it he is not in a position to understand the conditions of his own age, or to judge men, their motives and actions, except in the most incomplete and superficial manner.

Now, think over this, and if you can, come to Munich this winter. With kindest regards from all of us,—I remain, Yours very sincerely,

HENRIK IBSEN.[1]

141.

*To* LORENTZ DIETRICHSON.

MUNICH, 19*th December* 1879.

DEAR FRIEND,—Let me first of all thank you for sending me your polemic poem and congratulate you on it, as well as on the immediate demand for a second edition. I hope that others will soon be called for. It gave me much pleasure to read the light, adroit verse, in which I do not think you have many rivals. Your idea of basing the whole poem on the Kivleslaat legend is both an original and an effective one.

The cause in which you are labouring is unmistakably one of far-reaching import. But it seems to me very doubtful whether it will be possible to arouse and reform our good Norwegian people gradually—bit by bit; it seems to me doubtful if better artistic conditions can be arrived at before the

---

[1] Paulsen went to  Munich in October 1879.

intellectual soil has been thoroughly turned up and cleansed, and the intellectual swamp drained.[1]

As long as a people considers it more important to build meeting-houses than theatres, as long as it is readier to support the Zulu Mission than the Art Museum, art cannot really thrive, cannot even be considered as of immediate necessity. I do not think it is of much use to plead the cause of art with arguments derived from its own nature, which with us is still so little understoood, or rather so thoroughly misunderstood. What is needed first of all with us is to fall upon and eradicate all that gloomy medieval monasticism which narrows the view and stupefies the mind. My opinion is that at the present time it is of no use to wield one's weapons *for* art; one must simply turn them *against* what is hostile to art. First clear this away, and then we can build. Of course, I do not mean by these remarks that a poem like yours, ardent and full of conviction, will not have an arousing influence on many; I only mean that it will hardly succeed in changing the general, popular view of the matter.

But, old carissimo, do not let this influence you. Continue to write, and to speak, and to lay about you, for what you have chosen as your task in life. Even if no one of your different endeavours conducts to the goal, there is something in the spectacle of a man devoting all his powers to one task that arouses and incites to imitation. This is a swiftly progressive age; and you are a determined man, and have, I hope, still many years before you; so you will be certain to accomplish something. This is, briefly, what I have to say. I am sure that you will not misinterpret it.

I ought to have written to you long ago; but the publication of my new play and its despatch to the theatres has claimed my time to the exclusion of almost everything else; I have had a great deal of trouble with a German edition which was published simultaneously with the Norwegian. Feeling certain that

[1] Dietrichson's poem: *Kivleslaaten*, "Thema og Variationer over et norsk Folkesagn," was a plea for the recognition of art and of the national traditions as valuable civilising influences.

Hegel, our publisher, would bestow a copy of the play on you, I did not send you one myself.

I was on the point of forgetting something. Have you not noticed that you have in the division of your poem entitled, *A Norwegian Sculptor*, the subject for a five-act popular play (Folkeskuespil?) Act 1. In the Mountains. The wood-carver. The art-enthusiast from the capital discovers him and takes him away with him. Act 2. In Christiania. The boy the hero of the day; great hopes; sent to Rome. Act 3. In Rome. Life there among the artists and the Italian lower class. Act 4. Many years later. Return to Christiania; forgotten; everything changed. Act 5. At home again in the mountain parish; ruin. Write this with songs and dances and popular costumes and irony and devilry. It seems to me that it would be exactly the kind of theme for you.

Kindest regards to all of you from me and mine.—Yours ever,

HENRIK IBSEN.

## 142.

### To the "NATIONALTIDENDE."

MUNICH, 17*th February* 1880.

To the EDITOR.

SIR,—In No. 1360 of your esteemed paper I have read a letter from Flensburg, in which it is stated that *A Doll's House* (in German *Nora*) has been acted there, and that the conclusion of the play has been changed—the alteration having been made, it is asserted, by my orders. This last statement is untrue. Immediately after the publication of *Nora*, I received from my translator, Mr. Wilhelm Lange, of Berlin, who is also my business manager as far as the North German theatres are concerned, the information that he had reason to fear that an "adaptation" of the play, giving it a different ending, was about to be published, and that this would probably be chosen in preference to the original by several of the North German theatres.

In order to prevent such a possibility, I sent to him, for use in case of absolute necessity, a draft of an altered last scene, according to which Nora does not leave the house, but is forcibly led by Helmer to the door of the children's bedroom; a short dialogue takes place, Nora sinks down at the door, and the curtain falls.

This change I myself, in the letter to my translator, stigmatise as "barbaric violence" done to the play. Those who make use of the altered scene do so entirely against my wish. But I trust that it will not be used at very many German theatres.

As long as no literary convention exists between Germany and the Scandinavian countries, we Scandinavian authors enjoy no protection from the law here, just as the German authors enjoy none with us. Our dramatic works are, therefore, in Germany exposed to acts of violence at the hands of translators, theatrical directors, stage-managers, and actors at the smaller theatres. When my works are threatened, I prefer, taught by experience, to commit the act of violence myself, instead of leaving them to be treated and " adapted " by less carefully and less skilful hands.—Yours respectfully,

HENRIK IBSEN.

### 143.

#### To HEINRICH LAUBE.[1]

MUNICH, 18*th February* 1880.

HONOURED SIR,—It was a great pleasure to me to learn that my latest play, *A Doll's House*, is to be acted at the "Wiener Stadttheater" under your widely renowned management.

[1] Heinrich Laube (1806–1884), one of the best known authors belonging to the school known as Young Germany, was Director of the Burgtheatre in Vienna from 1849 to 1867. He afterwards founded and

You are of opinion that the play, on account of its ending, does not properly come under the category of " Schauspiel "; but, dear Sir, do you really attach much value to categories? I, for my part, believe that the dramatic categories are elastic, and that they must accommodate themselves to the literary facts— not *vice versâ*. This much is certain, that the play with its present ending has had an almost unprecedented success in Stockholm, Christiania, and Copenhagen.

The alternative altered ending I have prepared, not because I thought it was required, but simply at the request of a North German manager and of an actress who is going on tour in North Germany as " Nora." I herewith send you a copy of the altered scene, on reading which you will, I hope, acknowledge that the effect of the piece can only be weakened by employing it. I trust that you will decide to produce the play in its original form. With the assurance of my highest esteem, believe me, honoured Sir,—Yours respectfully,

HENRIK IBSEN.

## 144.

### *To* KRISTIAN ELSTER.

MUNICH, *25th March* 1880.

DEAR SIR,—You have been good enough to send me two of your later stories, and I herewith beg to thank you for the kind attention. You are mistaken in assuming that I very probably know nothing about these stories or your literary work generally. On the contrary, I have followed your career as an author with interest and sympathy from the time when your youthful dramatic productions first came under my observation. In these and in everything else you have published—in your

managed the "Wiener Stadttheater." He powerfully influenced the German stage in the direction of a more faithful representation of human nature.

stories, and very particularly in your descriptions of nature and the customs of the people in different parts of our country—I have seen evidences of a pleasing and distinctive talent, which, if I remember rightly, has also been acknowledged by the professional critics, and, what is of greater importance, by the best section of our reading public.

I believe, however, that it would be of extreme advantage to your future as an author, if it were possible for you very soon to make acquaintance with wider and freer spheres of life than those to which you have hitherto been confined. If it is in your power to give up your other occupations (of the nature of which I am not certain), I cannot imagine that a travelling-grant, either from the Schäffer Bequest or, better still, from the State funds for such purposes, would be denied you.

Should you make up your mind to apply for one, and should fortune favour your application, my strong advice to you would then be to include Germany in your plan of travel. Here there is up-to-date civilisation to study; and for observation, the manners and customs of a people related to, and yet different from, your own, and therefore perhaps of special interest to you.

I know what I myself owe to my acquaintance with the life of the wider world, and I often think with sympathy of the many gifted men and women at home who are hampered by the narrowness of the conditions under which they live. I need not, therefore, assure you that it would give me great pleasure if you succeeded in making your way out for a time, to gain experience and increased clearsightedness by instituting comparisons. Should you ever come to these parts, you will receive a hearty welcome from—Yours very sincerely,

HENRIK IBSEN.[1]

---

[1] Kristian Elster (born in 1841) died at Trondhjem in 1881. His stories were, for the most part, published in newspapers. In 1879 he brought out *Tora Trondal* separately, and after his death *Dangerous People* was published. His works were collected and published in two volumes in 1898.

## 145.

*To* VALFRID VASENIUS.[1]

MUNICH, 30*th March* 1880.

DEAR SIR,—I should have written to you long ago. For several months now I have had your kind letter and your book on my earlier works lying before me on my writing-table; and every day I have thought of acknowledging them; but something or other has always intervened, not only demanding my time, but scattering my thoughts in different directions, and depriving me of the tranquillity of mind without which I could not write the long letter I wished to send.

The same conditions still prevail, and there is no immediate prospect of anything else; but I cannot and will not delay any longer, though I must write much more briefly than I meant to.

Let me tell you, then, that I received your book and the pamphlet accompanying it with very great pleasure, and that the pleasure became even greater as I read.

It is, of course, difficult, nay, impossible for me to sit in judgment on my own writings; but I can safely say that I could not wish for a better pleader, in behalf of these writings and of myself, than I have found in you. Everything you say regarding my intentions, regarding the fundamental idea in the different works, regarding the characters and their relations to each other—this, and much, much more of what you write, is exactly what I very particularly desired to have publicly insisted on. Therefore I offer you my sincerest and heartiest thanks; you have truly done me an invaluable service.

Be assured that I appreciate equally highly that love of the

---

[1] Valfrid Vasenius (born 1848), first " docent " and then (since 1902) professor of Finnish and Scandinavian literature at Helsingfors University, published in 1879 a work entitled, *Henrik Ibsen's dramatiske digtning i dess förste skede* (*Henrik Ibsen's Dramatic Poetry in its First Stage*).

subject which manifests itself everywhere throughout your long work, and which will not fail to influence many of those who read your book. As regards knowledge of all the circumstances connected with my literary production, I believe that no one is in possession of so much as yourself. Many of the criticisms which you quote were quite unknown to me; and I could not but rejoice to see all the many misconstructions refuted and replaced by interpretations which are both friendlier and truer. It is my hope and desire that your book may become the chief source applied to by those who wish to gain an understanding of my literary work — its outward and inward coherence.

From the newspapers I see that at Helsingsfors, as elsewhere, *A Doll's House* is giving rise to a violent dispute. Your interpretation of the play, as far as I have yet seen it, has my entire approval, and I feel certain that the future will show that we are right.

I should like much to visit Helsingsfors and to make your personal acquaintance, and I hope some day to do both. In the meantime, please do me the pleasure of accepting enclosed photograph. One of yourself would be most acceptable to me.

Allow me once more, dear Sir, to return you my sincere and hearty thanks for all you have done.—Yours very faithfully,

HENRIK IBSEN.[1]

---

[1] At the time Vasenius received this letter, he was engaged in a violent dispute on the subject of *A Doll's House*. He had delivered a public lecture on it on the 12th of March 1880, by which he had drawn down upon himself the displeasure of those who considered the play "immoral."

Two years later, Vasenius wrote another book on Ibsen's works—the longest which had yet appeared. He also revised the Finnish translation of *The Pretenders*. On this occasion Ibsen wrote to him: "It always gives me special pleasure when any work of mine finds its way into Finland, a country with whose people I have a very strong sympathy —and where I have many dear friends." In 1899, Ibsen signed the address presented to the Czar by eminent European authors, artists, and scientists, on the occasion of the *coup d'état* in Finland.

## 146.

*To* LUDWIG PASSARGE.

MUNICH, 19*th May* 1880.

DEAR SIR,—It is most negligent of me only to be answering your friendly letter to-day, seeing that I have been in possession of it for nearly two months! I beg of you to forgive me.

And now let me first of all thank you heartily for the interest which you display in my writings. Your idea of *Peer Gynt* accords perfectly with what I had in my mind when I wrote the book; and I naturally rejoice that my poem has found a translator who has clearly divined its inmost meaning and aim.

I was, nevertheless, surprised to learn that you consider it a suitable work to translate, and to publish in German. I must admit that I have my doubts on the subject. Of all my books I consider *Peer Gynt* the least likely to be understood out of Scandinavia. Please remember that most of your possible German readers do not possess your own qualifications for understanding the book. You yourself are familiar with Norwegian nature and the manners and customs of the Norwegian people, with our literature and our national turn of thought: you know Norwegian men and women, and understand the Norwegian character. And is not all this necessary in order to be able to enjoy such a poem? I will not conceal my misgivings from you, although I take it for granted that you thoroughly weighed all these considerations before deciding to undertake such a difficult and lengthy task.

I entirely agree with your theory on the subject of translation in general. The specimens sent me I have read with great interest; it seems to me that they render the original with all possible accuracy.

I hope that you will not misconstrue my frank expression of the reasons which in my opinion make your undertaking a risky one. I have considered it my duty not to conceal my doubts; if they prove unfounded, I shall, of course, be only too pleased

My wife and my son well remember the pleasant meeting with you at Odde in Hardanger, and they request me to offer you their kindest regards.  Thanking you again most sincerel I remain,—Yours respectfully,

HENRIK IBSEN

### 147.

#### *To* FREDERIK HEGEL.

MUNICH, 31st May 1880.

DEAR MR. HEGEL,—Please oblige me by sending me 1000 Kroner, as usual in German bank-notes.

I have a new project, on the subject of which I should like to hear your frank opinion, and which I shall therefore briefly explain to you.

I do not think I am mistaken in my impression that the Preface to the new edition of *Catilina* has been read with considerable interest.  Suppose I were now to write a little book of 160 to 200 pages, containing similar information as to the outward and inward conditions under which each one of my works came into being?  In connection with *Lady Inger* and *The Vikings*, I should deal with my stay in Bergen; in connection with *The Pretenders* and *The Comedy of Love*, I should

---

[1] Ludwig Passarge (born in 1825) was originally a lawyer, until 1887 in Prussian government employment.  He travelled a great deal in Scandinavia, and published interesting accounts of his travels.  In 1877 he met Fru Ibsen and her son at Odde in Hardanger; and at Bergen he bought *Peer Gynt*, which he determined to translate.  He got into communication with Ibsen himself through Paul Heyse, who had some difficulty in persuading the " strange man " (as Heyse describes Ibsen in a letter) to reply to Passarge's advances.  The translation was published in October 1880.  In 1881, Passarge translated *Brand*, and in 1882, Ibsen's Poems.  In 1883 he published *Henrik Ibsen, Ein Beitrag zur neuesten Geschichte der norwegischen Nationallitteratur.*  He met Ibsen twice, at Gossensass in 1884 and at Munich in 1889.

describe the Christiania period following; then would come my life in Rome, in connection with *Brand, Peer Gynt,* etc. etc.

I should not, of course, attempt any interpretation of my books; in that domain it is best that the public and the critics should be allowed to disport themselves as they please—for the present at least; I should simply tell of the circumstances and conditions under which I wrote, observing the utmost discretion and leaving a wide field for all kinds of surmises.

Do you advise me to carry out or to give up this plan? Do you consider it a good idea, and do you think this the proper time, or would it perhaps be better to wait? Favour me, when convenient, with your expert opinion. But, please, let this matter be entirely between ourselves for the present. Whatever our decision may be, I shall spend this summer in preparing the manuscript; for I do not intend to write a new play this year, and I have nothing else to occupy myself with.

My wife and Sigurd are going to Norway soon, but I shall remain here.

With kindest regards to your family,—I remain, ever yours most sincerely,

HENRIK IBSEN.

### 148.

#### *To* LUDWIG PASSARGE.

MUNICH, 16*th June* 1880.

DEAR SIR,—Permit me to reply briefly to your esteemed letter of the 4th inst.

I am very glad to learn that you have found a first-class publisher for your translation of *Peer Gynt.* But, with every desire to oblige, I am not in a position to give explanations of the many allusions in the book which may be unintelligible to German readers; for it is impossible for me, as a foreigner, to judge what needs explanation and what does not. For the same

reason I consider that it would be useless for me to apply to
Dietrichson or any other Norwegian. I believe that no one
can judge better in this matter than yourself; and if there is
any particular point on which you feel uncertain, it should be
easy for you to obtain information during your approaching
visit to Norway. But it is my impression that you know as
much of matters Norwegian as any native.

Neither is it possible for me to give you an account of the
circumstances which led to the production of *Peer Gynt*. To
make the matter intelligible, I should have to write a whole
book, and for that the time has not yet come. Everything that
I have written has the closest possible connection with what I
have lived through, even if it has not been my own personal
experience; in every new poem or play I have aimed at my own
spiritual emancipation and purification—for a man shares the
responsibility and the guilt of the society to which he belongs.
Hence I once wrote the following dedicatory lines in a copy
of one of my books:

> At *leve* er krig med trolde
> i hjertets og hjernens hvælv;
> at *digte*—det er at holde
> dommedag over sig selv.[1]

It is only natural that you do not know the word
"pusselanker," for it does not belong to the written language
at all; it means "little legs or feet," and is only used by
mothers and nurses in talking to small children.

The meaning of the verses about which you ask is this:
*Peer Gynt* claims as a title of admission to hell that he has
been a slave-dealer. To this "the lean one" replies that there
are many who have done worse things, who have, for instance,
trafficked in wills and souls, and yet, from the fact that they

---

[1] To *live*—is to war with fiends
That infest the brain and the heart;
To *write*—is to summon one's self
And play the judge's part.

have done it in a "twaddling way," that is to say, without demoniacal earnestness, have not qualified themselves for hell, but only for the "casting-ladle."

This short answer is all I am able to give you at present. Wishing you a pleasant journey to Norway, and hoping that you will remember me to any of my friends and acquaintances whom you may happen to meet there,—I remain, Yours respectfully and sincerely,

HENRIK IBSEN.

## 149.

### *To* FREDERIK HEGEL.

MUNICH, 16th July 1880.

DEAR MR. HEGEL,—Thank you for your kind letter of the 6th June, and for the 1125 Marks contained in it. I take the liberty of sending you the enclosed bill of exchange, with the request that you will cash it and purchase for me Swedish Government Bonds or similar securities to the amount of about 4000 Kroner.

I agree with many of your objections to the literary project which I suggested; we will therefore leave the matter in abeyance for the time being.

My wife and Sigurd go to Norway at the beginning of next month; I do not think, however, that they will travel *viâ* Copenhagen this time. But you have probably heard all our news from Mrs. Thoresen.

That amiable man, Carl Andersen, came to see us some little time ago. He told us that you had bought a beautiful new villa, the one which formerly belonged to Orla Lehmann. May you and yours spend many happy days in it! I do not imagine, however, that you will part with your old place on the Strandvei, which possesses, in my estimation, the greatest of all recommendations—it lies on the Sound. Among the things wanting to me down here, the want of the sea is what I have the greatest difficulty in becoming reconciled to.

With kindest regards to yourself and to your family,—I remain, Ever yours sincerely,

HENRIK IBSEN.

## 150.

### *To* FREDERIK HEGEL.

ROME, 16*th January* 1881.[1]

DEAR MR. HEGEL,—Please accept our very best thanks, both for your kind Christmas and New Year's greetings and for the interesting books, which have given us much pleasure, and have brought home nearer to us during the Christmas season. Jacobsen's book [2] is a fine work in every respect; I venture to say that it is one of the very best of its kind which has been written in our day. When you write to him, please be good enough to offer him my heartiest congratulations. Also remember me very kindly to Drachmann. As to the latter's *Peder Tordenskjold*, it seems to me, between ourselves, that it is not on a level with many of the excellent things that he has written before. It is evident that this poem was not fully matured in his imagination before he committed it to paper.

We are spending a very agreeable and sociable winter. In the Scandinavian circle a number of pleasant people are associating on more or less intimate terms, in a manner which has never before been possible. The new Danish Minister, Hegermann-Lindencrone, is already very popular among the Scandinavians. I regret that the same cannot be said for the Swedish-Norwegian Minister; but as compensation,

---

[1] Ibsen went to Rome in November 1880. He had spent part of the summer at Berchtesgaden in company with Jonas Lie.

[2] *Niels Lyhne.*

we have in our Consul a man who knows how to keep the circle together, and who is himself most hospitable. Professor Heegaard is here; I was grieved to see him so ill as he was at the time of his arrival; now, however, he seems to be much better; but he is still compelled to lead a very retired and quiet life.

I am obliged to ask you to send me any interest on my money which is on hand, and any sums which may have been paid by the Theatre Royal or by Director Rasmussen. Kindly send a draft on Paris or Berlin this time; there is now a tax upon drafts on Italy which, though inconsiderable in itself, is the occasion of a good deal of trouble.

With our kindest regards to yourself and your family, believe me,—Yours most sincerely,

HENRIK IBSEN.

### 151.

*To* HAGBARD BERNER.

ROME, VIA CAPO LE CASE, 27*th March* 1881.

To HR. STATSREVISOR BERNER.

SIR,—Although I unfortunately have not the honour of your personal acquaintance, I nevertheless venture to address you in Björnsterne Björnson's and my own name, in a matter which to me, and probably also to Björnson, is of very great importance. It concerns an appeal to the now assembled Storthing. My observation of your journalistic career during a number of years leads me to the conclusion that you, more than most, are likely to be both willing and able to support the cause of which I shall now take the liberty to give you a brief account.

At the time when the Storthing voted, first to Björnson, and afterwards to myself, a State pension of 400 specie-dollars

22

(£90), every one regarded this pension in the light of a public acknowledgment and recompense of our literary labours; and as such it was gratefully accepted by us.

The conception of an author's right of property in his work was very imperfectly developed at that time in our countries, and has by no means arrived at maturity yet. Neither the Government nor the Storthing had then taken any measures to protect Norwegian authors—and more particularly the dramatists— from piracy. In other words, the laws did not secure for us, as they did for other citizens of the State, the certainty of enjoying the fruits of our own labour. From the Christiania Theatre we, as a rule, received a small payment, once for all, for our plays. For *The Vikings* they offered me 30 specie-dollars, informing me at the same time that if I was not satisfied with this, they would, being legally entitled to do so, play the piece without giving me any compensation whatever. The other theatres in Norway, and the travelling theatrical companies, naturally paid nothing; and the same state of matters prevailed throughout Sweden and Denmark, as far as the smaller theatres were concerned; indeed, even the Theatre Royal in Stockholm, as you may remember, once produced a play of Björnson's without paying a single farthing for it, although the author protested vigorously. Since then, perhaps thanks to the sensation this matter aroused, the Theatre Royal in Stockholm and the Danish Theatre Royal have made an agreement with us to pay such a sum as they think proper; an arrangement which we are obliged to accept and even to be grateful for, as neither the Government nor the Storthing has protected our interests by means of literary conventions with Sweden and Denmark.

In this manner almost the whole series of Björnson's and my own dramatic works have been taken from us, one after the other, without our having enjoyed the pecuniary rewards which fall to the lot of authors in other countries. How great the loss which we have suffered really is, I have only learned since copyright conventions have at last been concluded with Sweden and Denmark. But for Björnson and myself these conventions have come too late, seeing that almost everything we have produced in the dramatic line has been, under the previous lawless conditions, either taken from us, or acquired at a ridiculously low rate.

But this is not all; indeed the part of the case which I have just explained is the part that affects us least seriously. What does us much more harm is that Norway has not concluded a literary convention with Germany or any other country outside of Scandinavia. You must be aware that most of Björnson's and my books have been translated in Germany, and that many of our plays are produced in the theatres there. But if people at home infer from this favourable reception that we are probably well paid, or even paid anything worth mentioning at all, they are, I regret to say, very much mistaken; it is the translators or their publishers who reap the benefit; and we Norwegian dramatists have absolutely no legal means of preventing this. If we have translations made of our plays at our own expense, we may be tolerably certain that within a short time cheaper translations will appear and supersede ours.

That Norway should voluntarily take steps to bring about a general international copyright - convention, or, to put it more correctly, should become a party to the convention already existing between most of the European States, is, of course, not imaginable. Indeed, as a good Norwegian, I cannot even wish that such a step should be taken; because it is plain that such a convention would, with us, greatly increase the cost of every foreign scientific or literary work which it might be desirable to make accessible to our public by means of translation. And this would be equivalent to obstructing a great number of those streams of enlightenment which now flow gratis into Norway. Gratis? Yes, as far as the State is concerned, but not as far as Björnson and I are concerned. For it is we two who for a number of years have been paying, and still are paying, most of the tax on our country's import of foreign literary sources of information and culture. And this tax amounts to a by no means inconsiderable sum. I assert with a good conscience that Björnson and I are, comparatively speaking, the two heaviest-taxed men in Norway.

Therefore it is that I venture to ask if you would not think of taking up this matter and calling the attention of the Storthing to what I have here briefly touched upon. The State grants which Björnson and I have hitherto received are very far from being equivalent to the losses which we have suffered and are still suffering both abroad and at home. Might not the Storthing consider it equitable to grant us a reasonable indemnity by increasing our pensions? It constantly happens that citizens are indemnified for those which they have suffered from causes for which the State is responsible. And in Norway, authors, especially dramatic authors, have been suffering for a long time. It is characteristic that in our country edible game was protected by law before authors were. And as far as foreign countries are concerned, we are still in the position of noxious animals; all who choose may hunt us, without restriction; and the most galling thing of all is that we have to pay their expenses.

It is my duty to tell you that I have no authority from Björnson to write in his name. Distance has not permitted of my obtaining his assent; but I am fully convinced that he will agree in all essential points with what I have written. To me personally the matter is of great importance at the present moment, because the university legislation in force in Norway— and in Norway alone—having compelled my son to expatriate himself, thereby obliges me to extend my stay abroad for an indefinite period.

I shall not make bold to offer any suggestion as to the amount of the increase of pension proposed. I shall only with all due respect take the liberty of recalling the fact that, after Nordenskiöld and Palander discovered the North-East Passage, the Swedish Rigsdag granted each of them a pension of 4000 Kroner. I am bold enough to imagine it possible that Björnson and I, in the course of our poetic expeditions, may have discovered both north-east and north-west passages which may in the future be quite as much frequented by Scandinavians as that opened up for them by Nordenskiöld and Palander. Requesting you to use this letter in any way that you may consider most likely to further its purpose, and again urgently recommending the matter to your favourable attention, and through your intervention, to that of the Storthing,—I remain, dear Sir, Yours respectfully,

HENRIK IBSEN.[1]

## 152.

*To* HAGBARD BERNER.

SORRENTO, 14*th July* 1881.

DEAR SIR,—From a fellow-countryman at present residing in another part of Italy I yesterday received a note, in which he copies for me the following passage from a letter which he has received from a correspondent in Christiania :

" Do you know what they are saying here about Ibsen ?— that he has written to Berner and declared that, after having for a considerable time carefully followed the course of politics and the newspaper polemics, he has finally joined the party of the

[1] Hagbard Berner was from 1880 to 1888 one of the most influential members of the "Left" (Liberal and Radical) party in the Storthing. In compliance with Ibsen's appeal in this letter, he brought forward, and on various occasions supported, a proposal to increase Ibsen's and Björnson's pensions by the sum of 2400 Kroner per annum, in consideration of their services to their country, and of the small remuneration which they received for their works, owing to the existing state of the copyright laws. Some of the members of the "Right" party disputed the statement that Ibsen's writings had been of benefit to his country, and maintained—what was really the case—that the losses of both authors were not due to the lack of copyright laws in Norway, but to the lack of them in Denmark, in which country their books were printed and published.
Björnson was in America from the autumn of 1880 till May 1881.

Left; and that in the same letter he expresses the hope that Berner will interest himself in the procuring of larger pensions for the authors, as their present ones are very insufficient. The whole thing is, in my opinion, a malicious libel; but I think it right to inform you of the rumour, which is boldly propagated, and which it might be worth while to put a stop to."

As a rule I do not choose to refute rumours concerning myself and my affairs; but in the present instance the rumour has, in the course of its propagation, assumed a more than ordinarily base form, even for Christiania gossip. I therefore permit myself to ask a favour of you. Will you be kind enough to have my letter to you printed in full in the *Dagblad*, which I trust will grant the space necessary for the purpose.—Yours respectfully,

HENRIK IBSEN.

153.

*To* CAMILLA COLLETT.[1]

SORRENTO, *August* 1881.

. . . summer, including the doctor's degree, so that he now has to work pretty hard.[2] My wife suffers more than we do from the heat, and especially from the sirocco; but she manages to keep in health by bathing every day: I do not believe that

---

[1] In her remarkable novel, *Amtmandens Dötre* (The Sheriff's Daughters), published in 1855, in *Fra de Stummes Lejr* (From the Camp of the Dumb), published in 1877, and in other works, Camilla Collett raised all the questions connected with woman's position in society and woman's rights. Her writings, especially *Fra de Stummes Lejr*, were of great influence in bringing about a change in public opinion; and there is no doubt that they influenced Henrik Ibsen.

[2] Sigurd Ibsen, to whom the first sentence in this mutilated letter refers, took the degree of Doctor of Law in Rome in the summer of 1882.

you could have stood a whole summer down here. Walking is almost out of the question; one has to keep as still as possible.

I very well understand the depression caused by the many literary difficulties with which you, too, have to struggle. But if you imagine that things are quite easy for every one else, I am positive that you are mistaken. And it may also very well be that the "cold self-seeking" which you think you have observed in one and another, has rather been an entirely justifiable recognition of the necessity of living *by* the work we are living *for*. Most of us are not in such a fortunate position as to be able to discard such considerations. The mean, cold self-seeking exists, in my

.    .    .    .    .    .    .    .

But I am thoroughly convinced that in spite of all difficulties, you will yet, in your full strength and vigour, enjoy the victory to which the struggle that you are maintaining with so much talent and perseverance entitles you. The ideas and visions with which you have presented the world are not of the kind destined merely to live a barren life in literature. Living reality will seize them and build upon them. That this may happen soon, soon, I too wish with all my heart.

Excuse my putting you off with these few lines, dear Mrs. Collett. My wife will write to you very soon. I beg you to believe in my warm, complete sympathy with you and your life-task. Let no one persuade you to doubt that you possess this sympathy—not even myself, if I should at any time have given you apparent occasion for doubt.

We hope soon to receive good news of you. With our united kindest regards, I remain,—Yours very sincere'y,

HENRIK IBSEN.

### 154.

### *To* Ludwig Passarge.

Sorrento, *17th August* 1881.

Dear Sir,—I was grieved to learn from your esteemed letter that you had been much annoyed by a statement made in my letter to Statsrevisor Berner in Christiania. If I could have supposed that the statement would be thus misunderstood by you, I should certainly have worded it differently. In my letter I refer, as far as I myself am concerned, only to the payments made by the theatres; in mentioning publishers, I had in mind the publishers of the different editions of Björnson's stories.

*Peer Gynt* is not intended for the stage at all; and you will remember that I myself was very doubtful as to the wisdom of publishing the work in Germany. The idea of its being a source of profit to you or your publisher would never have occurred to me; and you must not doubt that I regard myself as deeply indebted to you for bringing it out.

The same holds good with regard to the announced translation of *Brand*. This poem is not intended for the stage either; and when, in spite of the fact that three German translations already exist, you see fit to make a fourth one, you evidence an interest in my writings which I can only regard as highly flattering.

I feel convinced that the passage of my letter in question has not been misunderstood by any reader in Norway; but, to make perfectly sure, I shall, when writing publicly again on these matters, as I intend to do ere long, make a special reservation, which you will, I hope, find satisfactory.

I am eager to make acquaintance with your translation of *Brand*, and also to hear how it is received in Germany. If you should think of honouring me with a few lines, please address until the end of October to Hotel Tramontano here; after that I shall be in Rome.

I am engaged this summer in writing a new play, which will appear in autumn, and which I shall then have the pleasure of sending you.

I entreat of you not to allow your temporary displeasure to affect the sympathetic favour which you have all along shown me as an author.—Yours sincerely and gratefully,

HENRIK IBSEN.

## 155.

### *To* OLAF SKAVLAN.

ROME, 12*th November* 1881.

DEAR FRIEND,—Forgive my not having found it possible to answer your letter sooner. A new dramatic work, which is to be published at the beginning of next month, has so entirely engrossed my time that I have had to postpone all letter-writing.

The magazine which you are about to start will, I am certain, receive a hearty welcome from a large circle of Norwegian readers; and if you could succeed in introducing it into Sweden too, it seems to me that its existence would be assured for a long time to come. But if you wish to secure Swedish readers, you will, I think, require to secure Swedish collaborators; and your preliminary announcement does not make it clear to me that such is your intention.[1]

[1] Professor Skavlan and Professor Sars began in January 1882 to publish *Nyt Tidsskrift* (the New Magazine), the speciality of which was the free discussion of all the questions of the day. They continued to publish it for six years. The public regarded it as above all else an organ of "the Left," which explains Ibsen's subsequent refusal to contribute (see Letter 161).

As regards myself, it will be an honour as well as a pleasure to me to be mentioned as belonging to your circle. But at this moment I really do not see how it will be possible for me to redeem my promise of furnishing contributions. Poems I do not write, and essays are not in my line. For some time past, however, I have been occupying myself at intervals with working at a book, which is to be called *From Skien to Rome*, and which is to deal with my experiences in much the same manner as the Preface to the second edition of *Catilina* does. If you think that a few selections from this work would suit your magazine, I shall be glad in course of time to let you have them.

As I am still very much occupied, I must limit myself to-day to this note. With our kindest regards to yourself and Sars, I remain,—Yours very sincerely,

HENRIK IBSEN.

### 156.

#### *To* LUDWIG PASSARGE.

ROME, *22nd December* 1881.

DEAR SIR,—I shall not attempt to make any excuses for having allowed such an unpardonably long time to pass without fulfilling my duty of thanking you for your kind letter of the 29th of August, and for the beautiful copy of your book, *Drei Sommer in Norwegen*, which came at the same time. All I shall say is that they reached me at a very busy time. I was at Sorrento, engaged in writing the new play which has just appeared.

I have read your book on Norway with the greatest interest and pleasure. Many of the districts which you describe I have myself visited, and I cannot sufficiently admire the graphic manner in which you communicate what you have seen. I believe that you at times regard the people of the country with more favour than they deserve; but this ought only to make us the more grateful to you for your excellent book, which is written with a most thorough k ꝺ wledge of the subject.

It will give me great satisfaction if you write my biography in some German magazine. You can obtain the complete materials for it by applying to Dr. Valfrid Vasenius, Librarian, Helsingfors, who about two years ago published, as the thesis for his doctor's degree, a book on myself and my earlier works (ending with *The Pretenders*), and who has since been engaged in writing a continuation of his book, which brings the subject up to the present day. I believe that this new volume is about to appear; and Dr. Vasenius will, I am sure, be delighted to send you a copy. No one else knows so much about my life and my literary career as he does.

I was agreeably surprised yesterday by receiving your translation of *Brand*. I shall read it as soon as possible; in the meantime please accept my best thanks for this new proof of the goodwill you bear me.

My new play has now appeared, and has occasioned a terrible uproar in the Scandinavian press; every day I receive letters and newspaper articles decrying or praising it. A copy will be sent you immediately. I consider it utterly impossible, however, that any German theatre will accept the play at present. I hardly believe that they will dare to play it in the Scandinavian countries for some time to come. Ten thousand copies of it have been printed, and it is very probable that a new edition will be required ere long.[1]

Permit me once again to offer you my best and sincerest thanks, along with all good Christmas and New Year's wishes.— Yours most sincerely,

HENRIK IBSEN.

[1] *Ghosts* was at first refused by all the theatres of Scandinavia. A second edition was not called for until 1894.

157.

*To* FREDERIK HEGEL.

ROME, *2nd January* 1882.

DEAR MR. HEGEL,—Accept my best thanks for your kind letter, which I received yesterday. I did not expect that you would be able to attend to the purchase of the Bonds during the busy Christmas week, otherwise I should have written some days ago and asked you to invest only 5000 Kroner in them I find that I shall be in need of money here sooner than I had counted on, and I cannot expect a remittance from Norway until late in the month. I am therefore obliged to request the favour that you will, with your accustomed kindness, advance me 1000 Kroner. Please do not take the request and the trouble I am giving very much amiss.

I am not in the least disturbed by the violence of the reviewers and all the folly that is written on the subject of *Ghosts.* I was prepared for it. When *Love's Comedy* appeared, there was just as great an outcry in Norway as there is now. *Peer Gynt,* too, was reviled; so was *The Pillars of Society;* so was *A Doll's House.* The cry will die away this time, just as it did on former occasions.

It is surely not possible that it is Molbech in disguise who is booming his *Upwards* in the *Dagblad?*

One thing troubles me, when I think of the large edition printed. Has all this uproar hurt the sale of the book?

I have this moment received your second letter and the newspapers. I shall write to-morrow to G. Brandes and thank him for his article, which gives me very great pleasure.

With hearty thanks for the books you sent me at Christmas and for all your kindness in the past year, and with our best wishes for a happy New Year, I remain,—Yours most sincerely and gratefully,                HENRIK IBSEN

## 158

*To* GEORGE BRANDES.

ROME, *3rd January* 1882.

DEAR BRANDES,—Yesterday I had the great pleasure of receiving, through Hegel, your brilliant, perspicuous, and flattering review of *Ghosts.* Accept my warmest and heartiest thanks for the invaluable service which you have again rendered me. All who read your article must, it seems to me, have their eyes opened to what my intention with my new book was—that is to say, if they have any desire to see. For I cannot get rid of the impression that a very large number of the false interpretations which have appeared in the newspapers are the work of people who know better. In Norway, however, I do believe that the blundering has in most cases been unintentional; and the reason is not far to seek. In that country a great many of the professional reviewers are theologians, more or less disguised; and these gentlemen are, as a rule, quite unable to criticise literature rationally. That enfeeblement of the judgment which, at least in the case of the average man, is an inevitable consequence of protracted occupation with theological studies, betrays itself more especially in the judging of human character, human actions, and human motives. Practical business judgment, on the other hand, does not suffer so much from the study in question. Hence the reverend gentlemen are very often excellent members of local boards; but they are, unquestionably, our worst critics.

And what can be said of the attitude assumed by the so-called Liberal press—of these leaders of the people who speak and write of freedom of action and thought, and at the same time make themselves the slaves of the supposed opinions of their subscribers? I receive more and more corroboration of my conviction that there is something demoralising in engaging in politics and in joining parties. It will never, in any case, be possible for me to join a party that has the majority on its side. Björnson says: "The majority is always right." And as a practical politician he is bound, I suppose, to say so. I, on the contrary, must of necessity say: "The minority is always right." Naturally I am not thinking of that minority of stagnationists who are left behind by the great middle party which with us is called Liberal; but I mean that minority which leads the van, and pushes on to points which the majority has not yet reached. I mean: That man is right who has allied himself most closely with the future.

This I have written as a kind of apologia, if such should prove necessary.

The storm against *Ghosts* I was prepared for; it did not seem to me that I could take any notice of it; that would have been cowardice.

I have to thank you not only for the article in the *Morgenblad*, but also, and quite as much, for your lecture on me, and your intention of having the said lecture printed. Hegel writes that you wish to make use of some passages in my letters to you. I have, of course, no objection to your doing so. I have perfect confidence in you, in this matter as in every other. If you wish to quote from the present letter also, you are at liberty to do so.

When I think how slow and heavy and dull the general intelligence is at home, when I notice the low standard by which everything is judged, a deep despondency comes over me, and it often seems to me that I might just as well end my literary activity at once. They really do not need poetry at home; they get along so well with the *Parliamentary News* and the *Lutheran Weekly*. And then they have their party papers. I have not the gifts that go to make a satisfactory citizen, nor yet the gift of orthodoxy; and what I possess no gift for, I keep out of. Liberty is the first and highest condition for me. At home they do not trouble much about liberty, but only about liberties—a few more or a few less, according to the standpoint of their party. I feel, too, most painfully affected by the crudity, the plebeian element in all our public discussion. The very praiseworthy attempt to make of our people a democratic community, has inadvertently gone a good way towards making us a plebeian community. Distinction of soul seems to be on the decline at home.

I must break off here to-day. Please give our very kindest regards to your wife, and assure her that we do not forget her. Thank you once more, dear Brandes, for everything that you have done and are still doing for me.—Yours always,

HENRIK IBSEN.

## 159.

### *To* SOPHUS SCHANDORPH.[1]

ROME, *6th January* 1882.

HONOURED SIR,—Accept my sincere thanks for the letter which you were good enough to write me, and excuse my not having found time to answer it until to-day. It came as a very welcome Christmas greeting at the time when my new play was being subjected to all kinds of misrepresentation and foolish criticism at home.

I was quite prepared for the hubbub. If certain of our Scandinavian reviewers have no talent for anything else, they have an unquestionable talent for thoroughly misunderstanding and misinterpreting those authors whose books they undertake to judge.

Is it, however, really nothing but misunderstanding? Have not many of these misrepresentations and distortions been presented to the public by writers fully aware of their being such? I can hardly think otherwise.

They endeavour to make me responsible for the opinions which certain of the personages of my drama express. And

---

[1] Sophus Schandorph (1837–1901). A realistic writer; an intimate friend of George Brandes.

yet there is not in the whole book a single opinion, a single utterance, which can be laid to the account of the author. I took good care to avoid this. The method, the technique of the construction in itself entirely precludes the author's appearing in the speeches. My intention was to produce the impression in the mind of the reader that he was witnessing something real. Now, nothing would more effectually prevent such an impression than the insertion of the author's private opinions in the dialogue. Do they imagine at home that I have not enough of the dramatic instinct to be aware of this? Of course I am aware of it, and act accordingly. And in no other play which I have written is the author such an outsider, so entirely absent, as in this last one.

Then they say that the book preaches nihilism. It does not. It preaches nothing at all. It merely points out that there is a ferment of nihilism under the surface, at home as elsewhere. And this is inevitable. A Pastor Manders will always rouse some Mrs. Alving to revolt. And just because she is a woman, she will, once she has begun, go to great extremes.

I hope that George Brandes's article in the *Morgenblad* will be of great assistance in producing a more correct impression of the play. The *Morgenblad* has on several occasions evidenced goodwill towards me; and I trust you will be good enough to convey to the editors the assurance of my gratitude.

Your letter was both a pleasure and an honour; and it has begun an acquaintance which I have long desired. Your writings have given much enjoyment to me and my more immediate circle; and I have followed you on your different literary and critical campaigns, with great pleasure and interest.

I hope that a meeting, somewhere or other, is in store for us.—Believe me, Yours very respectfully and sincerely,

HENRIK IBSEN.

*P.S.*—If any part of the above letter is likely to be of interest to readers of the *Morgenblad*, I have no objection to its publication.

160.

*To* RUDOLF SCHMIDT.[1]

ROME, *7th January* 1882.

DEAR SIR,—I shall make no attempt to excuse my negligence in not having thanked you sooner for your *Sketches.* I am, I regret to say, not at all to be relied on as far as letter-writing is concerned, and during the last few months I have been greatly engrossed by work.

I received your book at Sorrento; and a more welcome greeting from our Northern home we could not have had. It was a source of great enjoyment to us. I do not remember having read anything surer, truer, and more delicate than these sketches; the observation is remarkably keen, and the language is incomparable in its unerring rendering of exactly the shade of thought or mood which you intend it to express. But all this and much besides, you, as a critic, have, of course, seen and known yourself. I only want to give you an idea of the impression I received when I read the stories for the first time.

I cannot remember for certain whether I expressed any opinion to Mr. Hegel on the subject of *A Revival* or not. I was under the impression that I had carried out my intention of doing so, but it is possible that I forgot. We exchange letters only occasionally, and there are always a great many things to write about. Many of the incidents and details of your drama are, in my opinion, interesting and good; but it seems to me that the subject is better fitted for a story than for a play.

I hear that *Ghosts* has aroused a terrible uproar at home. This I was prepared for, and take very coolly.

Congratulating you heartily upon your latest book, I remain, —Yours sincerely, HENRIK IBSEN.

[1] Rudolf Schmidt published in 1881 his first collection of stories, *Haandtegninger* (Sketches). His play, *En Opvækkelse* (A Revival), 1877, was acted once at the Theatre Royal, Copenhagen.

23

161.

*To* OLAF SKAVLAN.

ROME, 24*th January* 1882.

DEAR SKAVLAN,—I am obliged to tell you, in answer to your last letter, that you cannot, for some months to come, reckon upon receiving any contribution from me for the magazine. Whether or not I shall be able to send you something after that, will depend upon circumstances which I am at the present time unable to forecast. In the meantime, please put me down as a subscriber; payment will be made by my agent, Nils Lund, the bookseller.

These last weeks have brought me a wealth of experiences, lessons, and discoveries. I was quite prepared for my new play eliciting a howl from the camp of the stagnationists; and I care no more for this than for the barking of a pack of chained dogs. But the alarm which I have observed among the so-called Liberals has given me cause for reflection. The very day after my play was published, the *Dagblad* rushed a hurriedly written article into print, with the evident purpose of at once rendering any suspicion that it approved of my play impossible. This was entirely unnecessary. I myself am responsible for what I write, I and no one else. I cannot possibly bring trouble on any party; for I do not belong to any. I stand like a solitary franctireur at the outposts and act on my own responsibility.[1]

The only man in Norway who has stood up frankly, boldly, and courageously for me is Björnson. It is just like him; he has, in truth, a great, a kingly soul; and I shall never forget what he has done just now.

But how about all these champions of liberty who have been

[1] It must in justice be recorded that the *Dagblad* declared itself in favour of the performance of *Ghosts* at the Christiania Theatre, and that it reprinted George Brandes's review of the play from the Danish paper in which it appeared.

frightened out of their wits? Is it only in the domain of politics that the work of emancipation is to be permitted to go on with us? Must not men's minds be emancipated first of all? Men with such slave-souls as ours cannot even make use of the liberties they already possess. Norway is a free country, peopled by unfree men and women.

I sincerely trust that I may find I have been mistaken in the discoveries I have been making these last weeks as to the nature of Norwegian Liberalism. I cannot but believe that there must be explanatory circumstances of which I am unaware.

I feel sure you will understand my considering it right to refrain from any kind of collaboration. No one contributor to a magazine ought to take up a totally different position from the others. Could I in the present case avoid doing so? I cannot say. I am very much confused as regards the situation at home, and need time to get my bearings. Remember me to all those who are silently my friends.—Yours most sincerely,

HENRIK IBSEN.

## 162.

### To OTTO BORCHSENIUS.[1]

ROME, 28th January 1882.

DEAR SIR,—Although I see that the *Dagblad* is annoyed with me because I write letters to Copenhagen,[2] I shall no longer delay answering the communication which I had the honour of receiving from you last autumn at Sorrento.

You desired at the time some little poem in my handwriting,

---

[1] Otto Borchsenius was from 1880–1884 one of the editors of *Ude og hjemme* (At Home and Abroad), a Danish weekly paper of Liberal tendencies.

[2] Ibsen's letter to Schandorph (No. 159) had been printed in the Danish *Morgenblad*, and had called forth an angry article in the Danish *Dagblad*.

to be published in *Ude og hjemme* (At Home and Abroad) with
marginal illustrations; and you referred me to the weekly in
question for guidance in the matter of size of page, etc.  I have
looked in it in vain for similar contributions from other authors
which could give me the hints required; and, concluding that
the editors' plan has for some reason or other been given up, I
have not sent you any contribution.  If, however, you still
desire one, be good enough to let me know, and it shall be sent
at once.  Only please remember that I have nothing to offer you
except what is already in print; it will simply be a copy of one
of the small poems in my collection—either the last, or any
other which your artist might propose as more suitable for
illustration.

Allow me to avail myself of this opportunity to offer you my
best and warmest thanks for your favourable and instructive
review of my latest play.  By writing of it as you have done,
you have rendered me a service for which I shall always feel
indebted to you.  It was most consolatory to me, in the midst
of the storm of excitement which has been raging both in
Denmark and Norway, to read your temperate judgment of the
work, unaffected as it is by any party considerations.

It may well be that the play is in several respects rather
daring.  But it seemed to me that the time had come when some
boundary-posts required to be moved.  And this was an undertaking for which an older writer like myself was more fitted
than the many younger authors who might desire to do something of the kind.

I was prepared for a storm; for such storms a man cannot
alter his course; that would be cowardice.

It is not the attacks that have depressed me most, but the
alarm manifested by the so-called Liberals in Norway.  They
would be poor fellows to man barricades with.  The Norwegian
*Dagblad* has refused to print any more articles by Björnson;
and many things, if the matter is thoroughly investigated,
indicate how isolated the positions are which both he and I
occupy in our own country.  If we had not Denmark, it would

be a bad lookout for us and for the work of intellectual emancipation in Scandinavia generally. Once more my best thanks.—Yours most sincerely,

HENRIK IBSEN.

## 163.

### To FREDERIK HEGEL.

ROME, 16th March 1882.

DEAR MR. HEGEL,—I ought long ago to have replied to your kind letter of February 16th. Of course, I have not the slightest doubt that it was written out of sincere regard for me; but I must entreat you not to lend an ear to advisers in my affairs, especially when they are persons who have no proper understanding of all the really new elements of the literature of the last twenty years.

I know quite well how greedy the gossips of our little provincial towns are for all kinds of information regarding the private affairs of authors and artists; but it seems to me that I am as cautious as any one can possibly be. Indeed, some of my friends are of opinion that I injure myself by being too reserved. Mr. Otto Borchsenius writes, on the 9th of February, that almost all my Copenhagen friends are agreed that this would be the right time for me to give a distinct and complete explanation of my standpoint. He adds (I quote directly from his letter): "Your publisher, too, asked me explicitly if there was nobody who could make you (me) speak." I only quote this to show you the medley of opinions on the matter. Your last letter places it beyond doubt that he must have misinterpreted your words.

I long ago abandoned the literary plan which I once mentioned to you; and I am now extremely busy with the preparations for a new drama.

It will be a very peaceable play this time, one which may

safely be read by the State councillors and the rich merchants and their ladies, and from which the theatres will not be obliged to recoil. It will be easy to write; and I shall try to have it ready early in the autumn.[1]

As regards *Ghosts*, I feel certain that the minds of the good people at home will soon be opened to its real meaning. All the infirm, decrepit creatures who have fallen upon the work, thinking to crush it, will themselves be crushed by the verdict of the history of literature. And the anonymous poachers and highwaymen, who have shot dirt at me from their ambush in Professor Goos's shopkeepers' newspaper and other such places, are certain to be found out.[2] The future belongs to my book. Those fellows who have bellowed so about it, have no real connection with the life even of their own day.

Therefore it is that I have taken this part of the affair so very coolly. I have made many studies and observations during the storm; and these I shall find very useful for coming works.

And now I have a request to make. Will you kindly again lend me 1000 Kroner? I expressly say "lend"; for I wish to pay interest on such advance payments as I receive from you. It would be too bad if I were to tie up my own money in securities and then take advance payments from you gratis. I do not wish to part with any of my Bonds, as I only require the money for a few months. I hope you will see the matter from my point of view.

With kindest regards to you and your family, I remain, dear Mr. Hegel,—Yours most sincerely,

HENRIK IBSEN.

---

[1] Ibsen completed *An Enemy of the People* in the summer of 1882, and it was published in November of the same year.

[2] Carl Goos (born 1835), Professor of Jurisprudence at the University of Copenhagen from 1862 to 1891, was from 1881 to 1889 the responsible publisher of the Danish *Dagblad*.

## 164.

*To* BJÖRNSTJERNE BJÖRNSON.

GOSSENSASS, 8*th August* 1882.

. . . . . . . .

In literature your works occupy, and always will occupy, a place in the first rank. But had I to decide on an inscription for your monument, I should choose these words:—" His life was his best work."

So to conduct one's life as to realise one's self—this seems to me the highest attainment possible to a human being. It is the task of one and all of us, but most of us bungle it.

. . . . . . . [1]

## 165.

*To* FREDERIK HEGEL.

GOSSENSASS, 9*th September* 1882.

DEAR MR. HEGEL,—I have the pleasure of sending you herewith the remainder of the manuscript of my new play. I have enjoyed writing this play, and I feel quite lost and lonely now that it is out of my hands. Dr. Stockmann and I got on so very well together; we agree on so many subjects. But the doctor is a more muddle-headed person than I am;

[1] On the 10th of August 1882, Björnstjerne Björnson celebrated, at his home in Gausdal, the twenty-fifth anniversary of his début as an author. On this occasion he received a long, cordial letter from Ibsen, of which only a fragment has been preserved.

Gossensass in the Tyrol was Ibsen's favourite summer resort. He was there in the summers of 1876, '77, '78, '82, '83, '84, and '89. Where he used to sit and enjoy the view of the surrounding country, there is now an "Ibsenplats"; and there is a tablet with an inscription on the wall of the house where he always lodged.

and because of this and other peculiarities of his people, will stand hearing a good many things from him, which they perhaps would not have taken in good part if they had been said by me. I expect you are of the same opinion, if you have read the manuscript.

Thank you very much for the numbers of *At Home and Abroad*; Brandes has sent me them too.

Please have one word in Act IV. corrected. A speech of Morten Kiil's reads as follows: "It will cost you dear." I wish it to read: "It may cost you dear." It probably occurs on the second page of the forty-third sheet of the manuscript.

I hope that my letter of the 30th of last month has reached you. We intend to remain here about a fortnight longer. When we leave I shall send you our new address.

With kindest regards to you and yours, I remain,—Yours most sincerely,

HENRIK IBSEN.

### 166.

#### *To* GEORGE BRANDES.

GOSSENSASS, TYROL, 21*st September* 1882.

DEAR BRANDES,—I got my manuscript off my hands about a week ago, and now I can resume my long neglected correspondence.

You are, naturally, the first to whom I turn; for I have to offer you my sincerest thanks for the literary portrait which you have drawn of me with such a friendly hand. I am, as you say, by no means indifferent to tokens of honour; but above all the others that have hitherto fallen to my share I place this careful and flattering analysis of my character and work, which has been made, while I am still here to read it, by you, the first critic of the day.

When you read my new play, you will observe how it has

interested and, I may say, amused me to recall many of the scattered and sketchy utterances in my letters to you; and you will understand how much it must have pleased me that your portrait of me was published just before this new play appeared. Yes, my dear Brandes, you have been a helpful friend to me this time, as always.

An inaccurate fact in your book I shall take the liberty of correcting. My parents both belonged to the most respected families of the Skien of their day. Chief Magistrate Paus, who for many years represented the town in the Storthing, and his brother, Judge Paus, were my father's half-brothers and my mother's cousins. And my parents were just as nearly related to the Plesner, von der Lippe, Cappelen, and Blom families—that is to say, to almost all the patrician families who were at that time the most influential in the town and neighbourhood. My father was a merchant with a large business and wide connections, and he enjoyed dispensing reckless hospitality. In 1836 he failed, and nothing was left to us except a farm near the town. To this farm we removed; and, in consequence, we got out of touch with the society to which we had until then belonged.

In writing *Peer Gynt* I had the circumstances and memories of my own childhood before me when I described the life in the house of "the rich Jon Gynt."

In your later letters you have repeatedly referred to two circumstances, the true and simple explanation of which I have not yet given you. On the occasion of my last two days' stay in Copenhagen, I was told that you were in the country; and as I did not see you and your wife at the dinner at Hegel's, the possibility of your being in the immediate neighbourhood never occurred to me; and I cannot but believe that Hegel, too, was ignorant of your whereabouts. The explanation of my not having read your book on Lassalle when we met in Munich is simply this, that Hegel had not as yet sent me the book; he always does send me those works published by him which he knows will interest me. Besides, I was occupied at that time planning *The Pillars of Society*; and under such circumstances I read hardly anything, and certainly never books which I know will engross me.

I do hope that your position and life in Copenhagen will be to your mind.[1] I hope to meet you there next summer. There are so many things I want to say to you and to talk over with you.

Our return to Italy is rendered impossible for the moment by great floods. We have no idea when we shall reach Rome; our first attempt must be to get to Bozen, and there is no possibility of that yet.

Please offer our kindest regards to your wife.—Yours very sincerely,

HENRIK IBSEN.

### 167.

*To* FREDERIK HEGEL.

ROME, *2nd December* 1882.

DEAR MR. HEGEL,—After a fatiguing journey, during the course of which we were more than once in real danger, we arrived here on the 24th of last month; and we have now settled down comfortably in our usual quarters.

I will not deny that I am awaiting the publication of my new play with nervous impatience. Its appearance has, I believe, been delayed by a combination of circumstances, and possibly also for prudential reasons; but I trust that it is out now; I hope to see it advertised in the Danish papers which come to-day. Generally speaking, November is a very good month for the publication of books; but it is not the best month for

---

[1] In the summer of 1882, George Brandes received an invitation from a number of his countrymen and countrywomen to return to Copenhagen and lecture there. They insured him a yearly income of 4000 Kroner for ten years. He at once accepted the invitation, and in February 1883 he returned to Denmark.

a play; it does not give it the chance of being produced before the best part of the theatrical season is over, more particularly in Sweden, for which country it must first be translated. But, on the other hand, seeing that such a very large edition of my book has been printed, it is undoubtedly desirable for us both that it should appear at a time when it can count upon the full and undivided attention of the public, undistracted by other literary novelties.

The immediate occasion of my writing to you to-day is, I regret to say, that I am obliged to ask you once more to send me a draft for 1000 Kroner. The last remittance came to hand duly at Brixen; my very best thanks for it.

And I have another great favour to request. Will you put down my name for Norwegian Mortgage-Bank 4½ per cent. Bonds to the amount of 4000 Kroner, face-value. I am informed that Norwegian Government Securities are at present regarded with distrust in the foreign money-markets, which makes it probable that this is a favourable time to purchase. I myself have not the slightest hesitation in investing in them; I know the ways of the politicians who are making such a noise in Norway, and know that they will never commit themselves to any serious action.

I hear that a good many Scandinavians have already arrived in Rome, but I have as yet met very few of them. Mrs. Heiberg has been so kind as to send me her interesting book; I shall write very soon to thank her for the truly valuable gift.[1] With kindest regards to yourself and your family, I remain, dear Mr. Hegel,—Yours sincerely and gratefully,

HENRIK IBSEN.


*P.S.*—If Björnson should happen to be in Copenhagen, please convey cordial greetings to him and his wife from all of us. H. I.

---

[1] In 1882, Johanne Luise Heiberg (1812–1890), the famous actress, published a book about her husband's parents, P. A. Heiberg and Thomasine Gyllembourg, which created a great sensation.

## 168.

*To* EDWARD FALLESEN.

TO HERR KAMMERHERRE FALLESEN.

ROME, 12*th December* 1882.

DEAR SIR,— It gave me great pleasure to learn from Councillor Hegel that you wish to produce my new play at the Theatre Royal, and I trust that you duly received my telegraphic answer.

My special purpose in writing to-day is to prevent a misconception and wrong rendering of one of the parts in the play. A Copenhagen newspaper, which gives an account of the plot, writes of Captain Horster as an "old man," an "old" friend of the doctor's, etc. This is a mistake. Captain Horster is a *young* man; he is one of "the young people" whom the doctor says he likes to see in his house. Horster must, especially in the brief dialogue between him and Petra in the Fifth Act, act in such a way as to suggest the beginning of an intimate and warm friendship between these two.

I, moreover, take the liberty of requesting that you will, as far as it is at all possible, give the minor parts in the Fourth Act to capable actors; the more figures you can have in the crowd that are really characteristic and true to nature, the better.

Pardon me, Sir, for making this request, which is probably a perfectly unnecessary one, and believe me to be,—Yours most respectfully,

HENRIK IBSEN.[1]

[1] *An Enemy of the People* was produced at the Theatre Royal of Copenhagen on the 4th of March 1883.

169.

*To* CAMILLA COLLETT.

ROME, 17*th January* 1883.

DEAR AND MOST ESTEEMED MRS. COLLETT,—A notable day in your life is approaching—a day which deserves to be celebrated far and wide. I cannot doubt but that this will be done, although the newspapers do not tell of preparations for it. But they are probably being kept secret.

You may be sure that in our little family circle here, the 23rd will not pass without our drinking your health and wishing you all that is good in the new decade upon which you are entering.

It is a great literary life-work upon which you will look back on that day, a life-work of which you may be proud. But I hope that it will not for a long, long time to come be a completed life-work. Your youthfulness of mind is unimpaired Your thoughts, your ideas, and your interests keep you still, as of old, in the vanguard of the fight; you have kept pace with the changes which time has brought; and we are entitled to hope that for a number of years to come it will be in your power to go on making valuable additions to the long series of gifted works which we already owe to you.

Ideas grow and propagate themselves slowly with us in the North; progress is unobservable; nevertheless it is made. The Norway now in process of development will bear traces of your intellectual pioneer-work. You are one of the fighters whom it will be most imperative for posterity to take into account in arriving at any understanding of that process.

But first of all I hope that gratitude and appreciation in full measure may fall to your share while you are still in the land of the living. There is something depressing, something terribly disheartening, in its constantly being too late before people begin to retrieve and make reparation for long neglect. It is a matter of indifference to me, as far as I am personally concerned; but it annoys, embitters, and enrages me when I observe it happening in the case of those whom I esteem and admire.

I hope, however, that the approaching festal day will not give occasion for any such reflections. It will bring you sunshine and a breath of warm air in the middle of the cold Northern winter. Let these lines from the South, from the Pincio, which you love so well, contribute a little to the warmth. Good luck and happiness that day and all the remaining days of your life!—Yours cordially and sincerely,

HENRIK IBSEN.[1]

## 170

### *To* JOHAN SVERDRUP.

To Mr. SVERDRUP, President of the Storthing.

ROME, 24*th January* 1883.

DEAR SIR,—The Norwegian papers which came to-day have brought us news of the sad event in your household.

Permit me, on behalf of myself and my family, to express sincere sympathy with you on the occasion of the great and painful loss which you have just suffered.

I may venture to speak in the name of all the Norwegians here, and assure you that the thoughts of one and all are with you in your sorrow.—Yours most respectfully and sincerely,

HENRIK IBSEN.[2]

[1] The 23rd of January 1883 was Camilla Collett's 70th birthday. Public congratulations and homage were offered her in several of the newspapers, and an address and gifts were presented by the women of Christiania. But in 1893, on the occasion of her 80th birthday, she was much more enthusiastically fêted by a much larger number of her compatriots.

[2] Johan Sverdrup lost his wife on the 8th of January 1883.

171

*To* LUCIE WOLF.

ROME, 25*th May* 1883.

DEAR MRS. WOLF,—At the beginning of this month we had
the unexpected pleasure of receiving a letter from you. The
letter was addressed to Mrs. Ibsen; but as it chiefly concerns
me, I take the liberty of answering it.

You wish me to write a prologue for the festival performance to be given at the Christiania Theatre in June, on the
thirtieth anniversary of your appearance on its stage.

I wish I could comply with your request. Nothing would
please me more than to be able to do it. But I cannot; my
convictions and my art-principles forbid me. Prologues,
epilogues, and everything of the kind ought to be banished
from the stage. The stage is for dramatic art alone; and
declamation is not dramatic art.

The prologue would, of course, have to be in verse; for such
is the established custom. But I will have no hand in perpetu-
ating this custom. Verse has been most injurious to dramatic
art. A scenic artist whose department is the drama of the
present day should be unwilling to take a verse into his mouth.
It is improbable that verse will be employed to any extent
worth mentioning in the drama of the immediate future; the
aims of the dramatists of the future are almost certain to be
incompatible with it. It is therefore doomed. For art forms
become extinct, just as the preposterous animal forms of pre-
historic times became extinct when their day was over.

A tragedy in iambic pentameters is already as rare a
phenomenon as that bird the dodo, of which only a few
specimens are still in existence on some African island.

I myself have for the last seven or eight years hardly
written a single verse; I have exclusively cultivated the very
much more difficult art of writing the genuine, plain language

spoken in real life. It is by no means of this language that you have become the excellent artist you now are. Smooth verse has never helped you to bribe any one's verdict.

But there is yet another argument, which appears to me to be the chief one. In a prologue all kinds of agreeable things are said to the public; it is thanked for its lenient and instructive criticism; the artist employs all the tricks of rhyme in making himself as insignificantly diminutive as possible. But is this an honest proceeding? You know, just as well as I, that it is not. The exact opposite is the truth. It is not you who are in debt to the public; it is the public that is deeply in debt to you for your thirty years' faithful work.

.This, in my opinion, is the standpoint which it is the duty of an able artist to maintain, out of regard for himself and his profession. And I am certain that you yourself will admit that I cannot well, holding such opinions, undertake to compose a prologue for the occasion in question.

But though I am unable to serve you in this matter, I trust that you will, nevertheless, accept the tribute of thanks which I herewith offer you, thanks for all you have been and still are to our scenic art, and my special thanks for the important share you have taken in the rendering of so many of my own dramatic works.

Hoping and heartily wishing that there may still be a long and bright artistic career before you, I remain,—Your attached old friend,

HENRIK IBSEN.[1]

[1] Fru Lucie Wolf, née Johannessen (1833–1902), an excellent actress, made her début at the Norwegian Theatre of Bergen in 1850; in 1853 she was engaged by the Christiania Theatre, and from 1899 onwards she played in the new National Theatre. Her real domain was that of comedy.

## 172.

To GEORGE BRANDES.

ROME, 12*th June* 1883.

DEAR BRANDES,—Once again I must begin by asking you to forgive my long delay in answering a letter of yours.

I was delighted to hear that your essay on me is about to be published in Germany; and I wrote immediately to Hanfstaengl, the Munich photographer, and requested him to send direct to the office of *Nord und Süd* two different cabinet photographs of me—which I hope he did at once. My signature I sent on a visiting-card.

Accept my best thanks for your great work on the Romantic School in France. I need not tell you that I have read it with the keenest interest. I had, while reading, the feeling that I was myself living in the period you describe. But it is impossible for me to give you my opinion of your book in a letter; I must tell it you when we are together. There is in your works a new element, an element of the future, by which I am often very much struck; they introduce something into the art of history writing which, so far as I am aware, was not there before. Your book on Disraeli, in particular, seems to me to be a profoundly original work. But, as already said, about these things I must talk with you; my pen is not accustomed to such subjects.

It seems strange to myself now that I should never have told you how *The Feast at Solhaug* came to be written; but I really never attached any importance to the matter. When, however, a preface was required for the new edition of that youthful production, I thought the occasion a suitable one to give a little correct information on the subject.[1]

As to *The Enemy of the People*, if we had a chance to discuss it, I think we should manage to come to an agreement.

[1] The second edition of *The Feast at Solhaug* was published in 1883.

24

You are, of course, right when you say that we must all work for the spread of our opinions.  But I maintain that a fighter in the intellectual vanguard can never collect a majority round him.  In ten years the majority will, possibly, occupy the standpoint which Dr. Stockmann held at the public meeting.  But during these ten years the Doctor will not have been standing still; he will still be at least ten years ahead of the majority.  He can never have the majority with him  As regards myself, at least, I am conscious of incessant progression.  At the point where I stood when I wrote each of my books, there now stands a tolerably compact crowd; but I myself am no longer there; I am elsewhere; farther ahead, I hope

My mind is running just now on the plot of a new dramatic work in four acts.  In course of time a variety of mad fancies (*galskaber*) are apt to collect in a man's mind, and he wants an outlet for them.  But as the play is neither to deal with the Supreme Court nor the right of absolute veto, and not even with the removal of the sign of union from the flag, it can hardly count upon arousing much interest in Norway.  I hope, however, that it may find a hearing elsewhere.

We were greatly pleased to read and hear of the reception you met with on your return to Denmark, and we sincerely trust that you may continue to find things there satisfactory in every way.

At the end of this month we go to the Tyrol, where it is our intention to spend the summer.

Our kindest regards to your wife and yourself.  Thanking you once more for all that I owe you, I remain,—Yours most sincerely,

HENRIK IBSEN.

173.

*To* EMMA KLINGENFELD.[1]

GOSSENSASS, TYROL, 4*th July* 1883.

DEAR MISS KLINGENFELD,—The letter you have been kind enough to write to my wife has made me feel doubly ashamed of my negligence in not thanking you at the proper time for the very beautiful and sympathetic verses with which you rejoiced and honoured me on my birthday, two years ago. Will you allow me to do so now, and not bear me too great a grudge for my dilatoriness?

I requested my publisher to send you the new edition of *The Feast at Solhaug*, because I thought that it might perhaps interest you to glance at the youthful production. I am delighted that you are translating it; I believe that you are particularly well fitted for the task, and that the translation will be a very successful one. That it will find a publisher, Reclam or some one else, I have not the slightest doubt; and it is not impossible that some of the German and Austrian theatres might be willing to produce your translation. But if I might take the liberty of advising you in the matter, I should recommend you to apply to a theatrical agent of good repute in Berlin, who would make all the business arrangements with the theatres for you. Please excuse my meddling with matters which do not concern me.

I hope that you will *not* translate the preface to the play; it would not interest German readers; in fact, it would not even be understood in Germany. I am sure that you and I are of the same opinion on this subject.

[1] Emma Klingenfeld, of Munich, was one of the first authorised translators of Ibsen. The German "original editions" of *The Vikings*, *Lady Inger*, and *Pillars of Society* are from her pen. Her translation of *The Feast at Solhaug* was published by Reclam, but not till 1888. She translated *Hedda Gabler* in 1891.

The reason why I did not send you my latest plays, *Ghosts* and *An Enemy of the People,* was that these pieces deal with problems which I did not imagine likely to be of so much interest to you; and I feared that my sending them might be construed by you as an invitation to translate them, an invitation which I did not think would be particularly agreeable to you.

I wonder if you have heard of the tremendous uproar which *Ghosts* produced in the Scandinavian press and among a large section of the public? No theatre dared to produce the play. Now, however, the tempest has calmed down, and several theatrical managers have acquired the right to perform it during the coming winter.

We were much interested to hear that you are soon to be off on a summer trip to Scandinavia. We hope that it will be taken under pleasant circumstances, and especially that you will have good luck in the way of weather. We hear from home that they are having a very fine summer there.

Allow me to congratulate you on the completion of your great undertaking, the translation of *Adam Homo.*[1] I do not doubt that you have been thoroughly successful, and 1 shall soon have an opportunity of convincing myself.

I have asked my wife to allow me to answer your kind letter for her; she sends you the enclosed card with her mother's address in Copenhagen.

Farewell for to-day, dear Miss Klingenfeld. Good luck on your expedition to the North! Please present our kind regards to your family. Remember us to the Heyses, if they are in Munich, and to any of our friends and acquaintances whom you may happen to meet in Scandinavia—particularly Brandes and his wife.—Yours sincerely and gratefully,

HENRIK IBSEN.

[1] Fräulein Emma Klingenfeld's translation of the Danish poet, Paludan-Müller's famous work, *Adam Homo,* appeared in 1883, with a preface by George Brandes.

## 174.

*To* KRISTIAN ANASTAS WINTERHJELM.[1]

GOSSENSASS, TYROL, 6*th September* 1883.

DEAR MR. WINTERHJELM,—I received your kind letter of the 3d inst. last night, and hasten to answer it.

Will you kindly inform Mr. Lindberg that, as far as I am concerned, he may produce my play on whatever stage in Christiania he thinks proper. Now that I know, thanks to you, what the present state of theatrical matters in the town is, I have no objection to offer to the People's Theatre (Folketeatret).

Accept my best thanks for the account which you sent me from Helsingfors of the first performance. And pray convey to Mrs. Winterhjelm the assurance of my sincere gratitude. Without her co-operation the victories and triumphs of these days would have been impossible; and it is a great pleasure and satisfaction to me to think that her name and mine will be mentioned together when the history of the stage in our day comes to be written.

I am sorry to be obliged to stop short here, in order to catch the first post.—Yours cordially and sincerely,

HENRIK IBSEN.

[1] K. A. Winterhjelm (born 1843), a Norwegian journalist and author, settled in Stockholm in 1880 as correspondent of the Norwegian *Aftenpost*. His wife was a well-known Swedish actress. Lady Inger and Mrs. Alving in *Ghosts* were amongst her finest parts. In the winter of 1883–84 she and the Swedish theatrical manager and actor, August Lindberg, made a professional tour in Sweden, Denmark, and Norway, performing *Ghosts*. The first performance (the first on any European stage) was at Helsingborg. They had large audiences everywhere.

175.

*To* OLE ANDREAS BACHKE.

ROME, 30*th November* 1883.

DEAR BACHKE,—Although I know that your time and attention are probably fully occupied at present with important matters, I nevertheless venture, emboldened by many evidences of goodwill towards me on your part, to apply to you in a matter which to me and mine is of very great importance.

As you perhaps remember, I applied in 1880 to the Department of Ecclesiastical and Educational Affairs for an order in council to the effect that my son, who had at that time been for a year and a half a law-student at the University of Munich, should be permitted to continue his studies in Christiania without previously passing the " second examination " (Andeneksamen), according to the Norwegian regulations. This application was refused, with the answer that to grant it would be a breach of the existing laws; and the proposal which you were good enough to make at the time, that these laws should be changed, seems to have been ineffectual; at least we are not aware of any change having been made.

As my son was thus prevented from attending the University of Christiania, he continued his studies here in Rome, and, as far as the University is concerned, brought them to a close by taking the degree of Doctor of Law in the summer of last year. Both while at the Universities and since taking his degree, he has chiefly occupied himself with studies which bear on politics—constitutional law, international law, political economy, etc.; and he is now in a position to present himself at any time for the so-called diplomatic examination here, which qualifies for appointments in the Foreign Office and in the diplomatic and consular services.

But before doing so it is necessary that he should be naturalised. And this is a step which we have great difficulty in persuading ourselves to take. It is a very serious matter for a man to separate himself completely from his country.

Therefore, at my son's request, I make a last attempt to preserve his Norwegian citizenship, by asking you if you will do what you can to obtain a promise from the Government that his claims will receive due consideration the next time the post of an Attaché falls vacant.

I may mention, as qualifying him for such a position, that in addition to his other acquirements, he speaks and writes German, French, and Italian like a native; and he will shortly be master of the English language also. His special inclination lies in the direction of authorship—in the domains of sociology and politics; and an appointment at a Legation would, he considers, place him in the most favourable of all positions for such work. At present he is engaged upon a treatise on "The Development throughout the Ages of the Conception of the State," the introductory part of which has appeared in the *Nyt Tidsskrift*.

I have much more to say on the subject, but dare not encroach further upon your time. I am unwilling to believe that I am what some people declare I am, namely, to such an extent a *persona ingrata* with a majority of the members of the Government that I cannot reckon upon any consideration whatever. As to the Head of the Ecclesiastical Department, I know quite well what to expect from him; but, fortunately, his vote is not likely to be decisive in this case.

If you are able to send me a few lines in reply to this, please address care of our Consulate here.

With our kindest regards, I am,—Yours ever,

HENRIK IBSEN.[1]

[1] In 1884, Sigurd Ibsen received an appointment in the consulate department in Christiania; in 1885 he entered the Swedish-Norwegian diplomatic service; he was sent to Washington and to Vienna. In 1890 he left the diplomatic service, for Norwegian nationalistic reasons. From 1890–99 he lived in Christiania, as journalist and author. In 1896–97 he lectured on sociology at the University of Christiania. In 1899 he again entered the service of the Government; in 1902 he became a member of the Ministry, and in 1903 was appointed Norwegian Minister at Stockholm.

176.

*To* FREDERIK HEGEL.

ROME, 27*th December* 1883.

DEAR Mr. HEGEL,—Just a few words of thanks from me and mine for the books which you have so kindly sent us, and which have done so much to gladden our Christmas by, as it were, bringing home nearer to us.

Let me at the same time thank you heartily for all the good-will and kindness shown to me throughout the year which is drawing to a close. Your intimation that a new edition of *The League of Youth* was in the press was exceedingly welcome. I hope you will forgive me for not taking any notice of it at the time. I was travelling; and I did not expect that the book would come out so soon; the beautiful copy which you sent me surprised me here immediately after my return.[1]

I see from the papers that a literary civil war has broken out in Copenhagen, and that severe fighting is going on. At this distance it is not easy to judge; but it seems to me that Drachmann ought to have been able to formulate his complaints of G. Brandes in a manner that need not have caused a rupture between two friends of so many years' standing.

Leaving this out of consideration, I, for my part, see no great misfortune in a disruption of the literary Left. I believe that the many highly gifted authors who belong to it will work better each for himself, without any side glances at a common programme.

There is quite a gathering of Scandinavians here now, but not such a large one as usual at this time of year. I have not seen many of them, as I am leading a quiet life and keeping much to myself this winter.

Once more, my thanks for all your kindness in the old year.

[1] The fifth edition of *The League of Youth* appeared in November 1883.

We all wish you and your dear family a good and happy new one.—Yours most sincerely and gratefully,

HENRIK IBSEN.

177.

*To* FREDERIK HEGEL.

ROME, 17*th January* 1884.

DEAR MR. HEGEL,—Thank you very much for the statement of our account for the past year. May I ask you kindly to send me a draft or Post Office order for 2000 Kroner?

I think you are likely to know Jonas Lie's address in Paris; if you do, will you be good enough, when writing, to let me have it, as I wish to write to him.

I have now read almost all the interesting Christmas literature you sent us. Lie's new story is a particularly attractive one; and I hope it will be very successful.[1] Henrik Pontoppidan's *Village Pictures* I also consider an excellent book. It is the first of his which I have read; I have no doubt that he is an author with a future. I presume that he is still a young man.[2]

Holger Drachmann has been kind enough to send me his *Shadow Pictures*. It seems that the reviewers are almost unanimous in considering the last story in the book the best. I am not of their opinion. I do not believe that the admiration excited by this story will endure. The world is not developing in the direction of national separatism and exclusiveness, but in the opposite. Some of the other *Shadow Pictures* are much more to my taste.

On the 2nd of January, Lindberg and his company played

---

[1] The book of Jonas Lie's here referred to is *The Family at Gilje*, the first of his stories of modern domestic life.

[2] Henrik Pontoppidan made his literary début in 1881. He soon became one of Denmark's best story-writers.

*Ghosts* for the 50th time in Sweden. In Denmark and Norway he has performed the play 21 times—in all 71 times in somewhat over four months.

There is no news to send you from here. We are having an extraordinarily beautiful winter; there is hardly ever a cloud in the sky, and it is just cold enough to be very pleasant.

Hoping that you are having a pleasant winter at home, I remain, with kindest regards to you all,—Yours most sincerely,

HENRIK IBSEN.

### 178.

*To* BJÖRNSTJERNE BJÖRNSON.

ROME, 28*th March* 1884.

DEAR BJÖRNSON,—The address to the Storthing which has been sent me has my entire sympathy; I therefore herewith return it signed.

But I must confess that I do not expect to see any outcome of the whole proceeding. If the majority of the Storthing had really been honestly in favour of Berner's motion, they would not have sent it to the Communal Councils for deliberation. In fact, they would not have asked men at all for an opinion on the matter; they would have asked women. To consult men in such a matter is like asking wolves if they wish to have the sheep better protected.[1]

No, indeed; that minority of our nation who possess all the

---

[1] In 1882, Hagbard Berner (see Letter 151) had introduced a Married Woman's Property Bill into the Storthing; it did not pass then, or in 1884, when the subject was again under discussion. The signatories of the address above referred to in favour of the Bill were Björnson, Ibsen, Jonas Lie, and Alexander Kielland. In 1888 a law entitling married women to hold property in their own right came into effect.

political, communal, and social privileges will certainly not voluntarily give them up or share them with the unprivileged majority. Hence I foresee, too, the fate of the proposals to extend the suffrage. None of them will obtain the necessary number of votes. Such things are not given away by their possessors; they must be fought for. And especially with us, where the decision really lies with a section of the peasant landowners. I have made acquaintance with the peasantry of many countries, but nowhere have I found them liberal-minded and self-sacrificing; I have, on the contrary, found them everywhere extremely tenacious of their rights, and very much alive to their own interests. Is it likely to be different with us? I can hardly believe it. I do not understand why our men of the Left are called Liberals. When I read the debates in our Storthing, I cannot discover in the views expressed by our peasants an atom more of real liberalism than is to be found among the ultramontane peasantry of the Tyrol.

I am therefore very much afraid that social reforms with us are still far off. No doubt the politically privileged class may acquire some new rights, some new advantages; but I cannot see that the nation as a whole, or the single individual, gains very much by this. I admit, however, that in politics, too, I am a pagan; I do not believe in the emancipatory power of political measures; nor have I much confidence in the altruism and goodwill of those in power.

If I could have my way at home, then all the unprivileged should unite and form a strong, resolute, progressive party, the programme of which should include none but practical and productive reforms—a very wide extension of the suffrage, the statutory improvement of the position of women, the emancipation of national education from all kinds of medievalism, etc. Theoretic political questions would be allowed to lie over for some time; they are not of great utility. If such a party were formed, the present party of the Left would soon be seen to be what it really is, and from its constitution must be—a Centre party (*centrums-parti* = the Moderates).[1]

But my paper leaves no space for any more pothouse politics. We are reading and re-reading your splendid "old document." I guess what is coming, and am eager to have the whole thing.[2] Remember me to your wife, the Jonas Lies, and all other friends and fellow-countrymen.—Yours,

HENRIK IBSEN.

179.

*To* GEORGE BRANDES.

ROME, 25*th June* 1884.

DEAR BRANDES,—My best thanks for your letter, which I ought to have answered long ago, especially as I know that you keep strict accounts in the matter of correspondence— although you assure me that you have changed somewhat in this respect.

I should most willingly have written sooner; but for these last months my time has been entirely occupied by a new dramatic work. And the writing of a letter is not the same easy matter to me that it is to you.

I have, like you, a distinct feeling that we stand much closer to each other now than we did during the first years of our acquaintance. The explanation of this I believe to be that

[1] In 1884 the Norwegian Left succeeded in passing a Bill for the extension of the franchise, and in 1898 one which introduced manhood-suffrage. In 1889 it introduced and succeeded in passing a measure which made the schools much more independent of the Church. It assisted in passing several other measures—1884, 1888, and 1894— which improved the position of women.

[2] "An Old Document" was the title of the introduction to Björnson's novel, *The Heritage of the Kurts*. It appeared in the January number of the *Nyt Tidsskrift*, 1884.

the process of development through which each of us has passed has tended to bring us together. On this subject and others of the same nature I should like to talk to you, but I cannot write.

A tone of depression pervades your account of your experiences since your return home. I was not surprised by it. I thought it perfectly natural that you should choose to go back, but I had an idea that disagreeable as well as pleasant experiences awaited you. You went back to Copenhagen with a European name. And intellectual rank and precedence and democratic principles are not things to agree well with each other. Moreover, it is much easier to manage a party and lead a movement from a distance than on the spot. One's personal presence irritates in various ways and for various reasons. I have had opportunities for observing this; and I have utilised my observations "in sundry wars."

The literary comedy which the press at home has been acting for the last year or so, I have followed with careful attention. I have not been surprised by the changes of parts that I have observed — least of all by the change in the part of the hero. But on this subject I shall not enlarge at present. I will rather, instead, thank you once more for your pleasant, frank letter, and also for the German version of my biography. I have not seen the magazine, but I have seen a separate reprint of the essay. Thank you again and again!

We have read in the German newspapers and heard from Danish tourists of the crowded attendances at your lectures. You see that your countrymen are proud of you after all, even if they cannot refrain from tormenting you at times. I know the situation by experience.

I have finished the first sketch of my new work, a play in five acts, and am now engrossed in elaborating it—moulding the language more carefully, and individualising the characters and speeches more thoroughly. In a day or two I go to Gossensass in the Tyrol, expecting to put the finishing touches to it there in the course of the summer.[1]　My wife and son go to Norway.

Please excuse this hurried letter.　Remember us most kindly to your wife and your little girls.—Your attached friend,

HENRIK IBSEN.

180.

*To* THEODOR CASPARI.[2]

ROME, 27*th June* 1884.

DEAR MR. CASPARI,—I do not remember whether I told you, when we were together here, that one of my faults was dilatoriness in the matter of answering letters.　At any rate you have now been made aware of it by experience.　I have had your kind letter and beautiful, warm-hearted verses lying on my table since the middle of April, and have looked at them every day, with the good intention of writing to you "tomorrow."　And not until now has my resolution become performance!　Forgive the delay, and accept my warmest thanks for the poem, which moves me every time I read it— and I read it often, for there is something in it which speaks to me of home.

You are greatly mistaken in imagining it to be my desire that you should break your lyre in pieces.　It most certainly is not.　There is not a single poem of yours which I could wish unwritten; and I hope that you will produce much in the future in the domain of metre and rhyme; for it seems to me that it is for this your natural gifts qualify you.　I have not forgotten certain disrespectful utterances of my own on the subject of the metrical art; but they were merely the

---

[1] *The Wild Duck* was written in the summer of 1884, in Rome and at Gossensass.

[2] Theodor Caspari (born 1853), a Norwegian lyric poet, had spent the winter of 1883–84 in Italy.

expression of my own temporary attitude to that art. I gave up universal standards long ago, because I ceased believing in the justice of applying them. I believe that there is nothing else and nothing better for us all to do than in spirit and in truth to realise ourselves. This, in my opinion, constitutes real liberalism; and you can therefore understand why the so-called Liberals are in so many ways thoroughly antipathetic to me.

All this winter I have been revolving some new follies in my brain; I went on doing it until they assumed dramatic form; and now I have just completed a play in five acts—that is to say, the rough draft of it; now comes the elaboration, the more energetic individualisation of the persons and their mode of expression. In order to find the quiet and solitude necessary for this work, I am going in a day or two to Gossensass in the Tyrol. My wife and son go to Norway. I wish I could have accompanied them; but that is not possible. At my age a man must make use of his time for his work; the work will never be finished; he "will not have time to write the last verse"; but still, one wishes to get as much done as possible.

I wish you and Mrs. Caspari a pleasant summer! You may be sure that we shall not forget either of you. Thanking you again, I remain,—Yours very sincerely,

HENRIK IBSEN.


### 181.

#### *To* FREDERIK HEGEL.

GOSSENSASS, *2nd September* 1884.

DEAR MR. HEGEL,—Along with this letter I send you the manuscript of my new play, *The Wild Duck*. For the last four months I have worked at it every day; and it is not without a certain feeling of regret that I part from it. Long, daily association with the persons in this play has endeared them to me, in spite of their manifold failings; and I am not without hope that they may find good and kind friends among the great reading public, and more particularly among the actor tribe—to whom they offer rôles which will well repay the trouble spent on them. The study and representation of these characters will not be an easy task; therefore it is desirable that the book should be offered to the theatres as early as possible in the season; I shall send the letters, which you will be good enough to despatch along with the different copies.

In some ways this new play occupies a position by itself among my dramatic works; in its method it differs in several respects from my former ones. But I shall say no more on this subject at present. I hope that my critics will discover the points alluded to; they will, at any rate, find several things to squabble about and several things to interpret. I also think that *The Wild Duck* may very probably entice some of our young dramatists into new paths; and this I consider a result to be desired.

I shall now take a thorough rest, until new plans begin to announce themselves importunately. Where we shall spend the winter I do not yet know. If cholera breaks out in Rome or the neighbourhood, we shall not be able to go there for some time. For the present I am staying on here, where, in spite of the altitude, we are still having real summer weather.

As you probably know, the Björnsons are at Schwaz, two or three hours by rail north of Gossensass. I have accepted an invitation to go and see them; it is now more than twenty years since we met.[1] Perhaps Jonas Lie will come to them at the same time, from Berchtesgaden; but this is quite uncertain.

Please accept my best thanks for all the kindness and attention shown by you and your family to my wife and son during their stay in Copenhagen. They have been at the North

---

[1] Ibsen paid a visit to Björnson at Schwaz in the middle of September 1884, immediately after the despatch of *The Wild Duck*.

Cape, and are now spending the summer at the Lake of Selbo, near Trondhjem. It is uncertain yet when they come south.

With kindest regards to yourself and your family, I remain —Yours sincerely and gratefully,

HENRIK IBSEN.

## 182.

### To BJÖRNSTJERNE BJÖRNSON.

GOSSENSASS, 29th September 1884.

DEAR BJÖRNSON,—I have been prevented, by having to answer some unexpected letters, from writing sooner on the subject of the Theatre.

When a man has had as much to do with the management of theatres as I have had, and has been occupied as long and exclusively as I have been in writing dramatic works, he cannot fail to long at times to have a hand in the practical arrangements. There is something peculiarly attractive about the theatre; and ever since you suggested the idea to me, a feeling of restlessness and desire has taken possession of me. Besides, I cannot deny that I sometimes feel the want of a settled and obligatory occupation. So there are motives which might be sufficient to induce me to go home and take the Directorship, if the thing were practicable.

But the misfortune is that at present it is not practicable. The party which is in power at the Theatre is certainly no more favourably disposed towards me than towards you. My wife writes to me: "I could never have believed that we were in such utter disrepute with the Right as numberless signs prove us to be." I do not doubt for a moment that she is correct in her observations. To offer me the Directorship of the Theatre would therefore be equivalent to placing the Management and the Theatre in a hostile attitude towards many wealthy families and persons, with whose support the institution cannot dispense.

25

Therefore it will not be done. You may be quite sure that 1 shall never be the Director of the Theatre as long as matters are under the control of the present Board of Management.

But you will perhaps argue that I ought to go home all the same, and do what I can in the meantime as a private reformer —hurry on the erection of the new Theatre, and thereby contribute to the establishment of such conditions as would make the selection of myself as Director a possibility. All this might be practicable if I had sufficient means of subsistence for the time being. But I have not. I have not yet saved nearly enough to support myself and my family in the case of my discontinuing my literary work. And I should be obliged to discontinue it if I were to live in Christiania. In affirming this I am not thinking principally of all the worries connected with the Theatre. What I feel is that I should not be able to write freely and frankly and unreservedly there. And this simply means that I should not write at all. When, ten years ago, after an absence of ten years, I sailed up the Fjord, I felt a weight settling down on my breast, a feeling of actual physical oppression. And this feeling lasted all the time I was at home ; I was not myself under the gaze of all those cold, uncomprehending Norwegian eyes at the windows and in the streets.

I must, at all events, have another year to think the matter over. If the Government and the Storthing see fit to increase the pensions sufficiently to place me in an independent position pecuniarily, I might, for the sake of the Theatre, let one or two dramatic works remain unwritten for a time. And it seems to me that the politicians at present in power ought to show us justice, and grant us some indemnity for the great losses we have suffered, and are still suffering, on account of the lack of literary conventions with foreign countries. The honourable gentlemen should remember that they certainly would never have held the position which they now hold in the estimation of the Norwegian people, but for the work done by us modern authors in awakening men's minds. And it does not seem to me that they are so particularly reluctant when it is a question of compensations and remunerations for themselves.

Then there is another consideration. Do you think it would be desirable for Björn that I should come to Christiania? I am not sure that it would. I believe that, as stage-manager, he will feel himself free and unhindered under Schroeder as Director.[1] And of what real use could I be as long as they play in that old, horrible, narrow box of a building? The artistic reforms which I might wish to introduce would be impossible in the present Theatre. Björn will soon recognise this, if he has not done so already. He will feel so unable to carry out his plans in the matter of artistic staging, that he will soon agree with me that if our theatrical art is not to perish altogether, we must have an up-to-date playhouse.

No more to-day, except hearty greetings to you all.—Yours ever,                                                        HENRIK IBSEN.

## 183.

### To " THE DAGBLAD."

GOSSENSASS, TYROL, 27th October 1884.

TO THE EDITOR OF " THE DAGBLAD,"—In your esteemed paper of the 20th inst. you publish a report that I have declared myself willing to assume the Directorship of the Christiania Theatre.

Allow me hereby to inform you that this rumour is entirely without foundation.

I have done nothing of the kind, and have had no opportunity of doing it, the position not having been offered me.

---

[1] Björnstjerne Björnson's eldest son, Björn (born 1859), began his theatrical career in 1884, as actor and stage-manager at the Christiania Theatre. He is now Director of the new National Theatre of Christiania. No Norwegian theatre has ever received state-aid; but the National Theatre has received assistance in various forms from the Municipality.

Should what seems to me impossible happen, should the present management appoint me Director of the Theatre, I should unhesitatingly decline the appointment.

It is a crime against our talented and capable staff of actors and actresses, and against our national dramatic literature, to go on any longer in the present miserable fashion, in the antiquated building, receiving no assistance from either State or Municipality. Such a crime I shall not aid and abet.—Yours respectfully,

HENRIK IBSEN.

184.

*To* FREDERIK HEGEL.

ROME, 2nd *March* 1885.

DEAR MR. HEGEL,—Accept my best thanks for the copy of *The Wild Duck*, for the different papers with notices of the first performance, and very specially for the telegram which you were thoughtful enough to send me.

I see that there was some hissing at the first performance, and possibly there has been more since. I am not at all surprised, when I remember the strained relations at present existing between the literary parties in Copenhagen. But I do not for a moment imagine that the demonstration can have been intended as a personal insult to myself.

Mrs. Thoresen has written to us about the acting, which she considers excellent. She specially praises the brothers Paulsen. Mr. Emil P. I know personally. If you should happen to see him, please remember me to him, and give him my best thanks.

There have been disquieting rumours in Norway of late regarding Björnson's health; but I have not been able to find out what is really the matter with him. I hope that whatever he is, or has been, suffering from is of a passing nature. I only wish he would abstain for a time from all exciting participation in our political controversies.

The immediate occasion of my writing to-day is that I find myself obliged to ask you to let me have a draft for 1000 Kroner. I have some money lying at Mr. Lund's in Christiania, but this I dare not touch until I know how much Sigurd will require in Stockholm before the month of August. After that time he will, presumably, be able to support himself.

We are having beautiful warm spring weather here now. This year we shall probably go to the country earlier than usual. We live more economically there, and it is quieter for my work; but we have come to no definite decision yet.

We hope that you are all well, and send you our kindest regards.—Ever, dear Mr. Hegel, Yours sincerely and gratefully,

HENRIK IBSEN.

185.

*To* LUDVIG JOSEPHSON

ROME, *9th April* 1885.

DEAR MR. JOSEPHSON,—I have received letters from Stockholm and a number of newspapers, all of which express themselves with extraordinary unanimity on the subject of the performance of *Brand* at the Nya Teater.

I was very much surprised to hear that the play had been produced. I had no idea that it was to be staged so soon; in fact I had begun to fear that it would have to wait till next year. Therefore it was all the greater pleasure to me to receive the telegrams from you and my son announcing that your courageous, I may almost say rash, undertaking had been so remarkably successful.

It is more than ten years since you first mentioned to me the plan which you have now carried out. I had in the interval almost forgotten about it; but you have kept firmly to your intention until it was possible to put it into effect. And I have more reasons than one for believing that you could not have chosen a more propitious moment than the present.

I thank you most cordially and sincerely for having devoted your great talents and skill as a theatrical manager to a task which will once more link our names together in the history of Scandinavian dramatic art. It is not the first time that we have stood in this kind of position to each other, and I hope that it will not be the last. I have still a store of mad ideas (galskaber) in my brain, out of which I believe quite good plays may be made.

You must please convey my best thanks to all your collaborators of the Nya Teater—in especial to Mr. Hillberg, without whose assistance you would, I suppose, hardly have been able to produce the play this winter.

I would gladly send my thanks to the Stockholm theatre-frequenters and the Stockholm press, if it were possible. But it is not. All I can do is to tell you that the cordial approbation of which they have now given me a fresh proof, is a source of great pleasure to me. It has effaced the impression made by all the cold, uncomprehending eyes which you yourself no doubt remember in a certain other northern city.

May fortune attend you in your present sphere of activity! Good-bye for to-day.—Yours most sincerely,

HENRIK IBSEN.

P.S.—My best thanks for the payment made to Councillor Hegel.

## 186.

*To* CHRISTIAN TÖNSBERG.

ROME, 25*th April* 1885.

To Consul-General TÖNSBERG.

DEAR MR. TÖNSBERG,—It is almost eleven years since I last had the pleasure of meeting you; but last autumn my wife, on her return from Norway, brought the good tidings that she had found you as hale and hearty as ever.

Though our paths these last twenty years have, except for an occasional meeting, lain very far apart, I beg of you to believe that I have always kept you in friendly remembrance. I have often, in foreign lands, thought with respect of you and of all your struggles at home, when you were, with characteristic undauntedness, engaged, during hard times, in planning and successfully carrying out great undertakings in connection with our literature.[1]

The course of your private life, too, I have followed with sympathy, feeling deeply for you when news came of the sad misfortunes which had befallen you and your esteemed wife. The coming 1st of May is an anniversary which my wife and I cannot allow to pass without sending you our best wishes. May a very happy old age be in store for the couple who are then to celebrate their golden-wedding!—Yours most sincerely,

HENRIK IBSEN.

[1] About the Fifties, Christian Tönsberg published many of the large works, both literary and pictorial, in which Norwegian national Romanticism found expression. His bankruptcy was the result of these extensive undertakings. He gave up business as a publisher and entered the Custom House service, receiving, on his retirement from this, a larger pension than usual, in acknowledgment of his services to literature. He was Consul in Christiania for several small countries.

187.

*To* FREDERIK HEGEL.

ROME, 25*th April* 1885.

DEAR MR. HEGEL,—At the same time that I send my best thanks for the draft received at the beginning of last month, I must request you to send me another, this time for 2000 Kroner, so that I may be fairly well provided with money for our summer travels.

We intend this year to leave Rome about the end of May, which is rather earlier than usual. I do not know yet where our summer quarters will be, but the probability is that we shall settle either in the Tyrol or at the Lake of Constance, in a place where I can work undisturbed at my new play, so as to have it ready in autumn, about the usual time.

Whether or not we shall return to Rome afterwards, is doubtful. For several reasons it would be advisable for me to spend a year in Germany again, where I could attend better to certain literary matters than I can when living here. Besides, I should be on the way home there; and I have of late begun to think seriously of the possibility of buying a little villa, or rather, small country house in the neighbourhood of Christiania— on the Fjord—where I could live in complete seclusion and give myself up entirely to my work. The sight of the sea is what I miss most here, and my longing for it increases year by year. Besides, I have, in the course of time, acquired a small collection of works of art, chiefly paintings; and all these things are now stored in a garret in Munich, giving us no pleasure at all.

The successful production of *Brand* at Stockholm has given me great pleasure; but the pecuniary profit I have derived from it has been small. On account of the many expenses connected with the staging of the piece, I was obliged to let Josephson have the permanent right of acting it for a single payment of 400 Kroner. But the money arrangements are, fortunately, of less importance to me now than when I was beginning to write *Brand* twenty years ago at Ariccia.

I see from the newspapers that Chamberlain Fallesen and a part of the staff of the Theatre Royal intend to give a series of Holberg performances at Stockholm during the summer. This is a very meritorious undertaking, for the Swedes themselves do not play Holberg as he ought to be played. I am much pleased that two of my pieces are also on their programme.[1]

May I trouble you to see that the enclosed letter is delivered on 1st May! That is the date of old Tönsberg's golden wedding, and I have been told that he hopes and expects to receive a few lines from me on the occasion; but I do not know his address in Copenhagen.

It is so hot here already that it is unpleasant to be out of doors in the middle of the day; but as our rooms are large and airy, we do not suffer.

I am following the course of political events in Denmark with eager interest; but I am unfortunately not nearly well enough acquainted with the real position of matters to be able to form an independent judgment as to the rights and wrongs of the case; and I am of course still less able to foretell how the conflict is likely to end. I am deeply interested, and hope for the best, for the sake of development and progress.

With our kindest regards to yourself and family, I remain—
Yours most sincerely,

HENRIK IBSEN.

---

[1] The proposed performances in Stockholm in the summer of 1885 were not given.

188.

*To* THE MANAGING COMMITTEE OF THE NORWEGIAN
STUDENTS' UNION.[1]

MUNICH, 23*rd October* 1885.

SIRS,—You have seen fit to write to me and enclose in your
letter a copy of a speech made by the President of your Union,
Professor Lorentz Dietrichson, on Saturday, 10th October, on the
subject of my refusal to receive a torch-light procession planned
in my honour by the Union.

You lead me to understand that a majority of the members
of the Union have seen fit publicly to signify their general
approval of the President's address as an expression of their
feelings in the matter.

This expression of approval, given, as it was, in advance, I
must characterise as precipitancy; and the fittest proceeding

---

[1] Ibsen spent the summer of 1885 (June to September) in Norway.
From the beginning of his stay he observed, or suspected, that his old
friend, Professor Dietrichson, was holding aloof from him. Dietrichson
was a strong Conservative—that is to say, he belonged to the party of
the Right. Letter 188 gives a sufficiently clear account of the story of
the torch-light procession. Dietrichson informed the students that
Ibsen had refused the honour offered him, because of his general objection to making public appearances, and also because he had already
refused a similar proposal from the Workmen's Association. The young
student, Ove Rode, contradicted this assertion, declaring that Ibsen's
real reason was his antipathy to the reactionary spirit prevailing in the
Students' Union. Thereupon Dietrichson telegraphed to Ibsen at
Copenhagen, and received a reply to the same effect. Then Dietrichson
made the speech referred to in the letter; and a demonstration against
Ibsen was made by the students of the party of the Right. The affair
gave rise to a violent controversy in the newspapers. A meeting of 600
admirers of Ibsen, all graduates or undergraduates of Christiania
University, was held on the 16th of October, at which an enthusiastic
protest against the behaviour of the Students' Union was made; an
address, expressing admiration, gratitude, and devotion, was forwarded
to the poet.

on my part would perhaps be to return both the documents sent me, without any remark whatever.

But out of regard for the members of the Union who are friendly to me, I will give an explanation, as short as I can make it, of my actual, true position in the matter.

When Mr. Lorentz Dietrichson, accompanied by one of his colleagues, called upon me on the morning of Monday, 28th September, to offer me the honour of a torch-light procession, he expressed himself in terms which led me to believe that the proposal to do me this honour had emanated from the Managing Committee, had, in fact, been made at its meeting on the previous Saturday.

This surprised me, for the Managing Committee had never shown any signs of goodwill towards me before—neither in spring, when I returned to Christiania after an absence from Norway of eleven years, nor during the earlier part of the autumn.

I, of course, did not for a moment doubt that the supposed initiative of the Committee was due to pressure of some kind from without. Still I regarded it as courtesy on their part to have yielded to this pressure. Therefore I made my refusal courteous, though it was short and decided. In the course of the interview I remarked that, not having observed that my presence gave the Union great pleasure, I did not care to have it expressing great joy on the occasion of my departure. No doubt I said this playfully, but the playfulness concealed a serious meaning, which I hope will be understood by many. I am only surprised that a serious person like Mr. Lorentz Dietrichson was not able to understand it.

The argument that I had refused the proposal of the Committee of the Workmen's Association, I did not employ till later in the interview, as an answer to an attempt by the Professor to make me change my mind with regard to the torch-light procession; I have no doubt he was sincere in making it, but it impressed me disagreeably.

I requested the two gentlemen to convey my thanks and

greetings—not to " the students," as the Professor has reported —but to " my friends among the students." From his speech I learn that he has appropriated these thanks and greetings for himself, for his colleagues of the Committee, and all the members of the Association. This is a misunderstanding. Not even at the moment when the torch-light procession was offered me was I foolish enough to flatter myself that I had none but friends in Mr. Lorentz Dietrichson's Students' Union.

The above is an account of everything essential that happened during the interview between the deputies of the Committee and myself. From the Professor's speech I see that I was right in the presumption, expressed in my telegram from Copenhagen, that his report of my refusal must have been incomplete. It was incomplete, and therefore—no doubt unintentionally—misleading.

Later in the day on which I received the deputation, I learned from various quarters that there was a history connected with the torch-light procession—a history which the two gentlemen had forgotten to tell me. I was informed, as a matter of absolute fact, that it was not to the Committee at all that the initiative in the matter was due, but that the proposal had been made quite unexpectedly by a section of the Union which as a rule is in the minority, but which on Saturday, 26th September, happened to be present in such numbers that it was able to carry its proposal.

I also learned from several quarters that a proposal to do me such an honour could not, with the present membership of the Union and the present Committee, by any possibility have been carried, if the ruling party among the students had known in time that it was to be made.

It was with all this in view, and thinking of all I had heard about the preponderance of reactionary tendencies in the Students' Union, that I gave utterance before a number of callers, one of whom was a student, Mr. Rode, to my sentiments regarding the Union and the spirit dominating it at present What I said seemed to interest the young student, and he

exclaimed that he would be delighted if he might repeat my
words to his "friends"—possibly he said to "the young
students."

To this I answered him that he was welcome to repeat them
to any one he chose, in the Union or out of it. But it never
for a moment occurred to me that what he had in view was an
official communication. This sufficiently appears from the fact
that in my telegram from Copenhagen I requested the President of the Union himself to inform the students of my real
meaning.

During my absence from Norway, an absence of many years,
I have never had any official deputy or spokesman in that
country. Had it been my intention to choose one on this
occasion, I should certainly have selected one of the older and
more experienced men of my acquaintance, and should also have
told him precisely what I wished to have communicated. But,
as already said, such a proceeding never occurred to me.

It is, in itself, a matter of tolerable indifference to me whether
my utterances were repeated at a formal meeting or over a bowl
of punch. But what I am not at all indifferent to, is the fact
that Mr. Rode has neither repeated my words nor reproduced
my meaning.

If I may rely upon Professor Dietrichson's account of the
matter in his address, Mr. Rode expressed himself to the following
effect: "Henrik Ibsen desires that the party of the Right, which
has a majority in the Students' Union, will do him the pleasure
of unseating Dietrichson and his colleagues, and electing a liberal
Committee of Management."

What I really said during the conversation was to this
purpose: "I have no wish for a torch-light procession or anything of that kind. The greatest pleasure the Students' Union
could give me would be this,—that the party of the Left in it,
the minority, should grow so large and strong as to become a
majority, when, as a matter of course, it would unseat Lorentz
Dietrichson and his colleagues in the Committee of Management
and choose liberal-minded men in their stead."

There is, it seems to me, some sense in this.  But in what
Mr. Rode is said to have reported there is no meaning at all.

I do not, however, blame the young student.  He no doubt
believed himself justified in behaving at the meeting as if he
were my official representative; and though he has reported my
words in a misleading manner, I make no doubt that he believed
he was repeating what he had heard me say.  He is probably
not yet skilled in making logical distinctions.

The gentleman whom I do blame very much is the President
of the Students' Union.  He himself refers in his speech to his
having known me for many years; and yet he puts on an
appearance of seriously believing that I wished the students to
be addressed in my name to much this effect: "What I demand
of you, good students of the party of the Right who belong to
this Union, is that at the next election of Committee Members
you shall vote against your own conviction.  I want you to
unseat Professor Dietrichson and those other members who
belong to your own party, and to choose a new Committee,
entirely composed of adherents of the party to which you are
opposed."

Can Professor Dietrichson persuade himself to declare upon
his honour that he really believed me capable of such a line of
argument ?

Dare he, who has known me for so many years, on his
honour deny that a private surmise suggested itself to him that
what I really had said was, that it was desirable, from my point
of view, that many students of the party of the Right should
soon become so liberal in their views that it would be a necessity
for them to get rid of the stagnationists, and to appoint in their
stead a Committee in touch with the thought and endeavours
of the age.

Dare Professor Dietrichson assert that this or a similar
surmise never suggested itself to him ?

But now I come to think of it—had he put such a surmise
into words, the Union would probably have taken time to procure
an authentic explanation direct from myself; in which case Mr.

Lorentz Dietrichson might have missed the opportunity of show-ing off before the new students from the country.

And it certainly was an opportunity which it would have been a sad pity to lose.

It was an opportunity to insult a poet. And poets are not popular in Norway at present.

And they are least popular in the circles whose standpoint and taste give the tone to Mr. Lorentz Dietrichson's banquet speeches.

It is, therefore, not at all inexplicable to me that Mr. Lorentz Dietrichson should at this particular time have seized on an opportunity to make a speech against me, especially as I was absent. And I consider that his introduction into the speech of all kinds of low innuendoes and charges was particularly well-timed and opportune. It seems to have pleased the Students' Union so much that the speech is recognised by it "as an expression of the feelings of the Union in this matter."

But now I have made it plain that "this matter" is in reality quite a different matter from that upon which Professor Dietrichson seems to have based his proceedings, and upon which those of the Students' Union really are based. The premises do not exist, and never have existed. Mr. Lorentz Dietrichson's speech, consequently, has nothing to rest on. It hangs in mid-air. The whole thing is nothing but an oratorical paper kite, which this serious man has let fly.

But what stands as firm as if it had been nailed to the ground, is the Union's approval of the speech.

I must, therefore, repeat what I began with. The Students' Union has on this occasion acted precipitately.

Neither the Union nor its President will succeed in doing me any enduring harm, except that this episode will leave behind a certain feeling which will remain with me for life. I shall be the same man I was the day before Mr. Lorentz Dietrich-son's assault. During the whole course of this torch-light procession affair, I have had no opportunity of proving myself either "small" or "great," either "narrowminded" or "wide-minded." The "spiritual tyranny" which has been imputed to me is an empty phantasm; and my behaviour during the whole affair has not at any point been (nor could it have been) a contradiction of my "theory" or my writings.

But I ask the majority of the Students' Union to say, after what has happened, whether or not the instinct was correct which bade me act according to my "real feeling" in the matter, and decline an honour which unwilling persons had been surprised into offering. For it will surely be acknowledged now that I had fairly good grounds for my suspicion of the genuineness of the goodwill displayed by the Students' Union, with its present views and representatives.

I expect what I have now written to be communicated by the Committee of Management to the students and to the general public.

I demand that, on the first Saturday after its arrival—previous announcement having been made—the whole letter shall be read from the same place in the hall of the Union from which I was insulted, without any provocation on my part, by the President of the Union, with the approbation of the majority of its members.[1]

And now I have said all that I have to say, both for the present and for the future, to the Committee of Management of the Students' Union.

HENRIK IBSEN.

[1] The letter was read at a meeting on the 31st of October, and was also printed in the newspapers. Dietrichson wrote a reply; and the newspapers continued the controversy for some time.

## 189.

*To* FREDRIK STANG LUND.[1]

MUNICH, 8*th November* 1885.

SIR,—It was with keen pleasure that I received, forwarded by you, the address from the graduates and undergraduates assembled in the hall of the Workmen's Association on Saturday, 17th October.

In its cordial words I find a confirmation of a hope which I have never relinquished—the hope that the great majority of the students of Norway, and of Europe generally, are really in league with the struggling, clarifying, ever-progressive life-forces in the domains of science, art, and literature.

I beg leave to offer my warmest thanks to the callers of the meeting and all who took part in it.—Yours respectfully and gratefully, HENRIK IBSEN.

## 190.

*To* BJÖRNSTJERNE BJÖRNSON.

MUNICH, MAXIMILIANSTRASSE 32,
22*nd December* 1885.

DEAR BJÖRNSON,—Once again you must pardon my negligence as a correspondent.

I will not sign a second application to the Storthing for a pension for Kielland; and I advise you to think twice before you interfere in the matter. I fear that such interference will injure, possibly even defeat, the cause you wish to further.

---

[1] The meeting on October 16th was held under the presidency of Fredrik Stang Lund, barrister in Christiania, afterwards State-Councillor.

26

As you no doubt remember, I was present when the proposal was last debated in the Storthing. The whole Ministry absented itself, and the explanation and excuse offered was that the motion was a private one—that application had not been made to the Government, but direct to the House—that the State Council had thus had no opportunity of submitting the matter to preparatory discussion, and, consequently, did not feel called upon to take part in the debate, etc. etc.

This excuse was actually by some regarded as genuine.

My opinion is that next time the Ministry itself must bear this heavy cross. We ought not to do anything to lighten the burden of the Ecclesiastical Department. If you can get the Liberal newspapers to exercise pressure, that might not be amiss. We should then see if the Government is favourably disposed towards this pension. I doubt it very much. I believe that our present Government sets far too high a value on the opinion of the priest-ridden section of the population.

I am aware that what I have said does not apply to the motives which impel you to act; nevertheless I cannot help believing that it would be for the good of the cause to wait and see what the Government will do. I am also of opinion that henceforth—or, at least, as long as we have parliamentary government—these direct applications to the Storthing ought not to be made. In times past they may have been suitable and necessary, but they are so no longer.[1]

I congratulate you upon *Geography and Love.* What a successful run it has had both in Christiania and Copenhagen!

I saw a great deal of Björn last summer. His frank, confident manner has helped him to win the favour of all, both friends and adversaries. Ejnar I saw only twice. I hear from Mr. Grönvold that Erling is attending the commercial college at Fürth, and is perhaps coming to Munich for the Christmas

---

[1] Björnson himself, unsupported, made the application in 1886. It was not granted; but Kielland was voted a sum of 1600 Kroner "as compensation for losses due to the lack of copyright laws."

holidays. In this case I hope to see him.[1] We expect Sigurd, too, about that time. He is going as attaché to Washington; but I hope he will have a few weeks' leave before he starts. My wife and I wish you all a merry Christmas and a happy New Year.—Yours,

HENRIK IBSEN.

191.

*To* CARL SNOILSKY.[2]

MUNICH, 14th *February* 1886.

DEAR FRIEND,—If you and your wife were to judge us by our long, obstinate silence, you would have good reason to pronounce us very ungrateful. The fact is that my wife is given to leaving all private correspondence to me; and nature and habit together are making me more and more prone to the evil practice of delaying the writing of all but necessary business letters till to-morrow, a day which, as you know, is long in coming. But to-day I really will put aside everything else, and send you a few lines, in the hope that our friendship has not suffered any lasting injury from my negligence.

In the first place, I must ask you to accept our best thanks for the books, which it gave us great pleasure to receive and read. The beautiful, graphic descriptions of travel brought the sunny shores of the Mediterranean most vividly before us, and made us long to see them again, and then, if possible, to cross over to Africa. As to your book of poems, it is, from beginning to end, a work well worthy of Scandinavia's greatest living lyric poet.

---

[1] The Ejnar and Erling referred to are Björnson's sons.

[2] Count Carl Snoilsky (see Letter 80) published collections of poems in 1871, 1881, 1883, and 1887. He lived much abroad. His wife, Countess Ebba Snoilsky, published (anonymously) in 1881, *Momentary Impressions received in Northern Africa and Southern Italy.*

And it is not only for the books that we have to thank you, but also for all the pleasure we had in your society at Molde. It was a great gain to us to be with you again, and to make acquaintance with the noble and high-minded lady who is your wife. The recollection of those days is the most inspiring of all the memories of our stay in Norway.

We read in the newspapers about your trip to Finland, and with special interest about the visit to Topelius.[1] Sigurd sent us an account of the festivities in Stockholm.

.    .    .    .    .    .    .    .

So you are in Dresden again. I hope that you will carry out your project of writing a dramatic work; I cannot but believe that it will be a success.

I also am engrossed in writing a new play, which I have been planning for a long time, and for which I made careful studies during my visit to Norway last summer.[2]

We have our son with us just now. Next month he goes to his post as attaché at the Legation in Washington, and then we shall again be quite alone.

I enclose a photograph which I hope you will accept, along with our most cordial greetings to you both, and repeated thanks for all your kindness.—Yours most sincerely,

HENRIK IBSEN.

## 192.

#### *To* EDWARD FALLESEN.

MUNICH, 28*th February* 1886.

To Chamberlain FALLESEN,
Director of the Theatre Royal.

HONOURED SIR,—I received a letter from Councillor Hegel yesterday, informing me of your inquiry as to whether a new dramatic work from my pen may be expected soon.

---

[1] Zakarias Topelius (1818–1898), a famous Finnish poet.
[2] The play referred to is *Rosmersholm.*

I beg leave to inform you that it will be late in the autumn before the new play, on which I am at present engaged, can be offered to the theatre.

At the same time I take the liberty of reminding you that two of my earlier plays have not yet been acted at the Theatre Royal.

One of these is *Love's Comedy*, a play of three acts, in rhymed verse. Its performance occupies a whole evening; and it has proved exceedingly attractive wherever it has been played. At the Theatre Royal it would have a chance of being particularly well produced, as all the parts are well adapted to the present staff of actors. For the sake of the Danish audiences, a little cutting of the speeches here and there might be advisable, and could easily be done. If the piece is accepted at once, and staged as soon as possible, I am convinced that the result will be a triumph both for the Theatre and for myself.

The other play of mine which has not yet been performed at the Theatre Royal is *Ghosts*. It was offered when it was new, but was not accepted. Now, however, public opinion is more enlightened as regards this serious drama; and I believe that if you could persuade yourself to produce it, all enlightened and unprejudiced people would consider that you were doing the public a service.

If either of these proposals meets with your approval, I trust, Sir, that you will be good enough to intimate the fact to me.—Yours most respectfully,

HENRIK IBSEN.[1]

---

[1] *Love's Comedy* was accepted by the Theatre Royal, but never acted there; but both it and *Ghosts* were played at the Dagmar Theatre in Copenhagen in 1898. *Ghosts* was not acted at the Theatre Royal till 1903.

193.

*To* FREDERIK HEGEL.

MUNICH, 25*th February* 1886.

DEAR MR. HEGEL,—I wrote at once direct to Mr. Fallesen in answer to the inquiry contained in your letter of the 17th inst. At present I have no new dramatic work to offer the Theatre Royal; it will be autumn before I have anything ready.

So much for this matter. I have also to acknowledge a communication received from you on the 12th. The list which you were good enough to send of my securities in your keeping agrees exactly with my own list. Your receipts for the Bonds redeemed last year I herewith return. The receipts for the Bonds of the Norwegian Mortgage Bank will be sent later, as I cannot lay my hands on them to-day. Please excuse all this not having been done before.

At the time of his stay in Munich, Henrik Jæger mentioned to me that he had some thoughts of writing my biography. I expressed neither approval nor disapproval, as I did not know what style of book he meant to write. I have only a dim recollection of any photographs taken of me as a young man. I consequently cannot say whether they resembled me at the time or not, or whether they would be worth reproducing for publication.

There is none taken so early as the period when *Catilina* was written. The oldest was done by Edward Larssen, the author, either in 1861 or 1862. Another, by a Christiania photographer, a Dane named Petersen, dates from about the same time. Those taken by Jäger of Stockholm in 1869 and Budtz-Möller of Copenhagen in 1870 are very unsatisfactory as regards expression. In Rome I have been photographed by Alessandri, in Dresden by Eich, in Munich by Leed and Hanfstaengl, and in Copenhagen (quite lately) by Hohlenberg. Hanfstaengl's and Hohlenberg's portraits I consider very good.

In this connection I had better mention my busts, as the

sculptors probably own photographs of them. The earliest were done in 1867, by Wilhelm Bissen and Walter Runeberg. That done in Rome in 1885 by the Danish sculptor, Johannes Hoffmann, is considered a fine piece of work, and I have seen excellent photographs of it. And the Norwegian sculptor, Fjelde, made a very good bust last summer.

There are three portraits of me done in oils. One, by Ejlif Peterssen, dates from about 1876, and belongs to the Norwegian Students' Union. A large three-quarter length portrait by Prof. Julius Kronberg of Stockholm, painted about the same time, is in my own possession. I do not believe that my expression and character are very felicitously rendered in either of these. Then there is a portrait by Olrik, painted in Rome, I think, in 1883.

My own drawings probably possess no artistic value whatever. If they were to be reproduced, it could only be as curiosities.

But the most important matter of all has not yet been mentioned. All Mr. H. Jæger's biographical data must have been procured second-hand, if not third or fourth hand. I have a strong suspicion that a good deal of his information is not quite correct. Absolutely reliable data he can only obtain from myself, and as yet he has not applied to me. To send me the manuscript of a completed work for correction would not be a good plan at all. He had much better wait until we have had a personal interview. There is no hurry. In two years I shall be sixty years old, and that might be a good time to bring out such a book. Its appearance would give me great pleasure if it were published by you, but not if it were published by any one else.[1]

---

[1] Henrik Jæger (1854–1895), a Norwegian writer on literary subjects, published a long biography of Ibsen in the spring of 1888. He received a considerable amount of information from Ibsen himself. They spent some time together at Sæby in Denmark in the summer of 1887. In 1892 Jæger published a more purely literary book, *Henrik Ibsen and his Works*, of which Ibsen himself read the proofs.

I hope that your daughter-in-law and the baby are well.—
With our kindest regards to all of you, I remain, Yours most
sincerely,　　　　　　　　　　　　　　　HENRIK IBSEN.

194.

*To* GEORGE BRANDES.

MUNICH, 10*th November* 1886.

DEAR BRANDES,—I hardly know whether I dare count upon
your willingness to receive a letter from me, now that more than
a year and a day have passed without my giving any direct signs
of life. But I rely on your good nature and on our old friendship, which I do not believe could ever really be destroyed.
As far as I am concerned, at least, it would be an impossibility.

The explanation of my obstinate silence is that I am getting
more and more into the habit of occupying my thoughts with one
single thing at a time; they keep circling round one set of ideas;
and as long as this goes on, everything else is set aside. Ever
since I returned to Munich I have been tormented by a new play,
which was determined that it should be written. I did not get
rid of it till the beginning of last month. That is to say, I got
the manuscript out of the house then. But afterwards came all
the unavoidable writing connected with the publication and
translation of a new book.[1]

It was late, too, before I set properly to work at this same
play. Not till well on in June did I begin to put pen to paper
in good earnest.

The experiences of my journey in Norway last summer—
the impressions received, the observations made—had a disturbing
effect on me. I had to come to a distinct understanding of the
whole, and draw my conclusions, before I could think of transforming the experiences into fiction. Your visit to Christiania,
and your experiences there, also gave me much to think about.

[1] *Rosmersholm* was published in November 1886.

They were of valuable assistance to me in my characterisation of our Liberals. Never have I felt myself less capable of understanding, and sympathising with, the "Thun und Treiben" of my Norwegian compariots than after the lessons taught me last year—never have I been more repelled, never more disagreeably impressed. Nevertheless, I do not relinquish the hope that all this crude immaturity may some day clarify into both the substance and the outward form of genuine civilisation. But such a possibility is for the moment of no interest to any one in Norway; nor do I believe that the present active forces of the country would suffice to accomplish any subtler, deeper-going reforms than those that are now the order of the day. And perhaps hardly even those. It was an unlucky hour for progress in Norway, the hour when Johan Sverdrup came into "power"—and was muzzled and handcuffed.

I have attended to what has been happening in the outside world this year, so far as to know that you were at Warsaw again in spring, lecturing. We half hoped that you would return by way of Munich; but of course you did not. I do not believe you know how many warm admirers you have here among those interested in literature.

Accept our best thanks for your articles on the state of Poland and on Luther's utterances on the subject of celibacy. It was kind of you to send them. That on Poland made a deep and lasting impression upon us; the other amused us immensely.

Please thank your wife from us for the letter of introduction she kindly sent Sigurd. He will probably have an opportunity of making use of it in the course of the winter.

We often talk of our visit to your peaceful, comfortable home. Please remember us to your wife and the girls. We shall perhaps come to Denmark next summer. We both have a great fancy to spend some months at the Skaw. If we gratify it, I hope we shall see you in Copenhagen.—Yours sincerely and gratefully,

HENRIK IBSEN.

195.

*To* LUDWIG PASSARGE.

MUNICH, 16*th December* 1886.

DEAR FRIEND,—I grieved, and reproached myself bitterly, as
I read your letter.

My long silence has really been nothing but a result of that
disinclination to express myself by means of letter-writing which
has of late been getting the upper hand of me, but which I shall
hereafter try to combat.

An exception certainly ought to have been made in your
case. You had, I regret to say, every right to consider it an
insult that I should allow such a length of time to elapse
without giving any sign of life. Your letter has made me
feel keenly that I have behaved very badly to you. I shall
not try to excuse myself. I shall only beg of you to pardon
me.

When your great critical and biographical work came to
hand, and I learned from it that you had procured some of
your most important information from those two men who,
among all my literary friends and acquaintances in Norway,
have been least capable of entering into what I consider the
essential spirit of my life-work as an author, I must confess
that I felt alarmed. And there is no doubt that here and
there throughout the description it becomes evident from what
sources the writer has drawn his facts. I must also say that in
your translations of poems I came upon one or two expressions
which did not seem to me exactly to reproduce the meaning
or the spirit of the original.

But what are trifles like these in comparison with the friendliness and the warm sympathy perceptible in everything you
write! Silent though I have been, I beg of you not to doubt
that I have appreciated this. I am keenly sensible, though it is
not in my nature to say much, of the great debt of gratitude

which I owe you, not only for having written about me, but for your disposition towards me.[1]

Please remember me very kindly to your noble, warm-hearted wife. Tell her that I do not forget the meeting in the Gossensass express train.—Yours most sincerely, HENRIK IBSEN.

196.

*To* FREDERIK HEGEL.

MUNICH, *5th January* 1887.

DEAR MR. HEGEL,—Will you be so kind as to send me 1000 Kroner, either in German bank-notes or per draft?

I am at present leading a kind of wandering life to which I am not accustomed. I was just beginning to settle down after the week of festivities at Meiningen; and now I must be off again. I leave the day after to-morrow for Berlin, where *Ghosts* is to be performed on the 9th, at the Residenz Theatre. I would much rather remain at home; but I have received so many urgent invitations that I cannot well refuse to put in an appearance, especially as *Ghosts* has become a burning literary and dramatic question in Germany.

I am prepared for a considerable amount of opposition on the part of the Berlin Conservative press—a reason the more that I should be on the spot.[2]

[1] L. Passarge's book on Ibsen was published at Leipzig in 1883. It was dedicated to Lorentz Dietrichson and Hartvig Lassen.

[2] *Ghosts* was produced in Berlin at a private matinée at the Residenz Theatre on the 9th of January 1887. The performance was epoch-making as regards the attitude of Germany to Ibsen. A large number of Berlin representatives of art and science took the opportunity to do homage to him at a banquet on the 11th. A public performance of *Ghosts* was proposed, but was forbidden by the authorities. On his return to Munich, Ibsen wrote to Hoffory: "My visit to Berlin (and everything connected with it) I regard in the light of real, great good fortune. It has had a marvellously refreshing, rejuvenating effect on me; and it is quite certain to have an influence on my future writing."

At Meiningen the Duke conferred on me a very special token of honour by investing me, the day after the performance [1] —"als Zeichen seiner Verehrung und Bewunderung"—with the insignia of a knight of the "Sächsisch-Ernestinisch" Order— the First Class, with the Star.

Please do not think that it is vanity which makes me tell you this. But I do not deny that the honour gives me pleasure when I think of it in connection with the stupid denunciation of which the play was so long the object in Scandinavia.

With many thanks for the books sent me, and with our kindest regards to yourself and your family, I remain, dear Mr. Hegel—Yours most sincerely,

HENRIK IBSEN.

### 197.

#### *To* BJÖRN KRISTENSEN.[2]

MUNICH, 13*th February* 1887.

SIR,—Kindly accept and convey to the Debating Club my sincerest thanks for its friendly letter of the 4th of December of last year.

It should have been answered ere now, had I not been away from home, or, when at home, overburdened with business which could not be postponed.

The call to work is, undoubtedly, distinguishable throughout *Rosmersholm.*

But the play also deals with the struggle which all serious-minded human beings have to wage with themselves in order to bring their lives into harmony with their convictions.

---

[1] *Ghosts* was the play performed at Meiningen.

[2] Björn Kristensen was, in 1886, the chairman of the debating club connected with Aars and Voss's Privatgymnasium in Christiana. At this club *Rosmersholm* had been read aloud, and a letter of thanks had been subsequently written to Ibsen.

For the different spiritual functions do not develop evenly and abreast of each other in any one human being. The instinct of acquisition hurries on from gain to gain. The moral consciousness—what we call conscience, is, on the other hand, very conservative. It has its deep roots in traditions and the past generally. Hence the conflict.

But the play is, of course, first and foremost a work of fiction, a story of human beings and human fates.

With a friendly greeting to each one of the members of the Debating Club, I remain—Yours sincerely,

HENRIK IBSEN.

## 198.

*To* JULIUS HOFFORY.[1]

MUNICH, 26th *February* 1888.

. . . . . . . .

*Emperor and Galilean* is the first work which I wrote under German intellectual influences.

When, in the autumn of 1868, I came from Italy to Dresden, I brought with me the outline of *The League of Youth*, which play I wrote in Dresden during the winter. During my four years' stay in Rome I had occupied myself with all kinds of historical studies in view of writing *Emperor and Galilean*, and had made notes for it; but I had evolved no distinct plan or plot, much less written any part of the drama. My view of life was still that of the Scandinavian nationalist, and I could not accommodate myself properly to the alien subject.

Then came the experiences of Germany's great time. I was

---

[1] Julius Hoffory, a Dane by birth, was in 1887 appointed Professor of Scandinavian Philology at the University of Berlin. He did much to make Ibsen known in Germany. The above letter, of which only a fragment has been preserved, relates to a German translation of *Emperor and Galilean*.

in Germany during the war, and the development consequent on it. All this acted in many ways on me with the force of a transforming power. My theory of history and of human life had until then been a national one; now it expanded into a racial theory, and I could write *Emperor and Galilean*. The play was completed in the spring of 1873.

. . . . . . . .

HENRIK IBSEN.

## 199.

*To* PETER HANSEN.[1]

MUNICH, 12th March 1888.

DEAR MR. HANSEN,—I ought to have thanked you long ago for the welcome proof of old friendship which you gave me by sending me your translation of Gœthe's *Faust*. But during the last two months I have been so overwhelmed with business, that I was compelled to give up all private letter-writing for the time. I hope that you will accept this excuse.

The thanks I send you to-day are not only for the gift of the book, but also for the enjoyment which I have had in reading it. And please accept, along with my thanks, my most sincere congratulations. For it seems to me that there can be no doubt of your having succeeded in producing the best translation of *Faust* in existence. The Romance languages do not seem to lend themselves to the rendering of this poem. Rydberg's translation is both noble and correct, but it does not seem to me that he gives due prominence to the Gothic ring of the language in the original. There is something academic about the Swedish language which perhaps makes the transference of such a quality difficult.

---

[1] Peter Hansen published a Danish translation of the First Part of *Faust* in 1881; a second edition was called for in 1887. In 1889 he published his translation of the Second Part. Rydberg translated *Faust* into Swedish in 1876.

Thanks once again for your valuable gift.—With kindest regards to your wife, I remain, Your old friend and fellow-Egyptian,         HENRIK IBSEN.


## 200.

### *To* OSCAR NISSEN.

MUNICH, 20*th March* 1888.

DEAR DR. OSCAR NISSEN,—It was with special pleasure that I received the telegram which you sent me on my sixtieth birthday, conveying a greeting from the Workmen's Association of Christiania. I return my most cordial thanks for it.

It is, unfortunately, not in my province or power to do anything directly for the benefit of the working class.

But will you tell the members of the Association that, of all the classes in our country, theirs is nearest to my heart ; and will you also say that in that future which I believe in and hope for, the circumstances and position in society of the workingman will be such that I already hail them with joy !—With kindest regards, I remain, Yours respectfully,

HENRIK IBSEN.


## 201.

### *To* HENRIK JÆGER.

MUNICH, *April* 1888.

.     .     .     .     .     .     .     .

And I thank you cordially for your long biographical work, two beautiful copies of which were received by us the day before yesterday.

I believe that I may confidently add congratulations to the thanks ; for it seem to me that the book is certain to be successful. It contains much new material of many different kinds, and it seems to me to be distinguished by a keen and intelligent comprehension of my literary works and of the periods of their production. . . .

202.

*To* The Reverend Christian Hostrup.[1]

Munich, *2nd April* 1888.

Dear Mr. Hostrup,—Kindly forgive me for not thanking you sooner for the telegram with which you and Mrs. Hostrup gave me so much pleasure on my birthday.

And I am no less grateful to you for the copy you sent me of *In the Snow-storm*. It was a real joy to read the beautiful work, and actually to live in it for the time being. Jutland, which has had a strong fascination for me ever since I made its acquaintance, was marvellously present with me whilst I read, although I have never seen it in winter. I hardly ever go to the theatre here, but I enjoy reading a play now and then in the evening; and as I have a powerful imagination where anything dramatic is concerned, I can see everything that is really natural, authentic, and credible, happening before my eyes. The reading of the play produces almost the same effect as its performance. This has made the reading of your new drama the great pleasure it has been to me.

My wife joins me in kindest regards to Mrs. Hostrup and yourself.—Yours sincerely and gratefully,

Henrik Ibsen.

[1] Christian Hostrup (1818–1892) wrote some amusing and pretty Vaudevilles in the Forties. During the following twenty years he devoted himself entirely to his clerical calling. The course taken by his own development, along with the influence of Ibsen's *Doll's House*, led him to begin writing plays again—this time serious ones. *In the Snow-storm*, published in 1888, was one of these. The old pastor's undaunted expression of liberal views in these later years often gave offence.

## 203.

*To* CARL SNOILSKY.

MUNICH, *6th April* 1888.

DEAR FRIEND,—Please accept yourself, and convey to your wife, my very best thanks for the telegram which I had the pleasure of receiving from you both on my birthday.

Some days ago I read with extreme satisfaction the article on you and your writings in the *Magazin für die Litteratur.* I have very often wished, in my desire for a more complete understanding of Scandinavian poetry here in Germany, that more of your poetry could be translated. For what Adolph Stern observes is perfectly true — you represent one of the characteristic developments which must on no account be neglected in a consideration of the whole. Now, I hope that the work will be undertaken. But it is of the greatest importance that you should have a translator with whom you can confer personally. The specimen verses in the magazine read very well in German. A perfect rendering of the inmost essence of the original poem in every respect is a thing which cannot in most cases be achieved. I know the editor of the *Magazin*, Wolfgang Kirchbach, and I am certain that he will, with the greatest pleasure, accept anything you may care to publish in it. He is himself a very gifted author. Several of his novels have been translated into Danish. I advise you to read his remarkable play, *Die Waiblinger.*

With our kindest regards to yourself and your wife, I remain—Yours most sincerely,

HENRIK IBSEN.

## 204.

*To* CHRISTIAN HOSTRUP.[1]

MUNICH, 18*th May* 1888.

REVEREND AND DEAR SIR,—Remembering the anniversary which you are to celebrate on Whitsunday, I send you my sincerest good wishes and congratulations. Please accept them —and along with them, thanks for that gleam of the joy of life and the joy of youth of which a reflection was borne by your writings to me and my contemporaries in overclouded Norway.—Yours faithfully,　　　　　HENRIK IBSEN.

## 205.

*To* LAURA KIELER.

MUNICH, 23*rd July* 1888.

DEAR MRS. KIELER,—The explanation of my not answering your kind letter of the 13th of June until to-day is that I am engaged in writing a long new play, and have consequently been obliged to give up letter-writing for the time being. I will, however, make an exception in your case, and send you a few lines.

I have read *Men of Honour* with the greatest interest. It is, in my opinion, a play which all our theatres ought to put on the stage as soon as possible. A few cuttings and a few abbreviations of the dialogue might be made. This can easily be done while the parts are being studied, unless you prefer to do it yourself.

I am not surprised that you feel unwilling to make any alteration in the ending of the play. But give the matter due consideration. Some expedient may suggest itself. Your name, as author, does not appear on the manuscript sent me.

[1] The 20th of May 1888 was Christian Hostrup's seventieth birthday.

This is an omission which positively must be rectified. Your reputation as an author will provide the well-written, interesting play with one recommendation the more.

Should the theatres, contrary to expectation, not accept your play, you must on no account do what you threaten in your letter—lay it away in a drawer. You must rewrite it as a novel. With your talent and with your great experience in novel-writing, such an adaptation will present no difficulty to you.[1]

Do not trouble about the advice of others. It is not the first time I have told you that you must not keep things lying in your drawer. This you owe to yourself.

My wife sends you her kindest regards, and I wish you all possible success with your work.—Always yours sincerely,

HENRIK IBSEN.

206.

*To* GEORGE BRANDES.

MUNICH, 30*th October* 1888.

DEAR BRANDES,—After many months of incessant work upon a new five-act play, which is now completed, I once more begin to have time at my disposal, and can think of a little letter-writing which is not purely business correspondence.[2]

Allow me now, late though it is, to thank you for the telegram with which you gladdened me on my birthday; also for your essay on *Temperament and Reality in the Case of Émile Zola*, which you were good enough to send me at the time of its publication, and which I have repeatedly read with great interest; and, lastly, for your new, long work: *Impres-*

---

[1] *Men of Honour* was acted at the Kasino of Copenhagen, and at the Christiania Theatre in 1890. There were great differences of opinion regarding it.

[2] *The Lady from the Sea* was published in November 1888.

*sions of Poland*, in which I am beginning to absorb myself, to the neglect of everything else. It is a whole "dark continent" which is here opened to the ken of Western Europe! Thanks for this new enrichment!

We have learned from the newspapers of the large attendances at your last course of lectures; but except for this, we know very little of how things are with you, and how the life at home suits you. I myself feel as if it might be possible to live very happily in Copenhagen. But then I have only tried it at intervals for a short time.

It would be quite impossible for me to settle for good in Norway. Nowhere should I feel less at home than there. A man of reasonably well-developed intellect is no longer satisfied with the old conception of nationality. We can no longer be content with the political community to which we belong. I believe that national consciousness is on the point of dying out, and that it will be replaced by racial consciousness; I myself, at least, have passed through this evolution. I began by feeling myself a Norwegian; I developed into a Scandinavian; and now I have arrived at Teutonism.

I follow with attention and interest all the manifestations of life in the old home. They are not particularly pleasant observations that one has the opportunity of making. But I cannot say that the political development has been a disappointment to me; for what has happened is exactly what I was prepared for. I knew beforehand that this, and no other, would inevitably be the course of events. But the leaders of our party of the Left altogether lack experience of the world; and consequently they had been cherishing the most unreasonable illusions. They imagined that a leader of the Opposition would and could remain the same after he got into power as he was before.

*4th November.*—DEAR FRIEND,—I had to leave this letter unfinished, as I have not been well for some days, and have, besides, been overburdened with business connected with theatrical matters, which could not be postponed.

To-day, just as I was sitting down to continue where I left off, there arrived a packet from Copenhagen addressed in your well-known writing. How good of you to send me your *Impressions of Russia*, too! I dare not now continue to hold forth upon affairs at home. This letter, conveying my sincerest thanks, must go at once. The pencil inscription in the book, too, warns me that I must not, by continued silence, put your friendship and your indulgence to a more severe test. I acknowledge that I have fully deserved the silent, and yet eloquent reproach. But it does not cause me any real alarm; it only awakens the conscience of the bad correspondent. A serious and lasting misunderstanding between us is to me something unimaginable.

While I am on the subject of my sins as a correspondent, may I ask you to convey to your brother my warmest thanks for his review of *Rosmersholm*. It made an ineffaceable impression on me. The first time I read it I felt as if I were reading a beautiful, profound, sympathetic poem on my work.

. . . . . . . .

My wife joins with me in sending very kind regards to you and your wife and the girls.—Your faithful, affectionate, and grateful,                                    HENRIK IBSEN.

## 207.

### *To* LUDVIG DAAE.

MUNICH, 20*th November* 1888.

DEAR LUDVIG L. DAAE,—I cannot resist the inclination to send you a few lines, while the first, fresh impression produced on me by reading your article in *Vidar* on Botten-Hansen is still strong.

You have enriched our literature with a masterly picture of the times and an exceedingly clever character-study. It

affected me strangely and powerfully to be so vividly trans-
ported once again into surroundings which have exercised such
a decisive influence on my subsequent development, and which
I have never in my innermost soul separated myself from—have
never had either the power or the will to separate myself from.

My sincerest thanks for your fine historical work on "the
Dutchman." Remember me to all—all the survivors.—Theirs
and yours sincerely,

HENRIK IBSEN.[1]

208.

*To* BREDO MORGENSTIERNE.[2]

MUNICH, 21st *November* 1888.

HONOURED SIR,—I do not think that I am mistaken in my
surmise that the genial, sympathetically cordial article with
which the *Aftenpost* gladdened and honoured me on my
birthday, the 20th of last March, was from your pen.

I have, therefore, requested my publisher to send you a
copy of my new play, which I hope you will accept as an
expression of the debt of gratitude which I feel that I owe you.

I have still a vivid recollection of my different meetings
with you. The first was in Christiania in 1874, at the great
fête with which the Students' Union welcomed me at that
time. Three years later we met in Stockholm, chiefly at the
Hotel Rydberg; and again in the train on the return journey
from Upsala, when we were in the same carriage with
Madvig, State-Councillor Steenstrup, and Professor Panum, then
Rector of the Copenhagen University. The very thought of
these meetings brings back the festive feeling.

---

[1] For Botten-Hansen and "the Dutchmen," see Introduction, p. 11.
[2] Bredo Morgenstierne (born 1851), a Norwegian journalist; from
1887 onwards Professor of Jurisprudence and Political Economy at
the University of Christiania.

When I come to Christiania again—if such a thing ever happens—I shall seek admission into the circle in which I feel that I am most at home. Farewell until then.—Yours very sincerely,

HENRIK IBSEN.

209.

*To* CAMILLA COLLETT.

MUNICH, *3rd May* 1889.

DEAR MRS. COLLETT,—A deeply interesting letter from you has been in my possession for more than two months without my giving you a sign of life. What can you think of me?

I can only say that a great deal has been happening since it came—a great deal of a nature to keep me away from the writing-table. First I had to go to Berlin, and then, quite unexpectedly, to Weimar. Only now am I beginning to settle down again.[1]

Allow me, then, to-day to send you a few words of very sincere thanks for your comprehension of *The Lady from the Sea.*

I felt pretty certain that you, you in particular, would understand it; but it gave me inexpressible pleasure to be confirmed in my belief by your letter.

Yes, there are suggestive resemblances — indeed, many. And you have seen and felt them, seen and felt that of which I could only have a vague premonition.

But it is many years now since you, by virtue of your

---

[1] Ibsen had gone to Berlin to be present at the first performance of *The Lady from the Sea* at the Theatre Royal. During the week of his stay in Berlin he saw *The Wild Duck* played at the Residenz Theatre, and *A Doll's House* at the Lessing Theatre. At Weimar he was also present at a performance of *The Lady from the Sea*, on which occasion he was called before the curtain after each act.

characteristic spiritual and intellectual development, began, in one form or another, to make your influence felt in my writings.

You may be sure that my wife and I do not forget you; we both think and talk of you. We heard during the winter that you were in Berlin, and we felt certain that we should have the pleasure of seeing you here in Munich again. But it was not to be, this time. We have not, as yet, been able to make any plans for the coming summer. But it is not impossible that circumstances will lead to our turning our steps northward, in which case we are sure to meet.

With kindest regards from my wife and myself, believe me, dear Mrs. Collett—Yours very sincerely,

HENRIK IBSEN.

## 210.

### *To* JENS BRAAGE HALVORSEN.[1]

MUNICH, 18*th June* 1889.

SIR,—My excuse for not answering your kind letter of the 30th of May until to-day is that the most important part of the information requested in it was conveyed to you in my jottings on the proof-sheets, which I returned to you as quickly as possible.

For the sake of correctness, however, I now supplement these notes with a few more particulars.

1. As a boy I attended the Drawing School at Skien for a year, and there learned a little pencil drawing. At the same time, or a little later, I had some instruction in oil-painting from a young landscape-painter, Mandt, from Telemarken, who sometimes stayed at Skien. At Bergen I did some

[1] J. B. Halvorsen (1845–1900) was the planner and publisher of a long work, *Norsk Forfatter-Lexikon*, 1814–1880. The third volume, published in July 1889, began with an article upon Ibsen, extending to eighty-four pages.

water-colour painting under the supervision of the late Mr. Losting. After my return to Christiania I painted a little in oil under the direction of Magnus Bagge. But in 1860 I began to be much occupied with preparations for writing *Love's Comedy* and *The Pretenders;* and thenceforward the art of painting was entirely neglected by me.

2. With the Working Men's movement I had, strictly speaking, nothing to do. I was a friend of Abildgaard's, and through him became acquainted with Marcus Thrane. I knew a good deal about their plans; and when they were arrested I feared that I might be called as a witness. But, fortunately, my letters to Abildgaard, and possibly also some manuscripts, were among the papers burned—as Henrik Jæger tells.

3. This matter is sufficiently dealt with in my notes on the proof-sheet.

4. The above remark applies here also.

5. I have no objection to the extract from my letter to King Charles being printed, although the style of it now strikes me as decidedly bombastic.

Accept my best thanks for the immense amount of labour which you have spent upon your article on me, and for the form you have given it.—Yours most sincerely,

HENRIK IBSEN.

## 211.

### *To* MORITZ PROZOR.[1]

MUNICH, *25th October* 1889.

DEAR COUNT PROZOR,—I have had the great pleasure of receiving your esteemed letter of the 20th inst. The enclosed

[1] Count Moritz Prozor (born 1849), a Russian diplomatist, saw *Ghosts* played at Stockholm in 1881, when he was Secretary of Legation there. It made a strong impression on him, and led him to study Ibsen's works. At Berne, in 1887, he and his wife, a Swedish lady, translated *Ghosts*

letter to Mr. Roger of Paris, I signed and forwarded at once. I am unable to express all the gratitude I feel for what you have done for me.

The introduction of my dramatic works into France has long been my dream. But I dared not think seriously of it, as it seemed to me to be something quite unattainable. I had no connections in that country to speak of. And I was already so fully engaged, attending to my literary business in Scandinavia, Germany, Austria, England, America, and elsewhere, that it was quite out of my power to make any attempt to extend my field of operations to that great and very inaccessible city, Paris, or what in matters literary is the same thing—to France.

And now you, Sir, have already done so much for me. The start has been made, and therewith the greatest difficulty has been overcome. Attention and interest have been aroused in influential circles. The thing is set going.

All this I owe chiefly to you. My earnest request to you is that you will continue to take charge of my French affairs and everything connected therewith. If you do so, then I may hope for good results.

But whether my plays succeed in Paris or not, I beg you, dear Sir, to believe that I shall always gratefully acknowledge and appreciate all that you have wished to do, and have done, for me. I will, of course, with the greatest pleasure, sign a declaration that your translation, and no other, is the one I wish to be accepted, if you will only be kind enough to send me a form of words for the said declaration.

My best thanks for the copy of the translation which I

and *A Doll's House* into French. Edouard Rod, a great admirer of Ibsen, procured him a publisher in Paris. Jules Lemaître introduced him to the Director of the Vaudeville Theatre, Purel, and his wife, the famous actress, Madame Réjane. *A Doll's House* was performed at the Vaudeville Theatre in 1892, with Madame Réjane as Nora. *Ghosts* was staged at the Théâtre Libre in 1890. Prozor has translated most of Ibsen's plays.

received yesterday. It is a very handsome volume, better got up than I have, as a rule, been accustomed to here in Germany.

And for the money-order, too, please accept my thanks. I had no real right to payment in this case.

I have had a very friendly letter from Count Snoilsky. May I take the liberty of asking you, when opportunity offers, to give him my kindest regards and best thanks.

Assuring you of my profound esteem, I am, Sir—Yours respectfully and gratefully,

HENRIK IBSEN.

## 212.

*To* WILLIAM ARCHER.

MUNICH, *3rd November* 1889.

DEAR MR. W. ARCHER,—I have this moment received, with very great pleasure, your kind letter of the 1st inst., which I hasten to answer.

I shall always feel that I owe you a great debt of gratitude for all that you have done, and are still doing, to introduce my works into England.

. . . . . . . .

The beautiful and valuable edition of *A Doll's House* reached me in good condition. For this gift, too, I send you my best thanks. I should have done so long ago. I have the book always lying on my table, and it is greatly admired by all who see it and are able to appreciate works of art in the typographical line. I do not deny being proud that a work of mine should have appeared in great England in such a garb.

. . . . . . .

Yours most sincerely,

HENRIK IBSEN.

213.

*To* PETER HANSEN.

MUNICH, 5*th December* 1889.

DEAR P. HANSEN,—To-day, just as I was preparing to write
and thank you for the Second Part of *Faust,* your letter arrived;
so I can now thank you for both at the some time. The great
work I have, as yet, only glanced at, here and there, while
cutting it. But I have seen enough to make me acknowledge
that you are probably right in your theory regarding the
language, although I still think that even in the First Part it
is about as good as it can be. I am studying the introduction,
and hope to be thereby enabled to understand this Second Part
of the work, which has hitherto appeared to me to suffer from
obscure allegorisation.

Whether or not Heyse will be able to notice the translation,
I cannot say for certain. But I am sure that he will do it if
he can.

What I decidedly advise you to do, is to send the work,
accompanied by a letter, to Dr. Suphan, Keeper of the Goethe
Archives at Weimar. These Archives are under the special
protection of the Grand Duchess; and application made in that
quarter is sure to result in everything possible being done to
direct the attention of Germany to your translation.

You should also at the same time, and in the same manner,
apply to Professor Erich Schmidt of Berlin. His department
is literature, and more especially Goethe literature, in which
he is probably the most eminent specialist of the present day
in Germany. I may also mention that he is one of my most
enthusiastic adherents, and that he is interested in Scandinavian
literature generally.

I entirely agree with you that this important work of
yours ought not to remain unknown in Germany; and I
beg of you to trust to my doing whatever I can to prevent

this happening. It is an honour to Denmark, and through Denmark to the whole of educated Scandinavia, that such a classical rendering of a foreign classic can be produced among us.

We are wading in snow here, and I, like yourself, often call to mind our voyage of adventure twenty years ago.

With a respectful and cordial greeting to your wife, I remain—Your sincere friend,

HENRIK IBSEN.[1]

## 214.

### To CARL SNOILSKY.

MUNICH, 29th June 1890.

DEAR FRIEND,—You probably wonder why I have not yet answered the letter which I had the pleasure of receiving from you nearly a fortnight ago. The reason is that I wished to be able to tell you if we are certain to be here about the middle of next month.

Our intention has all along been to spend the summer in the Tyrol again. But circumstances are against our doing so. I am at present engaged upon a new dramatic work, which for several reasons has made very slow progress; and I do not leave Munich until I can take with me the completed first draft. There is little or no prospect of my being able to complete it in July; on the contrary, the probability is that we shall have to stay here, in town, until well on in autumn; and it will give us great pleasure to see you at the time you mention.

The effect produced by *Ghosts* in Paris was very satisfactory

[1] P. Hansen sent his translation of *Faust* to Dr. Suphan and Professor E. Schmidt, and friendly literary relations with both these gentlemen resulted from this step. Ibsen exerted himself, according to promise, in the interests of the Danish *Faust*—he induced Dr. Elias to write a notice of it in the *Allgemeine Zeitung*, etc. etc.,

to me.  But I was exceedingly sorry that Count Prozor's
translation was not the one used.  I have no idea why it was
not; but often, when I think of the matter, I blame myself for
not having made a formal protest, even though it might have
been to no purpose.  My reason for not doing so was that
Count Prozor himself wrote to me that he did not wish it.  But
I should be deeply grieved if the matter were to cause any ill
feeling towards me on the part of one to whom I owe so much
If you have an opportunity, will you be good enough to tell
him this.  Our very kind regards to you and Countess Snoilsky
We hope soon to bid you welcome here.—Yours most sincerely,

HENRIK IBSEN.


215.


*To* HANS LIEN BRÆKSTAD.[1]


MUNICH, *August* 1890.

[I have had my attention called to a letter from Berlin
relating to myself in the *Daily Chronicle* of August 13; and
as several of the statements in this letter seem susceptible of
misconstruction—have, in fact, been already miscontrued in
the Scandinavian papers—I shall be very much obliged by
your having some of the expressions attributed to me corrected.
It appears to me that certain of them are not exact and complete
reproductions of my utterances to the correspondent of the
paper.]

I did not, for instance, say that I have never studied the

---

[1] H. L. Brækstad (born 1845), a Norwegian-English man of letters
(since 1877 resident in London), who has done much for the spread
of Norwegian and Danish literature in England.

Letter 215 has been reconstructed from the extracts from the original
letter (which is no longer in existence), inserted by Mr. Brækstad in the
*Daily Chronicle* of the 28th of August 1890, and the *Münchener Post*,
No. 200.

question of Socialism—the fact being that I am much interested in the question, and have endeavoured to the best of my ability to acquaint myself with its different sides. I only said that I have never had time to study the extensive literature dealing with the different socialistic systems.

Where the correspondent repeats my assertion that I do not belong to the Social-Democratic party, I wish that he had not omitted what I expressly added, namely, that I never have belonged, and probably never shall belong, to any party whatever.

I may add here that it has become an absolute necessity to me to work quite independently and to shape my own course.

What the correspondent writes about my surprise at seeing my name put forward by socialistic agitators as that of a supporter of their dogmas is particularly liable to be misunderstood.

What I really said was that I was surprised that I, who had made it my chief life-task to depict human characters and human destinies, should, without conscious or direct intention, have arrived in several matters at the same conclusions as the social-democratic moral philosophers had arrived at by scientific processes.

What led me to express this surprise (and, I may here add, satisfaction) was a statement made by the correspondent to the effect that one or more lectures had lately been given in London, dealing, according to him, chiefly with *A Doll's House*.[1]

[Here you have, briefly, what I wish explained to my friends. Please make such use of these lines as you yourself consider best.]

---

[1] The lecture referred to was one given by G. Bernard Shaw on the 18th of July 1890, upon the socialistic aspect of Ibsen's writings. It formed the basis of his book, *The Quintessence of Ibsen*.

216.

*To* Karl Hals.[1]

Munich, 30*th October* 1890.

Dear Mr. Hals,—Accept my best thanks for your kind invitation to the festivities of November 3rd.

I am sorry that I shall not be able to be present—you knew, of course, that it was not possible—but I send you my heartiest congratulations and good wishes.

I dare not affirm positively that I saw you working at piano No. 1; but it was certainly one of the very first of the enormous number, which you and your brother Peter were making when we met for the first time. This was in the autumn of 1850, and it was Ole Schulerud who took me to see you. You and your brother were living at that time in Cappelen's house; and your little workshop was there too. I remember that you were both taking part in the work. Your assistant was Thornam, afterwards an actor at the Christiania Theatre.

Your brother Peter was very dear to me. He left us long ago; but his fine, noble presence is still life-like in my memory.

And so forty years have passed since we made each other's acquaintance! Neither of us possessed many of the good things of life at that time. I, at least, did not. In the interval we have both done fairly well, each in his own line.

You learned early to love work. It was later before I understood the happiness it gives. But then I, also, learned to appreciate it thoroughly.

At present I am utterly engrossed in a new play. Not one leisure hour have I had for several months. For, besides the play, an oppressively large correspondence has to be attended to. But all this shall not prevent my being with you in

[1] In 1847 the brothers Karl and Peter Hals started a pianoforte manufactory in Christiania, which in 1890 produced its 10,000th piano.

thought, in your festive circle, on the evening of November 3rd.—Yours most sincerely,

HENRIK IBSEN.

## 217.

*To* MORITZ PROZOR.

MUNICH, 20*th November* 1890.

DEAR COUNT PROZOR,—Accept my very best thanks for the letter which I received yesterday. I herewith return the power of attorney duly signed. It affords a great sense of security to be able to hand over the care of pecuniary matters to the French Literary Society; and the terms seem to me to be very fair and advantageous.

My new play is finished; the manuscript went off to Copenhagen the day before yesterday. According to the agreement we came to when you were here, the proof-sheets will be sent to you straight from the printer. Should there be anything in the play requiring explanation, I am, of course, at your service—willing and grateful.

It produces a curious feeling of emptiness to be thus suddenly separated from a work which has occupied one's time and thoughts for several months, to the exclusion of all else. But it is a good thing, too, to have done with it. The constant intercourse with the fictitious personages was beginning to make me quite nervous. Please present my respectful compliments to Countess Prozor, and believe me to be—Yours most sincerely and gratefully

HENRIK IBSEN.

218.

*To* JULIUS ELIAS.[1]

MUNICH, 27*th November* 1890.

DEAR DR. ELIAS,—Accept my best thanks for your telegram and letter. Some of the matters to which these referred are already attended to, and the rest do not demand immediate attention. They are not the cause of my writing to you to-day.

The object of this letter is to make you aware of the present sad and serious mental condition of Professor Hoffory. He arrived here from Weimar about a fortnight ago, and put up at the Hotel Roth, where he is still. It struck me at once that his thinking powers and ability to express himself were affected. He had difficulty in finding the words that he wanted, and especially in remembering the names of persons, even those with whom he is most closely connected.

His condition has grown worse day by day. Dr. Brahm saw him and spoke to him a few days ago, and will be able to give you information. I can only add that since Brahm left, Hoffory has become still more unlike himself. Yesterday I tried hard to persuade him to return to Berlin immediately But it was quite in vain. He talked foolishly about some love-affair which kept him here, and said he could not leave until this was finally arranged. What I believe is that his will-power has given way to such an extent that he cannot make up his mind to pack, or to ask for his bill, or to go to the railway station. I consider him quite incapable of taking care of his money. Both last night and the night before, at the Café Maximilian, he wanted to pay his bill over and over again. I was witness to this myself.

I think there is no doubt whatever that he ought to leave here. But I cannot imagine how he is to be induced to do it.

[1] Julius Elias (born 1861), a German literary critic, resided in Munich from 1881 to 1890, and knew Ibsen there.

Will you talk over the matter with Erich Schmidt, who lives not far from you. He is a man for whom Hoffory has a very great regard. Perhaps an earnest request from him might induce H. to return, and allow himself to be treated by the doctors who know the history of his illness. For it is most imperative that he should do this. There is no one here to give him advice—at least no one to whom he will apply. And the consequence is that he is growing rapidly worse.

I have had personal experience of your readiness to devote both time and labour to the service of your friends; hence I turn to you in this sad predicament. It is the future, possibly the life, of a human being which is at stake.[1]

With our kindest regards to yourself and Mrs. Elias, I remain—Yours sincerely,

HENRIK IBSEN.

219.

*To* MORITZ PROZOR.

MUNICH, 4*th December* 1890.

DEAR COUNT PROZOR,—I at once reply briefly to the letter which I have just had the pleasure of receiving from you.

The title of the play is *Hedda Gabler*. My intention in giving it this name was to indicate that Hedda as a personality is to be regarded rather as her father's daughter than as her husband's wife.

It was not really my desire to deal in this play with so-called problems. What I principally wanted to do was to depict human beings, human emotions, and human destinies, upon a groundwork of certain of the social conditions and principles of the present day. When you have read the whole, my

---

[1] Julius Hoffory (see Letter 198) was taken to a sanatorium. He left it apparently cured, but in 1893 the symptoms of mental alienation returned; and this time his case proved to be hopeless.

fundamental idea will be clearer to you than I can make it by entering into further explanations.

Before these lines reach you, you will probably have received forty-eight pages more from Copenhagen. And a few days later, the last sixty-four pages, together with the title-page and the list of characters, will come to hand.

Please present my respectful compliments to Countess Prozor, and believe me to be—Yours most sincerely and gratefully,

HENRIK IBSEN.

## 220.

### *To* MORITZ PROZOR.

MUNICH, 23*rd January* 1891.

DEAR COUNT PROZOR,—Mr. Luigi Capuana has, I regret to see, given you a great deal of trouble by his proposal to alter the last scene of *A Doll's House* for performance in the Italian theatres.

I do not for a moment doubt that the alteration you suggest would be distinctly preferable to that which Mr. Capuana proposes. But the fact is that I cannot possibly directly authorise any change whatever in the ending of the drama. I may almost say that it was for the sake of the last scene that the whole play was written.

And, besides, I believe that Mr. Capuana is mistaken in fearing that the Italian public would not be able to understand or approve of my work if it were put on the stage in its original form. The experiment ought, at any rate, to be tried. If it turns out a failure, then let Mr. Capuana, on his own responsibility, employ your adaptation of the closing scene; for I cannot formally authorise, or approve of, such a proceeding.

I wrote to Mr. Capuana yesterday, briefly expressing my views on the subject; and I hope that he will disregard his misgivings until he has proved by experience that they are well founded.[1]

At the time when *A Doll's House* was quite new, I was obliged to give my consent to an alteration of the last scene for Frau Hedwig Niemann-Raabe, who was to play the part of Nora in Berlin. At that time I had no choice. I was entirely unprotected by copyright law in Germany, and could, consequently, prevent nothing. Besides, the play in its original, uncorrupted form, was accessible to the German public in a German edition which was already printed and published. With its altered ending it had only a short run. In its unchanged form it is still being played.

The enclosed letter from Mr. Antoine I have answered, thanking him for his intention to produce *The Wild Duck*, and urging him to make use of your translation. Of course I cannot tell what he will decide. But as the Théâtre Libre is really of the nature of a private society, it is probably not possible to procure a legal injunction. There are, besides, reasons which would render the taking of such a step inadvisable, even if possible. However, I leave the decision of this question entirely to you, assured that you will act in the best way possible.

. With my very respectful regards to Countess Prozor, and with cordial thanks to yourself for all the favour and kindness shown me, I remain—Your sincere and obliged,

HENRIK IBSEN.

[1] Luigi Capuana (born 1839), an Italian novelist and dramatic critic, translated *A Doll's House* into Italian. It was the famous actress Eleonora Duse, who wished him to alter the last scene of the play; but she finally accepted and acted it in the original form.

## 221.

*To* HEDVIG STOUSLAND

MUNICH, 13*th March* 1891.

DEAR SISTER,—I thank you very heartily for the letter which I received last month, and which I must no longer delay answering.

I was very glad indeed to learn from it that Skien, too, is now to have its Public Hall. It is sure to be a large and fine one, up-to-date in every respect, and worthy of the modern town.

You tell me that a variety of entertainments are to be given to celebrate the opening of this Hall. I wish very much that I could have been present at them. I should probably have met but few of the acquaintances of my childhood—should have been surrounded by a new generation, all strangers to me. But I might not, perhaps, have felt myself altogether a stranger among them; for, through all these long years of absence, I have always had a feeling that I still belong to my native town.

Had these festivities taken place some years ago, I should if I had been told of them, have written a song or a poem and sent it home; and I hope and believe that it would have met with a kind reception there.

But I no longer write poems and songs of the kind required. So this is out of the question. And yet I would fain take part in the proceedings in some way.

Therefore please let this letter be read, so that all may know that I am with you in thought on this festive occasion, as I have many a time been with you before, both in your troubles and in your anticipations of brighter days.

It was in 1850 that I was last at home in Skien. Not long afterwards the town passed through a period of spiritual storms, storms which spread from there over a wider area.

I have always loved stormy weather. And, though absent I went through this tempestuous period with you; to this a part of my literary production bears witness.[1]

Then great calamities befel the town, devastating it again and again.[2] The house where I was born and where I spent my earliest years, and the church—the old church with the angel of baptism under the raftered roof—were burned down. All tne objects to which my earliest recollecuions were attached have been burned—every one of them. It would have been impossible for me not to feel myself deeply and personally affected, together with you all, by the blows which fell upon our common home.

But I beg of you to believe, too, in the keen pleasure which it has given me to read of the re-erection of the town in a handsome and beautiful style, of its growth, and of its progress in many directions.

It seems to me that gladness and hopefulness must be your feelings when you think of the future of our town.

I wish I could have said this, and more, to you instead of writing it. But, in my own way, I am among you, in spite of the distance that separates us.

And if I come to Norway again, as I hope I shall, I will come and see my home again, the old and yet new home.

This, dear Hedvig, is what I particularly wished to write to you to-day. I shall do my best to let you hear more from me soon. Farewell! Remember me to your own family and to other relatives.—Your affectionate brother,

HENRIK IBSEN.

[1] In the Fifties, Skien was the centre of a great religious revival. The leader of the movement was Pastor G. A. Lammers—of whom there are distinct reminiscences in *Brand*.

[2] The greater part of Skien was burned down in 1854, and again in 1886.

222.

*To* WILLIAM ARCHER.

MUNICH, 29*th April* 1891.

DEAR MR. WILLIAM ARCHER,—I have just returned from a
journey to Vienna and Budapest, and have had the great
pleasure of finding your friendly letter, telling me that *Hedda
Gabler* met with a unanimously favourable reception at its first
performance in London.[1]

I am fully convinced that this great victory is very largely
due to the kind and competent assistance and advice which
you have been good enough to give, both in the matter of the
text and of the staging.

It is a great pleasure to me to be allowed to send my
photograph, through you, to the two excellent actresses. The
inscription I have, as you see, written in Norwegian; will you
be so kind as to write the English below it?

I should like to send you a longer letter to-day, but want
of time forbids my doing so. I must therefore limit myself
to asking you to present our kindest regards to Mrs. Archer,
and to accept yourself the assurance of my keen sense of gratitude for all that you, in your unwearied friendship, have done
for me and for my literary interests in the great British
domain—and, consequently, also far beyond its borders.—Yours
sincerely,

HENRIK IBSEN.

[1] *Hedda Gabler* was played in London, April 20th to 24th, 1891,
by the two American actresses, Miss Elizabeth Robins and Miss Marion
Lea.

## 223.

*To* EDWARD BRANDES.

CHRISTIANIA, 27*th December* 1892.[1]

DEAR DR. EDWARD BRANDES,—Your friendly lines, received yesterday, gave me much pleasure, and also reassured me.

I had been upbraiding myself for not having at once telegraphed, or written, to offer you the thanks I owe you for the exceedingly kind manner in which you have reviewed my new play. Any notice of my works from your pen I regard as of great value and importance. And it was of very special importance to me in this case to have my characters correctly interpreted and explained, and, above all, to have them vindicated as being real men and women—which you have done.

I have been deeply and keenly interested in all your dramatic works. Amongst all the works of imagination with which I am acquainted, few have made such a profound impression upon my feelings as *Under the Law.*

Kindly accept these lines, together with hearty thanks and a cordial greeting, from—Your sincere and obliged,

HENRIK IBSEN.

## 224.

*To* JENS BRAAGE HALVORSEN.

CHRISTIANIA, 22*nd April* 1895.

DEAR MR. HALVORSEN,—Mrs. Wettergreen, the actress, called on me some days ago, and informed me that she is applying for a travelling-grant. I have, of course, nothing whatever to

[1] In July 1891, Ibsen removed from Munich to Christiania. In Christiania he wrote *The Master Builder*, which was published in December 1892.

do with such matters; but she entreated me very urgently to put in a good word for her with the Committee, of which you are a member; and it seems to me that I can do this with a good conscience. I may assume it to be generally acknowledged that she is a highly-gifted actress. But what I particularly wish to emphasise, is that she possesses in a very unusual degree the capacity of perfectibility. She belongs to the class of aspirants, by no means a large class, who may be sent abroad with a well-founded expectation of some real artistic result.

To me, personally, it is of importance that Mrs. Wettergreen should be made as clever an actress as possible, as I believe that I shall in future often find employment for her in my plays. I therefore request you, and through you the Committee, to do for her all that is in your power.—Yours very sincerely,

HENRIK IBSEN.[1]

225.

*To* WILLIAM ARCHER.

CHRISTIANIA, 27*th June* 1895.

DEAR MR. WILLIAM ARCHER,—Permit me to offer you my best thanks for the two drafts received. I return the receipt for Mr. Tree, duly signed; also the two letters.[2]

I knew of your discussion with Jules Lemaître, because the Norwegian papers gave an account of it, with quotations from what was written on both sides. You came off victorious from that encounter; and it seems to me that your French opponent acknowledged his mistake about Asta in a very frank and pleasant manner. I am exceedingly obliged to you for having

---

[1] Fru Ragna Wettergreen received a travelling-grant in 1898.
[2] *An Enemy of the People* was produced by Mr. Tree at the Haymarket Theatre.

cleared up this matter for literary France.[1]  Unfortunately, only too many mistakes still remain uncorrected.

I hope that I shall be able to write a new play next year; but I cannot yet be certain.  So many other things demand my time and attention.

The state of my·wife's health obliged her to spend the winter at Meran in the Tyrol.  Now she has gone to Italy to take the baths at Monsummano.  My son is with her.  I shall have the pleasure of sending her the kind messages in your letter the next time I write.

I regret ever more and more that I neglected at the proper time to learn to speak English.  Now it is too late.  Wére I conversant with the language, I should go to London at once, or, to be more correct, I should have been there long ago.  I have been revolving many things in my mind lately, and one of the conclusions to which I have come is that there are very strong traces in me of my Scotch descent.  But this is only a feeling—perhaps only a wish that it were so.  I lack the experience and knowledge necessary to judge.

With respectful regards to Mrs. Archer, I remain—Yours most sincerely,                                        HENRIK IBSEN.


226.

*To* JONAS COLLIN.

CHRISTIANIA, 31*st July* 1895.

DEAR MR. JONAS COLLIN,—I thank you heartily for your kind letter, and hope that you will excuse my sending only a few words in reply.

---

[1] In criticising *Little Eyolf* after its performance in Paris on the 8th of May 1895, Jules Lemaître (writing in the *Journal des Débats*) showed that he had so far misunderstood the plot as to believe that Asta Allmers was Alfred's half-sister—which would have introduced the element of incest into the play.

The poster you write about, I have already received from M. Lugné Poë, together with other printed matter belonging to it.[1] And I have received many other papers besides—much more than I care for. There is, of course, a certain satisfaction in becoming so well known in these different countries. But it gives me no sense of happiness. And what is it really worth —the whole thing? Well, well! Kindest regards from—Yours very sincerely,                                   HENRIK IBSEN.

227.

*To* GEORGE BRANDES.

CHRISTIANIA, 24*th April* 1896.

DEAR BRANDES,—You are right; your letter of the 16th of December last has never been answered, though it has lain on my table the whole time, constantly reminding me to write and thank you for it. I hoped that Hegel would send me your important work when it was completed.[2] But I have not received it as yet, and I am unwilling to ask him to send it. Consequently I am most grateful to you for your offer of intervention in the matter. I assure you that there is no book which I have such a desire to bury myself in at present as this new one of yours.

In your last letter you make the suggestion that I should visit London. If I knew enough English I might perhaps go. But as I unfortunately do not, I must give up the idea altogether. Besides, I am engaged in preparing for a big new work, and I do not wish to put off the writing of it longer than necessary.

---

[1] Aurélien-Marie Lugné, or Lugné-Poë, the founder and still the manager of the "free" theatre, *L'Œuvre*, has produced a whole series of Ibsen plays in Paris.

[2] The first volume of George Brandes's book on Shakespeare was published in 1895, the second in 1896.

It might so easily happen that a roof-tile fell on my head before I had "found time to make the last verse." And what then? —Yours ever, HENRIK IBSEN.


## 228.

*To* GEORGE BRANDES.

CHRISTIANIA, *3rd October* 1896.

DEAR BRANDES,—You know by experience what an incorrigibly bad correspondent I am; and therefore you will understand my not having given a sign of life for so long— even to you.

I have not only read the whole of your monumental work on Shakespeare, but have been absorbed in it, as I hardly remember being in any other book. I feel as if Shakespeare, and his age, and you yourself, lived and breathed in this most able work of yours. A thousand thanks for the mental enrichment!

I was particularly pleased with the young Parisian couple whom you sent to see me.[1] And I liked the Hungarian philologist very much, too. But I am glad that they did not come at present, when I am not at home to any one. I am hard at work at a new, long play, which must be completed as soon as possible.[2]

Therefore I must ask you to be satisfied with these few lines from—Your attached and faithful friend,

HENRIK IBSEN.

[1] Taine's daughter, Geneviève, and her husband, a son of the famous sculptor and painter, Paul Dubois.

[2] *John Gabriel Borkman* was published in December **1896.**

229.

*To* GEORGE BRANDES.

CHRISTIANIA, 11*th October* 1896.

DEAR BRANDES,—I herewith briefly answer your questions.

1. I declare, on my honour and conscience, that I have never in my life, neither in my youth nor at any later period, read a single book of George Sand's. I once began to read *Consuelo* in a translation, but stopped immediately, as the story seemed to me to be the production of an amateur philosopher, not of a poet. But I read only a few pages, so that I may be mistaken in my judgment of it.

2. The above makes an answer to this question unnecessary.

3. To Alexandre Dumas I owe nothing, as regards dramatic form—except that I have learned from his plays to avoid several very awkward faults and blunders, of which he is not infrequently guilty.

My best thanks to you for taking the trouble to correct these French illusions![1]—Yours ever,

HENRIK IBSEN.

230.

*To* GEORGE BRANDES.

CHRISTIANIA, 3*rd June* 1897.

DEAR GEORGE BRANDES,—Not until I received your letter did I learn that the illness from which you are suffering is

---

[1] In an article on the new influences from Scandinavian literature, Jules Lemaître had maintained that Ibsen's ideas were all already to be found in George Sand's early novels and in the plays of Alexandre Dumas. Brandes protested in an article in *Cosmopolis* (January 1897), entitled "Henrik Ibsen en France."

such a troublesome and tedious one as that old Capitoline
ailment of yours, phlebitis. It was mentioned for the first
time in the number of *Politiken* which I received yesterday.
I had imagined that it was merely some unimportant affection
of the throat that was preventing you from lecturing. And
how could anything else have occurred to me, seeing that I know
you to have published in the course of these last weeks long
articles on Helge Rode's new plays and his writings generally,
on Victor Hugo's monument, and on other subjects? Truly your
productive power is inexhaustible. I have not been able to
follow all the details of the great controversy into which you
were led by your French essay on me; therefore I shall wait
to talk it over, and to thank you, until we meet again.

When I write of our meeting, I am not making use of an
empty phrase. Can you guess what I am dreaming about, and
planning, and picturing to myself as something delightful?
The making a home for myself near the Sound, between
Copenhagen and Elsinore, on some free, open spot, whence I
can see all the sea-going ships starting on and returning from
their long voyages. That I cannot do here. Here all the
sounds are closed, in every acceptation of the word—and all
the channels of intelligence are blocked. Oh, dear Brandes,
it is not without its consequences that a man lives for twenty-
seven years in the wider, emancipated and emancipating
spiritual conditions of the great world. Up here, by the fjords,
is my native land. But—but—but! Where am I to find my
home-land?

In my loneliness here I am employing myself in planning
something new of the nature of a drama. But I have no
distinct idea yet what it will be.

Now, in the first place, see that you get well again, and that
with as little trouble as possible. And then, let us meet in the
new home, with the Sound lying open before us.—Yours
devotedly and faithfully,

HENRIK IBSEN.

[ 231.

*To* JULIUS ELIAS

CHRISTIANIA, 20*th June* 1897.

DEAR DR. ELIAS,—It was a great pleasure to me to receive and study your and Dr. Schlenther's plan for the new, complete edition of my literary works. In all essentials I approve of it. But I shall permit myself to make one or two remarks. The list of contents of Vol. I. includes Poems and Prose Writings. Of the last mentioned I have written none suitable for translation into German; and I would suggest that my poems should form part of the last volume rather than of the first, for this reason, that they have been produced singly during the course of my whole literary career; besides, a satisfactory translation could hardly be made by the time the first volume ought to be published.

*Herrin von Oestrot* (Lady Inger of Östraat) and *Nordische Heerfahrt* (The Vikings) are *my* exclusive property, as Fraulein Klingenfeld was paid by me for her work : consequently there will be no difficulty in making over these plays to Mr. Fischer, your publisher.

*Das Hünengrab* (The Hero's Mound) was published many years ago as the feuilleton in a Norwegian newspaper, and I hope to be able to procure you a copy of it.

The other two plays which I wrote in my youth, I would never publish, and I do not wish to have them translated.

*Catilina* has, as you are aware, been published by Albert Langen of Munich; and it would perhaps be right, from a professional point of view, that Mr. Fischer should, before taking any other steps, come to an understanding with Mr. Langen.

The copies of the original editions which you ask for, I shall request my publisher in Copenhagen to send you as soon as possible; and I shall also find out if it is possible to get hold of any photographs taken at an earlier period.

I hope, after entering into a few more particulars, to come to an agreement with Mr. Fischer. I shall very soon write to him about one or two little things which I should like to have rather more plainly stated in the contract between us.

To save myself the trouble of writing in a foreign language, I am not sending a letter of thanks direct to Dr. Schlenther. I trust that he will consider this one as addressed to him as well as to you. And I beg of you both to believe me,—Yours sincerely and gratefully,

HENRIK IBSEN.

## 232.

### *To* GEORGE BRANDES.

CHRISTIANIA, *30th September* 1896.

DEAR GEORGE BRANDES,—I have received your letter; and I am very grateful to the Bohemian composer, because he has induced you to break your vow never to write to me again— and still more grateful to you for your letter, such as it is.

You tell me about your illness. As if I did not know all about it! Each day during the critical period I read with eager anxiety the bulletins published in the newspapers.

The newspapers told that you were not allowed to receive any visitors. Was I to force myself in, to the very bed where you lay sick, with a scrap of a letter every now and then? I cannot possibly imagine that, in the condition you were in at that time, you can have been exceedingly anxious to hear from me. I believe that you are making a mistake now in thinking that you were. I, in your place, would have asked for peace— nothing but undisturbed peace and quiet—so as to get well again.

Then you know, only too well, my inveterate aversion from sitting down to write letters.

And what purpose would writing have answered? You surely know that I acknowledge with gratitude all that I owe you,

29

including what you have done for me quite lately. Supposing you to doubt it — would a written assurance make any difference? Good Heavens! you know quite well how easy it is to put together a kind of French Staff letter.

Taking everything into consideration, I cannot allow that my crime of silence is of such a nature as to justify you in addressing a friend of many years' standing as "Honoured Sir," or something to that effect. And I think that it ought to be beneath the dignity of a man like you to behave so because of one or two letters that have not been written—by a man whose chief passion is certainly not correspondence, even with his best and dearest friends.

Enclosed letter I must, unfortunately, answer myself, because it touches on matters which affect my contract with my German theatrical agents. Yesterday I received a letter direct from Mr. Fibich on the same subject.[1] Please remember us very kindly to your wife and Miss Edith.—Yours always,

HENRIK IBSEN.

### 233.

*To* GEORGE BRANDES.

CHRISTIANIA, 30*th December* 1898.

DEAR GEORGE BRANDES,—The newspapers have informed me of the loss which you and your family have sustained; and I well know the feeling of bereavement and emptiness which is oppressing you, for your relation to your mother was undoubtedly a more than usually close one. My thoughts have been much with you these last days, I can assure you.[2]

And now you must allow me to thank you warmly for the

[1] Zdenko Fibich (1850–1900), a Bohemian composer, wished to write music for one of Ibsen's dramas.

[2] Fru Emilie Brandes, George Brandes's mother, died on the 27th of December 1898, aged eighty.

valuable present which you sent me, with a kindheartedness for which I can find no words, immediately after receiving my last letter, which certainly was not of a nature to call forth such a truly friendly reply. Thanks, thanks for it! I am reading and re-reading your ardent, refined, soulful poems; and I now understand why you no longer write verse; for it is this same poetical gift which you employ in your grand epic on Shakespeare, in your works on Disraeli and Lassalle, and in all the others; no matter how historical the material may be, it is permeated with latent poetry, with your own poetry of the days when you wrote these youthful verses.[1]

The work on Julius Lange I found most engrossing, and consequently I have retained a very pleasant remembrance of it. But it has not really given me any warmer feeling towards Julius Lange. He still seems to me a little too academic, a little too correct, and rather irritating—with his excessively tender conscience. But then your own letters are wanting. I very much wish that they had been printed too; for it is not conducive to the understanding of a dialogue that we should hear only the one interlocutor's speeches, and be obliged to guess at those of the other. The friendship between you and Julius Lange is not very comprehensible to me. Have you not sometimes, without intending to do it, exercised a terrorising influence upon his epistolary style? Has he not, while writing these letters to his friend, given some consideration to the manner in which they were likely to be received? Such considerations do not, in my opinion, accord well with friendship.

But, good gracious! here have I, quite unintentionally, strayed into a domain where I am an entire stranger—so, " Schwamm darüber ! "

With thanks for all that you have been and done for me in the past year, and with our best wishes for everything that is good for you and yours in the year to come, I remain—Yours devotedly and faithfully,     HENRIK IBSEN.

[1] In 1898, Brandes published *Youthful Poems* and *Julius Lange : Letters written in his Youth.*

234.

*To* EDWARD BRANDES

CHRISTIANIA, 1st *March* 1898.

DEAR DR. EDWARD BRANDES,—To-day I come to you as a kind of petitioner, although not directly on my own account.

The person in whom I desire to interest you is a young countrywoman of mine, Miss Hildur Andersen, the pianist, whom you probably know by name. She has been asked to come to Copenhagen in the beginning of March to assist at a Palais Concert. She is a pupil of Leschetizky, and enjoys a very good reputation as a performer in this country; but she has a certain, not unnatural, dread of Copenhagen, where she has not as yet appeared.

As you may suppose, it is not my intention to try to influence in any way the criticism which will be published in your paper: all I wish to ask is that she may be received in a kindly spirit. She is an intimate friend of mine—a good, wise, and faithful one; and I am greatly indebted to her relations, in whose house in Bergen I lived when I was young. Therefore it is that I write to you.

I must avail myself of the opportunity to thank you very sincerely for what you did for me by starting the idea of a complete edition of my works. It is turning out a very satisfactory undertaking, as far as I am concerned.—Yours most sincerely,

HENRIK IBSEN.

## 235.

*To* ROMAN WOERNER.[1]

CHRISTIANIA, *7th July* 1899.

DEAR DR. WOERNER,—In answer to your friendly inquiry, permit me briefly to reply that I took the groundwork of *Emperor and Galilean* from no single historical work. Tillemont's I do not know. I went through, and made extracts from, a whole series of writers of ecclesiastical history. For access to these I was greatly indebted to the German library on the Capitol. Ammianus Marcellinus is the author whom I chiefly consulted for the historical facts; he was more useful to me than any other.

Excuse haste. I am much occupied just now—am working busily at a new play.—Yours sincerely,

HENRIK IBSEN.

## 236.

*To* JONAS LIE.

CHRISTIANIA, *15th January* 1900.

DEAR JONAS LIE.—I see that you are still the same faithful and reliable letter-writer that you always were—and that I, unfortunately, never have been. Many thanks for your letter, and many thanks for sending me your new book. I am glad that it has met with the unanimously cordial reception and appreciation which it deserved—and specially glad that it has

---

[1] Roman Woerner (born 1863), a German writer on literary subjects, since 1901 professor at the University of Freiburg, has made a particular study of Ibsen's writings. He published the first volume of a long work on Ibsen in 1900.

done so in this country, where comprehension is not always particularly profound.[1]

Do you not think of dramatising the story of Faste? It seems to me that there is the making of a very good popular play in it. Just listen!

Act 1.—Faste as the half-grown boy, eating the bread of charity and dreaming of greatness.

Act 2.—Faste's struggle in the town.

Act 3.—Faste's victory in the town.

Act 4.—Faste's defeat and flight from the country.

Act 5.—Faste's return as a victorious poet. He has found himself.

It is a fine adventurous career to depict dramatically. But of course you would have to get farther away from your story first. You perhaps think this a barbarous and inhuman suggestion. But all your stories have the making of a drama in them.

Now I must not ramble on any longer.

We are delighted to have such good accounts of you all. Could we not meet here in Norway next summer? I am thinking of allowing myself a holiday this year; and it would be splendid to talk about all kinds of things again, as we did at Berchtesgaden about twenty years ago.

Give our very kindest regards to your wife; and remember me specially to my unquenchable flame, Elizabeth. I congratulate you on your success at Monte Carlo. When the Captain comes home I hope to hear still more good news of you.—Yours ever,      HENRIK IBSEN.

[1] The book referred to is *Faste Forland*, which Jonas Lie published in 1899.

## 237.

*To* MORITZ PROZOR.

CHRISTIANIA, *6th March* 1900.

DEAR COUNT PROZOR,—Permit me in the first place to express the sincere pleasure which it gives me to know that Countess Prozor has bravely and successfully undergone the operation, and is making a good recovery. This matter has been daily in my thoughts.

Accept my best thanks for the draft for 1000 Francs which I received yesterday. I hope I may venture to expect that your translation will appear in book form in the near future.

I cannot say yet whether or not I shall write another drama; but if I continue to retain the vigour of mind and body which I at present enjoy, I do not imagine that I shall be able to keep permanently away from the old battlefields. However, if I were to make my appearance again, it would be with new weapons and in new armour.

You are quite right when you say that the series which ends with the epilogue, really began with *The Master Builder*. Into this subject, however, I do not care to enter further. I leave all commentaries and interpretations to you.—With kindest regards, I remain, Yours sincerely and gratefully,     |HENRIK IBSEN.

## 238.

*To* CORNELIUS KAREL ELOUT.

CHRISTIANIA, *9th December* 1900.

To Mr. C. K. ELOUT,
Editor of the *Algemeen Handelsblad*, Amsterdam.

HONOURED SIR,—You have done me the honour of writing me an open letter in *Politiken*, and I take the liberty of sending you a brief open answer in the same paper.

In the domain of politics I am, as you perhaps know, a man
of peace; and nothing was farther from my thoughts than the
possibility of my being entangled in the South African war.  In
the quarrel between the Boers and the Britons, I have hitherto
kept myself quite as carefully in the background, quite as
neutral, as the great Dutch colonial power itself.

And my aphoristic utterances in the Norwegian *Öreblad* were
most certainly not intended to injure the Boers in the estimation
of the great outside world of politics.

You write of a book which has not yet appeared, but which
is to convince me that the Boers did not acquire their territory
in an unrightful manner, and that the English have done no
more for the cause of civilisation in South Africa than the
Boers.

We shall see.

If this promised book or pamphlet succeeds in convincing me
of all this—which would be equivalent to revolutionising my
present view of the matter—I shall honestly acknowledge it.

I owe a deep personal debt of gratitude to your nation, Mr.
Editor.  But you could not expect me to be ready to pay off
part of this debt by doing violence to my convictions.

You conclude by saying that the Dutch are the natural
defenders of the Boers in Europe.

Why did your countrymen not choose a more useful place
in which to defend them while there was yet time?

I am thinking of South Africa.

And as to defending your kinsmen with books and pamphlets
and open letters—are there not, Mr. Editor, more effective
weapons than these?

I am thinking of . . . .

Yours respectfully,

HENRIK IBSEN.

# INDEX

*Figures in brackets indicate letters to individuals.*